# The
# Beyond
# Experience

## by **Michael Reid, Jr.**

edited by
**Annmarie G.K. Ruggiero**
and
**Heather Lynn Schild**

H Q T

PUBLICATIONS

Interior design and layout, kalzub design.

ISBN 9780997350098

Library of Congress Control Number: 2016918936

**To dad.**
If only I could have one more long
conversation with you.

# Contents

# | ONE |

## October 15, 2016

Dr. Ethan Lewis had finally tracked Lily's parents down to Poughkeepsie, New York with the help of Agent Mike Sims. Dr. Lewis promised it was a one-time thing so Mike agreed. Mike owed him one because, as he said, "Without Ethan the FBI wouldn't have found the 27 missing people."

Dr. Lewis sat in the passenger seat of the Mercedes AMG S63, his knee bouncing up and down nervously as he stared out the window. He was trying to focus on the beauty of the colorful trees and rolling hills but the scenery had little effect. His palms began to sweat and he sighed heavily as Junior wailed in the back. Junior was only 20 months old, but Ethan wanted to take the drive from Saint Louis to Poughkeepsie. He needed the time to think, to go over the conversation he needed to have with Lily's parents—a conversation 20 years in the making.

"Sorry about Junior," Annie said as she glanced toward Dr. Lewis.

"Don't be. It's not him," he responded shifting in his chair. He reached toward the dashboard and turned the temperature down on his side of the car.

"Wanna talk about it?"

"No. I know what I'm gonna say. Just not sure if they'll let me in," he said, sighing heavily once again.

A moment later they drove past a sign, "Welcome to New York." Dr. Lewis began to sweat. He reached forward once again turning down the air, pointing all the vents toward his face. He closed his eyes trying to stop the car from spinning. His heart was slamming against his thorax and his respiratory rate increased significantly. In that moment he saw her eyes; Lily's eyes. The eyes he'd dreamt about for the last 20 years. The eyes he saw just one week earlier. He couldn't handle thinking about what happened. The stress of the present moment was too great for him to handle the thought of seeing her.

Several hours and three pit stops later, Dr. Ethan Lewis, Annie, and Junior all pulled up outside the moderate two-story home. It was beautiful, white with lush, green grass and old growth trees throughout the neighborhood. Ethan sat motionless in the car staring at the front of the house. The hundreds of scenarios he ran through his head over the two-day road trip immediately evaporated into an empty mind. He had no idea what to say, how to start; but he was there and it needed to happen. He closed his eyes and, for the first time in a long time, said a silent prayer.

The smell of fresh cut grass and burning leaves leapt at him as he opened the door. Ethan walked to the trunk and grabbed a basket full of flowers, Lilies of the Valley.

"Are you ready?" Annie asked as she met Ethan at the rear of his car holding a smiling Junior.

"I don't know where to start," he said with tears piling themselves against his eyes making it hard to see Annie's dark red hair.

"At the beginning, Ethan. That's the only way it works."

"You're gonna hear things you may not feel comfortable with."

"This was all your idea, Doc," she said smiling, knowing it would make him laugh. It was what Kyle had often called him when they were giving each other a hard time.

"That's cheating," he said smiling back. "I miss him too."

"I'm sorry."

"Don't be. It was my fault."

"No. Don't do that. It was just as much my fault as yours. He wouldn't have been there if it wasn't for me," Annie said allowing herself to shed a tear as she squeezed Kyle Junior tightly.

"We've never talked about this before. I don't think now's the time," Ethan said wiping the tear from her face.

Annie nodded and they turned toward the house.

The three of them began to walk up the edged sidewalk, past the manicured flower garden, and up three small wooden steps onto the porch. Ethan wiped his hands on his pants several times and his eyes began to dart all around, looking for a way out. Annie stood rooted beside him, she squeezed his arm firmly, reassuring him he was making the right decision.

Ethan rang the doorbell at 4:00 p.m. on a quiet Saturday afternoon. The maroon door swung open and there stood Edward Fisch, Lily's father.

"Captain Fisch," he said to the former police officer.

"Well don't you clean up nice?" he blurted harshly.

"I'm sorry?"

"You look good. Apparently you found a way to move on," Edward Fisch said as he nodded his head politely toward Annie and Junior.

"No sir, we're just friends," Ethan said looking toward Annie.

"Been seeing you on TV over the years. Must be pretty well set up now huh?" Mr. Fisch said.

"Yes sir I've done well. But that's not why I'm here."

"Well spit it out Ethan I don't have all day," he said crossing his heavy arms as he stood in the doorway.

"It's about Lily. I've thought about her every single day since she left. I wanted you to know you should be proud of her."

"She didn't leave, Ethan, she died," he said as he shifted, accidentally hitting the front door and opening it wide enough for Ethan to look inside, revealing beautifully stained hardwood and a white with blue rug that lay just inside.

"She made me a believer."

"Is this a joke? She's been gone 20 years Ethan. In fact, I don't know why we're entertaining each other right now. What's your pitch? What are you selling?"

"Please. Let us come in and tell you a story. I'll start from the beginning and end with what happened last week."

"Pat!" Edward yelled through the house without taking his eyes off Ethan.

A few moments later a petite woman with long, silver hair stood next to her husband. It was the first time Ethan had ever seen Pat's eyes. She had never looked at Ethan before, let alone into his eyes, but as soon as she did, he saw where Lily had gotten hers. For a brief moment Ethan was taken back to the island, only to be immediately brought back by Mrs. Fisch's firm voice.

"Ethan?" she asked in shock. "Why are you here?"

"Mrs. Fisch, please. I'd love to tell you the story but can we come in? It's going to take a while."

"What about?"

"About how your daughter saved my life."

"Are those Lilies?" Pat asked.

"Yes. Lily of the Valley—"

"Her favorite," Pat said as she placed her hand over her mouth and began to cry. It had taken her years to allow herself to even look at a lily since her daughter died. They had often looked at flowers together; Pat had always been a gardener.

Ed and Pat both stood there for a moment with tears in their eyes. Ed placed his right arm around his wife and pulled her gently into his shoulder, kissing her on the head. Pat began to cry and nod her head.

"Let them in Ed. I want to hear this," Pat said after a moment of silence. The two of them stepped back allowing Ethan, Annie, and Junior into the home.

"Your home is beautiful," Annie said as she admired the 10-foot ceilings and the large living room where Ed had gestured them to go.

"Not as beautiful as that baby of yours," Pat said smiling. "May

I?" she asked holding her hands up toward Junior.

"Be my guest," Annie said gently passing Junior to her.

"Come on in here and we'll sit down. You can tell us that story," Ed said walking toward the couches.

Ethan sighed heavily, preparing himself. He envisioned this moment occurring, but never thought it would truly happen. His mind was a whirlwind of stories, of events that led to him meeting Lily. He thought of Harvard and Lily, the treatments, the secret commitment to each other with their tattoos and what ultimately killed her. He thought all the way back to the beatings as a youth, the courtroom decision that left him in foster care. But most of all, he thought about the research and how it led to so much more than they ever understood. He took out a rock, and a notebook that he had used in the car to make notes, ensuring he wouldn't leave out a detail.

"This is going to sound unbelievable," Ethan said as he placed the black lava rock down onto the glass coffee table that rested between himself and Lily's parents. He looked to Annie who smiled and nodded back. "But she's here to corroborate everything I say," he said looking at Annie again. "I love your daughter with every part of me. She's the only person who knows me completely. Nobody comes close. She's saved me more than once."

# | TWO |

## November 8, 2005

Dr. Ethan Lewis sat in a black leather kitchen chair in silence as the sun progressively brought the room to life. Steam gently twisted and rolled from a coffee cup, the swirling moisture matching the figured wood of the walnut table. Tall dark custom hickory cabinets hung over black granite counters speckled white, creating the illusion of the heavens. The backsplash was several shades of green glass tile that glistened in the crescendo of light. The counters had a few items: a toaster, a coffee maker, and a glass jar containing carrots in a preservative solution, bringing a pop of contrasting color, which the decorator had suggested.

Sitting at his kitchen table in the indigo light of a young morning, Dr. Lewis was gently running his finger along the surface of the table, craving a comforting sensation he felt in his youth. He remembered, the scarred wood on the bedpost from his finger tracing the circular pattern over and over again. The touch of the smooth wood gradually revealed its true texture as he wore away the polyurethane. It was his favorite game as a young boy, the only thing he was allowed to do in his prison cell of a bedroom.

It had taken opening up to Lily to realize how traumatizing his childhood was. He told her about the countless times he was beaten, then locked in his room, told to "stay on his bed or get another whoopin'." He rarely wanted to leave his bed. It was a safe zone, a place he could hide, where his parents wouldn't see or hear him. While sitting on the bed as a malnourished youth, he would imagine wonderful places he thought he'd never see. In his mind, he painted his dingy white walls with lively colors, crashing waves, and rockets launching skyward with a red and orange trail of fire. He allowed the visions to overwhelm him, to take him away, to be his reality; if only for a moment. His fantasy would often be broken when the yellow light from under his door became fractured by two long shadows. His anxiety would return and prayers would be silently said, only to be unanswered each time by his mother or father entering. But with Lily, things had been different.

Lily had broken him, like a young stallion, bucking wild and retreating from anyone's advance, Ethan always found himself alone until her. She found a way to calm him, to talk to him, to show him she could love him, and he loved her back. The treatment she manufactured for his anxiety had worked. Every time he went into treatment it was like being back in his room with vivid scenes laid out before him. However, during the treatments he was able to fully interact with the incredible sensory experience. When he awoke, he would always feel relaxed, happy, loved, which is why reminiscing still caused a deep ache in his stomach knowing she was dead and at his hands. All he wanted to do was show his beautiful fiancé what she had shown him through the treatments so many times.

Ethan stared into the black hole of coffee, its color remaining unchanged, just as his thoughts. It had been a sleepless night, something that had lately become customary. He was gathering a lot of momentum in his most recent study on the treatment of anxiety and depression. The research had been mocked and certainly was unorthodox, but with over a thousand positive outcomes and lacking any side effects, it was looking promising. He had tweaked the formulation of the treatment several times, and that morning would be no exception. It would be the most aggressive treatment to date, but he knew the effect he was searching for, and so naturally he would have to continue to push the envelope. But pushing that envelope always caused him to reflect on Lily.

Ethan allowed himself to think about her, to remember her soft blonde hair, her captivating eyes and her empathy for him. He thought about how they used to spend hours talking about his past and how she used to hold his head into her chest while he silently cried the tears that hadn't come as a youth. She would hum to him, running her fingers through his dark wavy hair and gently scratch the top of his head. It had been so soothing. And when the thoughts of the botany lab came rushing back he wouldn't fight them. He still remembered her scent, flowers and the sea, and he could never forget how her lifeless body felt in his arms.

Dr. Lewis allowed the anxiety of that moment to wash over him. It helped him focus on the person being treated, not the research he was trying to prove worked. He took out his laptop. After entering a four-digit code, an image folder popped up. The cover photo was a close-up shot of two blue-green eyes staring into a camera, the corners of the eyes lifting slightly. He clicked on the folder and several more photos spread across the screen in a grid. There were pictures of Lily sticking out her tongue, crossing her eyes, making kissing faces and funny gestures with her hands. Other images were candid shots of her working on an assignment, or in the lab, focused on getting things perfect. The best images were of the two of them together enjoying a playful kiss, a hearty laugh with friends while at a bar. His favorite picture was one where he was sleeping while she laid on him. She was awake, staring directly into the camera for whoever was taking the picture. She looked like a lioness watching over her lover; so powerful, so protective, so much in love.

One image stood out from the rest. He clicked on it and stared for several minutes. It was the last picture he ever took of them together. They had decided to commit themselves to one another, without the church she grew up in, without the government, just the two of them with Jimmy the tattoo artist. The picture was of both their left hands, hers resting on his, all ten fingers spread out with their ring fingers almost side by side. Their skin was irritated from the needle penetrating it hundreds of times, but essentially there was nothing to be seen. They had matching white tattoos where rings should be.

They didn't have money for a wedding. Lily's parents had all but disowned her after meeting Ethan. He was an atheist, and who could have blamed him, having dealt with regular beatings from both a mother and father who wore crosses around their necks and told him he "better be good because Jesus was watchin'!".

Dr. Lewis closed the computer. Reaching for his coffee he hesitated for a moment, watching the still present but fleeting steam rise up and out of the cup. What bothered him the most after her death hadn't been the police visits, the interrogations, or that everyone felt he had a larger part in her death than he was admitting. It was the fact that her parents kept him away from the funeral. They hadn't told him a single detail, but he gathered it in bits and pieces from acquaintances.

He had flown to New York City, and from there, took a cab to the church where a police officer prevented him from entering. He wanted to fight, to press his way through the large officer, slam through the doors, and see her one last time before she went under the ground. But he didn't, he couldn't; and when more family and friends passed him and entered the large, arched doorways he saw two more policemen standing inside.

He waited for hours, loitering against a brick wall of a building, watching for the casket to exit the church. The afternoon sun felt much hotter than the actual temperature, and he baked in his black suitcoat, pants, and tie. His white shirt was sticking to his torso and had become saturated, transparent at his chest. His mouth was dry, but when the church doors opened he saw her casket and began to walk quickly toward it.

He saw no policeman, only pallbearers carrying an all white

casket with brass handles. His heart quickened and so did his pace. He removed his hands from his pockets and he flexed them, swinging his arms back and forth attempting to walk even faster.

Then he saw them, Edward and Joey Fisch exiting the church directly behind Lily's casket. The look her father and brother gave him still brought a chill—cold, angry eyes, bloodshot from tears and tissues for days. Her mother, Pat, came next without even a glance in Ethan's direction, which at the time felt like nothing, but looking back was worse than the men's hateful glares. Joey Fisch pulled back his suitcoat and flashed his service nine millimeter freezing Ethan in place. He stayed there until the hearse pulled away and his eyes welled up so full that he could no longer make out the street scene spread before him.

As Dr. Lewis sat in the morning light he squeezed out tears he hadn't allowed himself to cry that day standing on the street in New York. He blinked hard and took a drink of the warm coffee. With each sip he gained a little more emotional control. The tears stopped forming and gradually his thoughts morphed from Lily, to the cocktail, to the research, and finally to the day's testing.

Today was finally the day he had been building toward. The anxiety and depression drug had been tweaked several times, each step of the way being tested and carefully measured out for the dosage, always getting closer to that elusive ratio Lily had used on him. It was her drug mix that finally allowed him to ditch his anxiety meds and feel his mind open once more, rather than the fog he was living in.

After Lily had died, Ethan had convinced his advisor and research coordinator to trial the cocktail while he was getting his PhD. They found the first preliminary results extremely successful—so much so, that he was asked to continue his research as a full-time faculty after he presented his dissertation. He had turned it down in order to pursue his career at Washington University in Saint Louis. He loved Harvard before Lily's death, but everything there reminded him of her.

An hour later Dr. Lewis walked the campus of Washington

University Medical School toward 4500 Parkview. It was a short walk after parking in the surface lot across the street from The Rehabilitation Institute of Saint Louis, but he was able to feel the warm sun hitting his face and arms as he carried a satchel across his body and over his right shoulder.

Upon entering the building, he took the elevator to the third floor, exiting into the treatment suite. He sat at his desk and reviewed the case file on Linda, their subject for the day. *Clinical depression diagnosed ten years ago, no history of suicidal tendencies, lost a father early in life, two children and a happy marriage. Full-time job she was satisfied with, no financial difficulties.*

He then walked to a couch that sat opposite a TV. He turned it on and tried to relax, waiting for Kyle his lab assistant to arrive. Kyle wasn't always on time and it was irritating Dr. Lewis today. Donna, the part-time receptionist, had told Dr. Lewis Linda would arrive at 10:00 a.m.

"You're late," Dr. Lewis said turning off the TV and standing up as Kyle walked into the office.

"Not really," Kyle said smiling and throwing his bag into the chair.

"We've got prep to do and now we've only got an hour before Linda gets here," Dr. Lewis said frustrated as he walked through the office and into the lab.

"We can do it Doc," Kyle said jokingly and grabbed Dr. Lewis playfully on the top of the shoulder.

"You're lucky we've been together four years. Otherwise I'd find someone new," Dr. Lewis said while trying to hide a growing smirk.

"You couldn't replace me!"

"Just get in the lab," Dr. Lewis said reaching behind Kyle and pushing him forward with his left hand.

Linda arrived promptly at 10:00 a.m. Donna led her up to the treatment suite where Dr. Lewis conducted a preliminary questionnaire and prepped her for the procedure. He also ensured all the recording devices and safety equipment were working before he had Linda enter the treatment room and get comfortable on the bed.

"You're going to feel a chill go up your arm when we start the titration." Dr. Lewis watched as Linda brushed the hair away from her forehead.

"I remember you said that," she faked a smile, something she had become quite good at.

"Just making sure you're as comfortable and relaxed as you can be Linda," he said. "Ready?"

"I hope so."

"Kyle how are we doing?" Dr. Lewis said looking through the glass window and into the observation suite where Kyle was reviewing the data coming in.

"Heart monitor's a go, EEG is recording, pulse is 85, BP looks good, pulse ox 100 percent."

"Cameras?"

"Cameras are all up and running."

"Start recording please," Dr. Lewis said as he squeezed Linda's hand and smiled. "This is test number 50-09, Linda Reynolds, age 36. No comorbidities, clinically diagnosed with depression and anxiety disorder. She has not taken medications in the last six weeks. Weight, 124 pounds, height 5'4". Titration of PB-50 has been determined to be 75 percent saline. Linda, do you consent to treatment?"

"I do Dr. Lewis," Linda said squeezing his hand.

Dr. Lewis' shoes made a scuffing sound as he walked several feet across the white tile floor. He took a deep breath as he tried to relax himself. The slight hint of rubbing alcohol and latex filled his lungs as only a clean research lab could. He reached the IV machine and checked the saline bag, still 90 percent full. He looked at the glass bottle containing the cocktail of ingredients he had become all too familiar with. A hint of ketamine, a dash of propofol, etomidate, thiopental, methohexital, and *her* secret ingredient, *Convallaria majalis* the Lily of the Valley.

"Beginning titration," Dr. Lewis said as he pressed several buttons on the IV machine, and checked to ensure there was not air in the line. The IV machine hummed to life, gears turned and gently pressed the fluid from the glass bottle, down into the main line, and into Linda's arm.

"Whoa," Linda said blinking her eyes hard then trying to open them wide.

"Everything ok Linda?" Dr. Lewis asked concerned.

"Yeah, just cold."

"That's what I was referring to. It should pass. Kyle, how are we looking?"

"Everything's green Doctor."

"Ok Linda get ready. Count down from 100. See you on the other side."

"99 . . . 9 . . . 7 . . . ," Linda said.

"How are the vitals?" Dr. Lewis asked as he watched Linda's eyelids close.

"Looks good Doc."

Dr. Lewis stood in the room with Linda for a while watching her breathe. She looked comfortable, and the wrinkles that screamed sorrow, worry, and regret had leveled across her face allowing her to look her age. He found it sad how the inner battles could often manifest themselves externally; as if it wasn't hard enough to bury the emotions, just to be reminded of them when you looked in the mirror. It was cyclical, and he was simply trying to break the cycle. He knew how rough the cycle could be.

"Doctor Lewis can you come to the observation room? It's starting," Kyle said after Linda had been unconscious for several minutes.

"What are we seeing?" Dr. Lewis said entering the room and peered over Kyle's shoulder trying to decipher the live data coming in.

"Her EEG is basically flatlining. Her BP is 95/60, heart rate is 55, pulse ox still 100."

"Ok good. Set the audible alarms for anything lower than 95 percent O2, less than 50 beats, and 85/50 BP."

"Done."

"Let's wait and see." Doctor Lewis crossed his arms and began watching the HD monitors feeding live video of Linda. There were several cameras monitoring her. One was infrared monitoring her body temperature, another was plotting her eye movements and graphing them, a third was a full body shot to monitor gross motor movements, and a fourth, which was automated, quickly responding to any noted movement, focusing its 4K camera on the object.

This moment was what Dr. Lewis felt was the most critical. It was where he felt he lost Lily, but also where he felt the treatment would reveal its deepest secrets. It hadn't happened yet, but he felt as though they were getting close to having someone experience the vivid world he had. Everyone had come out feeling anxiety free, but nobody described the vibrant colors, the depth of sound, or the physical sensations he had when Lily treated him.

"Doc, look at her eyes," Kyle said pointing to monitor four, breaking Dr. Lewis' thoughts.

"Hmm . . . What does her EEG say?"

"Still flat."

"What are the odds we have a bad lead?"

"Zero. We had a good read before and after she went under. It's accurate."

"She's smiling now," Dr. Lewis said with a smirk as he stared at the screen. "Still nothing?"

"Nothing Doc. Is this what we've been looking for?"

"I'm not taking the leap just yet, but it does look promising."
Dr. Lewis grabbed a microphone. "Twenty-three minutes 15 seconds, patient is exhibiting rapid eye movement and smiling without any

brain activity. Vitals are steady." His hands began to sweat and it was hard work focusing on the subtle details of the experiment.

"Oh my God, Dr. Lewis. She's talking!"

"Rewind the audio," Dr. Lewis said quickly.

"What . . . is this . . . ," Linda said as camera four focused on her lips.

"All the EEG readings are still flat Dr. Lewis."

"It's all being recorded right Kyle?"

"Yeah Doc. Can you leap yet?"

"I'm getting closer." Adrenaline surged through Dr. Lewis. It was the first time he saw documented evidence of the experience.

*Beep. Beep. Beep.* The alarm went off on the monitors. "I'm pulling her out Kyle, that's it," Dr. Lewis said when he spotted her BP had dropped to 80/45 setting off the prearranged alarms. Lewis jogged to the door, rushed through, and stopped the titration. He immediately gave her a shot of epinephrine directly into her IV line.

"Ahhh," Linda sighed deeply and smiled as her eyes popped wide open.

"How are you feeling Linda?" Dr. Lewis asked. She looked through him peacefully, as if she could see something behind the doctor's eyes. "Linda?" Dr. Lewis asked again.

She began to cry, then sob. She covered her mouth as she looked around the room. She began giggling and sputtering uncontrollably.

Dr. Lewis approached her bed. "Linda," he said and sat next to her, as she reached up to remove hair from her face once again.

"I want to go back," she said.

"I'm sorry?" Dr. Lewis said signaling Kyle to keep recording.

"I want to go back," Linda repeated.

"Where exactly?"

"Heaven."

Linda was all smiles. She danced a little with her fork as she ate a small plate of bland pasta, some melon, and washed it down with bottled water. It was really quite a terrible lunch but she seemed preoccupied with her bliss. She had already gotten dressed and was sitting alone in the small 10 by 20 recovery room humming a familiar tune.

"Hi Linda," Dr. Lewis said as he walked into the room with her. "Just so you're aware, we are still recording from that camera," he said pointing behind him into the corner of the room. "I'm going to conduct a small exit interview if that's ok with you. Thanks for retaking the written questionnaire."

"Sure Doc!" she said excitedly and capped her water, holding it in front of her with both hands, resting it on her cross legs.

"Well you sure do seem happy. On a scale of one to ten, how happy are you?"

"Ten!"

"When asked six weeks ago, you said you were taking your medications regularly, and you answered that same question with a three. Do you remember that?"

"How could I forget," Linda said smiling and throwing her hands gracefully up into the air. Her eyes glistened and her teeth were exquisitely straight, something only braces could have done. It was the first time Dr. Lewis had seen her teeth and the first time he wondered what had given her so much anxiety and sorrow. She was beautiful when she smiled.

"You have weaned off your meds as we discussed since we spoke six weeks ago, correct?"

"Sí."

Dr. Lewis smirked as he wrote down her response. "I think we are both happy with the results of today. Can you please describe the events you experienced during treatment?"

Linda sat for a moment with her face relaxed, still lacking the wrinkles she wore before the treatment. She opened her mouth, then closed it. Again she opened her mouth and scowled in frustration. She reached up and played with her hair for a moment.

"You described it as heaven—"

"Oh, I remember Dr. Lewis, I'm just having a hard time describing it."

"Well you can take your time."

"It was white on white, a little hazy. It was like when you wake up in the middle of the afternoon and the blinds are immediately pulled back. It was so intense but I didn't strain against the light. It smelled like every flower I've ever smelled mixed into one. I love flowers. I kept breathing deeper and tried to pick a few of my favorites out to see if I could differentiate a mum or a rose but it was useless; I gave into the intoxicating medley. It felt like I was floating, like I had no sensation below my feet but it was solid. I know it was because when my feet hit the ground they made a noise that was so rich, so full, almost musical. The longer I stayed, the more contrast developed between objects, but still lacked depth and character. I feel like if I spent more time there it would have continued to improve. It sounds terrible, but it was soothing having everything the same. I feel a little silly."

"Why?"

"I don't know. Seems a bit weird to have such an abstract dream affect me so much."

"Let it happen Linda. Remember, you're ten out of ten happy. Don't ask why."

"You're right doctor," she said laughing and pointing jokingly at Dr. Lewis.

"Last question. Do you have any adverse effects? Any headaches, nausea, things like that?"

"No. Completely perfect."

"Ok. Thanks Linda. That's it for now. I think you can go home. Your husband is out front waiting for you. He's going to drive you home. You were under anesthesia. I don't care how happy you feel you still need to let him drive."

"Thank you Dr. Lewis." She paused and looked at her water.

"What is it?" he asked reading the slight rounding of her shoulders.

"How long was I there?"

"Well, you were under for less than thirty minutes."

"Incredible," she said softly. She stood up and walked toward him. She threw her arms around his shoulders and kissed him on the lips. "Don't tell my husband. I just wanted to thank you for making me happy."

He stood, stunned. Even though he was a handsome man by most women's standards, he hadn't allowed himself to kiss a woman in close to a decade.

"Don't look so shocked Doctor. Nothing meant in it," Linda said and walked out the door and into her husband's arms. It took a moment for Dr. Lewis to turn around, but he was able to wave as the two lovers left the glass doors of the clinic.

Kyle sat in the control room still analyzing the data from Linda's treatment. He pored over the EEG readings looking for blips that could explain Linda's episodes of smiling, which involves over 40 different muscles in itself, talking, which would activate various different areas in the cortex: Broca's area, the primary motor cortex, and the anterior insula. Even her brainstem was showing no activity, despite clearly having basal metabolic functions, such as a heartbeat and breathing. Nothing was active. The fact that the EEG was receiving positive brain activity immediately following the administration of the epinephrine injection was driving Kyle mad.

"Hello Kyle," Dr. Lewis said leaning on the doorframe of the observation room.

"Dr. Lewis, what is it we've created here?"

"Same thing we've always been. A cure for psychological disorders."

"This is clearly different. I've gone through the data several times and she was brain dead for the entire time she expressed outward emotions, language, movements. I'm not sure I'm worthy of a PhD because I don't see how this is all possible," Kyle said half frustrated and bewildered.

"Well what makes a good experiment Kyle?"

"Controlling the variables."

"Have we done that?"

"I'd say we have."

"How's that?"

"Every patient has a background check, we eliminate those who have comorbidities and anomalies such as adverse reaction to anesthesia. We take only patients suffering from anxiety and/or depression. They are weaned off all meds for at least six weeks prior to our trial. Other than that we allow them to be as normal as possible leading up to the test to eliminate covariables that could otherwise affect our tests. We go through all of our pre-treatment discussions based on a script you have devised to eliminate a placebo effect, we don't feed them answers, no guiding questions."

"What else makes a good experiment Kyle?"

"I'm confused."

"Let's say you and I write a paper on Linda. One case study. What makes it more powerful?"

"More results, a bigger sample size, randomization across a population."

"How do we make that happen?"

"Reproducibility?"

"I think you might earn that PhD after all, Kyle," Dr. Lewis said with a smile.

"Ok," Kyle said looking at the computer and pulling up a schedule for the next day. "Looks like we have another woman, 142 pounds, 5'3", 43 years old. I can start calculating the percentages for the cocktail now if you want."

"How about for a male, 28, 6'2", and, I don't know, a buck eighty-five?"

"Me?" Kyle said pushing the chair back as he swiveled to face Dr. Lewis head on. He froze, eyes wide and pointing to himself.

"No time like the present. You heard Linda. Wanna' see heaven?"

"Not sure I'm a believer." He shrugged and his face went flat.

"That makes two of us. No pressure. Just a bit antsy is all. Been working on this for years, you know."

It was bittersweet for Dr. Lewis. He wanted to scream for joy, to tell Lily he finally got it right. He wanted to hold her, to tell her to take him back to where he felt the bliss. Maybe they could go together now. But it was too late. It had taken hundreds of different formulations to get it right. *How did she just randomly create such a wonderful cocktail? She was so brilliant compared to me.* His eagerness had taken her life so many years ago but nobody knew it was him. *She was too smart to kill herself. I should have tested it first.*

Kyle sat in the chair staring out into the open office space. His mind was relatively calm despite the looming question. He had thought about asking Dr. Lewis to allow him to be treated. He himself had suffered from depression and wanted the problem to go away, but now the proposition was made and it caused a reflective moment. *Would it be a huge change? Would I even notice a difference?*

"Ah screw it. Let's do it Doc," Kyle said and jumped out of the chair shaking his hand. It was worth the risks, if any were associated with the treatment.

The room was comfortable as the two men went to work. Kyle was lying supine on the bed in a standard hospital gown. Light was reflecting off most of the floor and walls; the glossy white tile acting as mirrors bathing the room from every angle with a bright white glow. A soft but steady drumbeat was present from the music playing in the observation room. Kyle heard it, and was a bit shocked that Dr. Lewis had never asked him to turn it down during testing. Kyle was always in the observation room listening to music and never knew it could be heard it in the treatment room.

Kyle had never been in the treatment room with a patient before. He smelled the alcohol, the latex. He felt the cool sensation from the alcohol wipe and the small sting as Dr. Lewis inserted the IV into his left hand.

"Good veins Kyle."

"Thanks Doc."

"You're going to feel a chill go up your arm when we start the titration."

"I'm aware."

"Just making sure you're as comfortable and relaxed as you can be Kyle. Ready?"

"Yes."

"Ok, I'm going to check on the readings, making sure we're all green and the cameras are running."

"Fair enough."

Dr. Lewis quickly walked into the observation area, taking off his gloves on the way. "BP is reading, heart rate reading, EEG is good, camera feeds are live, pulse ox . . . hey Kyle!"

"Yeah?"

"Wanna' put that pulse ox on for me?"

"Sure do," Kyle said and grabbed it, placing it on his right index finger. "So much for the script."

"Ah, shut up," Dr. Lewis said but not quite loud enough for Kyle to hear the joke. "Ok, pulse ox is 100 percent," he said to himself. He walked back out to Kyle. "You ready? I'm recording."

"Yes."

"This is test number 50-10, Kyle Braun, age 28. No comorbidities, no clinical psychological disorders. Right?"

"Correct," Kyle responded smiling.

"He has not taken medications in the last six weeks. Weight, 172 pounds, height 6'2". Titration of PB-50 has been determined to be 78 percent saline. Kyle, do you consent to treatment?"

"I do Dr. Lewis."

"Are you sure you want to do this Kyle? No lies."

"Yes, I'm good."

Dr. Lewis walked back across the floor, heels scraping tile several times along the way. He checked the saline bag, still more than 80 percent full. Next he checked the IV lines, and prepped the IV machine, making sure it was churning the way it should: no bubbles, no kinks.

"Wow, Doc it is a bit chilly."

"That's what I was referring to. It should pass."

"Back to the script I see."

"Ok Kyle get ready. Count down from 100. See you on the other side."

"99 . . . 9 . . . 7 . . . ," Kyle faded into the experience.

Dr. Lewis walked into the observation room and sat down in the soft cloth chair. He bobbed his head gently to Modestep playing through the speakers as he watched the monitors. He didn't care for Kyle's music, but never changed it either. He liked the predictability of the beat, the rhythm, the constant up and down swinging of the electronic sound. The song began to evolve, to fold together, to soften, and then it happened, the beat dropped. Dr. Lewis felt it in his entire body. The music was tinder for his adrenaline, his mind becoming more focused with each hit of the bass.

Dr. Lewis saw Kyle's vitals were leveling off: BP was 110/68, heart rate was steady at 62, O2 was 100 percent, and his EEG was flat. "Ok, let's throw some alarm values in 'er. BP, 90/55, heart rate, 50, O2 at 82," he said out loud to himself to the beat of the song.

Several more songs came and went as Dr. Lewis continued to watch the HD screens and tap his foot. Kyle's eyes were still, his body motionless, and his body temperature unchanging. The EEG was flat.

Camera four jumped to Kyle's mouth and Dr. Lewis caught the change out of the corner of his eye. Kyle's mouth was moving, slightly, but organized. It wasn't merely a muscle twitch. Dr. Lewis turned off the music and switched on the room audio. He placed headphones on to hear the subtle, quiet noises in the hum of the lights, the rhythmic clicking of the IV machine, and Kyle, whispering.

Kyle's EEG was flat, no brain activity. "We are 23 minutes into the test of Kyle Braun, he is whispering—" Dr. Lewis paused, "and exhibiting rapid eye movements. EEG is showing no brain activity."

*Bing, bing, bing.* The alarm sounded on the monitor. Dr. Lewis looked right and saw Kyle's heart rate had dipped to 42 beats per minute. He stood up, grabbed the epinephrine, and walked into the treatment room. After turning off the IV pump he grabbed an alcohol swab, quickly rubbing the IV port clean, and injected the drug.

Kyle snapped awake and took a deep, cleansing breath. He tasted the drugs in the back of his throat but the bitterness didn't ruin his state of mind. He felt whole; loved. "Doc," Kyle said softly and slowly turning to meet Dr. Lewis' eyes. "You've gotta try this."

Dr. Lewis smiled and rubbed Kyle's head, ruffling his brown hair. His eyes were sad but Kyle hadn't noticed. "I could tell you stories," Dr. Lewis said; only half joking.

# | THREE |

Dr. Lewis stood in front of the second-year med school students giving a lecture on the uses, physiology, and contraindications of beta blockers. The projector hummed overhead and his palm was sweaty from holding the remote for the PowerPoint presentation. He flippantly pointed the red laser at several recently published articles related to the drugs, but his focus was elsewhere.

"As you see, the p-value is .035, revealing a statistically significant finding related to the effects of beta blockers in this study. The inclusion criterion for this particular study was a past medical history of hypertension, no previous myocardial infarction, age range was 35 to 60, and if you see, the sample size was 1,198 individuals tested over six months, with 1,150 of them finishing the study. No explanation for the 48 drops, but I think we can assume they just didn't want to come in for their follow-up visits. That's only about a five percent drop out so we are ok with that."

Dr. Lewis sighed, clicked the remote, and threw the laser up at the next set of numbers. He was on autopilot. This was the twelfth time since joining the Washington University staff that he had given this lecture. He updated the PowerPoint annually, using teacher's aides to scour the research articles for appropriate content which he would ultimately comb through looking for holes in the study. He never wanted to be a professor, but it came with the contract if he wanted to do his research. Plus, it had its perks, such as weeding out who would make good lab assistants. It was how Kyle came along.

"All right everyone, I think that's gonna be it for the day. It's about eleven-o'clock and there's a really bad ice storm coming at noon.

Get home so you don't have to sleep in the building," Dr. Lewis said gratefully.

He was distracted by the previous day's results and eager to get to the lab. Kyle was going through the data from his own trial, taboo for a researcher, but this data wasn't going to be placed into the letter for federal funding.

Outside was a disaster. Saint Louis was known for its humid summers, however, very little is mentioned about its ice storms. Each step toward Dr. Lewis' lab was painful. He was being blasted by small ice crystals and cold rain making his face sting as he reached deep into his coat pockets trying to find relief. The collar of his black peacoat was up and he was trying to drive his head deep within the protective walls, making himself a turtle, but he walked with the speed of a hare.

His research lab was across campus, a frustrating situation on these days. When he began his contract with the university, administration had a difficult time deciphering where to place his lab. Technically, he was researching psychological disorders, however, his lab and research was conducted using anesthetics and required the use of a full operating room suite with all the trimmings. Ultimately, he was thrown into the top floor of 4500 Parkview. It was an industrial type building with big wonderful windows, but it was old. They had to do considerable renovations in order to maintain the clean, stable environment for testing.

The ground floor at 4500 Parkview had two large loading areas so bringing in lab equipment, oxygen tanks, drywall, large windows to replace the old leaky ones, and other non-essentials was easy. It did offer a 360-degree view of the medical campus, but that wasn't much to look at. It had taken a full year to completely buildout the suite. When it was finished they had a full waiting room, a testing room with observation suite completely isolated from outside stimulus, and a beautifully decorated office with nearly floor to ceiling solar windows wrapping around the suite.

Finally, Dr. Lewis entered the building, slipping on the ice with his last step, having let his guard down. He checked his watch, 11:30, and entered the elevator. The steel doors closed and he was gently carried to the top floor. He swatted at his arms attempting to shake loose the moisture before his coat soaked it in.

"Hey Ethan," Kyle said as he heard the elevator doors open.

"How we doing, Kyle?"

"The results are identical to Linda's."

"Well that's not surprising, but I meant how are you feeling?"

"Rested."

"Looks like we're gonna be stuck here tonight," Dr. Lewis said nodding his head toward the large, uninterrupted solar glass windows.

"It's that bad already?"

"Yeah, and according to the forecast it hasn't even begun yet. I think we need to get some pizza up here, a lot, because I don't plan on leaving."

"Imo's?" Kyle jokingly asked.

"I'm not from here. Can't get into that local crap."

"I know I'm just kidding. I'll make a call, grab some of the good stuff."

The hours drifted by as the two men ate pizza and went through mountains of data. It was all saved locally on servers inside the research office, as well as remotely for redundancy. In all, five gigs of data had to be combed through, compiled, and statistically analyzed. It was decided that they would exclude, for now, Linda's results. Dr. Lewis and Kyle had performed over one-thousand test results before Linda, and they were going to use that data to reach out to the federal government for money to conduct stage four clinical trials of the drug cocktail. They had been confident the findings would be significant; they just wanted a powerful study.

It was time to make it official.

"Ok Kyle, lets start running the numbers for MADRS and the

Hamilton Depression."

"Ok Doc. Two different analyses?"

"Yes, should be pretty well correlated between the two tests' results and I'd rather do more work now instead of backtracking if the numbers get ugly."

"We know they won't get ugly," Kyle said with a mouthful of pizza.

"I don't want a single shred of doubt about our results. Nobody is doing this type of treatment and I know there are more doubters than believers."

"Well I was a doubter of a few things before I went under. I think you should just invite the federal review board down here for a sample of the treatment. Guarantee they sign off then."

"Not a bad plan. Now get to work on the stats. I'm going to write the experimental design."

Several hours of icy rain pelted the windows in a percussive melody as the men worked tirelessly through the night. The increases in volume and frequency of rain was stimulating and welcomed. The wind would blow in gusts raising the noise to a feverish pitch, first on the east end of the suite, and then wrapped around to the west as the night progressed.

Kyle had fallen fast asleep on a sectional in the corner of the office, his laptop open, but on the floor were his statistical printouts thrown haphazardly in a semicircle around him. He was lying in a fetal position, head uncomfortably tilted to the left from lying on the arm of the couch. No doubt he would wake with a terrible neck ache but Dr. Lewis let him sleep. They had put in a week's worth of work over the last thirteen hours.

Behind Kyle through the windows shimmered a frozen paradise. The ice had stopped falling around midnight and the sky opened above, allowing the moon to illuminate the dark, reflective world below. The trees were coated in half-inch-thick ice. The streets were deserted and the buildings looked like giant glazed candies displayed on an oversized glass tray. There were more lights on than Dr. Lewis typically saw at 2:00 a.m. He assumed the faculty researchers were all taking advantage of the excuse to spend a late night in the lab. Classes would likely be cancelled.

Dr. Lewis stood facing out the east windows watching the sky begin to change into a lighter shade of night as the sun hinted at its ascent to begin the new day. He held firmly onto the printed research paper. He preferred to edit hard copies over digital media. In his left hand he sipped cold coffee. He wanted to finish the paper. He paced the room east to west as he mumbled the words slowly, aloud to himself, making sure each sentence felt right. After striking through a few sentences, adding a notation for a point here and there, he went back to the computer to make the final corrections.

### A Preliminary Investigation into the Use of a Multifactorial Anesthetic Approach to the Treatment of Clinical Depression and General Anxiety Disorder.

Dr. Ethan Lewis, MD, PhD; Kyle Braun, BS

*Abstract*

Depression and anxiety often result in reduced compliance associated with treatment due to the length of time required for the drugs to work. 1,056 subjects entered the trial involving an anesthetic approach for treatment of anxiety and depression disorders. The treatment proved beneficial in treating depression and anxiety both immediately following, as well as long-term at a statistically significant level.

*Introduction*

Major depressive disorder affects approximately 14.8 million American adults, or about 6.7 percent of the US population age 18 and older in a given year. Anxiety disorders are the most common mental illness in the US, affecting 38 million adults in the United States age 18 and older (16 percent of US population). Anxiety disorders are highly treatable, yet only about one-third of those suffering receive treatment. Both of these psychological disorders have been found associated with higher rates of myocardial infarction, high blood pressure, suicidal thoughts and decreased appetite. Current gold standard for treatment of depression and anxiety include drugs and counseling. Often times, compliance is an issue with regard to taking the medications as frequently as prescribed, and the drugs often take several weeks for effect. There may also be social stigmas to seeking professional counseling.

**Hypothesis:** The anesthetic treatment will show immediate results demonstrating improved symptoms associated with depression and/or anxiety.

**Null Hypothesis:** No observable or testable difference will be present following the administration of the treatment.

*Methods*

**Inclusion criterion**

**Age:** 25–60.

**Sex:** male or female.

**Diagnosis:** Presence of clinical depression and/or anxiety.

**Standardized tests:** Montgomery-Asberg Depression Rating Scale (MADRS) and the Hamilton Depression Rating Scale (HDRS) to be administered four times: once before weaning from meds, one immediately before test, the third immediately following, and the fourth was three months after treatment, medication-free.

**Exclusion criterion:** Adverse reaction to anesthetics uncontrolled hypertension, diabetes, COPD, history of concussions or TBI, stroke or TIA, other psychological disorders.

Sample size was 1,056 individual men and women, of which 1,008 followed through until the fourth written test. 386 men and 670 women were tested.

Subjects were interviewed by both Dr. Ethan Lewis and Kyle

Braun. Each subject was asked a series of background questions to ensure they met the inclusion criterion. A second set of questions was asked to determine the level of anxiety based off the multiple question test on the Anxiety and Depression Association of America. They were given both the MADRS as well as the DHRS at that time. They were instructed to discontinue use of any prescription medications for the six weeks leading up to treatment. An anesthetic tolerance test was issued to ensure the subjects did not possess any intolerance or opportunity for adverse effect.

The second stage begins with a retake of the written tests. The subject's treatment begins using a proprietary formulated mix of anesthetics being titrated in with a saline solution. Informed consent was given. Baseline vitals and brain activity monitoring with an EEG were recorded prior to administration of the drug. Once under, low-end vitals were noted and once those were violated, the patient was brought out of anesthesia immediately. EEG was recorded throughout, but no baseline or normalized parameters were set.

Stage three is retaking the written tests.

Stage four is a fourth written test to achieve long-term follow up.

**Results/Discussion**

Using statistical analysis, both the MADRS and DHRS demonstrated statistically significant improvements in scores during the third and fourth written tests with a p-value of .002, and .001 respectively. A slight worsening of symptoms was noted between the first and second examination but proved insignificant. No differences were noted between men or women, nor were there any differences noted when comparing those with only anxiety, only depression, or for those diagnosed with both.

The results reveal a strong and significant improvement with respect to depression and anxiety symptoms. Of particular interest are the results from the third and fourth tests, which show no statistical difference from one another, thereby indicating the treatment could

be considered for long term results even after one use. A treatment
requiring a one-time use could dramatically improve compliance and
consistent results, and is worth further investigation. It is also less
likely that this treatment option would be associated with negative
social stigmas.

"Kyle, wake up," Dr. Lewis said as he plopped down on the
opposite side of the couch.

"Oh man. Sorry Doc. How long was I—"

"No worries, Kyle you did great work. Read this. Wait, drink this
first." Dr. Lewis handed him a large cup of fresh coffee he made just
before printing the final version. Several minutes passed and Kyle
was fully awake and reading. His brow was furrowed, and he digested
every word slowly and methodically. Dr. Lewis appreciated this about
Kyle. He was not working with Dr. Lewis as a means to an end; he
truly believed in the research and what they were trying to achieve. It
seemed Kyle was even more dedicated since being treated himself.

Kyle finished the paper, skipping the citations. He had been the
one to put them together. "I would add one thing," Kyle said as he
handed the paper back to Dr. Lewis.

"What's that?"

"Our video of Linda."

"How will that help? How would we send it?"

"We submit it digitally, attach an edited video file. I used to
make some movies with my friends." Dr. Lewis gave Kyle a judging
glance and smirked. "Ok, don't judge me. Just trust me. Let me put it
together, it'll be five minutes tops and I'll reduce the quality so the file
is small."

"I've never heard of sending a video with a proposal. I think we'll
get rejected upon submission."

"I don't. It's about how insane that was. She was literally talking
without having any brain activity noted. Doc, trust me."

Dr. Lewis paused for a moment, performing a mental pros and

cons list. After careful consideration he smirked and looked at Kyle. "Show me what you got, Hollywood."

"Oh, I'll show you." Dr. Lewis once again looked sideways at Kyle. "Dang it just let me do it already!" Kyle said and smiled as he pulled up the videos on his computer.

The sun had fully risen and the world shimmered. It was incredible how beautiful ice was as it coated everything in existence. It was blinding, the light reflecting off of everything in sight, but the stillness was calming as the world appeared suspended in time.

Kyle was pasting the last of the footage together as Dr. Lewis watched over his shoulder. In total, the clip was four-minutes thirty-three seconds. It included a shot of Linda talking and her rapid eye movements. The videos were time stamped and synced perfectly with the instrument data that was shown in a smaller square box on the bottom right of the video displaying her EEG and vitals. He also included her interviews before treatment and after showing the visual and emotional differences.

"Great work, Kyle."

"Thanks, Doc."

"Let's send this off." Dr. Lewis sat down at the computer and gathered the article and the video. He submitted the article for publication in the American Psychological Association, in hopes to get his article approved and placed in the journal sometime in the summer of 2006. Afterward, he submitted his research findings, along with the video for a government grant in order to increase his research lab, and begin stage IV clinical trials on the treatment.

"You know," Dr. Lewis said quietly. "This is going to take a few weeks."

"Yeah, it always does."

"I . . . um . . . Kyle . . . what I'm trying to ask is uh . . . ha—" he said starting to smirk at his own struggles.

"Jesus Ethan, spit it out."

"Yeah . . ." Dr. Lewis paused and tried to wish away the volatile question that was swimming in his head. It is selfish to experiment once again with the fringes of human life, to explore a drug that was so capable of killing, which had killed the only woman he ever loved was. . . . In his mind he briefly went back to the Harvard lab where she exhaled her last breath, where her heart stopped beating and his world shattered like the ice currently surrounding him. He wouldn't be able to walk away this time. He had worked on the treatment for far too many years now and Lily was the reason, the motivation, the original creator. It was her that kept him from asking Kyle.

"Kyle, I think I'm going to get some sleep. Amazing work today. I cannot thank you enough for helping me the last several years. Let's hope they see the benefits of what we've achieved." Dr. Lewis extended his hand. Kyle grasped it firmly.

Dr. Lewis walked toward the treatment lab and closed the door behind him. He kicked off his shoes and the noise from them striking the floor echoed in the small room as he lay down on the treatment table. The comforting smell of the alcohol and the hum from the electronics soothed him to sleep. As his eyelids closed they forced the stubborn tears to fall, just as they'd done many times before in memory of Lily, the one who first taught him to release.

# | FOUR |

One week went by slowly, as Dr. Lewis waited patiently to hear about his federal funding. He was distracting himself by reworking his lectures, updating slides with the latest research, and eliminating the few items that were falling out of practice. He graded exams, held office hours, and actually attended the month's faculty meeting. All the busy work couldn't stop his mind from wandering to the question he refused to ask Kyle. It was like heroin; the more resistance, the harder it says yes.

"Hey Kyle, what's the word?" Dr. Lewis asked casually into the phone from the lab.

"Not much. Finally caught up on sleep."

"Do you have a few minutes to swing by the clinic? I'd like to run something by you." Dr. Lewis hands were clammy, his forehead in hand, and he clenched his jaw firmly in frustration. *What the hell am I doing, what the hell am I doing, what the hell am I doing?*

"Yeah, I can head right over. Kinda bored to tell you the truth."

"Um. Well, Ok then, Kyle. See you soon."

Dr. Lewis sat in the clinic and waited. He pulled up the research findings, reviewed them once more, making sure both Kyle and Linda had the same, lifeless EEG results. It had been the first time they had these specific findings. The prior 1,056 all had excellent clinical findings, but the difference was they all had active EEGs, a lot of which showed increased activity in the areas associated with opiates. He knew the funding may not come because of this, but the long-term effects of treatment, being as significant as they were, would hopefully get them through. If not, they would need to test this reformulation on another thousand individuals, and retry to submit.

He watched Linda's video again, leaned back into the swiveling chair, and twisted side to side, hands behind his head. *Was this what I looked like when she treated me? Did I talk? Did I laugh? I remember what I experienced like it was yesterday, but I still couldn't describe it. I hope she got to see what I saw, that would almost make it worth it; for her anyway.*

The steel doors of the elevator opened and out sauntered Kyle. He was bundled up from the walk to the clinic, but he had already taken his hat off on the ride up. His wavy hair was askew and he did his best to rub it back into a respectable style. He smiled at Dr. Lewis, his dimples hiding within brown stubble cheeks.

"Cold, isn't it?" Dr. Lewis asked as he stopped Linda's video.

"Frustratingly."

"Thanks for coming down. I'm not sure how comfortable I am with what I want to ask you, so before I ask, I want you to understand that 'no' is a welcomed response."

"Ok?" Kyle asked confused. "Just ask, Ethan."

"Do you want to be treated again?"

"Like with our cocktail?"

"Yes."

"For what? What would change?"

Dr. Lewis paused. It was a valid question. Of the dozens of times he went through the conversation in his head, this question hadn't come up. It wasn't easy. *What would we change?* "The parameters. I would hold off on bringing you out until we get to lower vitals. See if the event changes at all."

"How low are we talking?"

"Five percent difference. Should be negligible."

"When?"

"Your convenience."

"It's convenient right now." Kyle said and winked.

"Ok. It really, I'm really uh—"

"Shut up, Ethan. Let's do this already," Kyle said throwing off his jacket.

Kyle was in a hospital gown sitting up in the treatment bed. The cameras were running, the IV inserted, leads were placed on his head for the EEG, a blood pressure cuff on his arm, and the pulse ox on his finger was not forgotten this time.

"You ready, Kyle?"

"What, no script?"

"We're off the books now, kid. Wanna turn back?"

"All in the name of science, Doc."

"In all seriousness, Kyle. I need to know you're good with this. I can't have that on my conscience."

"Yes Doc, I'm good. Going to heaven again. Nothing wrong with that."

Dr. Lewis began the titration, and as before, Kyle felt the chill and fought hard to stay awake longer, counting down to 96 from 100.

Dr. Lewis went into the observation room and sat with his face in the glow of screens projecting data and HD video which continuously updated. He entered the low end parameters into the monitors: BP 85/52, heart rate . . . 39, O2 at 78.

He sat and waited, sweat moistening his armpits, his back, and palms. He was forced to clean the lenses of his reading glasses several times due to the fog that was accumulating, limiting his ability to read the values on the monitors.

Thirty minutes into the test and the signs began. Camera four came to life and focused on Kyle's face, his lips mouthing inaudible words, a smile—one that continued for the next several minutes. Dr. Lewis began to feel a knot in his stomach churning, cramping, forcing him to move to the edge of his chair for relief. He could see his own heartbeat through his shirt, hear it swooshing in his ears. He focused solely on Kyle's vitals, wishing for them to drop soon so the treatment would end quickly. He stared and stared, searching for a book, a magazine, anything to avert his eyes from the monitors but found nothing. *I'm going to need a distraction if we do this again.*

Finally, after 53 minutes and 23 seconds, the alarm sounded. Dr. Lewis was already in the room, having walked there at the forty-fifth minute, epinephrine in hand, waiting for the sound from the observation room. He injected the stimulant and Kyle woke up in a storm of laughter.

"Oh my Lord, Doc," Kyle said as he grasped Dr. Lewis' hand. He looked into his eyes. "How long was I under?"

"Fifty-three long, torturous minutes."

Kyle wiped his eyes with his hands trying to bring the experience back to life. "But I can't even see paradise. It's like I have some sort of block to where I can't see it when I close my eyes, but I remember it. Strangest experience ever, Doc. When can I go back?"

*I know that feeling . . . what have I done.* "Minimum three days, Kyle. Was the experience more intense?"

"Not on a quantifiable level but yeah, I believe it was."

# | FIVE |

Another two weeks passed, and like clockwork, every three days, Kyle was given the treatment. His BP was set at a hard 55/30, his heart rate 30, and oxygen 75 percent. Most often, it was his BP that was tripping the alarm but he was experiencing no ill effects. The time he was under anesthesia also became longer, but it was fairly linear. The longest he was under had been just over two hours. What was more incredible, was that Kyle had no concept of time when inside. "It's like time stands still," he said each time he came out, seemingly more amazed at every treatment.

The experience was becoming more visceral, more cumulative. "It's like finding out you have more than five senses and you come back a little frustrated, but mainly euphoric," Kyle had said. The sounds were more rich, the visuals were hard to decipher, but the more he went under, the more defined the objects were becoming for Kyle, as if his own system was recalibrating.

Kyle had once participated in a test at a neuro lab. He had to throw little rubber balls at a target 10 feet away while standing on one leg. It was a joke, nonsense, a waste of time. He had been a scholarship-earning swimmer, not a throwing sport athlete, but it was beyond easy to hit the target 50 out of 50 tries. He then had to wear goggles, which distorted his vision, and asked to throw again. The first ten throws he missed horribly to the right. The next three sets of ten became progressively closer, and, during the final ten, he hit the target ten times. The last part of the test was to take the goggles off and toss another fifty times. Of the first ten he missed six, but by the time he threw 25 he was striking the target every time. It was an example of how the cerebellum can adapt, retrain, and reorganize complex motor movements. Kyle felt this was happening with his entire brain while in the treatment, except at a much higher level, as if dormant synaptic events created more connections, heightening sensations he'd never felt before.

Dr. Lewis walked into the lab office and sat at his desk. It was Friday, just over three weeks since submitting his request for federal funding. The thought of another weekend of boredom and second-guessing was driving him crazy. He methodically entered his login, taking his time, delaying the disappointment. His inbox was full of unread messages, which made it hard to find the one he had been waiting for. Another faculty meeting next week, several questions about the last lecture topic, anesthetics, presumably because of his area of research, and a few messages that somehow got past the spam filter.

Then there it was. Once he saw the subject line, he froze. His hands began to sweat and his finger stuck to the mouse. *If it's a no ... it can't be a no ... the evidence is strong. We nailed the research, had powerful data.*

He clicked on the email.

Dr. Ethan Lewis:

On behalf of the Unites States Government, we would like to inform you that your request for a grant in the area of Healthcare, specifically under the submission Behavioral Interventions to Address Multiple Chronic Health Conditions in Primary Care, has been granted. Below you will find the details.

We have deemed it appropriate to grant you ten million dollars in federal funding. Our decision was not an easy one, being that your study involving a proprietary blend of anesthetics and a known poison, *Convallaria majalis,* we were reluctant to allow the study to continue. However, the compelling nature of your long-term follow-ups and the video of the woman was fascinating. We decided the research shows a compelling amount of evidence which needs further follow-up, as it could greatly reduce the overall cost of treatment and improve the quality of life of the individuals included in your research study.

Speaking specifically about the woman in the video, it appears her results were not included in the actual numbers within the study data. Her EEG on the video was flat reading zero activity. We felt this should have been discussed in the results section, and would like a follow-up explanation as to why this wasn't included before we allow the funding to finalize. Our assumption is that it was an inadvertent mistake.

Dr. Mitchell Raymond MD, PhD

"Thank you, Kyle, for making that video," Dr. Lewis said out loud as he clapped his hands.

Dr. Raymond,

Thank you for the funding. Our decision to exclude her data was due to a differentiation of the proprietary blend, and therefore, was technically not a part of the same study. We will, however, in our next phase of testing, explore this new blend due to the findings associated with her response to treatment. Mainly, as you have noticed, her EEG results. We have conceded that there may be hallucinogenic effects of our drug mix, and by association, people were reporting euphoric and vivid visual, auditory, and olfactory sensations. However, with the final subject exhibiting a lack of brain activity, we found it particularly interesting and worth exploring since, as you saw, she also had these sensory experiences, as well as physical manifestations while under treatment which are currently unexplained.

We are very appreciative of your large grant. It will be put to good use, as you've certainly seen in the plans we've submitted.

I await your continued correspondence,
Dr. Ethan Lewis MD, PhD

Dr. Lewis exhaled, picked up the phone, and called Kyle. He was relieved, almost empty, as he sat in his chair waiting to hit send on the email. He had spent years with his myopic vision dominating his world, leaving room for nothing else; not that he wanted anything else. His dreams of a family died with Lily.

His whole life was changed in that moment. He was a biochemical student working on his PhD, performing special research in drug development, specifically in the area of analgesics. He was studying natural plants, rather than synthetic drugs, which was where she came in. Lily studied botany in undergraduate school and knew thousands of species that could be tested. Her favorite plant was Lily of the Valley, because she always said she was from "the Valley." Most people assumed San Fernando, California, but what she actually meant was

The Valley of Ashes which separates Long Island and the glitzy world of Manhattan in *The Great Gatsby*. She giggled every time she said it. Harvard couldn't contain her brilliance.

"Kyle!" Dr. Lewis exclaimed into the phone.

"Dr. Lewis, sounds like you've got some good news for me," Kyle said happily on the other end.

"You're right, I do. Haven't hit the send button yet so why don't you get down here and we can celebrate by looking over the plans of the new clinic. Maybe even search for a couple lab assistants from our current classes."

"I'll head over after my lecture. I have a 10:30, I'll make it quick, cancel my office hours. Go ahead and hit that send without me."

"Fair enough. Bring lunch up when you come."

"What do you—"

"I don't care what the hell I'm eating just bring it."

"You read my mind, Doc. I'll bring whatever I please."

Dr. Lewis was reviewing the new research facility. One requirement of the grant was to have a complete, itemized list of expected costs. The biggest item for Dr. Lewis and Kyle was the expansion of the clinic.

The plan was to renovate the entire second floor, making four treatment rooms in total with a centralized observation suite. In order for privacy, there had to be a dividing wall that split the observation rooms into four pods, each having large glass windows looking into each treatment room. At the center of the second floor was the elevator, along with storage rooms, oxygen tanks, servers, ducting, and electrical. It was beautifully symmetrical on the plans. The exterior windows would all have to be removed in order to facilitate as much control over external stimulus, and with the windows being terribly inefficient, it would help with climate control. Each treatment room was exactly the same size, color, and temperature to ensure that even the smallest variables were controlled.

The first floor was to be beautifully built out with large windows, dozens of chairs, a few couches, multiple flat screens hung throughout. There would be hardwood flooring and plenty of artwork to hang on the wall in the center of the room, which would inconspicuously hide the elevator shaft. The designer had suggested an orange paint for that wall, but Dr. Lewis immediately rejected it for a much more subdued seafoam green. Dr. Lewis' other touch was to place a variety of faux lilies throughout the waiting area.

"What ya up to?" Kyle asked as he walked to the large wooden table that delineated the office workspace from lounge space.

"Reviewing our new research suite. It's a work of art. Look at the symmetry in the second floor. Truly artistic."

"Yeah. Well here's lunch," Kyle said plopping down a brown bag.

"Should have known."

"Yup."

Dr. Lewis opened the bag and started spooning the rice, beans and chicken into his mouth. "At least you got my order right."

"Everyone loves Chipotle, Doc. You send that email?"

"Yes, they were asking for an explanation as to why Linda wasn't included, but we still sent her video. They noted her EEG findings. Our money won't come until that's explained, but I explained it."

"Great. So how much did we get?"

"All of it."

"No!" Kyle exclaimed, his mouth full of burrito.

"Ten million."

"We've got to celebrate!"

"How?"

"We're getting drunk!"

"Oh Kyle, I'm too old for that. I'm not even sure I've ever been able to do that."

"Ok Doc, but you are, so man up!"

The bar was walking distance. As the two researchers entered the poorly lit establishment there was a slight smell of cigarettes that had penetrated deep into the walls and the thick lacquered tables. The music from the radio was bland, but fresh to them because the two of them had exclusively listened to songs from their online accounts over the last several months.

"You guys are a little early for the dinner crowd. I'm Eric. You can sit at the bar. We aren't seating tables."

"Hey we're good with that, right Ethan?"

"Yeah, fair enough." The men meandered through several worn tables, their feet sticking slightly to the floor but not from filth, from old, degraded polyurethane. The staff was using a chemical on the floor that was reacting with the sealing agent, but at least they were cleaning. They took seats side by side at the dark, walnut bar. It appeared new, smooth to the touch, a sheen over the entire surface that was reflecting the variety of overhead lights and neon signs displayed behind the bar. Behind them and to the left, a stage, and on the bar counter was a flyer for karaoke night.

"What we drinking tonight, gentlemen?" Eric asked taking his place behind the bar and turning on the TV mounted above.

"Shot and a beer," Kyle said quickly.

"The same I guess," Dr. Lewis said shrugging at Eric as if he'd never drank a day in his life. Quickly, Eric grabbed two Buds and gave them both a two-finger pour of whiskey.

"To success," Kyle said holding up the whiskey.

"To the grant," Dr. Lewis responded with a smile.

"Whoa, Doc!" Kyle shouted as Dr. Lewis slammed the thick bottom glass onto the bar. "Didn't think you drank much?"

"I don't, but that doesn't mean I don't know how," Dr. Lewis said raising the glass back into the air. "Eric, another round."

"You guys wanna start a tab?" Eric said pouring the firewater.

"Yeah, I got it," Dr. Lewis said handing over his credit card. "What time you start serving food?"

"'Bout an hour or so."

"Well I'm not slowing down before then," Dr. Lewis said and slammed the second two-finger pour in one gulp, feeling the burn branch out through his chest like a warm, comforting fire without the smoke.

"Oh my God!" Kyle said laughing as he stood witness to the spectacle that nobody on campus would believe. A hermit of a researcher, an antisocial professor watching the clock every second he lectured, avoiding any faculty function, gathering, and holiday party. People rarely saw the man eat, let alone cut loose. "I'm getting a video of this," Kyle said and pulled out his phone.

"Better get it quick!" Dr. Lewis said as he snapped his head back throwing whiskey down for a third time, still having neglected his beer.

"I missed it!" Kyle shouted and laughed as Dr. Lewis raised his eyebrows wide and stuck his tongue out.

"I'm winnin'!" Dr. Lewis said straight into the camera while Kyle laughed silently.

"Ok, we can do that," Kyle responded and put his phone away, slammed his first double shot and yelped quietly to reduce the burn. "Eric, just leave the bottle."

"Am I gonna have to watch you two all night?" Eric said as he placed the bottle of whiskey down, his hand still grasping the neck.

"We'll be good boys," Kyle said.

"Scout's honor," Dr. Lewis said holding up his hand.

"Well that explains a few things," Eric joked.

A few drinks later, several plates of half eaten appetizers, and a table front and center for karaoke was the best night of Dr. Lewis' last twelve years. It was exhilarating cheering for the younger crowd while they sang and danced. Most of them were terrible, but that's when he and Kyle would cheer even louder. A couple of the songs they knew, but most times, the music was as foreign as durian fruit and haggis.

"Next up on the mic . . . Ethan and Kyyllleeee!" the emcee yelled to the crowd gathered in the bar. By now, the bar had become standing room only and everyone in the bar knew the two, drunk cheerleaders who were making everyone feel confident.

"Did you put our names in?" Kyle yelled.

"Hell no, I don't sing!"

"Screw it, let's do this!" Kyle said grabbing Ethan by the arm and hauling him on stage.

"What are we gonna sing?"

"Hmmm," Ethan said as he paged through the book. "Haha, we're doing this one," he said pointing.

"Yes. They'll know it too. Let's rock this mother!" Ethan said without smiling.

The music started, slowly, a melody that everyone knew and they erupted. Kyle raised his hands above his head to quiet the crowd, whose eyes were all transfixed on the two men.

"Every now and then I get a little bit lonely, and you're never coming round. Every now and then I get a little bit tired of listening to the sound of my tears."

Slowly the music began to build, Kyle had dropped to a knee several times already and Dr. Ethan Lewis had even performed a leg kick and a pelvic thrust, which he did while throwing his tie back over his shoulder to an incredible crescendo of applause. The climax of the song hit and everyone began to sing it through to the finish.

"I really need you tonight! Forever's gonna start tonight, forever's gonna start to—. Once upon a time I was fallin' in love, but now I'm only falling apart, there's nothing I can do, a total eclipse of the heart."

The song had finished, both men on knees, heads down and both hands on their mics in a folded hands position. They were sweaty messes having done very little in the way of aerobic exercise over the last several years of compiling research. Everyone was clapping and cheering.

"Encore, encore, encore," the crowd cheered and the two men rose and looked at each other.

"What d'ya say, Doc?"

"I'm not a doctor tonight. Let's bring the house down."

The two of them sang two more songs and they shut the place down. It was only 1:00 a.m., but nobody was willing to go on stage after they completed their set-list of 80's love ballads. With their appetizers wolfed down and their warm beers finished, they walked to the bar, steadying themselves along the way on the shoulders, hips, and tables of their best fans.

"Hey Eric we're gonna head out now," Ethan said once he got to the bar.

"Impressive night Doc. Impressive night," Eric said as he handed him the bill and his credit card.

"I do what I can Eric. This is for you." Dr. Lewis handed the man five hundred dollars.

"Hey wait! Wait! Dr. Lewis!" Eric yelled as Ethan walked away. He didn't turn around so Eric ran around the bar, pushed through a sea of shifting people, and finally reached Ethan just outside the doors to the bar.

"You want my number or something?" Ethan joked as he turned to see Eric.

"This is too much. I can't take it."

"You're a good man, Eric. I can see that, even though I'm really, really drunk."

"I'll second that!" Kyle said throwing a finger in the air.

"Listen Eric," Dr. Lewis said placing a hand on Eric's shoulder in order to steady himself enough to look into his eyes. "I had a really good day today. I'm paying it forward because tomorrow, I know I won't be as generous."

"Thanks Doc. You ever need anything, you come see me." Eric reached up, took Dr. Dr. Lewis' hand off of his shoulder, and shook it.

"Will do."

It was as planned, a short walk back to the research office and they would crash there overnight. The air was brisk, a slight southern breeze kept it comfortable, but neither of the two felt the cold. They stumbled down the sidewalk, pulling themselves together as best they could whenever they saw a pair or headlights or another person walking down the streets. The last thing they wanted was a scandal over two drunk researchers getting arrested for public intoxication.

"Hey Ethan, if I may call you that, sir," Kyle said and tried to bow, almost falling face first onto the concrete.

"Yes you may good man," Ethan replied with a proper British accent.

"I would like you to take me deeper in treatment. Screw the blood pressure, just put me on oxygen and make sure I don't drop below 70 percent."

Dr. Lewis sobered up a little. His mind was trying to race through the sludge of the alcohol. It did make sense, if his tissues, particularly his brain, were getting adequate oxygen it shouldn't matter what his blood pressure, or heart rate was reading.

"I think it's a valid suggestion Kyle, one worth considering in the morning," he said continuing the British accent.

They walked in silence, both thinking independently about how smart they felt, but how stupid their ideas would seem in the morning.

The two men walked into the office in the top floor of their building. "You take the couch," Dr. Lewis said haphazardly pointing into the sitting area to the right.

"Thanks Doc," Kyle said with a deep sigh and rubbed his eyes with numb hands. When he brought them down his eyes were moist.

"Kyle?" Dr. Lewis paused, seeing the sadness on his assistant's face. "Yeah?"

"You an emotional drunk?" he said smirking, trying to lighten the awkward mix of drunken sadness.

Kyle smirked, "No Doc, not usually." He conceded to the
moment. Kyle could never lie to his father either. "My dad died."

"Oh my God Kyle, when?"

"Seven years ago. Pancreatic cancer."

"Wow, I'm so sorry Kyle. I had no idea. It may sound a bit harsh
but I'm glad you didn't say it happened today."

"No worries, Doc."

"You wanna talk about it? No time like the present."

"I don't know," Kyle said as he looked at Dr. Lewis. He admired
his boss, who challenged him to think. His father, who was an
engineer, had often done that. "Kyle, help me figure this out," Ray
would say even though he knew the answer. He wanted Kyle to use his
reasoning, his logic, to come to the same conclusions. Kyle's ability to
use creative reasoning and problem solving made him so appealing to
Dr. Lewis.

"I don't like to talk about it. Too many bad memories drown out
the good. I'm hoping one day it'll change. Sometimes I remember the
good stuff. He came to all my swim meets even through my freshman
year at Missouri. After that, his health slipped, I took a year away
from school to help him and we dug through the research articles
on pancreatic cancer treatments. We made two different trips to
Europe to talk to oncologists. One trip was Germany and the other
was Spain, both clinics showed promising results from a vitamin and
micronutrient super-dose. Dad showed some improvements early,
but after a month back home he took a nosedive. We went from
talking about life, about women, about how to raise a family, to never
speaking again. For six weeks I watched him in hospice."

"Your mom?"

"She walked out several years before."

"Kyle I'm so—"

"I know Doc. You don't have to say it. I just miss telling him about things. I miss the way he used to ask questions that made me think, the way he used to be able to get me to talk about my problems. I miss hearing his voice after a race as he yelled louder than all the other fans. I miss pointing to him and smiling, knowing that I made him proud. Mostly though," Kyle said walking across the room and throwing himself down onto the couch, his left arm draped over his weeping eyes. "Mostly I think of the things he won't be here for. He would have loved grandkids. I can't stop thinking about him laying in the bed, snoring, his tongue swollen from the dehydration. That's not the man I want to remember, but it's the one I can't get out my head."

"Go to bed Kyle. If you ever want to talk though, I'll listen. I've lost a loved one too."

"Thanks, Doc. One thing I hated about him dying, was that in the end, he accepted it. Felt safe, like he had a place to go. He went to church so I guess he felt he was going to heaven." They were silent for a few moments, except for a sniffle once or twice from Kyle who lay motionless.

"You know what'll help, Doc?"

"No."

"Never having to see this stupid tattoo anymore." He held his left forearm into the air revealing a tattoo of the Missouri "M."

"I don't understand—"

"Of course not."

"We can talk tomorrow if you'd like."

"I guess. Thanks, Doc." Kyle didn't speak anymore, but by the pulsing of his chest up and down, Dr. Lewis knew he wasn't just breathing and decided to leave him to his thoughts. Dr. Lewis walked into the treatment room and onto the table. He closed his eyes and drifted to sleep.

As he slept, he found himself in a familiar place. He was surrounded by emotion, by music, and the smell of flowers. He saw nothing but light, and the hint of something beyond a thin, white veil that seemed miles away in every direction. His movements seemed slow, methodical, guided by an unseen force. As he glided through the open world full of sensations, he began to wonder what it was all about. He'd been here before, but it was different each time. The music wasn't familiar, but comforting, and seemed to come from every direction even though he saw nothing was around him.

He looked down toward the ground, which revealed footprints like one would find in soft earth or sand, but the ground appeared firm and seamless. He heard footsteps from far off, moving in a rhythmical fashion, playing in sync with the cello and viola he heard all around him. The footsteps were coming closer and Dr. Lewis began to feel uneasy in his paradise. He could hear them echoing off walls that didn't exist. Louder and louder they grew until they drowned out the soothing music from the strings. He was distracted from the smells, the veiled objects seemed to disappear into shadows, and he focused only on the footsteps.

He felt a tap on his shoulder that startled him. He spun around shying away from the touch and saw her. Lily. She was standing with her blonde hair gently blowing back revealing her tan skin, and the handful of freckles he loved on her nose. Her eyes were glowing like the ocean but her expression was lifeless. Her beauty was tainted by the hate that breached her eyes. She clenched her jaw more than once, biting back the words. She took a step closer, and grasped his waist with her hands. They stood together, locked eye to eye for a long time. Tears began to lay tracks down his face as he tried to match her gaze. He missed her so much and his guilt was overtaking him in the moment.

"I love you," he managed to say with a whisper, words being too hard to say aloud.

"Do you, Ethan?"

"Of course I do." The question laid yet another wound onto the guilt stricken man.

"It didn't hurt, you know. When you killed me."

"It was an accident!" he exclaimed grasping her face in his hands as he squatted down to meet her level gaze. She grabbed his hands and gently squeezed them.

"Accident or not. I'm dead and it's your fault."

"I don't know what to say Lily. Please, please forgive me."

"Forgive yourself. You mean nothing to me now." She slapped him and walked away. His feet were frozen to the spot.

He was helpless, screaming "Come back!" over and over while she continued to walk away. Her shoes clicking more quietly with each distant step. His perfect world started to collapse around him. The thin veil thickened and it grew darker making the world beyond it impossible to see. The experience was closing rapidly around him and the stringed instruments were playing out of tune. He began to panic, to rip at his feet with both hands. Lily was far from sight, enveloped by the quickly swelling darkness. He was alone and the walls that seemed so distant, so unreal, were now closing tight around him. It was hard to breathe, his heart was racing, and he felt only fear.

He awoke, springing up from the treatment bed and gasping for air. He quickly got his bearings, noting he was in the treatment room in his lab. His head was less fuzzy from the alcohol, but he felt sick. His heart continued to race and his mouth began to salivate. He ran to the observation room and grabbed the trashcan from under the computer desk. He vomited over and over. For a moment, the spasming in his abdomen erased all thoughts that were scrambling around his head. He sat in the office chair, head and shoulders rounded forward looking at the ground. He wished the vomiting would return. If nothing else, he wouldn't be thinking about how she said he meant nothing to her now.

Dr. Lewis had forgotten how hard it was the morning after. A splitting headache, dizziness, and the taste of vomit in the back of his throat were continuously making him feel nauseous. He stood with noodled legs and guided himself to the bathroom with his hands, while his eyes stayed closed to avoid the inescapable rays of sun that came through the large windows on all sides.

Kyle was awoken by the unmistakable sound of retching. He too was suffering from the blinding light entering the room, unable to open his eyes, which caused a slight panic in the fogginess of his morning mind. After a few minutes Kyle opened one eye allowing him to see toward the bathroom where Dr. Lewis lay in a fetal position next to the toilet.

"Hey Ethan, you all right?" Kyle yelled, immediately regretting his decision, as the back of his head lit up in pain.

"It's Dr. Lewis," he moaned from the bathroom. "Never call me Ethan again." Ethan felt like an alter ego, which last night, went a little overboard and wasn't present for the after effects.

"Fine with me, that guy's nuts anyways," Kyle said attempting to joke as he cradled his head in both hands, lying back down on the sectional. "Hey Doc."

"Yeah," he barked.

"Give me an IV."

"Kyle, that's the best idea I've ever heard. You're gonna learn how to give an IV today, too."

It took a few hours, but both men were starting to come around. The earth slowly turned and the day marched on, placing the sun in a disadvantaged position, allowing the men to open their eyes and experience the world. They spent the afternoon relaxing in the office, piecing together the entire night. They even laughed a little about the karaoke. One thing they didn't laugh about was Kyle's proposal at the end of the night.

"I just don't know how comfortable I am with allowing your stats to drop that low," Dr. Lewis said, taking a long drink of Gatorade. He hated the sweet stuff but needed to replenish his electrolytes, plus it had some sugars, and he wasn't in the eating mood.

"I know. I just think there's something there that we aren't seeing yet," Kyle said still laying down on the couch, an arm across his face to shield his eyes.

"Is it worth potentially dying for? We already know the experience is more vivid when you are deeper, but what's the point if it doesn't really benefit you any more once you come out?"

"To know! I want to know how far we can go, Doc."

"I'm not entertaining this anymore." Dr. Lewis stood and walked back toward the bathroom and closed the door. He sat on the toilet, lid down, with his head in hands. The grain pattern on the floor guided his eyes as he reflected back to Harvard, the lab, the girl.

"Forgive me," she had said just before she slipped away. *Forgive me? Why did she say that? Was it even for me?* Her hair was wonderfully soft, dirty blonde waves, and her eyes were like coves of tropical waters from the South Pacific. Her hands had been rough from the chemicals, the latex, and the constant hand washing. *I miss you.* Ethan sighed in frustration. Her limp body, the pale color to her skin. He now felt the same pangs in his stomach as he did then, when he walked down the halls of Harvard's Goldenson Biomedical Research Building and left her lying there. He wished he could go back there and try to do more. Panic had taken him and he fled, hoping it would save his career, which it did, but he couldn't have stayed at Harvard.

Ethan was reminded of a time he had last been drunk and allowed himself a break from the grief. He had just received his MD–PhD from Harvard, along with an offer to continue his research at the just built New Research Building. However, he got a call from Washington University in Saint Louis with a similar offer, to build his own research suite. It gave Dr. Lewis cause for celebration, because it allowed him to continue his experimental research, as well as distance himself from the place that still haunted his daily thoughts.

He felt nauseous, but not from the booze. It was grief, he was embarrassed, angry at himself for thinking that a simple relocation could have helped ease the pain. It had been years and it hadn't changed.

# | SIX |

## Spring 2006

It was just after midnight as Dr. Lewis walked into 4500 Parkview; time for his weekly check in on the progress of the new facility. He had been refused entry into the first and second floor about a month ago, due to his constant attempts to tell the contractor which step should come next in the buildout. Dr. Lewis knew to trust a man like Bill McCreary, having been the general contractor on the construction of numerous lab buildouts across Washington University, as well as other commercial institutions in the area.

"Dr. Lewis I understand you want everything done the right way, but for the last time, I know what I'm doing. Please Doctor, I'll ask you to avoid coming onto the first and second floor during our working hours. You are forcing us to slow down quite a bit, and I know damn well you want this done sooner than later." Bill was right, on all accounts.

Upon entering the building, Dr. Lewis immediately saw the telltale signs of progress. Scraps of drywall, cardboard boxes, dust hanging in the air, highlighted by the glow of LED work lights that were scattered throughout the first and second floor. The elevator shaft on the main floor was roughed out, taking away some of the square footage but Dr. Lewis could see how much tidier the room would appear without the elevator shaft in plain sight. Industrial was what he was trying to avoid. The exterior walls and windows had also been installed on the ground floor. They looked immaculate. His vision was coming together— the green colors of the tropics, the faux lilies, the wonderful artwork displayed on the walls, all the things that reminded him of Lily.

He walked into the elevator and rode it to the second floor. Upon exiting, he saw the framed treatment rooms, storage areas, and observation suites. He could see through the forest of wooden two-by-fours to the exterior walls. The windows had been removed and replaced by bricks which he had seen from outside as he approached the building 20 minutes earlier. As he stood on the second floor looking toward the exterior walls he saw no brickwork. Instead, spray foam covered the entire wall with two-by-fours pressed into the insulation like fork tines through frosting.

He walked slowly through the maze of wooden beams, imagining the blueprints as he meandered along, building his treatment suite in his mind. He saw the large oxygen tanks, four in all, one for each treatment room. It was easier to place one for each room rather than a massive tank that would service all four rooms. Plus, it looked much more symmetrical to have four. The storage rooms were fairly sizeable and he saw where the refrigeration units would be, the long wall where cabinets would be hung and materials stocked. Through the framed doorway, he walked into the observation suite.

Dr. Lewis pictured himself sitting at the aluminum desk he and Kyle chose for each room, while staring at the four, 24-inch monitors, waiting for the treatment to take effect. It was a surreal feeling knowing the five million dollar renovation for this building was all a direct result of his work. He stood staring through the opening in the wall that would soon be the window into the treatment room.

Finally, Dr. Lewis went up to the top floor and began taking inventory. He knew they were short three research assistants, and some part-time undergraduate assistants to handle compiling the data and assisting in maintaining the stock for the labs. Dr. Lewis had already begun to calculate the amount of each ingredient he would need for the cocktail in order to treat the projected 80 individuals per week. That's 16 people, five days a week; which would allow for each of the four labs to see two people per day. It was possible, but with preps, treatment times being somewhat unpredictable, and the interviews, it would be a close call.

Dr. Lewis sat down to check his email. He was waiting for a response from botanists all over the country. He needed a way to grow the *Convallaria majalis*. For several weeks, he had gotten rejection after rejection. Knowing that it was poisonous caused a lot of fear and misunderstanding.

Dear Dr. Lewis,

We unfortunately do not have the facility that would support such a large quantity of *Convallaria majalis* for the longevity of your study. We wish you the best of luck.

Dear Dr. Lewis.

Unfortunately, we do not feel comfortable supplying you with such a large quantity of the *Convallaria majalis*. As you are aware, it's known to cause abnormal heart rhythms, decreased consciousness, and death in high doses. We wish you luck and hope you find success.

Dr. Lewis—

We feel as though your request will open us up for liability should something go wrong with the study. Furthermore, we would suggest removing this ingredient from your study, as it does have considerable side effects. Either way, wishing you the best of luck. You are doing God's work.

It was beginning to feel as if these rejections were a form letter sent from every botanist in the world. He had investigated making his own greenhouse and growing the flower himself, but it proved just as costly as his entire new treatment center. It was nonsense to be stopped by something as small as a flower. There were still several options, botanists he hadn't heard back from, but he was starting to feel desperate and scared that the study might have to stop before it even began.

Dr. Lewis scanned through his email with care.

DEAR DR. LEWIS I HAVE YOUR FLOWERS . . . SORT OF.

Immediately he clicked on the email. It was from an address he didn't recognize, but the title was an attention grabber.

Dear Dr. Lewis,

My name is Elias Grant and I heard of your study from a researcher to whom I have donated funding in the past. I read through your research paper and I am intrigued by the possibilities. You see, my son, Gregor, took his life three years ago last Christmas. We spent limitless amounts of money in an attempt to cure his depression and anxiety disorders but with no success. I am willing to help in any way I can, including funding a lab for your flowers, Lily of the Valley. Please contact me at your convenience. I've told my assistant to put your call through no matter what I am doing.

Your partner,
Elias Grant

Dr. Lewis wasted no time and quickly picked up the phone. He paused when he saw that it was 1:30 a.m. *No,* he thought and slammed the phone down. He turned off the monitor on his computer and saved Elias Grant's contact information on his phone. A small pang of concern grew in his chest. *Who is Elias Grant?* He turned the computer back on and quickly searched "Elias Grant."

*Elias Grant, CEO of Whitestone, becomes largest donor in school history.*

Dr. Lewis searched "Whitestone."

*Whitestone rated most lucrative firm for last three years.*

*Whitestone purchases twelve firms in first quarter, marking the largest purchase of private equity firms in history.*

*Elias Grant, CEO of Whitestone, rated 23 in the top 100 most influential people in the United States.*

The articles satisfied Dr. Lewis' curiosity enough for him to stop his search. He felt reassured it wasn't a risk to call the random person. The small amount of anxiety he felt moments earlier were replaced with nervous excitement as he walked to the couch and lie down to sleep.

It was 8:01 a.m. when Dr. Lewis allowed himself to call. He had been distracting himself for hours as he scoured the internet for individuals who owned greenhouses, gardens, wildflower suppliers, anyone who could possibly be growing *Convallaria majalis,* but found no success. The problem wasn't that the plant was hard to grow; in fact, it was relatively easy to and could be found growing wild. The problem was the quantity, and what it was being used for. *Convallaria majalis* was never used as a drug, and doing so was a scary proposition. The volume required for a study of this magnitude was incredible, and they couldn't rely on finding it in the wild, or purchasing it through a variety of small growers. They planned on testing over a thousand people this year, a 500 percent increase in the volumes he and Kyle had done historically.

He dialed Elias' number and it began to ring.

"Oh hello Dr. Lewis," a sweet, but raspy voice said on the opposite end of the phone. "He's been waiting for your call. Can you please hold for a moment while I get him?"

"Sure can, Miss—'

"It's Mrs. White, Dr. Lewis. I'll be right back," she said emphasizing the "h" in White.

"I'm sorry."

"Oh no need to apologize sweetie, just letting you know. Please hold," Mrs. White said, allowing her South Carolina accent to sneak through her filters.

Several moments passed as Dr. Lewis waited patiently in front of his computer reviewing the Excel spreadsheet that he and Kyle had worked on for the past month. They knew it would take 100 milliliters of 50 percent *Convallaria majalis* extract, and 50 percent distilled water in order to facilitate the 80 subjects per week. The solution would last for two days before a fresh batch needed to be made. They found the half-life was too unpredictable after that amount of time, causing inaccurate testing. This would require roughly 250 individual plants every two weeks, and talking to the botany team at Wash U, that would require approximately two acres, growing the plants on a staggered schedule to ensure a constant fresh product.

"Dr. Lewis," a male voice calmly said.

"This is, and I assume this is Mr. Grant?"

"You assume correctly. I appreciate you calling me back. I realize it was probably a bit strange to receive my email, but, I see you found my words sufficiently comforting."

"In a way. I must confess I searched you online, and your company as well. Congratulations on being named in the top 100 most influential Americans."

"It's just words. So, what do you require of me, Dr. Lewis?"

"I uh . . .," Dr. Lewis hesitated, caught off guard by the sudden directness to Elias' question. "I do need the *Convallaria majalis*—"

"Lily of the Valley," Elias said cutting Dr. Lewis off.

"Yes, exactly," Dr. Lewis said dismissively. "It requires approximately two acres of staggered growth cycling, a full-time botanist, and all the necessary soil, irrigation system, et cetera. We had estimated that a complete green house buildout would exceed five million."

"Well that's a pretty serious price tag doctor. I can see why you would be looking to outsource this. Found anyone yet?"

"No," he said sighing.

"Well, just my luck then," Elias paused.

"Why's that?" Dr. Lewis said, playing along, but annoyed all the same.

"I just so happened to purchase a greenhouse in central Illinois, capable of producing approximately one-point-five acres of produce."

"What's the catch?"

"If you get this past stage four trials, I want a small piece of the action, and I want inside knowledge of the results before they are released in order to notify my clients."

*There it is,* Dr. Lewis thought. The truth came oozing out through the phone like lukewarm pudding causing him to pull the phone away in disgust, almost hanging up.

"Was the story even real?"

"My son? Sadly, yes, we are truly trying to help other families avoid our tragic end. You do believe me, right, Dr. Lewis?"

"Sure," he lied, but who else was going to come to him with a blank check and a complete working greenhouse that was within three hours of his lab.

"Glad to hear it. I'll have Seth, my assistant, call you later in the week to work out the details on when we should start growing your Lily of the Valley."

*"Convallaria majalis."*

"Why must we use that name?"

*Because when she said it, it sounded like poetry,* Dr. Lewis thought to himself. "I'm a scientist. Can't help it."

"Fair enough I guess. Talk to you soon, Doctor."

Dr. Lewis looked at his watch, 9:05 a.m. He sipped on his third cup of hot coffee for the day. He'd been awakened by the sounds on the floor below around 5:30. *If I get past stage four trials,* he thought as he walked to the couch and turned on the TV. *Arrogant prick.* He watched the Today Show while his mind was elsewhere. It was always wandering to thoughts about the study—the numbers, the formulation, the results, the success, but never the prestige. He hadn't ever thought about his reputation or legacy. Disgusted at himself for daydreaming, even for a moment, about the level of success he may obtain, he picked up his phone and called Kyle.

"Kyle, glad I got you. We need to start getting our assistants selected. Can you post on the website that we are looking for three research assistants and some techs?"

"Sure, we can just interview as they come in. I don't think it should be a problem. Any specifics?"

"They must be biology or chem majors, lab experience, even if it was just coursework, we can teach them before the study begins. Preferably graduate students for the assistants and those could come from the nursing or medical school."

"I'll see what I can do."

"Kyle, I got us our *Convallaria majalis.* Don't ask me too many questions though."

"Well, I won't ask any. How's that?"

"Perfect."

# | SEVEN |

Two months marched past and Dr. Lewis had lined up over 800 individuals who were ready for treatment. He had hired an assistant, Donna, to handle the scheduling. It was a massive undertaking on its own. They needed interview times at least six weeks prior to the actual treatment. If Dr. Lewis was concerned about anesthetic sensitivities, they would need a screen at least two weeks before their treatment date. They also needed time after the treatment for an interview, as well as their long-term follow-up three months after the treatment. But Donna seemed up to the task.

Donna had previously worked in research for Dr. Lewis on a part-time basis. She also worked as a secretary for one of the department chairs at the undergraduate campus. Dr. Lewis had always respected how hard Donna worked for him when called upon, so when he knew he got the funding, he offered the red-headed thirty-something a full-time position. She accepted immediately and he gave her a key to the top floor. That made her one of only three who had access to the topmost floor at 4500 Parkview, now nicknamed The Shack by the students on campus because of the research building's small size.

The Shack had come together nicely. The main floor was now painted, beige furniture in place with black and white pictures of Saint Louis adorning the walls. The floor was real bamboo stained moderately dark. Lilies were beautifully arranged around the room, primarily white and yellow, but a few were red and orange standing out in stark contrast to the rest of the room. The end tables each had lamps, though they were merely decorative because the amount of light that streamed in through the windows was more than adequate during late June afternoons.

Dr. Lewis entered the elevator and took it to the second floor. Kyle was waiting along with Donna and several students that would comprise his team. His lab assistants would be Malcolm, a nursing student; Traci and Veronica both were graduate students studying neurotransmitter physiology; and Adam, a pre-med student.

Upon exiting the elevator, he smiled. Every time he entered the treatment suite he was in awe of how well it turned out. He walked through the lobby and into Treatment Room One, where his team waited patiently. Dr. Lewis walked into the observation suite and smelled the static from the electronics as their fans hummed, quietly cooling the machines. He looked through the large ten-by-four-foot window into the treatment area and saw his team waiting for him. He opened the door and walked in, closing it silently behind him. The stillness was wonderful in the room, almost allowing him to hear everyone's breath echoing off the white walls and tiled floor.

He walked to the treatment table, pushed it slightly to the right, and reached behind it toward the wall. He turned a green knob and a tiny metallic ball rose inside a thin plastic tube, indicating ten liters of oxygen was flowing. He smiled, turned the O2 off, and spun to address his staff.

"I appreciate you all coming here on a Saturday. I promise it's not my intent to make this a habit. That being said, I think it's time we go over everyone's expectations. To begin, Donna has done an amazing job of scheduling over 800 patients into our system, and we will begin seeing them in just three short weeks. We need to understand our roles. We'll start with two rooms working simultaneously, I will be administering all the treatments, but observations will be performed by myself and Kyle. Adam, Malcolm, Traci, and Veronica you will all eventually be monitoring the patient's vitals from the observation room. Once I feel confident in your abilities, we will open all four rooms. This will likely lead to long days for the first two weeks, but it's critical we are all approaching the patients the same way." Everyone nodded in approval.

"You will also be responsible for pre-treatment written tests, post test, and a long-term test. You will administer all four tests per patient. You'll also be responsible for checking inventory on miscellaneous items in the treatment labs from IV bags, gloves, needles, laundry, and cleanliness."

"We're going to go through a couple scenarios today, just so you're not looking like deer in the headlights when we're seeing patients," Kyle said breaking into Dr. Lewis' monologue.

Six people fit snugly in the observation room, but it was doable. It was vitally important that the team understood the objectives, and it was simpler to do it all at once. Veronica clicked her pen nervously as they waited in the room. She was scared of needles since she was a child, but she hadn't told Dr. Lewis or Kyle during the interview. It was an amazing opportunity to see the physiologic brain activity during the treatment being administered. She would get over it, especially if she had to. After all, she had made it through getting a tattoo of her favorite Nirvana lyrics on her shoulder blade.

"Ok, so Kyle is being treated. I will be going through a scripted conversation, not leading him with questions or answers, simply asking my questions and explaining the situation. Again, you will not be administering the drugs, only asking the questions from the depression and anxiety questionnaires we've already used." Dr. Lewis walked into the treatment room. "So," he projected his voice for all to hear. "We will pretend I already asked all the questions, and I am preparing to administer the treatment." The group of them all nodded their heads, including Donna. She wanted to be present for everything so she could feel comfortable working there, and answer any questions that Dr. Lewis would allow her to answer.

"Once I walk into the room the recording should start to ensure anything that is said will be recorded. This is test number XX-XX,

Kyle Braun, age 28. No comorbidities, no clinical psychological disorders."

"Correct," Kyle responded smiling.

"He has not taken medications in the last six weeks. Weight, 187 pounds, height 6'2". Titration of PB-50 has been determined to be 55 percent saline. Kyle, do you consent to treatment?"

"I do, Dr. Lewis."

"This is a very important step. If for any reason I do not get informed consent, we will scratch the treatment session."

Dr. Lewis walked back across the floor, his steps echoing in the room. "This is where I will be turning on the medication," Dr. Lewis mimed the task for them to see, his hands held in an exaggerated overhead position."

"Ok Kyle get ready. Count down from 100. See you on the other side."

"99 . . . 98 . . . 97 . . .," Kyle faked as though he went under.

"Any questions so far?" Dr. Lewis asked looking through the glass and into the observation room. "Great. Now I'll come back into the observation room and watch. Our objective is to see where the vitals dip down over the next ten to fifteen minutes. Once that's established, we allow them to drop another ten percent before I administer epinephrine to help them come back around. That simple. Malcolm, I talked to your advisor and they are very confident in your abilities, and I was told you already passed your boards. You will be the only one allowed to titrate the cocktail and administer the epinephrine if I am busy with another subject. I hope everyone understands that."

"Thanks for the confidence, Dr. Lewis. I'm very excited to work here. Always been fascinated by research, and this seems like a great experience. Plus, it pays better than some of the offers I got."

"Well, we should reconsider your compensation then," Dr. Lewis said smiling.

It broke the tension in the room. Everyone thought Dr. Lewis was a bland, myopic perfectionist without a balanced personality. In all their interviews he seemed distracted while Kyle asked all the questions. Prior to Dr. Lewis arriving, the group had all been questioning Kyle and Donna about how it was to work with the doctor. Initially, Donna had fun with the new lab assistants by talking about how terrible Dr. Lewis was, how he never smiled, rarely talked, and demanded that Kyle work around the clock. She said, "The good doctor doesn't sleep, so he feels all those hours should be productive." Kyle sighed and nodded his head, but the moment didn't last long because he let himself smirk and Traci called his bluff.

"One more thing, everyone. The confidentiality agreements are legally binding. I appreciate you all signing them and I want to reiterate the importance. You have the opportunity to be a part of something amazing and on the ground floor. I would say groundbreaking, but Kyle and I already broke ground with our previous paper that has now been published. I'm not going to quiz you on it, but I suggest you read it if you haven't already."

"They all have," Kyle said as only a proud mentor would.

"Good, well, I think we can let the kiddos up onto the third floor for a viewing, what do you think, Kyle?" Dr. Lewis asked as he walked to the elevator.

"Seems fair to me." They all followed like young school children on a field trip. The elevator was cramped but having to rub shoulders with each other helped break the ice a little more. Upon exiting the elevator, they were in a small, poorly lit lobby with one door. The entire lobby was built out of cinder blocks except for the lonely metal door. Dr. Lewis had this area put in for security purposes after the buildout was completed. He felt it was a good idea to have an isolated treatment suite, separate from prying eyes, in case he and Kyle decided to do more work, off the books.

Dr. Lewis unlocked the door and, opening it, allowed for everyone to walk through, smiling at Donna who brought up the rear.

"Ok everyone, please go sit on the couch, Kyle and I are going to be bringing in two videos to watch; both are subjects in our study. The first video will represent one of the thousand which were included in our research paper. The second, well, I'll let you deconstruct it on your own."

A few moments later Kyle had placed the two full treatment videos on a thumb drive and plugged it directly into the 60-inch TV. The first video was a middle-aged woman, normal BMI, and she stated that she was suffering from depression. Kyle walked her through the questionnaires and also confirmed she had weaned off her meds for six weeks. Dr. Lewis entered the room, explained the procedure, and received informed consent from the woman. Several moments later she was unconscious. For 30 minutes they sat and watched the woman sleep on the bed, unmoving, expressionless. Her vitals were displayed across the bottom of the screen, and above, four different video feeds were revealing things about the woman in different ways. One was infrared monitoring of her body, another plotted her eye movements, a third was a full body shot catching any large motor movements, and a fourth, which was automated, quickly responded to any noted movement and focused on it.

*Beep, beep, beep,* a familiar alarm began to sound on the feed. Malcolm's palms began to sweat and he became slightly uneasy in his seat on the couch. Having worked in the ICU, those chimes often meant something was wrong and he needed to respond. The video then showed Dr. Lewis entering the room, administering the epinephrine, and the woman waking up, calm but groggy. Malcolm relaxed back into the couch, hoping that nobody picked up on his subtle response. He wasn't alone, however. Adam had also felt a quickening of his pulse.

The subject was then asked the same set of questions by Kyle, and it was clear that her subjective feelings had improved. The recording quickly changed venues.

"This is her three-month follow-up," Dr. Lewis interjected. Kyle walked into the office where the woman was waiting. She smiled politely. Kyle, once again, began asking the same questions to which she stated the same answers as the post treatment.

"So, what questions do you have?" Dr. Lewis asked once the video screen changed back to icons.

"I think it's too neat and clean," Veronica stated disappointedly. "It was clear in the video that her brain was lit up like a Christmas tree after you gave her the treatment. How do you know you just didn't get her high?"

"It's valid, and honestly why we chose to do the long-term follow-up as well. Knowing that three months later they were still feeling the improvements, the data speaks for itself."

"Yeah, I'm with Veronica," Traci said. "We've both studied the way the brain responds to a narcotic intensively, and I'm starting to wonder if that's why you brought us on. This looks a lot like a hallucinogenic."

"You've got me," Kyle said with his hands in the air.

"Yeah, we brought you on for that reason, and Malcolm for his ability to treat a patient, and Adam for his background in biochemistry and botany. Sorry Adam, we are certainly going to be using every bit of your knowledge, but filling you in on very little; and now you know your roles." The room felt more comfortable after that. With one statement Dr. Lewis had made everyone in the room stick their chest out and feel needed. They had felt replaceable, like pawns on a chess board waiting to be sacrificed, used to perform a task and discarded. But now they felt like part of a team.

"Before you get cocky Veronica, Traci. I think you need to watch the second video."

Dr. Lewis played the video of Linda. He stood near the TV and focused his attention on their responses. He had already watched it dozens it times, mainly reassuring himself it actually happened. It was the first time anyone outside of himself, Kyle, and Dr. Mitchell Raymond, the head of the committee who reviewed their submission for funding, had viewed the recording. It was exciting seeing a group of people who understood the significance of this particular set of vitals and response to treatment. Dr. Lewis saw Malcolm respond first, showing his experience with patients showing no brain activity. He looked confused when Linda smiled, and uncomfortable when she talked. Kyle noticed Malcolm's reaction too, and glanced toward Dr. Lewis, smiling.

*Beep, beep, beep,* the monitors began to chime and Malcolm's expression was unchanged. Dr. Lewis came into frame and administered the epinephrine. Linda woke up with a smile ear to ear. She almost seemed distant, distracted by some unseen variable when she first started talking with Dr. Lewis. She was bubbly, flirtatious, and objectively changed. The HD feed showed the same woman, but she was visibly different. Her eyes were brighter, her skin less aged, her smile, authentic. The video then cut to her three-month follow-up where she continued to exhibit the same personality noted immediately following the treatment.

"Malcolm, what did you see?" Dr. Lewis said cutting right to the chase.

"I saw something I can't explain. Never seen a brain dead patient move, smile, or talk. She was also describing things she experienced when she was under. No idea how that happened," he said staring down at the floor and throwing his hands in the air.

"How about you," Dr. Lewis said looking at Veronica as he leaned against a sturdy shelf next to the TV.

"I'm all in. If what Malcolm said is accurate, I need to know why she wasn't displaying any synaptic events in her brain while all that was happening."

"Was the EEG working?" Traci asked in a suspicious manner, assuming this was a test.

"Yes. I'm confident." Kyle said straightfaced, making sure everyone knew he wasn't trying to play a prank. He could never keep a straight face if he was joking.

"Have you gotten these results with anyone else?" Adam spoke for the first time. He understood the importance of reproducibility more than any of the assistants. He had worked in several labs during undergraduate school, and continued to do the same since starting at Washington University. In fact, Kyle poached him from a current lab in the biochemistry building.

"Uh, well, I guess we may as well tell you. Yes, we did. We used Kyle." They all directed their eyes toward Kyle who stood smiling widely.

"Yeah, it was pretty much like she described it," Kyle said matter of fact.

"Before anyone asks, no. Nobody in this room will be allowed to have the treatment." Kyle was relieved the doctor spoke up.

"Dr. Lewis, what was different with this woman, and then with Kyle? I mean, why did they have such a different response?" Malcolm asked, still in awe of the vitals.

"We slightly altered the formulation, which is now the formulation we'll be continuing this research with." He saw the assistants all internalize the discussion, analyzing the experiment, imagining what their day to day would be like. "Seemed more interesting to listen to people describe these amazing experiences without any explanation. Sounds like we have a couple variables to solve."

"When can we start? Donna?" Veronica asked.

"Doctor?" Donna said passing the question.

"Well, I'm glad I got you guys all riled up for this. But here's the problem. One of our ingredients is a flower, a poisonous variety, and I've had a hell of a time getting enough to treat as many people as we are planning for. I still have several letters, phone calls, and contacts that I haven't heard back from. We'll see what comes through in the next few weeks."

Dr. Lewis looked at Kyle with veiled frustration. It had been several weeks since talking with Elias Grant and his assistant, Seth. The conversation was uncomfortable, feeling as if he would be selling out to a businessman who would eventually try to control his research and use it for his own financial gain. It was obvious that was Elias' intent, and Dr. Lewis wasn't even sure what he was asking was even legal. It sounded akin to insider trading, letting Elias know his research before it was published. If Elias had his way, he would be considered a partner. It wasn't that Dr. Lewis wanted all the fame and glory, nor did he even care that Elias may get a pat on the back as well. It was the nature in which he originally reached out, through an emotional email using his own son's death as a way to generate money for his clients. *If he was willing to use that as leverage, what wasn't this man capable of?*

"Ok class over. Starting Monday, we will meet from four to seven p.m. for the entire week in order to train on the equipment, practice Q and A, and get used to how the computer systems work. I would like this to be as smooth as possible when we start seeing patients." Each one took their turn shaking hands with Kyle and Dr. Lewis on their way out. They all left through the metal door, and into the elevator. It was such an eyesore, having a cinderblock box disrupting what used to be a very well decorated and beautifully laid out office and treatment suite. It cut off some of the light that came in through the east windows in the morning, which wasn't the worst thing, but the aesthetics were just destroyed. However, it was of the utmost importance to have the top floor secure, especially because Dr. Lewis was seriously considering Kyle's proposal; to go deep into the experience without safety parameters.

"Kyle, I don't know how much longer I can avoid Elias."

"Still getting no from everyone?"

"Yes, and I've even tried to split it between two or three facilities, nobody wants to touch it."

"Jesus, I mean, man it's not that poisonous!"

"I agree. If it's not solved by the time we end training next week then I'm just gonna pull the trigger. Enough is enough and we need this to move forward or we'll never get more funding."

"Sounds good Doc. Just make sure you negotiate. Lawyer up buddy."

# | EIGHT |

The week had gone by too quickly for Dr. Lewis. The training went well and he felt confident in Kyle's choices, but it was difficult to let people in. Malcolm was demonstrating a strong propensity toward empathy and an irreplaceable way of looking at a patient that gave them a warm and comforting feeling. Adam was a sponge. "I think Adam could run this study right now and we could just go on a vacation," Kyle had told Dr. Lewis one evening in their office space. It wasn't that Adam was cocky, in fact, he rarely spoke, he just took careful note of all procedures and directions given.

Veronica and Traci spent a lot of the time watching videos of previous subjects, analyzing their activation sites that lit up the EEG, and compared them to classic distribution patterns for narcotics use. Kyle wasn't exactly sure of the purpose, but Dr. Lewis knew. The two researchers were attempting to find a pattern, a way to predict what was happening to the neurons at the most basic levels. He knew the two women would compare it to other known narcotics studies to determine what neural pathways would be involved. From there, he was confident they would try to decipher how the brain in Linda's study was able to flat line. The more he sat quietly in his office, the better he felt about the team. They were already proving to fit the exact combination of empathy, intelligence, and brilliance that he and Kyle were hoping for. In only ten days the trial was going to begin.

Dr. Lewis shifted in his chair at the thought, his stomach cramping and he began to sweat a little. He reached into his desk drawer and took a large swig of Pepto-Bismol, finishing the second bottle of the week. He had called a lawyer Monday and they discussed the situation briefly. He was supposed to call her today and discuss possible contract options to offer Elias.

He picked up the phone and dialed Michelle Adams.

"Hello, Dr. Lewis," she said smiling into the phone.

"Ready."

"Well what was the original offer Elias Grant made to you?"

"He wanted me to guarantee early results of the research before it was submitted. Something about wanting to give his clients a heads-up."

"Hmmm, that does sound questionable, Dr. Lewis. You were good to trust your gut. He was going to enter a contract to provide you with a certain plant, of which you didn't specify, nor do you need to. Not necessary for our discussions."

"Correct."

"I understand, but please understand that our conversations are confidential."

"Thank you. Do you think I have any other options? I'm desperate for this plant and I need it soon or my study is never going to happen."

"Are you paying him?"

"No."

"Men like Mr. Grant love money."

"Tell me about it. He watched his son die and all he cared about was money."

"I don't follow."

"It's a long story. Please continue your thought."

"I'm assuming there will be some long-term financial gain following the study, which is why he wanted a heads-up, so to speak."

"Likely so, yes."

"Find a way to guarantee him some money."

"I'd like him to keep his mouth shut too. He used the word partner and that really rubbed me wrong."

"Well we can place that in the contract. A confidentiality agreement, a guarantee that information does not come out about the plant, the study, et cetera. We can even stipulate he is in no way directly affiliated with the actual study, and therefore, not a partner."

"I'd appreciate you writing all this up for me. I'm focused on the research, Michelle. I just want to ensure I'm not being taken advantage of."

"Give me the afternoon. I'll send you a tentative draft around three p.m."

"I appreciate your work."

"Well I hope you appreciate how much I charge."

Dr. Lewis wanted Kyle in the office when he called Elias Grant. The businessman was slimy, but a smooth talker. He whispers charms in his adversaries' ears while stabbing them in the back and convinces them to thank him for it. Dr. Lewis didn't have experience with a man like Elias. He felt vulnerable, overthinking every sentence that came out of the man's mouth. He wished he could just focus on his study and leave the money and legalities to someone else. He knew it was going to cost several thousand dollars to have Michelle work this contract, but it was well worth it.

"Kyle, you free?" Dr. Lewis said walking down Euclid and toward Tom's Bar and Grill, where he was hoping Eric was working.

"Yeah, just got done swimming."

"Can you meet me at Tom's Bar?"

"Haha, sure what are we celebrating this time?"

"Nothing. I've gotta call Elias. Want you with me. Michelle, my lawyer, is working on a draft of a contract."

"Yeah I can be there in like 20."

"See ya soon."

Dr. Lewis reached the bar at one and walked in. Immediately he saw Eric serving a few tables.

"Hey Doc!" Eric said walking right over. "You alone?"

"No, I've got Kyle coming."

"I got no tables right now. I promise I'll try and push some people out the door for ya—"

"No, no Eric that's a nice gesture but we'll just eat at the bar if that's ok," Dr. Lewis said cutting him off. Eric smiled through his thick beard, relaxation setting in like an old friend.

"Get on over there then. Want a shot'n a beer?"

"No, just water when you get a second. Not in a rush. Here killin' time."

"Fair enough, Doc. You're the boss," Eric said shrugging his shoulders then looking back at the tables. "Ah, well they're looking pretty restless. Gotta check on their food. I'll be at the bar in a minute."

"See ya there."

Fifteen minutes passed slowly and Dr. Lewis had already read the long list of microbrews that Tom's had to offer. He was fighting the urge to pull the trigger on a wheat ale when Kyle finally came through the door, hair still wet from his workout in the pool. He waved at Eric and worked his way through the maze of tables to the bar with Dr. Lewis.

"How we doin' Doc?"

"Better. I was about to start drinking. I'm so anxious to get this phone call over with," he said checking the clock on the wall for the fifth time since being there.

"What are we gonna say?"

"Michelle advised me to give him a way to make long-term money. I told her I'm not allowing him to be a partner, nor am I allowing him to divulge any information about what the flowers are, who they are for, and how much they are growing. I'd prefer it if he didn't mention he even had a greenhouse."

"Yeah, it's his greenhouse, can't really tell him not to talk about his own stuff."

"Agreed. Kyle, how can we offer him long-term money?"

"I don't know. How are we guaranteed long-term money?"

"Kyle, that's it buddy," Dr. Lewis said slapping him on the back. "I swear without you this study wouldn't exist."

"You gonna fill me in?" Kyle said with wide, green eyes, his face showing no hint of emotion.

"When this study proves itself to be an effective treatment, you and I are going to be rich. We'll likely need an even larger stream of the *Convallaria majalis* and we can guarantee him exclusive rights to grow it for the drug."

"I think that should do it."

"I hope so. Otherwise I'm not sure this study is gonna happen."

The two of them sat at the bar enjoying their greasy burgers and people-watching. It was fun to actually get out and see what was happening. The TV was showing the Saint Louis Cardinals playing an afternoon double-header at Wrigley. It was nice to watch a bit of the game. He couldn't tolerate watching a whole game let alone the devout loyalty of a fan who watched every game. They sat long enough to watch two full innings and the Cardinals go up three runs before Dr. Lewis got an email from Michelle.

"She's good, Kyle. Real good." He handed Kyle his phone.

"I'm certainly not going to disagree with you. I'm just not going to hold my breath. Elias probably has a team of lawyers advising him."

"Yeah, but I'm still making the call right now. Let's go." He motioned for Eric, who came immediately.

"What can I do for my all-star karaoke duo?"

"Just checking out," Kyle said.

"Ok, this one's on me Doc," Eric said winking.

"No it's not," he responded and slapped a fifty down on the bar. "Thanks Eric."

"Doc, you can't keep doing this."

"I will and you'll like it. Otherwise I'll go someplace else." The two of them locked eyes, Eric showing gratitude with a nod. "Just keep treating us like kings."

"I can do that, Doc."

"And call me Ethan. I'm not a doctor when I'm in here."

The walk back to the office at the top floor of The Shack was nice. The air was humid but the breeze was a neutralizer. The smell of the air was highlighted by random wafts of sewage and fertilizer as they crossed the street. The campus was alive with students despite the time of the year. Most of the Medical School was still in session. The pharmacy and physical therapy and occupational therapy programs were located just near their research building, and down the street was the Nursing School. South from them was the main medical school building, Olin Residence Hall, and Barnes Jewish Hospital dominated everything west of that. There were hundreds of students, faculty, patients, and workers all over campus enjoying the wonderful weather.

As they entered their office, Dr. Lewis closed the door and locked it behind him. He walked to the office phone, and dialed Elias' cell phone directly.

"Good afternoon Ethan. How are you doing?"

"I'm well, and I'd prefer Dr. Lewis if you don't mind." He looked at Kyle who was listening through speakerphone. Kyle gave him a reassuring nod.

"Very well, Doctor. It's a well deserved title. Have you called to accept my offer? I have a confession, I started growing the Lily of the Valley about three weeks ago. I thought you might come around."

Dr. Lewis was furious. He raised his hand and brought it to the phone. He wanted nothing to do with the businessman on the other end of the phone and it took everything he had to convince himself to call. *What arrogance!* He thought as he ground his teeth and appealed to Kyle with his eyes, wishing for him to simply nod as a signal that it was ok to hang the phone up. Kyle stayed frozen, green eyes focused on Dr. Lewis' steely blues.

"Well I'm not sure yet."

"Oh, well you have another grower then? Please tell me who, if you don't mind me asking."

"It's not that. I have a counter offer." His heart beat forcefully. His mouth was dry and that wheat beer sounded so good at that moment.

"I'm listening, but I'm going to have to bring in my lawyer. If you don't mind."

"It's ok. Better to get it out of the way." Several moments passed and Dr. Lewis muted the call. "Kyle please grab me some water I can't even swallow right now." Kyle nodded and ran to the refrigerator grabbing a bottle and hustling back.

"Are you still there, Dr. Lewis?" Elias asked.

"Yes."

"Ok you may continue."

"As you recall, I wasn't thrilled about the terms you laid out before. I would like to counter your offer, with another. If my study proves the treatment a success, I will need an abundance of the *Convallaria majalis* in order to synthesize the treatment at a massive level. You will have the exclusive contract to produce the flower." There was a pause. Kyle and Dr. Lewis froze in a staring contest with one another, not focused on what they were seeing, but on the silence that was so telling. Elias was calculating possibilities, forecasting projections, looking for loopholes in the deal. He was clearly caught off guard by the counter and was likely staring at his lawyer, or his team of lawyers, in the same way Kyle and the doctor were.

"I'd say that's a fair deal."

"I have two more stipulations," Dr. Lewis quickly said. "One, you will refrain from calling yourself a partner. In no way shape or form will this be insinuated or blatantly stated. Not only do I wish not to be openly affiliated with you, but it shows a clear conflict of interest and will poison the study."

"A little harsh, but I can see the conflict," Elias said losing his charming candor.

"Last item is there will be no mentioning of what is in your greenhouse, who it is for, and to what purpose it is serving. I cannot express the delicate nature of what we are working on, and for someone to obtain the ingredient could be bad for everyone involved financially. In the wrong hands, *Convallaria majalis* can be lethal, and this could set you up for liability in a lawsuit."

"Understood. I'm assuming you contacted a lawyer. Have him go ahead and send us a finalized contract and we can comb through it. If that's all there is to the agreement we're going to be in business real soon."

"I'll have Michelle send it right over."

"Ah, a woman. Real firecracker I'm sure," Elias said with his usual tone. The blow from Dr. Lewis staggered the giant, but didn't put him down.

"One more thing. When you sign those papers today, send them down hand delivered with a sample of those flowers."

"I can arrange that. You have a good day, Dr. Lewis."

"Well, we got him," Kyle said slapping his hands together and smiling ear to ear.

"That we do. I'm calling Michelle right now and getting this over with."

"Michelle. I need the deal finalized and sent over to Elias Grant right now. He verbally agreed to the deal. Thank you so much for your assistance."

"It was a pleasure."

"You'll get your money, plus some."

"Oh I know I'll get my money. You can keep the plus some. Save it for a rainy day, Doctor. Have a good one."

"Kyle. This calls for a celebration," he said calmly staring at his hands for a moment.

"You don't look right Doc."

"I'm good, Kyle. Really good. Just crossing some mental t's. We're ready aren't we?"

Dr. Lewis wasn't all right. He was battling his inner desires. He had an addiction and he just gone through an emotional event that left his defenses down. For months he had denied Kyle's urge to go deeper into the treatment but at this moment he was struggling. Dr. Lewis wanted to know how deep they could go, how visceral the experience, how long one could stay in. It was never something Lily or Ethan could have tried to experience. They lacked the knowledge, the equipment, the data. The two lovers had no idea what was happening physiologically, let alone the formulation. Now, so many years and experiments later, it was perfect, and Dr. Lewis wanted to know what perfect looked like.

"Yes we are. Ten days out now and we finally have all the pieces."

"We still have one unanswered question though."

"We do?" Kyle sat, brows furrowed over stubbled cheeks.

"We don't know how far we can go."

"Are you serious?" Kyle sat straight up and his eyes were wide. "You're gonna let me—"

"Yes. Tonight," Dr. Lewis said cutting him off.

"Whoa!" Kyle screamed and clenched his fists. He hadn't brought the idea up since the morning after they had gotten drunk. He was suspicious Dr. Lewis was considering it, especially when he placed the lock on the office suite. He figured it would happen sooner rather than later.

Dr. Lewis just laughed and crossed his arms. "We have to make the cocktail Kyle. Let's get to work. Those flowers are coming tonight."

"That's why you asked for them?" Kyle said loudly, his emotions were clearly getting the best of him as he was now standing and pacing the room.

"Yep."

Behind the cinderblock wall, just left of the treatment lab was a full lab for creating the cocktail—burners, glassware, titration equipment, pipettes, centrifuge, and cold storage. It was a simple lab, only possessing what was required to extract the ingredients from the *Convallaria majalis,* and mix it with the other anesthetics in the right proportions. Kyle and Dr. Lewis had even devised a way to determine the strength of the *Convallaria majalis* potency, and if it was too strong, they found distilled water helped with diluting the concentration.

The two men worked methodically. Dr. Lewis had already cancelled his office hours for Friday morning and didn't have any lectures to attend. Kyle was also free, making both of them available for a long night at The Shack. They placed each anesthetic into an IV bag that contained 1,000 milliliters. Dr. Lewis then gathered one-hundred milliliters of distilled water and placed it directly into a sterile syringe, and put all their work into the refrigerator.

The bench was cleared off and the burner brought out, along with the equipment for titration: mortar and pestle, scissors, and several flasks and test tubes. They grabbed their makeshift kit for determining the strength of the isolated ingredient from the flower, which included litmus paper, a urine test for barbiturates, and table salt. The litmus paper tested the acidity. If it was too high, the sodium acted as a buffering agent to help neutralize the compound. Once an appropriate pH was achieved, they tested for the presence of barbiturates. Depending on the intensity of the color, they knew how potent the extract from *Convallaria majalis* was. It took the men months to figure out the pH was crucial. If that wasn't accounted for, the strength test was completely invalid.

"That's it for now," Dr. Lewis said to Kyle as they both stood going through a mental checklist. It had been a few months since they worked on the cocktail.

"Yeah, I'd say that's it," Kyle responded with a furrowed brow and hands on hips. "It's only 4:30. What do you wanna do? I guarantee we have at least two more hours till the courier gets here."

"Well, let's just go see Eric then shall we?"

"I'm game."

"Absolutely no booze. Agreed?"

"Agreed."

They walked toward the bar, leaning forward as the strong winds tried to blow them back upright. The sky above was morphing into a sinister mix of purple, gray, and green, which slowly suffocated the brilliant blue sky from a few hours earlier. Dr. Lewis' tall, lean frame was struggling against the wind. He was getting a workout as the wind tried to twist him, stand him up, and push him steadily to the right. More than once, his legs scissored from a gust and he almost stepped into the road. He found himself growing frustrated until he heard Kyle laughing from behind. The more muscular lab assistant had no problem with the wind. Dr. Lewis laughed with him after realizing how funny he looked.

Finally, they reached the door to Tom's and walked in. The room was dark, but their eyes quickly adjusted, seeing the pictures on the wall and a sea of empty table. Their friend, Eric, was leaning on the bar with both forearms, cell phone in hand.

"You guys again?"

"Yeah. Gotta kill a few more hours. It's the name of the game," Dr. Lewis said trying to sound matter-of-fact and shrugged.

"So, beer and a shot?"

"Absolutely not," Dr. Lewis said throwing both hands in front of himself, displaying the universal symbol for "back off."

"Ok Doc, it was just a question," Eric said smiling.

"We'll take a couple burgers though," Kyle said. Dr. Lewis looked sideways at him. "I worked out today. I can eat as much as I please, Ethan!"

"Oh Doc," Eric said grimacing slightly. "I mean Ethan. I forgot you told me not to call you Doc in here."

"It's all right. Glad you remembered."

The food was good, greasy, but that just helped it slide down. It was also nice because they didn't look to quench their thirst with a tall glass of wheat ale. The two of them sat silent, slowly eating. Dr. Lewis was very methodical, eating only the fries at first. Once those were done, he moved on to the burger. He hated burning his mouth with scalding hot cheese and liquid fat that oozed out with each bite. It wasn't enjoyable to quickly chomp down in between inhaled breaths meant to cool the scalding meat. He enjoyed eating. As a man who leaned toward the savory, he was enjoying the crunch from the bacon and the salty chewiness of the pretzel roll.

"I can't believe you're letting me back in."

"Neither can I," Ethan sighed and waved Eric over. "I'll take one of those wheat beers."

"No drinking Ethan," Kyle said quickly, pointing his finger at him with wide eyes.

"You're gonna cut me some slack. I'm essentially going to watch you die on my table tonight."

"That's why you should be clear headed!" Kyle joked and threw a couple fries in his mouth.

"Huh," Ethan said with a mouthful of food. He chewed it slowly and turned to look at Kyle.

"What?"

"You should stop eating. Anesthesia and a full stomach don't mix."

"I'll be fine."

"So will I. Eric, the beer please."

"Sorry Kyle, I'm siding with Ethan. And I have no idea what the hell you two are talking about, but I'm not asking any questions either."

Eric walked down the bar and opened the top of a microbrew from the Central West End. "Figured you didn't specify, you wanted my pick," Eric said.

"Smart man Eric," he said with a tense smile, veiling his anxiety. Ethan was beginning to regain control of his emotions that had led to his decision just hours earlier. He was feeling his strength of will, his ability to say no to the addiction. It was such a dichotomy, the yin and yang of his inquisitive side versus his fear and morality. He was wishing to both concede to his addiction and overcome it.

Ethan looked up at the TV. The Cardinals second game of the double header was a blowout. Cardinals were already up by eight runs and it was only the second inning. He finished the inning and his beer, afterward feeling a bit more at ease. He glanced at Kyle who was talking to Eric, gesturing at the TV with his left hand. A strong thunderstorm warning starting at 6:00 p.m. was scrolling across the TV. He saw Kyle's tattoo and remembered their drunken conversation in the office from months ago.

"Kyle, can I ask you something. It's a bit personal."

"I guess so," Kyle said adjusting his hat.

"Your tattoo. You said you'd rather not see it again. Why?" Kyle looked down at the bar and again adjusted his hat, this time uncomfortably shifting in his stool while doing so. "You don't have to tell me. I'm sorry I asked."

"No Ethan it's fine. It's just my dad. He took me to get it after I went All-American my freshman year. A lot of the guys on the team did it as a thing, but it was my dad who made me feel like I earned it. Not them."

"Did you ever go back to swimming?"

"Yeah but it wasn't the same. Never PR'ed again."

"PR?"

"Sorry. Personal Record. Never got a fast time again. It felt meaningless. I only did it to keep my scholarship."

"Isn't having that tattoo on your arm a good memory then?"

"No. It's a constant reminder of how I failed to help him," Kyle said coldly, leaving no doubt he carried his father's death as a burden.

"Kyle, that wasn't your fault. There was nothing—"

"I'm aware Ethan. Just can't get it to go away." Kyle said looking at the doctor. He smiled a little, "I'll be all right. I'm all right."

"All right Kyle, let's get back. We'll beat the rain most likely," Dr. Lewis gestured toward the TV screen, which was scrolling the warning for a second time.

"Good plan. I've been eyeballing that Blue Moon tap since we've been here. After talking about my dad, I'm thinking about getting it."

"Eric," Ethan said throwing down another fifty and waving his hand above his head.

"Take it easy guys. Don't go dying on me. Or whatever the hell that meant."

"I'll try not to," Kyle said, mostly joking.

Dr. Lewis was completely wrong and the two men were caught in the rain. It started coming down in sheets as they got a few blocks away from the lab. It was pointless to run, they were already soaked through their clothes and their shoes were gushing with every heel strike but they laughed until their abdominals cramped while in the elevator to the top floor.

They entered the office, went into the treatment room, and both put on hospital gowns. The two grown men sat on the couch and watched the Cardinals game while they waited for the courier. It was the weirdest form of normalcy; two men on a couch watching a baseball game in a research office, drinking deionized water from beakers, while waiting for a poisonous flower to extract a compound used to bring a man to the edge of death. In a different world, the two men would likely have never crossed paths, but in the moment, they were best friends with a deep secret; deeper yet, was the one Dr. Lewis still held close to his heart.

The Cubs were coming back and it was the bottom of the eighth. The score was now ten to nine, in favor of the visiting Cardinals.

*Ring, ring, ring.*

"Hello," Dr. Lewis answered, annoyed to be interrupted while watching the comeback by the loveable losers. He and Kyle had gotten so into the meaningless game they had forgotten why they were sitting in the office rather than at home.

"This is the courier sent by Elias Grant. I'm in the lobby of your building."

"Ok, thank you."

"Courier is here. You're going to get it," Dr. Lewis said looking at Kyle, smiling.

"Really?"

"Well I'm sure not going. Your idea, you're going."

Kyle stood up, tied his hospital gown around the back, and went to meet the courier.

It must have been a sight, but the courier was all business. No smirk, just "Hello," as he shook Kyle's hand. "I need you to sign here."

"Sure thing," Kyle said as he took the pen. "How's the rain?"

"Slowing down a bit. Would have been here by 7:00 p.m. but had to pull over for a minute. Couldn't see past the windshield."

"It's only 8:00, you did all right."

"Thanks, have a good one."

"You too."

Kyle walked back into the office suite and locked the door behind him. He set the contract down on the desk and brought the box containing the flowers to the couch. Dr. Lewis sat unflinching as he watched the top of the ninth. The Cubs had just taken the lead, so the Cardinals needed to score. There were two outs, nobody on base, and the batter had two strikes. Kyle sat down to join him for the remainder of the game. As soon as his butt hit the couch, "Strike three!" the umpire called and the Cubs fans went nuts.

"Good thing that ended quickly," Dr. Lewis said as he turned off the TV. "To the lab."

They made quick work of breaking down the plants. They

removed several red berries that highlighted each plant. They looked appetizing, but extremely poisonous. They then removed the two large broad leaves and threw them away exposing the small, white, bell-shaped flowers. They sliced each stem lengthwise with a razor knife. They placed the stems, flowers, and berries into a large mortar and began pulverizing the plant materials.

The berries went first, excitedly bursting with the first stroke from the pestle causing a vibrant red to fill the vessel. Slowly, the flowers were dyed red as well, and they too began to concede the crushing blows from Kyle; their delicate petals rolling and shearing apart. The stem was the last to fall victim to the pestle. The stems were a resilient and stubborn being, but after five minutes of Kyle's consistent barrage of varying strokes, they had given in leaving a warzone of thin filaments of what they used to be.

Dr. Lewis poured 50 milliliters of water into the mortar. He made sure all of the sides were washed down into the center of the vessel. Following this, he poured the mortar out over a filter and into a large beaker that was resting over a burner. He lit the burner and waited for the water to boil. It was a slight pink hue, one that reminded him of a single drop of blood in an IV line.

As the mixture boiled off, the extract from the Lily was becoming more concentrated, more potent. For Dr. Lewis it was like his Lily, becoming more potent each time he saw her in his dreams. Her words had become more powerful in death than they had been in life. The most recent dream still gave him a hollow feeling and now, he wished she wouldn't come to him in dreams. He knew it wasn't really her, it was impossible, but her words still cut deep troughs in his soul. *You mean nothing to me now,* he heard the words, a whisper in his head but so real he looked at Kyle for reassurance. Kyle was busy prepping for the next step as he stood with his back to Dr. Lewis.

"I think we're good here, Kyle," Dr. Lewis said, noting the water level in the beaker was just under 75 milliliters. He shut the burner off and let the mixture cool to room temperature. Kyle brought the litmus paper and the table salt. He also brought the IV bag and 100 milliliter syringe of deionized water out of the refrigerator.

After 20 minutes, the solution had cooled enough and they tested the acidity with the litmus paper.

"Looks good, Kyle," said Dr. Lewis who showed him the color of the paper, a shade of light blue, indicating a slight alkaline solution. They knew from prior testing that the *Convallaria majalis'* working ingredient fell into the spectrum of alkaline. Next, they tested for the presence of barbiturates.

"Wow Kyle, this is a strong brew. We're gonna likely need that whole 100 milliliters." Dr. Lewis grabbed the syringe and began squirting the clean water into the beaker. Once approximately 75 milliliters had been added, he paused for a retest. He dipped the paper into the water, "Perfect. Hand me a clean syringe." Kyle was ahead of Dr. Lewis and had it held out for him to grab. "It's like we've done this before," he responded with a smirk, catching a glimpse of the tattoo on Kyle's forearm.

He drew up 50 milliliters of the *Convallaria majalis* solution and injected it into the IV bag that already contained the ketamine, propofol, etomidate, thiopental, and methohexital. Dr. Lewis then picked the bag up and tipped it back and forth, rolled it right and left and flipped it upside down and back several times to help the mixture spread in the bag. The hint of pink that once existed in the beaker was now completely untraceable in the much larger IV bag.

They repeated the last step two additional times in order to make three hanging bags for the treatment session. Because Kyle had been staying in longer and longer, they quickly learned that more of the cocktail would be required. The longest he had been under was five hours, 32 minutes, and it required Dr. Lewis to pull him out just before the second bag was drained completely.

"We ready?" Kyle asked Dr. Lewis as he stood looking at the IV bags resting on the counter.

"I am. You still have to place your cath. I'm not helping with that. I'll take these into the lab. Meet you in there."

Kyle thoroughly lubricated the catheter and slid it inside. It was never a comforting experience but he had gotten used to the odd sensation. He inflated the small air bladder, ensuring the device would stay in place, and walked into the lab where Dr. Lewis was working. He had taken out the AED and laid it on a small tray next to the treatment table.

"Comforting," Kyle said gesturing with his hand that held his catheter bag as he pointed toward the AED.

"Well, I'm not taking any chances. Last thing we need is for you to die," he responded sharply, which Kyle read immediately.

"We ok here, Ethan?"

"Yes. Just a bit nervous about this whole thing. I don't want to regret this when it's all said and done. I'm pulling you out at the first sign of distress. Is that understood?"

"I agree. Please do. I'd like to tell you what happens. That's the point."

"I'm going to be giving you five liters of O2 with the mask. A nasal cannula will likely be irritating."

"You're the boss."

"Get on the table, Kyle. We're all ready then."

Kyle climbed up onto the table and laid his head back against a thin, cheap pillow. He grabbed the wool blanket and placed it over his body. In the study, they needed a full view of the body to note any motor movements, but because Kyle had been under repeatedly, they already knew his movements, and were more interested in his subjective findings. Kyle grabbed the EEG and placed it on his head. He also placed the O2 monitor on his finger and all the heart monitors on his body. After finally placing the O2 mask over his mouth and nose, Kyle placed his left arm on an armrest.

Dr. Lewis had walked back into the office to make sure all the equipment was on. He then returned to Kyle, placing a blood pressure cuff on his right arm and cranked up the O2. He then gloved up and took out an alcohol wipe. He gently ran the wipe across the back of Kyle's hand. Both men saw the "M" and shared a wordless glance. "Little prick," Dr. Lewis said.

"Don't call me a prick," Kyle attempted a joke.

"You've got air coming in the mask?"

Kyle took a deep, reassuring breath, "Sure do."

"See you on the other side."

"You'd better."

Kyle felt the menthol sensation enter his hand, creep up his arm, and then through his entire body. With every pump of his left ventricle the drug cocktail surged through his arteries.

"99, 98, 97."

Quickly the mixture reached his brain and he was unconscious to the world.

The bright light came quickly for Kyle this time. He had noticed each time he went under the perfect world came quicker. It was as if his body was learning, adapting to this other place. He was soon seeing mountains in the distance draped in shadows, contrasted with brilliant light beyond them. Where he stood was cream-colored ground, soft underfoot and made a small halo of fine dust around his feet with every step. The dust would never fall back to the ground. On a previous visit, Kyle had knelt down to watch the cloud of fine dust for the entire experience; it never changed once he stepped down no matter how he tried to manipulate it.

He began to walk; he knew the direction. He was looking for the ocean of blue water that stretched itself in all directions, except behind him. It called to him every time he entered the experience, and every time he got there, he woke up. Something had guided him there the third time he went into the experience, but it wasn't until the seventh time he saw the water, and the twelfth time in the experience that he reached its edge.

Kyle began to run. His arms and legs pumping, his lungs expanding and his will strong. The sensations he felt in life weren't present in this place. His lungs didn't hurt, his heart was steady, his muscles didn't burn or fatigue. He saw a red bird flying with him, singing a beautiful song, a richness of tone, and with the fullness of an entire orchestra. Behind the bird, a small white cloud traced his path back to his origin, flowing with the turbulence from each stroke of its wings. Kyle smiled, in awe of the beauty.

Time didn't exist there. He was running because that's all he knew to do. He needed to get to the water. He hadn't told Dr. Lewis his real reasons for going deeper. He never told Dr. Lewis about the water or the strong sensation of something urging him in that direction. He felt the answer was on the other side of the water.

Then he saw it: the blue horizon that he had seen at least a dozen times now. It was different from any water he had experienced on earth. He had seen the Pacific, the Atlantic, the Gulf, the Great Lakes, swimming pools, but nothing compared to the blue-green brilliance that swept the entire horizon. The sounds were incredible, waves crashing sending a full barrage of sensory stimulation to a height he couldn't even describe, making him a bit weak in the knees. The ground quaked, his eyes could see ghosting of the previous wave inside of the next, almost building one on another. The sound was so crisp and clear he swore he could hear the individual grains of sand washing across one another as the last wave returned to the sea. The smell was the most soothing for him. Instead of the ocean, he smelled the hot, humid air, the chlorine, the rubber from flippers, goggles, and swim caps; he smelled a pool.

He reached the water's edge and watched a wave to crash down shaking the ground and causing him to lose his balance. He recovered and felt the warm, cleansing water on his feet, his toes hugged sand as they sunk into it. As the water pulled back and took sand from around his feet, he saw something in stark contrast against the fine cream and white sand of the beach. He reached down and grabbed it. The feeling was unmistakable in his hand.

He lifted goggles from out of the sand and placed them onto his head. They felt like home, having worn a dozen of these exact pairs over his college career. His father bought him these goggles his freshman year, and after he died, they were the only ones Kyle would buy. He looked out at the sea and placed the goggles on. The entire sea morphed into a swimming pool, with an infinite number of lanes to his right and left. He looked down, and he was standing on a starting block. "Take your mark," echoed faintly across the infinite pool deck. Kyle reached down and grasped his starting block, the toes from his right foot grasping over the front edge.

*Beep!* The race was on. Kyle swam hard. His stroke had always been butterfly, smashing age group, club, pool, and state records as he climbed through the ranks. He rode on top of the water like a dolphin, burying his head for four strokes, then a breath, four strokes then a breath, over and over again. He gained strength with each pull of his arms and each dolphin kick. It felt as though he was covering ten yards with every stroke. He saw the "T" at the bottom of the pool and knew it was time to turn. *Boom!* He exploded off the wall and rocketed underwater with a powerful series of dolphin kicks, a stream of bubbles exiting his nose and traveling down the center of his torso as he sped through the water. Before he knew it he saw the "T" at the bottom again and—*boom!* He heard the roar of the crowd as he came off the wall for a second time, and took his first breath.

He felt strong, no fatigue, full of hope. He had never felt this good after 100 meters before. Looking right while coming off the wall, he had seen his rival at nationals, Mark Williams, from Stanford. Four more strokes and a breath, he looked left and saw Hal Rosenthal the one who beat him freshman year at conference. *Boom!* He exploded off the wall, breaking the tile on the side of the pool and shot out to a full body length lead. He had always been a great turner but this was beyond incredible. He took one last breath at the 20-meter mark and buried his head, working anaerobically toward the finish. He reached out, extending his arms overhead in the longest streamline of his life. He hit the wall and turned to look at the scoreboard high above the sea, large enough for all to view. He had a new PR: 1:56.54.

Kyle yelled and pumped his fist in the air. He looked around and saw nothing but a brilliant white sky with a beautiful blue horizon. It was as if the sun shone so bright all things above ceased to exist. He grabbed the starting block and began to climb out when he felt someone grab his arm.

*Dad,* he thought but was too afraid to look up. It was unbelievable but he couldn't bring himself to do it. It had to be his dad. It would explain everything—the drive to come to the water, the goggles his dad bought, seeing Hal, the only one who beat him the last time his father saw him race before he died.

He looked up and saw his father. "Dad!" he yelled getting out of the pool and standing in awe of the moment. He was now taller than his dad, having grown three more inches late in college. They now stood eye to eye, Kyle dripping wet and trying to grasp the moment. "How is this, my God! Dad!" He yelled again trying to hug him. His father put up both hands as an indication not to.

"Kyle, my beautiful boy. I'd love nothing more than to hold you and squeeze you tight like when you were a little boy but right now it can't happen. We have only a moment to talk."

"Why?"

"I think you know why. Solve the problem son. We both know you aren't staying long. I've been trying to get you here to see me for some time now."

"I felt it. That's why I kept coming back. I had no idea it was you. How is this real?"

"Well, I'm not exactly sure but I'll leave that problem solving up to you. You always knew how to solve the problem."

"I miss you, Dad. So much. I don't even know where to start."

"I'm so proud of you. I've seen you, watched you. I'm glad you finished your career at Mizzou. Made me so happy to watch you finish even though I know it was hard. I want you to know that I love you and no matter what, I am ok. Do not burden yourself with regrets about what happened."

Kyle nodded, too shocked to say anything. He just wanted to stay in this experience forever with his dad, his mentor, his best friend. "When can I see you again? How does this work?"

"When the time is right," his father said waving.

Everything began to fade. The brilliant sky began to turn a pale gray and Kyle knew his father would be gone.

"Dad, I love you."

"I love you!" he yelled as he came back to life in the treatment room.

He was supine, the bed was flat and he had large patches stuck to his chest and abdomen. Dr. Lewis straddled Kyle with both hands on his chest.

"Normal rhythm, discontinue CPR, and monitor patient," the calm, female voice from the AED said.

"Oh thank God," Dr. Lewis said as he rolled off the bed and lay on the tile floor of the treatment room. "We are NOT doing that again."

"Did I die?"

"Yes. Your BP bottomed out at 20/10 and then everything went to hell. You were gone for two minutes."

"Dr. Lewis," Kyle said calmly. "Dr. Lewis," he repeated a bit louder.

"Yeah."

"I, I don't really know how to say this without sounding crazy."

Dr. Lewis slowly stood up from the floor, still breathing heavy and feeling a bit lightheaded. The adrenaline was running low and the gravity of the last ten minutes weighing him down.

"Tell me, Kyle. Did something happen?"

"I've been hiding something from you. Every time I went in I felt this feeling, an unexplainable pulling toward something."

"Is that it?"

"No."

"Well?"

"Was everything the same on the monitors?"

"Kyle, I'm not playing games. You died. Spit it out!"

"I need to know. Was my EEG quiet?"

"Yes. Same everything except you tanked and I just spent the last two minutes pressing down on your chest and shocking your heart back into a normal rhythm so excuse me if I don't have time to answer questions you already know the answer to. Now if you were lying to me this whole time how can I ever tr—"

"It was my dad. I saw my dad! I talked to him."

Dr. Lewis stood in disbelief. He would have called Kyle a liar, but Kyle had already done that to himself moments ago. He felt uneasy, jittery, wanting to scratch everywhere at the same time. He wanted to scream, to run, to never come back, or even continue with the study. He secretly hoped the experience would reveal itself to be something grander, more worthwhile than a way to treat psychological disorders. He too had felt the pull toward something when Lily brought him to that place but he had personally never followed it. He was too involved with taking in the sights, the sounds, the overload of sensory input that nobody could fully explain, but anyone could experience.

Ethan thought of what Lily had said when she lay dying. "Forgive me," she said just before her last chilling breath exited her soft lips.

*Who had she seen? Why was she asking forgiveness? Had she killed someone like I killed her? Is that how she knew of the cocktail?*

Dozens of questions began streaking through his head. The uneasiness and fear began to morph into anger and frustration. He wasn't going to be able to answer these new questions. No amount of research was going to be able to answer the questions he had. The thoughts began to evaporate allowing for clearer thinking, and he began to focus on Kyle who still lay in front of him waiting to tell the story.

"Ok Kyle, tell me all about it."

Over the next hour Kyle told Dr. Lewis about everything. He told him about the sensory details, how it seemed as though he was unlocked, able to fully experience the world around him for the first time. He explained how each time he went under his ability to adapt, understand, and experience the environment was faster and more inclusive. He went from a blank white veil, with a mix of gentle shadows and echoing music, to the details of the dust that came up with each step, the red bird, and meeting his father after a swim race. He told Dr. Lewis about his conversation with his father and how he felt much more at peace with the choices he made.

Kyle reached down to his tattoo, "I don't regret this anymore. I'm so glad I never got around to taking it off." He gently stroked his palm over it remembering the day he got it. His father laughed at him as he winced, waiting for the needle to pierce his skin for the first time. Once it started, the sharp burn turned numb and he was able to relax into the moment.

"I think it's time we both get some sleep. You can take the treatment bed. I'll take the couch."

"All right Doc. Thanks."

"For what, saving your life?"

"More than one way." He smiled, staring at Dr. Lewis. The two men understood each other.

# | NINE |

"You'll feel a bit of a chill as we start the medication," Malcolm said to the middle aged man who lay on the treatment table. "Do you consent to the treatment?"

"Yes I do, Malcolm."

"Ok, Marcus. Here we go. Start counting down from 100."

"Wow, that it is cold. 100, 99, 98, 97 . . ."

"Ok Traci you got 'em?"

"Sure do Malcolm. He's looking good." Treatment Room One was running smoothly. Dr. Lewis felt Malcolm was ready, and last week he decided to let him proceed without Kyle or himself administering the drug.

Treatment Room Three was also beginning, Adam was performing the pre-treatment interview, followed by the treatment he would be initiating himself as well. He had been performing the treatments on his own for over a month now. Dr. Lewis was very impressed with how Adam was able to absorb information and demonstrate true understanding of material.

"Ok, Veronica, we're looking good," Adam said watching his patient's eyes close and begin entering the experience.

"Thanks, she looks good. Now come on in here and keep me company."

Treatment Rooms Two and Four were being handled by Dr. Lewis and Kyle, each taking one by themselves. The entire four-room suite was able to communicate through intercom, each letting Dr. Lewis know when the patient was ready to come out based on their vitals. Nobody, except Kyle and Dr. Lewis, knew how far they could actually allow the vitals to slip. Once each subject's specific number was hit, Dr. Lewis would leave his observation room to administer the drug. Depending on the room he was entering, Veronica, Traci, or Kyle would trade and watch his patient. It had only taken a few days to smooth out the switching, and the study was running smoothly as they finished their second month.

It took another hour, but they had all finished the interviews and data entry. It was only 3:00 p.m. and the whole crew was excited. The days were becoming very consistent starting at about 7:00 a.m., and in the last week they were able to streamline the scheduling quite a bit more. They had planned on each treatment and interview session taking four hours per person, however, they had cut it down to three. It allowed them to tighten the scheduling and create shorter days for everyone.

"I'll work for you forever, Dr. Lewis. These hours are great!" Veronica said. She then walked over to Adam, looked up toward his face, and received a kiss on the forehead. She then nuzzled herself into the space between his arm and chest, forcing him to place an arm around her. She closed her eyes and smiled, smelling the cologne on his chest. He kissed her again on the top of the head and gave her a squeeze.

"Aren't you glad you decided to help the good Doc out?" She looked up again and smiled at Adam.

"Oh my God," Adam said rolling his eyes and gently pushing her away. The rest of the group chuckled at the bashful gesture.

It was fun for Dr. Lewis to watch the two of them. He knew they were good, smart kids. It reminded him of how Lily and he used to be. He was confident the two would make it for the long haul. He then looked away and stared blankly at the floor, the wall, and finally found a cabinet door that needed shutting so he walked away. He sighed heavily as he reached the door, taking his time to close it gently and leave his hand there for a brief moment, giving the two of them time to finish their moment together.

"Ok, love birds, take it somewhere else," Dr. Lewis said motioning with his hands toward the door. "I'm starting to feel like a broken record, but it's a good thing; great job today. See everyone tomorrow," he said forcing a smile, which everyone bought.

Kyle and Dr. Lewis stayed in the treatment suite and waited for everyone to leave. It only took a few moments, but finally they were alone. They silently went to the elevator and took it to the top floor. Upon exiting, Dr. Lewis unlocked the office door, opened it for himself and held it for Kyle. He made sure to lock it and the two men finally spoke.

"We're ready?"

"Sure are Doc. I prepped the cocktail last night and placed them all in the refrigerator. Five IV bags full."

"Last time you were under for twelve hours. If that happens again, we're gonna have to prep six just in case."

"I hear ya, Ethan."

"Let's get going."

Kyle was resting on the bed waiting for the treatment to begin, thinking about seeing his father again. The second time he saw his father, Kyle was able to keep his emotions at bay and have an actual conversation. They talked about a few things, mainly how Kyle's mother left because she was unfaithful. They also talked briefly about Kyle's lack of relationships, to which they both agreed was a combination of distress related to his mother leaving and his father dying. Kyle agreed it was time to try and find someone. When Kyle was pulled out of the experience on the second occasion, he hadn't yet died on the table.

"Ok Kyle, ready?" Dr. Lewis said as he glanced at the clock on the wall, 3:35 p.m.

"Yeah," Kyle said nodding and sighing deeply.

"See you in a few hours."

Dr. Lewis began entering the treatment parameters.

Third time into deep experience.

Parameters: BP 20/10, heart rate 30, O2 85 percent. Predicted time under, 12 hours.

Dr. Lewis was prepared. In their isolated observation room, he had brought in a refrigerator, a blue-ray player, and two books he hadn't read. People had always given him books for Christmas and birthdays, as if books were something he talked about regularly. In actuality, Ethan hadn't read a book for pleasure in decades. He picked up a book and began to page through it, reading the preface, in pieces, then the first paragraph of chapter one. It was a book about terrorism, an unhappy, unaccepted boy who wants to join the army. It piqued his interest, but his mind had other plans.

He glanced up to check on Kyle who was likely already in the experience. *Is he running yet? Has he seen the water? Has he started talking to his father?* Kyle never moved like the others while under, no matter what stage. He also never talked or showed emotion. Not even the first time he saw his father. The clinic had seen dozens of patients over the last two months with the newest variation of the cocktail, and each one of them had a motor response while inside the experience. Ethan chalked it up to variability inherent in every study, but it did make it difficult for Dr. Lewis to comprehensively study Kyle.

Kyle had gone in the second time after Dr. Lewis gave into his own curiosity once again. The shock of seeing Kyle's death and the trauma of having to revive him kept Dr. Lewis up for a week, but after that, a seed of wonder was planted. He was able to fight it for two full days, but on the third, he propositioned Kyle.

"Kyle, can you come into the office?" Dr. Lewis had asked him nervously. "I was thinking about how you saw your father. I have to admit, I'm curious to see if that was an anomaly."

"Me too," Kyle responded, his eyes looking toward the floor.

"I honestly don't feel comfortable with you going in that deep again."

"I would love to talk to my dad. I was too shocked. He told me when the time was right."

"Is the time right?" Dr. Lewis asked.

"It's always right for me."

Dr. Lewis had plans to go beyond the current research parameters. He wanted to find a way to keep the test safe, while allowing others to go very deep into the treatment. Kyle was the test subject in helping Dr. Lewis determine the safest parameters to use, while still getting everything out of the experience. He hadn't let Kyle know his plans, but he would after this third deep probe.

Ethan had once, long ago, watched a special on near death experiences. He saw the program shortly after Lily had died and it really affected him. It wasn't because she was gone, or that he wondered if she experienced it, but rather because he knew he had experienced it himself. When Lily gave him the drug, he was taken to a place very similar to what the individuals on the program were describing—the bright light, the sensation of being drawn to something or someone, the energy, the lack of ability to fully explain the experience despite being able to recall every subtle feature of the event. Some of the people described talking with or seeing lost loved ones. He knew Lily had experienced it too; that everyone who was part of the test since Linda had also experienced it to some degree. The hardest part of the whole thing was determining what everyone was experiencing and establishing norms. Dr. Lewis had tentatively determined that it hadn't mattered how deep everyone was taken, their experiences were all individualized. However, he was now wondering if one were to go deep enough, would everyone give into what was guiding them, and would it be a loved one like Kyle? *Who did Lily see?*

Ethan reached into the refrigerator and grabbed a sandwich; turkey and ham on a sub roll. He had thrown it together that morning on his way out the door. He never considered packing a lunch before, nor did he usually plan out meals. He moved the refrigerator into the observation room the day before so he felt obligated to fill it with something. Plus, working seven to three without a break left him hungry most days, and with grinding away for another 12 hours, he was going to need food. If nothing else, it would help him stay awake.

An orange glow began to bleed into the observation room from under the door as the sun began to set. It was eerie, but Dr. Lewis had seen it before on many occasions. It resembled a scene from a horror movie, and at any moment a monster would break through the door. Dr. Lewis was so bored he would've welcomed the opportunity to battle a beast. He sat and read, watched a movie, doodled on a notepad, but the time crept by.

He looked through the window and into the treatment room. He watched Kyle breathe slowly, eight times per minute. It was an odd experience no matter how often he watched this. It was clear Kyle's body was working on autopilot, allowing the deepest reflexive systems in the body to keep him alive. Each breath was more of a large gulp of air that slowly escaped his lungs followed by a long pause; then repeat.

Dr. Lewis looked at the monitors and noted the BP was currently 60/45, and his heart rate was 34. Kyle still had 100 percent O2, thanks to the five-liters of oxygen pumping into the mask continuously. He then looked at the cameras, three of them continuously recording while the motion sensor camera stayed black. Dr. Lewis had to remind himself of the fourth camera's function quite regularly, since it had been so inactive with Kyle during their testing over the last year.

Two more hanging IV bags, six hours, and an entire novel later, Kyle's BP hit 20/12. Dr. Lewis walked into the room with stiff legs, epinephrine in hand. He rubbed his eyes with his free hand and then opened his blue eyes wide. He looked at Kyle and moved his own brown hair from his face, catching a few strands on what sporadic stubble he had. He then grasped the IV line and injected the epinephrine.

"Lily?" Kyle asked quietly with eyes closed.

Dr. Lewis felt numb all over. The room began to spin and he felt like crying. He rubbed his hands through his hair and furrowed his brow, the needle just inches from his own forehead. *Does he know? Why would he see her? What do I do? What do I do? What do I do!* Dr. Lewis thought to run, to leave the treatment room. *Where am I gonna go?*

Kyle began to stir, "Wait dad! Lily?" Dr. Lewis began to panic. The epinephrine hadn't brought Kyle out and he needed an answer. He ran to the AED and placed the pads on Kyle's chest. He grasped the bed firmly, the whites of his knuckles were indiscernible from the white of the rail. He closed his eyes just as firmly in an attempt to reset his mind, but it was of little use. The harder he closed his eyes, the brighter the vision. It reminded him of the botany lab years ago, Lily lying on the floor and his instinct to run. Only this time, he couldn't.

Dr. Lewis opened his eyes and saw the syringe sitting on the bed. He saw only half of the dose had been administered. He had inadvertently pulled the needle when he heard her name. Quickly, he administered the remaining portion and held his breath, hoping it would still work.

"Dr. Lewis? Is everything ok?" Kyle asked softly, raspy from his dry mouth and throat.

"Perfect," Dr. Lewis said sweating.

"That's great. So when are we gonna do this again?"

"Never."

"Why?" Kyle asked aggressively. "I don't understand. What's changed?"

"Kyle you said a name. You never speak when you're under, and you said Lily. Who is Lily?"

"It was my dog. When I was a kid we had a Lab named Lily."

"And you saw Lily?"

"No," Kyle said smiling. "My dad told me he saw her."

"Nothing else?" Dr. Lewis wasn't sure he should believe Kyle. He had already lied once after all.

"No Doc, you pulled me out. It was a bit random, but I loved that dog. She died a few years before my dad. We had her for twelve years. It made me very sad when she died."

"Ok Kyle. Go grab some food. I've got something to talk to you about but it can wait."

# | TEN |

It was early on Saturday but Dr. Lewis found it was necessary to call Michelle Adams. He was fuming over the latest press release from Whitestone. It was showcasing this quarter's latest and greatest purchases, mergers, and new happenings. Elias Grant, the prick, had stated, "Whitestone was currently integrally involved in a major medical research project which promised to be a very vital and prolific medical advancement." He also went on to say, "Beyond the medical benefits for multiple millions, it has the potential to generate enormous money making opportunities and open doors to further medical research opportunities for our company."

"Hello, Dr. Lewis," the sweet voice of five-hundred dollars per hour answered the phone.

"I need you to decipher something for me," Dr. Lewis spat into the phone without pleasantries. He then went on to read the quarterly report, adding accents to every point referencing research. "What the hell do I do with this? I feel like he is in breach of our contract!"

"Dr. Lewis, please calm down and email me the article. I'm not going to charge you for this call, but please remember I charge by the hour. Don't read to me when I could read it for myself. I'll try and get back to you by nine a.m. Is that ok?"

"Yes, and I'm sorry for being abrupt. The last thing I need is for him to blow my research project up, especially because we are really rolling now."

"No apologies needed, Doctor. I've seen worst reactions to less. Talk soon, sweetheart." Michelle said before hanging up.

Dr. Lewis immediately emailed her the article and walked to the kitchen. He started his second pot of coffee for the morning. It was 7:30, but he hadn't slept that night. It was a conscious decision, the previous two nights were filled with nightmares of Lily disowning him, blaming him, hating him for what had happened to her. He couldn't stand another night of hearing the words that made his every day grief stricken and monotonous. Instead, he spent the entire night watching YouTube videos, reading articles, and searching blogs for persons who talked about having out of body experiences. The deeper treatments were going to focus on the individuals who claimed to have felt death, seen themselves from the outside, been drawn into a light, or talked to deceased loved ones. He wanted to answer his new hypothesis: Will persons who claim to have experienced an NDE or Near Death Experience describe it as the same sensation given by the deeper treatments? He knew it would be a strong correlation. He just needed the bodies to prove it.

Dr. Lewis had also made a post on several blogs.

To those who have survived an NDE:

Hello, I am a research physician who is currently looking to study those who have gone through a near death experience. My goal is to simply have a conversation in which I listen to your experiences, allowing you to describe them in great detail. Please consider sending me a direct message, so your information can remain confidential.

Sincerely,
NDEDOC1

Dr. Lewis paused before hitting send at 3:00 a.m. It seemed wrong, awkward, and completely uncontrolled. *Who knew if anyone on these forums tells the truth? Are they attention seeking? Are they unstable? Will they think I'm unstable?* Dozens of unanswered questions left him feeling frustrated, but instead of closing the browser window, he clicked send.

It was difficult for Dr. Lewis to relax. The waves of anxiety crashed heavily upon him over and over again each time he thought of the news from Whitestone, but at least it took his mind off of the web posting. It took everything he had not to call Elias Grant at that moment and scream at him through the phone, citing breaches of their contract and threatening to sue. He thought of how nice it would be to take ownership of the greenhouse and eliminate the need for Elias all together. He fantasized about watching Elias drop to his knees and beg him not to tarnish the name of Whitestone. Dr. Lewis would love to see Elias squirm, to feel anxiety, nervousness, vulnerability. He wanted Elias to pay for using his own son's death as leverage.

*His own son,* Dr. Lewis thought to himself. He smirked. *What if I put that selfish man into the experience and let him talk to his own dead son?* Thinking about the possible effects that would have on a man like Elias was comforting. He allowed himself to imagine even selfish monsters like Elias would be able to feel emotion when faced with a lost loved one returning to tell them how upset they were with how they were treated in death.

Dr. Lewis grabbed his black coffee and sat himself down in front of the TV to watch the news. He felt less anxiety since his fantasy of watching Elias meet his own son while in the experience. It was a start. The news was rarely eventful but this morning there was talk about a terrorist attack in Europe. Dozens of people had died and many more injured in the shootings. It was a fresh story so updates were coming about every ten minutes which kept him well distracted. By the time Dr. Lewis was getting back up for another cup of coffee, it was close to 9:00 a.m.

*Ring, ring, ring, ring, ring, ring.* His phone went off. He walked to his desk and answered the phone. "Hello Michelle."

"Hello Dr. Lewis. I'll get right to it. The good man Elias, unfortunately, has not broken our contract."

"Michelle, how can that be? He all but mentioned us directly!" he said angrily into the phone.

"That's exactly it, Dr. Lewis. He didn't mention your research, your name, or anything official. He hadn't mentioned your name or what specifically you were researching, nor did he mention what he was doing for you."

"So that's it then? We have nothing on him?"

"I'm afraid so. I know it's challenging. I can see that you feel vulnerable in this agreement. He's a businessman, make no mistake about it. He will exploit anything he can to make a buck."

"I plan on calling him. Giving him a piece of my mind."

"I would advise against it, but if you do, make sure you aren't threatening with him. Just stick to the facts. He's likely discussed this entire scenario with his team and the release was likely a joint decision."

"Thanks, Michelle. I appreciate you working on it so fast."

"And I appreciate your business. Call anytime. For anything."

"I'm sure I will."

Dr. Lewis hung up the phone and called Elias Grant.

"Hello," a sweet voice said softly on the other end.

"Hi, Mrs. White. This is Dr. Lewis. I was wondering if Elias would have a minute to speak?"

"Hello, Dr. Lewis. I hope you're well."

"I am, thank you. And you?"

"I am as well thank you. Hold on please, Dr. Lewis." Several moments passed and Ethan knew the longer he waited, the less likely Elias would be available. *He's likely discussed the entire scenario.* Michelle's words echoed in his head. He also revisited her final words: *For anything; what did that mean?*

"Dr. Lewis, I'm sorry but he will have to call you back at a later time. He is currently busy talking to other board members regarding the feedback from their quarterly release."

"Well, I would love to have a word with him about that as well. Can you please let him know I called?"

"Of course I can, Dr. Lewis. Is the number you called from a good one?"

"Yes, it's my cell phone. That works best."

"Ok, you'll hear from him as soon as he can. He assured me of that."

"Thanks, Mrs. White."

Frustrated, Dr. Lewis squeezed the phone as he ended the call. The anxiety returned and he was angry about being blown off. Elias had clearly done this to twist a knife into him. *Why else would this be happening?* It may simply be that Dr. Lewis had no understanding of business, or bottom lines, or future planning venture capitalism. All he knew was his research, which was driven by his memory of her.

Dr. Lewis sat back down on the couch, coffee in hand. Kyle was supposed to be at the office sometime in the early afternoon to discuss something Dr. Lewis had promised would be "important and revolutionary." He now had more fuel for the fire, Elias Grant's press release, and it meant they may have to move the timetable up on their federal research. It was looking like a full Saturday afternoon.

A few hours had passed but Dr. Lewis hadn't paid much attention. The news had ended and a much less entertaining daytime schedule began smearing itself across the screen. The TV was once again background noise for the constant thoughts parading through his head. The second pot of coffee helped sharpen his mind as insomnia twisted his thoughts. *How many should we test? What variability should we expect? What if the person tested had no lost loved ones?* But of all the questions that he had, the one item eluding him was how to explain the experience. The brain was lifeless, not producing anything within the cerebral cortex. He refused to believe that was the case, but could find no way to explain what people were experiencing. This is what drove him mad, why he often gave in to his curiosity, and allowed Kyle to go deeper. But not again, not after he heard her name from Kyle's mouth.

*Click.* The deadbolt from the door twisted and Kyle entered. Dr. Lewis' thoughts halted like hundreds of bubbles, bursting into remnant memories, most of which were soon forgotten. "Morning," Kyle said closing the door and taking a bite of a bagel full of cream cheese.

"Morning?" Dr. Lewis said checking the clock on the wall.

"Come on Doc, it's Saturday!"

"I'm still working. So let's get to work, shall we?"

"What ya got?"

"I asked you to come here for a reason, but that'll have to wait until I get this out there." Dr. Lewis gestured toward the desktop and Kyle followed, bagel in hand.

"What we got?" Kyle asked with a hint of whimsy.

"What we got is a big mouth monster working with us," Dr. Lewis said striking the mouse aggressively, clicking the window that had been minimized. He couldn't keep it open on the desktop, the press release made his stomach turn.

"What a jerk."

"I already talked to Michelle, she said there's nothing legally we can do."

"You know as well as I do there's only a short amount of time before someone figures out what he's referring to."

"Mhm. Which is why I called him this morning. Mrs. White said he's busy with quite a bit since the press release came out."

"Yeah, I'm sure he is. He may have done this to let you know you didn't get the last word on the deal."

"Could be I guess, but that selfish prick has to realize this could screw us both," he said sighing through his teeth. "I swear Kyle I would change things if I could do it over again. Never get wrapped up in this guy's deal."

"It's the only option we had at the time. I'd say look at the bright side. It took him a few months to stick it to ya. Think you did a good job."

Dr. Lewis smirked, did a long, circle with his head loosening his neck, and said, "Could be worse I guess. I still wanna give him a piece of my mind though."

"I know. But relax. We need this study to finish, not get bogged down in trying to find another supplier for the flower. So what's the other thing? Why did I really bring my breakfast here?"

"Ok, well, I've been thinking. You went under deep three times now, each with replicating experiences more or less. I want to try something bigger."

"You said I couldn't go in again," Kyle said, probing for a sign. He wanted to read Dr. Lewis, he wanted to see he was going to let him go back in.

"That's correct. Not you."

"Then who?" Kyle said cramming the last, large bite into his mouth. He had been hungry from another strenuous swim.

Dr. Lewis then brought up a second browser window, this time with three separate tabs. The first, was a general website for persons looking for knowledge of near death experiences. The second was a YouTube video in which someone was being interviewed about their NDE, and the third was a forum. This was where Dr. Lewis placed his post about the study.

"Can you see what I'm getting at Kyle?"

"Yes Ethan. But what if these people have other issues? Other comorbidities. I had been under a dozen times before I went that deep. I knew how it felt, you know how I responded, how to get me out. These people will have no clue, and on top of that, you will be asking them to be hush-hush. How can you possibly expect that?"

"I'm hoping the experience enough will keep them quiet."

"If you're willing to risk it all, I'll go along with it, but I'm not excited right now. This seems reckless. I didn't think you were reckless—"

"I'm not reckless!" Dr. Lewis said cutting him off and looking sternly at Kyle. If you'd quit blabbering you'd hear me. We are going to take everyone into the experience one step at a time just as we did for you. If we get a bad sign, they are done. Clearly this is a much more strenuous process but one that can be incredibly rewarding for those involved. We need to figure this out Kyle. We need to know what's out there. We need to see if it's reproducible, if it's dangerous, if it's a manifestation in the mind."

"I can tell you without question my father was not in my mind Ethan. One-hundred percent sure."

"We need to test it. Over and over again."

"How, when, we already have to increase the speed of our federal testing because of Elias. Where will we get the time?"

"Kyle," Dr. Lewis said calmly, reassuringly. He was aware of the emotional toll Kyle was under. Dr. Lewis had the benefit of working out all of these scenarios in his head for weeks before he tested Kyle a few weeks earlier. He had already generated schedules for them to follow, how they would mix the cocktail, see patients after hours and on the weekends, and still perform their federal study despite the increased productivity demands.

"Kyle I have it all figured out. Sit over on the couch and review this spreadsheet." He handed it to his trusted, work-hardened assistant who walked to the couch and plopped down, burying his head deep within the walls of his light hoodie. For several minutes Kyle reviewed the work, tracing line over line with his index finger making sure he hadn't missed a single point. He was looking for a reason to say no, a chink in the armor, a hole in the wall. He wasn't afraid of the work; it was something much more personal. He wanted to be the one who got to go in. He wanted to keep seeing his father.

"Kyle," Dr. Lewis said staring at the lump of man balled up on the couch. Without waiting for an acknowledgement he said, "I want you to know I'm going to do this with or without you. But would much prefer you come with me. Your father was right. You are a problem solver."

Kyle felt a small flame ignite inside him. He knew that Dr. Lewis may have been playing to his sentimental side, but in the moment he remembered how much the good doctor reminded him of Ray, his father. He reflected on how he used to feel when he looked at the Mizzou tattoo on his arm just a few months earlier, wanting to have it removed. He looked at his hands, vascular and strong, the way he used to look when he was lean and in race shape. He had recently found his way back into the pool very regularly, putting in 30,000 yards a week now. He had quit drinking beer, stopped eating out, started flirting with girls again. His jealousy, his childish transparent grumblings that were only fooling himself started to slowly melt away. He took his hood down, allowing Dr. Lewis to see that he had cut his hair the preceding afternoon, leaving a smooth look of stubble on his temples and around the back of his head, and long, waving hair arching back over the top of his head.

"Nice haircut, Kyle."

"Haha," he laughed out loud rubbing the sides vigorously. "I can't even fake that this is a bad idea," he said looking up with sorrowful eyes and smirking. "I'm sorry Ethan. I should be thankful for what you allowed me to do. I don't know what else to say."

"Say yes. Otherwise I'm never gonna be sleeping."

"Yes," Kyle said laughing at Dr. Lewis' joke.

"Now we wait and see who wants to share their stories. It might take a while to find a few good candidates."

"Let's take our time with it. What are we gonna call this thing?"

"Oh, I'm glad you asked," Dr. Lewis said pointing a finger at him. "I was thinking The Beyond Experience," he gestured his hand across the sky in a dramatic arc.

Kyle sat for a moment contemplating the idea. "As stupid as you just made it with that hand gesture I think it's pretty spot on. Almost like you've been there before, Ethan."

"Well, must just be all those research studies I wrap up. Doing the interviews. Seems fitting doesn't it?"

"I could give you a treatment, then you'll know firsthand."

Dr. Lewis did well holding back. He smirked and lied the lie he practiced for years. It the easiest way out. He had, after all, been under for a simple procedure when he was in his early 20s. He had torn his meniscus and needed a scope performed. "I don't do anesthesia well, I'm afraid. Got pretty sick about 20 years back. I'll live through the thousands I treat I'm afraid."

"Seems unfair to know what it's like and never experience it, but I'll let it slide. I guess better to have never known or whatever that saying is."

*You have no idea*, he thought as he looked at his young lab assistant. "Better to have known love and lost? That one?"

"Yeah you got it. Speaking of—"

"That's gonna take a lot more buttering up and another night of karaoke."

"All right, all right. Thought I'd try asking again. It'd been a while and thought we were feeling a moment."

"Let's do some work. Grab a laptop and get reading these blogs."

The two men worked for a couple of hours scouring the internet for first person accounts of NDEs. It was difficult to determine which were fake and which were real. So many of the stories were similar, but some, on rare occasion, were very dark. They would talk about complete loneliness, screaming, ripping of flesh, and breaking of bone. Kyle and Dr. Lewis both felt these versions would certainly be outside of the study, at least initially, but both agreed it may be something worth investigating down the road. After all, it wasn't as if The Beyond Experience was by the book.

"Looks like we'll have a couple of weeks to interview some of these people before we start testing," Dr. Lewis said pushing back from the computer, having checked his blog post for the twentieth time that afternoon. He had been hoping for a flood of people interested in participating, but so far none had messaged him.

"Yeah, looks like it may be a bit slow. A lot of these posts date back several years. I don't think there's tons of action."

"Likely not. A lot of negativity in the responses from some people. Probably scares people away from talking openly."

Dr. Lewis checked his email. A wave of nervous anxiety crept over him as he was immediately taken back to Harvard, to the research lab, to Lily on the floor, pale and breathless. It was an email reminding him of the Harvard Annual Research Report. Every year Harvard hosted a weekend-long research symposium where faculty were allowed to present their current work, finished or not, to their peers. The report also allowed previous students of Harvard graduate studies to apply for a spot in the presentation.

Ethan attended every year, but mostly as an excuse to get away. The weekend had always coincided with his anniversary with Lily. It was a pleasant memory of love, commitment, the kind of thing married couples reflect upon years after their vows have been given. The two of them had committed themselves to each other long ago. He wasn't sure if it was the guilt or the love that drove his tradition, but he did know the magnetism was undeniable.

"Kyle, next weekend I'll be in Boston for the Annual Research Report. Everyone's got that Friday off. Make sure I remember to tell them would you?"

"Yeah Doc, I'll shoot them all an email right now just to get it over with. I'm sure they're gonna love it, especially since we're telling them it's time to increase the numbers."

"Good plan."

"Doc, how come we never apply for that report?"

"I'm not big on giving speeches, just like to get the research out there, let the evidence in our papers speak for themselves." He was lying. He loathed mingling, small talk, and introductions, so bringing Kyle would make it impossible to blend into the surroundings. Kyle was easy to like, handsome, and talkative—three qualities Ethan lacked. Plus, and likely exponentially more important, he wanted to be alone as he relived his past with Lily. He certainly didn't want to risk her being brought up in a reminiscent conversation or a probing joke from Kyle.

"It's your call, Doc, but eventually people need to know what we're doing. No place like unveiling our work at your old stomping grounds."

"Maybe next year."

# | ELEVEN |

## Chicago, Illinois | Fall 2006

Adam and Veronica were driving north on I-55 in Illinois. The sun
was bright orange on the horizon, and fading to yellow as it marched
vertically into the sky. Adam drove with one hand on the wheel and
his other gently holding Veronica's as she slept in the passenger seat.
He stroked her thumb lightly, feeling the subtle creases in her thumb
at the knuckle, and the smooth cool sensation of her nail that was
freshly painted. She was nervous to look her best. It was going to be
the first time meeting Adam's parents, both physicians themselves in
the northern suburbs of Chicago.

Adam's father was a family practitioner and his mother an
anesthesiologist, both still working full time and both eager to meet
the first woman to capture their son's attention. "We can't believe
our Adam is bringing home a girl!" his mother said via Skype the
previous night. She has also asked to be called Julie when Veronica
had repeatedly called her Dr. Nicholson. Adam's father also insisted on
being called by his first name, Harmon. Adam laughed when his father
said that, because it was an ongoing joke that his father had a man
crush on Harmon Rabb from the show JAG. Everyone was giddy on
the call and laughed loudly when Adam brought it up.

It was Adam's idea to drive to Chicago. After hearing the plans
to start seeing more patients he made an uncharacteristically snap
decision and asked Veronica to come and meet his parents. Kyle had
told the lab assistants Dr. Lewis never took days off, and this would be
the only three-day weekend they had coming. Adam thought it best to
leave by 5:00 a.m. Friday morning, which would allow them to beat

traffic out of Saint Louis, and miss Chicago's after the morning rush. Both of his parents would be working in the afternoon but planned on driving into the city to join them at Quartino Ristorante.

Adam had the small VW Golf on cruise control and was speeding, but only a little. It didn't matter what time they got to Chicago, as long as Veronica got to see it. Having never been, she had no idea what to expect. He wanted to show her Michigan Avenue, Navy Pier, the Art Museum, Soldier Field, and the train station. He had so many stories about school trips and family outings he wanted to tell her about and showing her the places was exciting for him. He was nervous, hoping she loved it all.

Adam realized he was smirking to himself. He looked over to Veronica, who was curled up in her seat sleeping, despite the grande Americano sitting in the cup-holder next to her. He laughed quietly, *I can't sleep in cars,* her words passed through his head. She looked angelic lying there in the seat, the hues of the morning sunlight were revealing the golden highlights in her dark hair and her skin seemed to glow a light shade of bronze. Her breathing was like long rhythmical beats of a baton as a conductor guided a symphony through a gentle, beautiful melody. He sat listening to the tires roll over the road and thinking of how happy his mother would be to meet his beautiful Veronica in person. He sighed heavily, attempting to shake the nerves that he knew would grow as the day pressed on. He knew he was in love, just didn't want to say it yet. Or, was the nervousness caused by the fact he planned on telling his parents he was dropping out of medical school to continue researching full time for Dr. Lewis?

## Boston, Massachusetts | October 2006

It was a day easily forgettable for most as Dr. Lewis walked down the street in Brookline, Massachusetts—average boring temperature, a slight breeze, and fluffy skies allowed for a mix of shadow and sunlight all day. There were the same traffic noises, the same familiar streets, and the usual smells of greasy pub food; the same buses taking the same students to the same classes they had every Friday morning. However, for Dr. Ethan Lewis, it was a day he would remember; the same as all the last ten October sixths before it.

"How we doin' today Doc?" Jimmy asked as Dr. Lewis entered the door, and chimes sounded.

"Same as last year Jimmy."

"Every year I hope you don't show, but every year here you are standing in this doorway soon as we open."

"It won't change Jimmy."

"After ten years Doc, I'm starting to believe you."

"Ethan, Jimmy. Call me Ethan."

"You got it. What'll it be Ethan? You wanna' change it up at all? A back piece? An arm sleeve?" he said holding both hands slightly up in the air, a tattoo gun grasped in one.

Ethan just looked at Jimmy who smirked, "I have to ask!"

Ethan placed his hand on a soft tray while Jimmy took out the essentials: a pair of gloves, a coloring needle, and white ink. Jimmy told Ethan several years back he liked the action of the needles with the rubber bands around the gun. Ethan noted that Jimmy had added yet another band, now totaling four.

"Ok we ready?" Jimmy said snapping the gloves on and releasing the familiar scent of latex into the air.

"Ready, Jimmy."

Jimmy then dipped the multi-tipped needle into the ink, running the gun a few cycles to distribute the paint load. He brought it toward the base of Ethan's ring finger and plunged the tips in. Ethan always felt closer to her in this moment, when needle pierced flesh. The ink left no trace but it was the moment he remembered most. Jimmy was there the first time he placed ink within his skin, and so was Lily. With matching ink, they paired themselves, silent in the lack of color, but fully committed. It was as permanent for him as any ceremony in a church or paper sealed by a court of law; which they planned to do once they both finished school.

Ethan allowed a tear to roll down his cheek. He didn't care Jimmy knew how emotional he still was. How could Jimmy not have known? The first year Ethan returned to the tattoo shop they talked about Lily. Plus, there was nobody in the tattoo shop at 10:00 a.m., let alone anyone in Cambridge, Massachusetts Ethan would be concerned about running into. It had been over a decade since he walked these streets regularly, not a soul would recognize him.

"There ya go man," Jimmy said wiping down Ethan's hand and fingers, removing the excess ink.

"Thanks Jimmy," he said taking out a hundred-dollar bill.

"I told you last time, I'm not taking your money for this."

"Either you will or your tip jar will. At least this way you get it all."

"I'm doin' all right. Drop it in the jar. Let the kids fight over it right?"

"Your place, your rules." Ethan stuck out his hand and Jimmy took it, squeezing firmly.

"I hope you find someone man. You're a good guy."

"I'm in a good place Jimmy. Thank you though. Till next year."

"Same time, same place."

Dr. Lewis took a taxi across the river and onto the medical campus. The buildings would likely never change during his lifetime, and he immediately felt a small wave of anxiety. He frequently went back to the campus, walked the hallways, and remembered the smells in his nightmares. Outside of those terrible dreams, he may have enjoyed the annual conference. He never mingled, rarely waved, and always tried to sit in the back in order to leave as soon as the clapping began. The conference was set to begin at noon, which was in thirty minutes.

He exited the car and began meandering down Avenue Louis

Pasteur toward the New Research Building. The New Research Building was a gem to some and an eyesore to others. It stood in contrast to most other buildings on and surrounding campus, having more curves, windows, and technology. Dr. Lewis was finding comfort in refusing the offer of a great office in the New Research Building with an expansive view of the medical campus, in turn for his Washington University position. It was difficult for him to imagine dealing with the anxiety and constant reminders of how he walked away from her. He kept his eyes up, paying careful attention not to find himself next to someone he knew or recognized from graduate school.

Dr. Lewis walked through the glass doors that rested within an entire wall of glass, supported by a network of steel wire, rods, and bolts fastening the windows. He walked toward the registration desk that was full of a mix of researchers, former students, persons attending the conference for continuing education, each one of them using the opportunity to network. All except Dr. Lewis, who mysteriously snaked his way through the crowd unnoticed, and into the Joseph B. Martin Conference Center.

He found an isolated spot in the last row on the main level. The center sections had already filled and he saw several familiar faces, none of which would likely know him. They were the faces everyone would likely know—the primary researchers and keynote speakers everyone was attempting to talk shop with. Dr. Lewis sat slouched into the corner of his chair, his palm covering his jaw and his fingers stretching up the entire right side of his face.

For the first time in more than an hour, he felt the slight burn on his left ring finger, a small reminder of the vows he took. The burn always seemed to reignite the flame within him, kept him focused.

The lights in the Conference Center dimmed twice and the conversations around the room began to come to a close. He watched as several groups of intellects nodded their heads, or shook hands, or waved to associates as they scrambled to find a seat. Dr. Lewis almost laughed watching the large game of musical chairs they struggled with.

"Good afternoon, everyone, and welcome to Harvard's Annual Research Report. As you can tell by the name of our building, we are great at naming things," the speaker paused as the room rumbled in a chuckle. "We've got some exciting news for everyone this afternoon, and even more tomorrow for those who are lucky enough to stick around. I'd like to kick the event off with our latest news on stem cell epigenomics and Dr. Edgar Chiang. Dr. Chiang, the room is yours," he stood back from the podium and clapped with rest of the attendees.

Dr. Lewis clapped and waited for the middle-aged researcher to finish his short walk to the podium.

"Good afternoon everyone. I am excited to say, that we have been able to mark several proteins that are directly involved in bonding to the genome, activating sequences in genes associated with fat metabolism as well as muscle growth and development." Several members of the crowd applauded when the findings were announced.

Dr. Lewis was impressed, but distracted. He paged through the welcome registration packet and noted the two lectures he would likely come back for tomorrow: Dr. Marcus Stelious' *Deep Brain EMG Studies*, and Dr. Brian Lacey on *Long- and Short-Term Effects of Repetitive Use of Anesthetics*. Both lectures were scheduled for the next day: Dr. Lacey at 9:00 a.m.; Dr. Stelious' not until 4:00 p.m. He knew Dr. Lacey, they attended Harvard together and had been acquaintances, having only spent time together socially on one or two occasions.

He took out his phone and began searching both doctors, learning as much as he could about each. He read a few previously published studies by Stelious, and was quickly very intrigued by the research designs. He was studying comatose and stroke patients in order to decipher complex deep brain chemistry and neural pathways. He saved a couple webpages, and also emailed them to Veronica and Traci.

Clapping brought Dr. Lewis out of his focus and he looked up to see Dr. Chiang graciously accepting the praise as he left the podium and returned to his seat. Dr. Lewis then returned to combing over research papers and their websites. For the next several lectures he sporadically caught a glimpse of a slide, a point of interest, or an attempted joke. It only took about two hours, but his phone ultimately died. He sat in distracted silence for the remaining three hours of talks, thinking of what the next day's lectures may hold.

The morning came slowly as Dr. Lewis continued to struggle with sleep. He spent most of the dark morning hours combing through the same research articles he read while sitting through the previous afternoon's lectures. He had already drunk the entire hotel room supply of coffee while doing so. He looked up from his computer screen and wiped his eyes from underneath his glasses. He gazed out the large bay window to see the horizon just starting to become blue. He checked the time, 6:45, and decided to get ready.

By 7:15 he was walking the streets with the die-hards. It was a Saturday morning and everyone out was on a mission. People weren't conversing with one another, if they were speaking, it was aloud in order to solve a problem they had still been working on from the night before, assuming that hearing it out loud may shed a new angle on the material. There were no recreational activities at 7:15 on Saturday mornings. The only places open were out of necessity: Starbucks, McDonalds, gas stations, all having their lights on and patrons inside, each buying the black plasma.

Dr. Lewis found himself in a small, signless café he used to frequent when attending school. They roasted their own beans in-house every morning and had a limited number of cups they'd make. The café didn't have any cream, sugar, or soy. The coffee there was meant to stand on its own two legs. Dr. Lewis forgot how much he missed the house-roasted beans. He was early enough to drink a cup at a table, taking his time, enjoying each sip. He bought a second cup, to go.

Dr. Lewis walked back into the New Research Building and meandered down its halls toward the conference hall. He was late for the first lecture, but he wasn't interested in hearing about white blood cell phagocytosis in persons with complex autoimmune diseases. He entered the hall and slowly closed the door with a click. He found his seat from the day before empty, as were the seats immediately to the right and left. It gave him a small thrill knowing he could hide there for the morning, assuming nobody would fill in the seats around him.

He glanced down at the schedule, noting that one remained before Dr. Brian Lacey's lecture on *Long- and Short-Term Effects of Repetitive Use of Anesthetics*. He decided to use the next 20 minutes reading Dr. Lacey's bio and searching for him online. He hadn't realized it before, but Dr. Lacey was a guest lecturer from the University of Wisconsin–Madison. Former graduates of Harvard had the option to submit their research and present it during the Harvard Annual Research Report. It was difficult to gain acceptance, which meant his research evidently showed strong proof of an innovative idea. Dr. Lewis continued to read through some of his old schoolmate's research as time permitted.

"Well, thank you again, Dr. Grainger," the organizer said as the room clapped in respect for the man who just finished his talk on *Protein Structure Analysis of Cellular Transport Mechanisms in the Presence of Viral RNA*. It was a very specific topic, one which most in the room wouldn't need the details on, but nonetheless, helpful in treating patients suffering from a viral born illness in the relatively near future.

"Next we have a former Harvard grad who comes all the way from the University of Wisconsin–Madison. He has been studying the effects of anesthetics on individuals who've had them administered more than once. His findings have brought up very valid questions in the surgical community. Without further ado, Dr. Brian Lacey from Wisconsin–Madison."

Dr. Lacey strode toward the podium, each step of his long

legs covering significant ground. Most of the other lecturers stood comfortably at the podium, but Dr. Lacey had to adjust the mic as tall as it would allow, and had it not been for his large booming voice, he would have had to lean forward when speaking in order to be heard. He was equally as wide, struggling to bring his broad shoulders within the width of the podium.

"Good afternoon, everyone. Thank you for your kind welcoming," Dr. Lacey said while grasping the podium with large, thick hands. "I'm here to ask and answer the question, should we be allowing people to be administered anesthesia as if there are no consequences? Simply, no; but as you may know, medicine isn't black and white." The room chuckled at the attempted joke.

"Our research was performed retrospectively, involving a questionnaire that we administered in-house, as well as with each follow-up visit from any surgical patient within the greater Madison area. We were looking for any possible side effects. The findings are on this chart." Dr. Lacey clicked the remote and a complex chart was shown on the screens in the front of the room. Several findings were highlighted in yellow.

"As you can see, we have several correlated findings which were concerning to us. One: the percentage of individuals who suffered from a minor episode of low percent $O_2$ following anesthesia was five percent. Low percent was defined as 90 percent $O_2$. Furthermore, of those five percent, only ten percent complained of dyspnea, which meant 90 percent were below 80 percent $O_2$ and had no symptoms. A second finding was that 15 percent described a migraine-like headache within two weeks of the surgical procedure. We know that most of these drugs have a half-life of 48 hours, so why are they suffering for longer than two days? These migraine complaints have no correlation with persons suffering from insufficient $O_2$ findings, so there must be a separate mechanism. We have begun a second study to determine if there is a localized decrease in oxygen to the brain following the anesthetic treatments. Our preliminary results have been shocking."

Dr. Lacey hit the button on the remote again pulling up another graph. He directed the red laser toward the screen. "As you see, we introduced a catheter with a pulse ox into the Basilar artery and monitored intra-arterial blood oxygen numbers throughout the administration of the anesthetic. Immediately following anesthesia, a drop of oxygen is noted in over 90 percent of those in the study. It returns to normal after several minutes, but upon awakening, you see a plummeting of the oxygen to less than 80 percent in over 50 percent of individuals. Why is this happening? Is it a phenomenon worth looking into or should we just assume that because this drop only lasts fifteen minutes it's an acceptable risk? What about the individuals in my initial slide who still complain of headaches two weeks later? Are they suffering from chronic O2 insufficiency, which is being reinforced through a terribly negative feedback loop? We all know the importance of the Basilar artery and its role in bringing blood to the brainstem, what happens when our regulatory centers aren't properly regulated themselves?"

The room was silent. Dr. Lacey had paused for a moment looking the room over. His large presence almost seemed fatherly, shamefully judging everyone in the room who had ever placed someone under without thinking it through. After hearing the findings, Dr. Lewis shifted in his chair. Anesthesia was completely safe, or so he thought. Nobody had awoken with these complaints during his own study. He had placed thousands of people under and not a single one was expressing headaches, low O2, or shortness of breath. He decided to include a follow-up oxygen measurement at the long-term follow-up visit, along with a short questionnaire related to symptoms cited in Dr. Lacey's research.

"My hope is to come back here in two years and give you more conclusive findings on our newest research. We haven't, however, received more funding so hopefully our newest results will get us more.

Thank you all for allowing me here and listening. It's an honor to stand here in this hall and discuss my work. Thank you."

A gentle roar of clapping grew as the large man made his way back to his seat, stopping for several handshakes on his way.

The rest of the morning was a blur for Dr. Lewis. He had made his way out of the lecture hall following Dr. Lacey's presentation, and walked down the familiar streets to his hotel, lost in his own thoughts. Dozens of patients flashed into his mind, each of which he re-examined through memory, verifying they were happy and free from any episodes of anxiety or depression following the treatment. Most of his patient's pulse ox had never dropped below 88, but he had never taken intra-arterial oxygen levels at the Basilar artery.

As Dr. Lewis left for the afternoon weather was pleasant, a sunny 70 degrees, with a slight breeze out of the east bringing a slight smell of the ocean. He had missed that smell when he moved to the Midwest. He looked past the tops of the stone and concrete buildings at the infinitely deep blue sky above. He took a deep, cleansing breath of the air and decided he would spend the afternoon outside waiting for Dr. Stelious' lecture.

He walked a while with the sun beating on his face. It was comfortable, warm, like a loving embrace. Thoughts that he typically fought off he decided to allow. *What if they had been married? What if they had their honeymoon in Bora Bora? When would they have had the three kids they talked about? Their names?* It was an odd sensation to relive the moments he spent too much energy burying, but it was as if the warm sun and the salty air was a treatment for his sorrow.

He recalled Lily's eyes, the blue-green color that matched the cove in Bora Bora; at least based on the pictures they would look at together. The small specs of brown which resembled tiny islands in her eyes were his favorite. He used to have a picture of just her eyes, pupils small, allowing her iris to spread broadly as she stared into the camera. Around the camera lens was a bright florescent bulb which flooded her eyes with light allowing for a fast shutter speed and a crisp, sharp image. He had it hung up in his room right next to an aerial picture of Bora Bora.

He smiled recalling the moment he showed her the pictures side by side and even she admitted there was a strong correlation between the two. They kissed sweetly afterward.

Ethan remembered her smell, like flowers and the ocean. Her skin was soft and smooth but her body hard from exercise. She loved to run, to lift weights, to sweat. She had made him that way too by showing him how it felt to exercise. He became confident, strong, and impressive while they had been together. Before her, he had been a simple man who was myopic in his endeavors, just as he was now. It was as if his life had reached one massive crescendo stretching limitlessly upward into heaven, and, when she died, it returned to a quiet, lifeless melody.

It was 1:00 p.m. by the time hunger got the best of him and he stopped into a greasy pub. Without looking at the menu he ordered a burger and took a seat at the short, sticky bar. It was familiar looking, but he hadn't been there before. It had the same signs, the same beer taps, and the same type of stools every other bar seemed to have. The large picture frames that hung behind him on the wall were different, featuring what he assumed were local regulars engaging in drunken selfies. Ethan quickly concluded the images were taken using the bar's camera, as the digital frames changed images every ten-seconds, each picture more wild than the last. After seeing several more photos of college kids with their tongues out and drinks in the air, he decided to email Kyle, asking him to examine the research finding for anyone who was complaining of symptoms following the treatment, and to mark anyone who had experienced oxygen levels lower than 80 during testing. He wanted to reach out to those individuals and question them for symptoms.

A couple more hours passed and Dr. Lewis found himself back

inside the dimly lit conference room waiting patiently in the back for his most anticipated lecture. Dr. Stelious would be coming on stage in ten minutes, and following his lecture, they would conclude for the day. It would give him the opportunity to try and talk to the researcher about his deep brain EMG scanner. He shifted in his chair several times, and constantly checked his watch attempting to will the time by faster.

"Our final lecture of the day is our own Dr. Marcus Stelious. He will be discussing his recent advancements in deep brain EMG studies. Please welcome, Dr. Stelious." Once again, the drone of respectful clapping echoed around the conference hall as the Greek doctor waddled up to the front, the light from the projectors bathing him in an eerie blue.

"Good afternoon," he said with an accent he struggled to overcome. "I have come to demonstrate our advancements to the world of EMG studies." Dr. Stelious then reached into a case and pulled out a strange-looking device. He placed a short tube on the small table adjacent to the podium. He then removed a small aluminum box and placed it next to the tube, plugging in a coiled rubber cord. Lastly, he removed a device meant to be placed onto someone's head. The device held a cylinder in a small cup, which was allowed to move on a track. The track moved anteriorly to posteriorly, and right to left in arcs across the surface of the head. It allowed for the cylinder to be fixated above the brain at any specific location they were interested in studying.

"As you can see," he said placing the tube in the device and then the device on top of his head, "we can scan any specific spot on your head. But, what makes this different? We wanted to study the deepest parts of the brain in great detail. We wanted to know how the most primordial pathways are running through the brainstem. Here is one of our subjects."

Dr. Stelious cued up a video. "What we are seeing here is an individual who has suffered from a severe TBI. He had been labeled brain dead and was awaiting a recipient match for organ donation. We placed the typical EEG device on his head and found essentially no activity. However, we then placed our device on and focused our readings into the brainstem. We were able to find a small and distinct signal originating in the *medulla oblongata*. More specifically, the medial portions. We then conferred with the treating physicians, and based on our findings, they allowed us to remove him from the respirator." The video showed a physician and a nurse shutting down the respirator, and the patient continued to breathe on his own for several minutes. "With this knowledge of deep brain scanning, we may be able to determine which patients could return to a high enough life state, defined by the Rancho Los Amigos coma scale, or which are not saveable with a higher degree of certainty."

Dr. Lewis was at the edge of his seat, his arms resting on the back of the chair in front of him. The thought of knowing what was happening in the brains of his patients was almost too much for him to bear. His leg subconsciously bounced up and down attempting to burn off his nervous energy.

"We are now attempting to gather a wider subject base for the deep scanning. Obviously, it is a very small number of people we are capable of testing on due to the nature of the specific requirements. We need brain dead patients in the most sincere way possible," he said playfully throwing his hands in the air, the dark humor hitting a homerun in a room full of undemonstrative researchers.

It took every fiber of control for Dr. Lewis not to yell out "I've got thousands of subjects," in the conference room full of people. His palms were sweating and he took a drink of water trying to calm his nerves. He realized he was going to have to mingle with people as Dr. Stelious dodged conversations himself.

The lecture ended and Dr. Lewis shot up from his seat like a Rottweiler after a bone. He made a direct line toward Dr. Stelious, turning sideways and sliding through several people as they crossed paths down the aisle. He was several rows away when he saw a familiar stride paralleling his own walking down the other aisle. It was Dr. Lacey. He also had his eyes locked onto Dr. Stelious who was still putting his equipment back into his large black case and fended off several conversations without much more than a glance upward. Ethan knew he was going to have to talk with Lacey.

Dr. Stelious looked up after snapping his case shut and his gaze immediately went to the largest object entering his field of vision: Dr. Lacey. The two men nodded to one another and Dr. Lewis decided to slow down and allow them to visit for a moment. He waited a few feet away, patiently leaning on the back of a chair. He strained to hear their conversation.

It was a bit numbing knowing the large Dr. Lacey was so opposed to what Dr. Lewis was doing in his lab. He knew Lacey may have heard of his research, but they hadn't been great friends in college, so he may not even recognize him. Dr. Lewis only recognized him by his large size. At 6'9" he was always the largest man in a room full of researchers and that would never change. What Dr. Lewis noticed had changed was the hair that had receded, the 40 or so extra pounds that he hid well in a suit, and pockmarks that had replaced his acne.

As he listened, he heard Dr. Selious' accent compliment Lacey on his findings. Fortunately for Stelious, his research was on individuals who were unconscious, but not from anesthetics. "I would like to see more subjects, but there aren't thousands of TBIs coming into the greater Boston area that we can test," Dr. Stelious said with a shrug. It was an opening Lewis hadn't seen coming. He turned and faced the two other researchers, neither of them returned his gaze. He paused, not sure how to interject himself into the conversation.

The momentary pause allowed for Dr. Lacey to react. He turned to Dr. Lewis and his face immediately changed. The slight upward slant to his eyes and jovial smirk morphed into a dark, hollow eyed grimace. Dr. Stelious continued to vent about the limited number of subjects he was finding and how their mapping of the brainstem was suffering due to the variability of the subtle pathways they were discovering. He explained how it originally was thought to be a primordial and well established neural pathway but revealed itself to be markedly more variable than imagined, and due to this, it was impossible to establish norms without thousands more studies performed.

But Dr. Lewis processed none of that information and neither did Dr. Lacey. Both men had stayed locked eye to eye while a hundred conversation starters went through their head, each being weighed against the next. Dr. Lewis could tell Lacey had recognized him, and he was aware of his research.

"Excuse me Dr. Stelious," Dr. Lewis said while remaining locked onto Lacey. "I couldn't help but hear the main limitations of your study." Dr. Stelious looked toward him, and Dr. Lewis finally peeled his eyes from Lacey.

"You are?"

"Dr. Ethan Lewis, Washington University, formerly Harvard," he said extending his hand, which Stelious took.

"Pleasure meeting you, Doctor."

"As I was saying, I can help you with your subject number. My research—"

"Yes, what about your research?" Dr. Lacey blurted out loudly, much more so that necessary and his gravelly voice drew the attention of many in the room. Dozens of conversations trailed off and Dr. Lewis felt their eyes converge onto him. He began to sweat, he shifted uncomfortably on the gently sloped floor. He tried to gaze around the room but the longer he stood frozen in the spot, the more uncomfortable he became. The red walls all seemed to scream caution as he thought out his next few words.

"I've received funding to complete a clinical trial on a new treatment for anxiety and depression. My preliminary results have 100 percent success rate both long- and short-term." The room slowly began to darken as black and gray suits converged in toward the three men standing around the small podium.

"It is great to hear of your successes, but how will that help me with my subjects Dr. Lewis?" Stelious said.

"I'll tell you," Dr. Lacey once again rumbled in disgust. "He places each of his patients under a 'cocktail'." Dr. Lacey aggressively placed quotes around the word and glared at Dr. Lewis. "And puts them out. He monitors their vitals and EEG, pulling them out when they reach a certain low threshold point in one or more of their vitals. Did I get it?" he asked folding his large arms. Dr. Lewis noticed that most of the weight Lacey had gained was the kind every man wanted.

"Nearly yes."

"Well what did I miss doctor? Did you monitor their oxygen through arterial blood gas? Did you determine whether they had long- or short-term effects following your anesthetic cocktail? Speaking of that, what's in it?"

Dr. Lewis was angry, annoyed that he was being attacked in front of a room full of men who press into the boundaries of science, often finding that they are just as wrong as they are right. Clearly Dr. Lacey was trying to bully his way into proving himself more righteous but had no definitive proof to date.

"First, no, as it stands the current guidelines for monitoring oxygen does not include an invasive arterial line, especially one into the Basilar artery. Secondly, we have had questionnaires similar to yours, and not a single one of our patients to date has complained of any side effects whatsoever. As for what's in it, most of which you know, a little of this a little of that, but I have my secrets as well. It's called proprietary formulation. Try asking anyone who develops a drug their secrets and see how well it's received." By now the entire conference room was focused on the two men exchanging verbal blows. Dr. Stelious was pinned in between the two like a pudgy referee without a whistle.

"Excuse me," a faceless voice said, slightly muffled by the crowd. "I'd like to hear more about this study." Several men nodded in approval and a few claps sporadically erupted throughout the hall. A moment later one giant clap let loose, then a second, then several for a third, and a fourth, louder and more organized for a fifth, sixth, seventh, and by the eighth the room crescendoed to a high volume of quickening, organized clapping.

The organizer for the event pressed his way through the crowd and found himself immediately next to Dr. Lewis.

"You're a former Harvard grad are you not?" he yelled into Ethan's ear over the clapping and cheering that had continued to elevate in volume.

"Yes I am."

"Do you want to speak? I think you could take the floor," he continued to yell as they both laughed at the moment.

"I could give it a go." Dr. Lewis couldn't have planned on this. A room full of men he cared little about, who's lectures he'd skipped, and others he sat distractedly through were now wishing him to the podium. All because of the loud bully, Dr. Lacey. The organizer waved his hand toward the media booth, who immediately understood to turn the mic back on.

"Well, well my goodness. I'd have to say this is certainly a first. So without further ado," he paused and looked toward Dr. Lewis. "What's your name?" he asked while covering the mic.

"Dr. Ethan Lewis."

"Dr. Ethan Lewis from," he paused once again and looked at Dr. Lewis laughing.

"Washington University in Saint–"

"Washington University in Saint Louis." He made a subservient gesture toward the podium, inferring that Dr. Lewis was the king and the organizer walked back to a seat.

"Well good evening I guess I should say," Dr. Lewis said while pausing at the podium. He chuckled, "It's an honor being asked to speak impromptu but I guess I should thank Dr. Lacey for the borderline assault he was placing on me verbally." The room rumbled with polite laughter and Lacey took it in stride, waiving his hand high into the air. "As most of you heard, I have performed an initial study on a treatment for anxiety and depression. You also heard the methods for the treatment, and that the results were found to be effective for short- and long-term, with long-term being defined as three months. We also had no adverse effects."

He paused for a moment, recalling why he had even been standing there. He looked into the first row and saw Dr. Stelious very attentive and still trying to work out exactly how this was relevant to his studies. Dr. Lewis chuckled again and looked at the round, bearded doctor. "Dr. Stelious," he waited for a response.

"Yes Doctor." The room barely heard the man respond.

"You asked me how my research could help your research."

"Yes."

"A picture is worth a thousands words, right doctors?" Several heads nodded, trying to stay on the hook. "What about a video? Does anyone have a powercord for a MacBook? I must confess, I used up my battery hours ago." The room roared a bit louder at the admission of guilt. "Thank you," he said when a random doctor from the second row handed him the cord.

Dr. Lewis then opened his laptop, quickly found the video of Linda, and plugged the HDMI cord into the side of his MacBook. "What you are going to see is one patient in our latest formulation. Dr. Stelious, I want you to pay careful attention to her EEG for the entirety of the video."

Dr. Lewis began the relatively short video that chronicled the entire procedure, and included her long-term follow up. As he stood and craned his head to watch along, he felt a sense of overwhelming joy and completion. He was sure the room was going to react warmly, just as Dr. Mitchell Raymond from the Federal Review Board, Malcolm, Adam, Traci, Veronica, and Donna had. He even imagined most of them felt the goosebumps cascade down their arms when they saw Linda talk, even while her EEG was registering no brain activity. The entire day had seemed to fall right into Dr. Lewis' hands from the coffee he had this morning, to the lecture that opened the door to a possible use for Dr. Stelious' ingenious new machine. All eyes stayed fixed on the screen for the entire five-minute video. When it was finished, the room erupted.

For two more continuous minutes the room was standing and applauding Dr. Lewis and his patient Linda. It was surreal how much everyone was coming together in that moment to support his work, the work they had only seen the very surface of. He was envisioning Dr. Stelious' machine to work on The Beyond Experience more than this treatment protocol, but even this superficial application was hitting home in this room. The room quieted down and slowly they sat back into their seats in ones and twos, then by the dozen and soon the room was once again quiet.

"So as you can see Dr. Stelious, I am in need of your deep brain scanner. If you wouldn't mind allowing me to borrow it, we can both benefit from it greatly."

"I have three, you can take one!" the jolly man said with a wave of his hand and the room laughed the loudest yet. He stood from his seat, turned, and took a quick playful bow as he belly laughed at the new found friendship.

"Thank you very much Doctor. Maybe you and I can co-present next year, same time same place?"

The room clapped and cheered loudly at the suggestion. Dr. Lewis smiled widely and waved. Everyone seemed to be clapping except for one man who was taking the moment to try and sneak out of the conference hall. The man's back was turned, but he was easy to spot: Dr. Brian Lacey.

The next hour Dr. Lewis mingled with several researchers, but the conversation was rushed at best. He said as few words as possible, and answered most questions with "I don't have my research with me." He watched Dr. Stelious, taking note of his every move, making sure the short, portly man was never out of sight.

As the conversations died down, the room became much easier to scan. It wasn't as hard to see Dr. Stelious, and on more than one occasion, Dr. Lewis saw he was also watching. It made them both feel at ease.

Dr. Stelious wrapped up his discussion with the last of the stragglers, and found his way to Dr. Lewis who was still talking with his graduate school professor Dr. Franklin. They were joking about how Dr. Lewis had rejected the Harvard research offer, despite his advisor's constant recommendations to the faculty. Initially, Dr. Franklin had been very offended, but enough time had passed. Ethan was very happy, Dr. Franklin was someone he emulated while at Harvard.

"It appears Marcus might be ready to court you," Dr. Franklin said jokingly as he saw the bearded Stelious approach with a smile that nearly hid his eyes beneath silver rimmed glasses.

"Are you ready to see my lab Dr. Lewis?"

"Absolutely, but please, call me Ethan. If we're going to be working together, I'd prefer it. Saves time."

"Ok, and you can call me Marcus, but Dr. Stelious is fine too if you prefer."

Dr. Lewis looked toward his former advisor with wide, playful eyes as if to say, *I've got my hands full don't I?*

"Seems you two have a lot to discuss and it's already six. I'll leave you to it. Great seeing you Ethan. Good luck this next year. Can't wait to see the results." Dr. Franklin left the room, with Marcus and Ethan following slowly behind.

"My research office is in this building, let's go there and discuss." The walk was slow as the short Marcus waddled through the hallways. The building was quiet, the only noises came from the soles of their shoes, the hum of the lights, and Marcus' heavy breathing. Dr. Stelious cleared his throat and sniffled loudly several times only adding to the list of annoying little habits Ethan would likely have to deal with during the partnership. *At least I know he's not self conscious.* Marcus also wore suspenders, which were revealed when he removed his suitcoat, and Ethan could make out the edges of a sweat ring forming between the man's scapulae on his back.

"Here we are my friend," Marcus finally said as he reached into his shallow pockets, pulling out the keys Ethan saw outlined through his snug pants. He unlocked the door and entered the room, the lights turning on automatically upon sensing the motion.

It was a humble office, with a small round linoleum table with four chairs, a nice wooden desk, and a modest bookshelf with several books about neurology and the anatomy of the brain. He also had a few shelves bolted to the wall with several jars containing cross sections of brain tissue. Against the far wall, Dr. Lewis noted two boxes that were identical to the one Dr. Stelious brought into the lecture.

"Are those your other scanners?" he asked pointing across the open space toward the black boxes resting on the tile.

"That is them, yes," he responded and walked the thirty feet and grabbed them, placing them gently onto the round table.

Ethan walked over and lifted one of the boxes. "Heavier than I thought," he said curling the steel box several times with a pouty look on his face.

"I had them over-engineer the box. Make sure it's not going to get broken in transit."

"I'd say that's a good plan."

"Well what's your plan Dr. Lewis? You said you could get my

scanner working on more subjects. I'm all ears."

"Ok, Marcus, we have twelve patients being seen per day, running in four rooms simultaneously, so in reality, if we only have one scanner, we can only do four subjects per day." Dr. Lewis wasn't nervous asking for two scanners, just realistic in thinking a researcher, especially one whose technology is patentable, wouldn't want to part with two-thirds of the inventory. "Which is why I was hoping for two now, and another two as soon as you can."

Dr. Stelious crossed his arms, placed one hand on his face and exhaled loudly. He stared at the floor for an uncomfortably long time. Dr. Lewis started to speak but Marcus simply stifled the attempt with a glance, only to return to staring at the speckled tile floor once he was silent. Thirty seconds felt like several minutes and Dr. Lewis began to shift uneasy.

"I can do that, but we will need the data sent immediately via Wi-Fi."

"You tell me how to set it up, and we'll send it direct to you," Dr. Lewis said holding out his left hand, wanting to make the agreement official but his right hand was busy holding on to a prototype of the device that had been resting on the desk. It was a bit awkward, and he felt the soreness in his ring finger when Dr. Stelious squeezed his hand firmly, but at least they had sealed the deal.

# | TWELVE |

Kyle woke with the alarm on Sunday morning. It was the first time in years he forced himself out of bed before 9:00 a.m. on a Sunday. Dr. Lewis had, on occasion, beckoned him to the lab for various reasons, all of which he had been happy to do, but this time he got up for himself. It was 6:00 a.m. and he grabbed his small gym bag, goggles, towel, and swimsuit, and headed for the pool.

It wasn't a long swim—four-thousand meters, mainly freestyle, breaking the yardage into some smaller sets. He thought while he swam, mostly about his dad, which was why he was up so early. Before Ray had died, he tried to bring Kyle to church with him. The two had attended off and on after his mother left but both had drifted away when Kyle began traveling on the weekends for swimming. When Ray was diagnosed, the first thing he did was fall back to the church where he found happiness, peace, and the support he leaned on when Kyle was away at school.

Kyle had been angry initially with his father's decision, thinking it was a copout and an admission he was ready to die rather than fight the cancer. He often yelled at Ray when he asked him to come to church with him. In contrast, Ray was determined to bring Kyle back into the church before he died.

Kyle jumped out of the pool, walked into the locker room and, after a quick shower, put on a pair of jeans and a white button up shirt. His shoes were casual brown, with red laces, and he also quickly threw a little product in the wild new fauxhawk he had been sporting since getting back regularly in the pool. As he stood and glanced quickly in the mirror, he noticed how much he had changed in the last few months. His hair had changed from a wavy mess to a different sort of wild, his physique had morphed into one from a decade ago, his shoulders broad and his waistline hidden beneath a shirt that flowed down from his lats and reached his hips. His belt buckle was using the last hole, which was three inches to the left of the hole much more worn.

Kyle had searched the internet for churches in the area on Saturday, and settled on Chesterfield Presbyterian Church. It was located about 20 minutes west of the city, and he planned on making the 10:30 service. He was speeding, even though he was running ten minutes early, and he found himself constantly playing with the keys that dangled from the ignition. He hadn't even noticed that the radio was off until he had exited Interstate 64/40 and entered the city of Chesterfield. He didn't bother to turn it on, the music would be lost on him at the moment.

The parking lot was moderately full, but he could see several people entering behind him. He was, after all, relatively early for a church service. He paused in his car for a moment, watching a husband and wife exit their black Honda Accord. The husband walked around the rear of the sedan and opened the right rear passenger door, released their four-year-old from the carseat. The toddler put both of his parents to shame, wearing a clip on tie, khakis, and a pair of nice brown shoes. The boy grabbed one hand from each parent and skipped toward church, the parents lifted him off the ground once or twice as he skipped, sending him into a loud, playful laugh. Kyle sat for several more minutes and quickly made a few observations about the congregation: first, that it was relatively young, mostly families with young children and second was that the dress code was fairly lax, which made Kyle feel right at home.

The church he grew up in, so to speak, was very similar. In fact, the reason he chose this church was because the inside looked so similar to his own—at least he thought so from the website pictures—a stage with a drum set, two guitars, a piano, a bass. In the photo he saw there were even a few brass instruments.

Kyle exited the car at 10:25 making sure not to walk into church too early and run into unwanted small talk and conversation. He wasn't there because he was interested in learning about God. He'd had that lesson many times over throughout his childhood, and ultimately several more times while his father was dying. He was there to feel closer to his earthly father, the one Dr. Lewis wasn't allowing him to see anymore.

He entered the white doors and was immediately greeted by two men in button up shirts and dress slacks. They smiled politely at Kyle and gestured toward the sanctuary. Kyle heard the muffled sounds of a full band, the roar of a church singing together, and felt the bass drum hit with each beat. He felt alive and a smile crossed his face as he opened the doors and the muffled music became a crystal clear worship song he remembered from years ago.

*Your grace is enough,*
*Your grace is enough,*
*Your grace is enough,*
*For me.*

Kyle found a seat toward the right side of the sanctuary, halfway toward the front. He made sure he had a great view of the stage and spent the time watching the drummer. The sanctuary was tall, 25 feet or more, with a row of lights strapped to scaffolding near the ceiling, all pointing down at the stage and the back wall. The obtuse-angled walls in the front were all a medium shade of purple whereas the walls to his left, right, and rear were cream.

The music dropped off and the entire congregation was singing *a cappella* for the final chorus. It made Kyle focus only on the voices around him, the emotion of it, the fact that some of them were incredibly off key and nobody cared. He watched the worship team in the front of the church, all clapping their hands to a beat that carried over from their playing. The head of the worship team was walking around the stage, waving at a few people near the front, and singing with a smile as he clapped loudly. The song came to an end and everyone clapped and praised Jesus.

A man with white hair and a matching goatee walked quickly onto the stage while the worship team walked off. As this happened, several ushers walked toward the windows that lined the walls to Kyle's right and left, and they pulled down the blinds creating a darker sanctuary. That one change focused more attention to the stage, where the man stood alone for a moment, struggling with turning on his headset microphone.

"Let us pray," the pastor said after turning on the headset. "Dear Heavenly Father we ask that You allow our hearts to hear Your word today. Allow it to speak to our souls, and guide us in whatever way You see fit. Thank you for bringing us together in this place of worship and please give me the words to speak which would allow this congregation to become more connected and informed Christians in this ever increasing time of need. Amen."

The congregation all looked forward to their pastor who stood with a projected image of the verses and the message he would be preaching, clearly displayed on a large screen.

Revelations 4, A Glimpse into Heaven.

Kyle grabbed a piece of paper from the seatback in front of him, and grabbed a Bible as well. The projector had listed the page number in the pew Bibles, however, Kyle wanted to take notes.

"We see that John is experiencing a vision given to him by an angel of heaven. In this vision, it is established that Jesus is at the center, sitting on a throne, with a group of 24 other thrones, each being occupied by an elder . . ." the pastor continued to deliver his message but Kyle was drawn into his own reading.

Kyle noted at the start of Revelation 4 John was escorted into the presence of Jesus, and begins to describe all that he sees in great detail. He reads of creatures with eyes surrounding their heads, of wings covered with eyes as well, and of other elders that are worshiping the one who is in the center. It was beyond confusing, whether it was symbolism or not, Kyle needed to look elsewhere. He opened up his internet browser and began searching for "visions in the Bible," getting several hits immediately. He began scanning through the infinite amount of information and quickly realized that it was futile. Like all things on the internet, he was vulnerable to false testimony, sermons that were not founded in biblical truths, and no way to tell the difference.

He closed his phone and sat in his soft bottomed chair, listening intently to the pastor preach his sermon on the vision of heaven, and how it gave a glimpse into the ultimate authority of God. Following the sermon, the offertory was passed and Kyle placed 20 dollars inside, despite being told that visitors were not expected to give. Kyle was antsy. He had a million questions to ask someone, anyone, and even more than that, he had a secret he was trying to keep. If he asked even one question, they may all start spilling out and that could lead to some serious questions in return, or even worse, a full investigation into their research.

The benediction was said after one last song, and Kyle immediately made a beeline for the door. He didn't trust himself to stay a moment longer. His heart was pounding and his head racing with questions he couldn't even gather into a coherent thought. The possibilities were too great to imagine, too improbable to believe, and yet, the only thing that came to his mind when he got into his car and screeched out of his spot was *what if we found a way to see into heaven?*

# | THIRTEEN |

Adam woke up next to Veronica early Monday morning and quietly got out of bed, allowing her to sleep. It was cold in the apartment, the weather had finally begun to cool at night, and she hadn't turned the heat on. He walked into the large, carpeted living room, and checked the thermostat: 58 degrees. He turned on the heat and the smell of warming metal quickly filled the air. He rubbed his hands together allowing friction to do its thing, and walked into the kitchen. He placed a K-Cup into the Keurig, slapped the lid down, and stood at the counter checking his phone while it brewed. The Keurig was one condition he negotiated into the agreement when she asked him to stay over occasionally. He said he needed it in the morning, whereas she hated clutter on the counter.

The gurgling alone was enough to wake him; the conditioned response was almost humbling. Finally, the coffee began to stream out of the bottom and the aroma slowly entered his nose causing an involuntary deep inhalation. A few moments later, Adam quit browsing his phone, grabbed his coffee, and walked into the living room. He sat on the white, tweed couch and turned on the six o-clock news, catching the latest on the baseball playoffs, where the Cardinals won again the previous night. He remembered driving into the city the night before and running into bumper to bumper traffic as he came across the Poplar Street Bridge into Saint Louis. The lights of the stadium to the north was a dead giveaway as to the reason.

They were both still happy from the events of the weekend. Adam's parents took the news of him dropping out of medical school very well. "As long as you're happy sweetheart, and clearly you are," his mother said and hugged Veronica for the tenth time that night. The hugging had started to become awkward for everyone, including his father, but nobody said a word. Adam was simply happy his parents weren't mad.

Adam sat and watched the news recap the same weather reports, sports updates, and crime that happened the night before. He did this until 7:00 a.m. when he was forced to wake Veronica up to go to The Shack. He walked back into the bedroom and knelt next to the bed. He hated the thought of disturbing her sleep. She was so relaxed, so peaceful sleeping on her side facing toward the window blinds, which were now allowing slivers of light to penetrate the room. She was buried to her neck in warm blankets and it took a tremendous amount of willpower not to jump back into bed with her and skip work. He brushed her hair gently away from her face, his rough fingertips scraping gently across her soft face. She stirred briefly, then made a gravelly whimper as she opened one eye and knew it was time.

"Come on baby, let's go. It's 7:00 a.m."

"Ugh," she said playfully. "Can we just quit?"

"I already quit something, can't quit everything," he joked back.

"Have you heard from them at all?"

"No, I think I'm in the clear."

"That's good. Ok, I'm getting up. But can you please grab me my sweater? It's cold in here."

"Sure. I already turned the heat on. It's up to 65."

"65!"

"Well it was 58 when I got up, so you're welcome."

"Why don't you just get in here and snuggle with me. Warm me up," Veronica said flirtatiously, with a pouty voice.

"Don't make it more difficult than it already is. I'm going in the living room. Hurry up. We gotta be there by eight."

"You're no fun," she said swinging the blankets off of herself and walking to the windows, opening the blinds allowing the sunlight and cold air to wake her up. "Today's the day we start seeing more, right?"

"Yes, so let's be on time please."

"I will. Make me some of that coffee I smell."

Adam looked at her, raising an eyebrow and smirking.

"Oh I know, I know, just make it!"

"It's growing on you already I see," he joked and slowly closed the door, making sure to look queerly through the opening, making her laugh.

Adam and Veronica were the last to arrive at the treatment center. They strolled in hand in hand, Veronica squeezing his arm with the other, leaning on his shoulder. Dr. Lewis saw them as they arrived, locked in loving embrace, and he smiled outwardly to hide the small bit of jealousy inside. He was truly happy for them, but missed his own happiness immensely.

"Ok everyone, thanks for coming early today. Well, most of you. As Kyle told you last week we are going to be kicking the numbers up from here on out. The bastard Elias Grant has all but told the world what we are doing, so we need to wrap it up and get our papers written."

"Sounds good, Dr. Lewis," Malcolm said with little emotion. He had grown to love the research.

"Ok. And now one more bit of very exciting business for the ladies in the room," Dr. Lewis said smirking at both Veronica and Traci. He tapped the top of two silver boxes that sat to his right and left on the treatment table immediately in front of him. "Any idea, ladies?"

The two women glanced awkwardly at one another, trying to get a read on the situation.

"No trick questions here. Come on. What drew you in when Kyle first got us all in the same room? I know it wasn't the Q and A sessions with the patients. Or was it?" he said shrugging and smiling.

"The brain activity. And for the record, I hate the quiz game, Dr. Lewis," Traci said frustrated slightly at the buildup.

"These are new tech, never been seen before, deep brain scanners for electrical activity. We'll finally be able to see what's happening in these brains when we are taking them under."

"Oh finally something for us to do!" Traci said throwing her head back as if she had been freed from torture she had been enduring for months.

"How does it work?" Adam asked letting go of Veronica for the first time since leaving the house. He walked over to the treatment table immediately in front of Dr. Lewis.

"How did everything go with your parents this weekend, Adam?" Dr. Lewis leaned forward asking softly across the table.

"Much better than expected. It helped Vero was there," he said smiling.

"Yeah, I'm sure she helped." Dr. Lewis considered other words, but none were appropriate for the situation. "All right everyone, gather round the table. I think we'll only need to do this once."

Dr. Lewis took out the headpiece, placed it on his head, showing everyone how the grid worked by sliding it across a y-axis, as well as an x, trying to pinpoint an exact spot. There was a separate control box for the head unit. The small box had a dial allowing them to study the brain activity at precise depths. Dr. Lewis knew the device could be irreplaceable when it came to determining the source of the experience during his patients' treatment sessions. The box also housed the recording device, the Wi-Fi and Bluetooth chips, and the on and off switch. "We'll only be observing one area initially, and that's the brainstem. We will be mapping out any signals and those findings will automatically be sent to Dr. Stelious at Harvard who is conducting different research with these results. We struck a deal. Unfortunately, we only get two machines, but the good doctor is having more made and will be coming down next month. So, let's have some good results by then."

The afternoon began quickly, and soon they had four patients, one in each of the identical suites. Dr. Lewis in Treatment Room One,

Adam in Two, Kyle in Three, and Malcolm in Four. Each of the men had conducted the primary interviews on their corresponding patients several weeks beforehand, and had now completed the second round and subsequently each patient was under. Dr. Lewis had Veronica with him watching the new EEG machine read the deep brain activity, while in Room Three, Traci assisted Kyle. The plan was for them to gather data independently and compare their findings after the first treatment was completed.

"Thank you for participating and I'm glad you are feeling better with your anxiety. Remember, continue to refrain from using your medication and please return for your follow-up at three months," Dr. Lewis said to Trini, a 42 year-old patient he was dismissing from the treatment room.

"So?" he said to Veronica as the elevator door closed in Trini's face.

"So? The results are in," she said with a pause and a smile.

"Out with it, woman," he said smiling and throwing his hands in the air.

"I finally have a job to do!" she said waving the results in the air.

"What are you swinging around missy?" Traci asked as she strutted out of Treatment Room Three.

"Oh, nothing, just some deep brain activity to go through. No big deal," she said in a playful voice, fanning herself with the paper.

"Huh, that's funny," Traci said pulling results from behind her back and throwing them down on the floor in front of her. "Looks like we're gonna have to start working for our money now, sister!"

Everyone cheered but nobody knew what it meant, just that they could prove, at some level, the subjects were having deep brain activity.

Dr. Lewis allowed them to have their fun, but inside he was feeling anxious. For him, a lot depended on the results they would find during these deep scans. There had to be a way to experience the vivid sensations during treatment. It would likely win him an award, but more important, solidify his belief in the science.

# | FOURTEEN |

## Friday, December 8, 2006

Three men sat in the top floor of The Shack, painted by the colors of the setting sun. It was dusk, the magic hour, where all the spectral colors spring forth as if trying to be remembered, just before the darkness wins over the light. It added drama to the topic of conversation. Jack, a 45-year-old man sat on the large couch, while Dr. Lewis and Kyle pulled office chairs onto the throw rug in front of him. Dr. Lewis had been contacted by Jack on the forums. Jack was deemed the most stable individual who had written the doctor. He had a job, two children, and a social life. The other five individuals who reached out to Dr. Lewis had all been solely focused on their experience, and, in Kyle's opinion, were attention seekers. The researchers sat with elbows on knees, having stopped taking notes 20 minutes earlier in favor of soaking up the moment with the man. The glasses on Jack's face shielded his moist eyes as he recounted the moment in his history that brought him to his near death experience.

"We really appreciate your willingness to share your story," Kyle said smiling at Jack.

"Not a problem guys. Jut happy to talk about it without annoying anyone. I used to talk about it quite a bit," Jack said nervously rubbing his sweaty hands together.

"I suffered a massive heart attack at the age of 37. I was sitting in my home office early on a cold Monday morning when it started to snow, hard. The weather at 6:00 a.m. reported the Saint Louis area would be 'eight inches deep in snow by noon.' They had one of those information bars at the bottom of the screen. Saw the kids school was cancelled. I went upstairs and told them the good news so they could sleep as long as they wanted.

"By 9:00 a.m., I stood staring out the large front window watching the snow fall. I remember not even being able to see the large maple tree in our front yard." He chuckled. "It wasn't even 30 feet from where I stood. You could tell the snow was heavy, and wet. The flakes were the size of a credit card, when they could be distinguished from one another.

"I was 37. What the hell did I need a slow blower for? I was in great shape, ran more days than not, had weights in the basement I used," Jack said throwing his hands up in the air, then wiping them on his jeans. "It was about ten or so when I threw my coat and hat on. Just before that, I had made some breakfast for the kids, assuming they'd be up any minute. . . ." he paused. "Pancakes, they loved pancakes back then."

"Where was your wife?" Kyle asked breaking into the story and causing Dr. Lewis to lose focus.

"She worked nights at the hospital. She's a nurse ironically. ICU," he sighed and looked into Kyle's eyes. It almost made the researcher shudder. "So I opened the garage and the cold air froze my lungs good, I'm tellin' you what. That's about the last thing I remember. The rest was told to me by my wife later. I had apparently started shoveling and didn't get too far, maybe half the walkway was done from the driveway to the front porch. My wife found me, by the grace of God, in the front lawn. She said the only thing she saw was the handle of the shovel sticking out of the snow. She parked the car in the garage and went out to grab it, when she tripped over my foot. I had been buried under two inches of snow during the thirty minutes I had spent face down in the ground. She immediately got the children to dial 911, and she began pressing on my chest over and over."

He removed his glasses and shifted uncomfortably on the couch. His eyes could no longer contain the fear that overwhelmed him when he discussed the events of that day. Several tears streaked down his face. "I'm sorry, guys," Jack said wiping his eyes and clearing his throat several times in an attempt to remove his emotion from his story.

"Take your time, Jack," Kyle said gently as he reached forward to hand him a tissue.

"Oh, man," Jack said with a smile. "Want to know the most ironic part? I love snow. Grew up with it in Colorado. I moved to Chesterfield for my wife. She got a job at SLU hospital and I could do sales anywhere. I was excited to see a big snow again. Told work I wasn't even gonna make any calls that day from home to enjoy it with the kids."

"So what happened after the ambulance arrived?" Dr. Lewis asked with a furrowed brow.

"Uh, well, from what my wife says, they shocked me three times with an AED and they got my rhythm back. They ended up taking me to Barnes Jewish and I don't remember anything, except, well, you know, till five days later. Doc said the only thing that saved me was the snow."

"How's that?" Kyle asked, then looked to Dr. Lewis for reassurance. Dr. Lewis was nodding slightly and watching Jack, as if knowing the answer.

"Slowed your metabolism?" Dr. Lewis asked and Jack nodded.

"Can you believe that? Snow saved my life. Doc also told me it was likely the shoveling in the cold. Shocked my system good. Apparently I have a congenital problem with my heart. Rough way of finding out."

The room was uncomfortably quiet for several moments as the men sat stationary and digested the information. The sun had now fully set, which made them feel isolated from the world, the dark windows acting as featureless walls closing them in. Dr. Lewis was the first to break the silence.

"Jack, you reached out to me for a very particular reason. Is it ok if we talk about that?"

"I think that's appropriate. It's why I'm here. I appreciate a good listening ear without judgment. For the first year I told everyone who would listen, but I lost a lot of friends at work and in my personal life. After a year, I began attending church regularly again, and began making new friends, my wife and kids go with me now too. I don't know. Hearing about God makes me think the whole near death experience happened to bring me back to Him."

"Well Jack, let's hear it," Kyle said with a smile.

"Ok, here goes," Jack said sighing deeply and blowing the air out slowly.

"I remember seeing a light, a bright one, steadily getting bigger in front of me. Exponentially, if that's the word. It didn't even matter which way I turned, I still saw the light you know? It was incredible how bright it was but I could still look at it.

"I began hearing things, in the distance; beautiful sounds. The roaring of the Colorado River, the sounds of a choir of birds, and the smell of sap and firewood. I felt warm and bare, but I had clothes on. The ground beneath me was thick green prairie grass, like the kind my grandfather and I hunted in when I was a boy. Just feeling the way grass bent under my boots brought memories flooding into my mind. I felt strong, solid, young. I was fearless and complete without anything else around me." Jack sat staring across the office as if trying to grasp at a long lost dream he secretly wished he could be taken back to.

"Anything else?" Kyle said, trying to draw information out.

"No, no. Nothing. I woke up five days later, but to me, no time had really passed."

Kyle looked to Dr. Lewis with a questioning look. It was something they had discussed before Jack had arrived. Prior to Jack coming in, Kyle asked Dr. Lewis if it was ok to lead or guide the conversation with questions. For their main study, it was not allowed, seeing that it could be misconstrued as tampering. This was different and completely experimental. Plus, during the last three weeks with Dr. Stelious' new technology they were able to determine, without question, that the parts of the brain that were active had nothing to do with sensory information. Veronica and Traci had mapped the pathways that were active in several dozen patients. None of them were active in the cortex, or the cerebellum, all activity was in the brainstem associated with regulation, not sensory stimulus. With that information, Dr. Lewis was confident no amount of questioning could lead to a conjuring of a dream.

Dr. Lewis nodded to Kyle and then watched Jack closely.

"Jack, we asked you here for a reason. Remember, you can trust us, no matter how weird it may seem."

"I don't know guys. There are some things I'd like to keep to myself, you know?"

"Ok," Kyle said shrugging his shoulders. "But, let me ask you something," he said holding up a finger. "Did you feel compelled to go anywhere? Any sensation pulling you into a direction?"

"Yes."

"Did you go?"

"Yes."

"And?" Dr. Lewis asked quickly breaking their dialogue.

"And, I didn't seem to get there."

"Why?" asked Kyle with a smirk.

"I ran out of time I guess. I woke up confused, angry, afraid I missed something amazing."

"Who was pulling you in?" Kyle asked very pointedly. He had been there himself, finally seeing his father. He remembered the sensation and it was intoxicating, creating a myopic drive to find the source.

"I don't understand," Jack responded, his calm face now wrinkled, not in frustration, but unease.

"I think you do," Kyle said willing the man to talk.

"Ok gentlemen I think I'd like to be done now. We're reaching the point where this has now become uncomfortable," Jack said placing his large hands on his knees, rocking forward to stand up from the couch.

"Hold on please, Jack," Dr. Lewis said holding a hand up in the air and gesturing to sit back down. "I'm sorry you're feeling uncomfortable, I genuinely am. What Kyle is not telling you is we believe we have stumbled upon something that allows people to experience what you have, but without having to die."

"Ok?"

"Jack, I've felt what you felt. I've done it at least two dozen times." Kyle paused, once again checking with Dr. Lewis to see if he can go further. "In fact, the last three times, I made it to the source that was drawing me in."

"What happened?"

"I saw my dad. He died several years ago. Cancer."

"We're trying to determine if it's a hallucination—"

"Or something real," Kyle said cutting Dr. Lewis off.

"We're tracking the activity of the brain and frankly, it's very scarce. We know it's something more than just a weird dream, and you may be the one to help us."

"How can I do that?" Jack said nervously. There was a pause as the question hung in the air. Both researchers knew how to answer, but it meant that The Beyond Experience would go from talk, to action.

"Well, for starters, you'd need to be placed under anesthesia. We need to determine some baselines. Then you go under for longer, and we push deeper with the treatment parameters."

"How dangerous is this?"

"It's experimental. Nobody has died, but you're looking at the only person who's gone that far," Kyle said sitting back into his chair.

"I don't know guys. Can I think about it? I'm not terribly

comfortable with experiments."

"That's fair. But I can tell you with a very high level of confidence, the normal treatment is incredibly safe. We could show you what it's like and give you a baseline assessment first, then you can decide from there if you want as well. No pressure," Dr. Lewis said with an honest smile that Jack responded to warmly.

Jack stared blankly at the printed floral rug spread out beneath his feet. He traced the stems, the leaves, and the petals with his eyes. It was soothing his mind and slowing his heart rate. Jack was excited, not nervous. For the first time he was sitting with two people who not only understood what he went through, but could actually reproduce the experience, or so they claimed.

"Thousands of people?" Jack asked breaking the silence but still tracing the carpet with his eyes.

"Literally thousands," Dr. Lewis said sitting up straight and folding his hands.

"How long does this treatment take?"

"Somewhere between fifteen and forty-five minutes once everything is prepped."

Jack lifted his hand, 7:15 p.m. "Can we make it happen right now?"

"Uh, sure yeah. Yeah, we can make it right now. I can drive you home afterward and Kyle can follow in your car."

"Ok. Let's do it."

"I just want to remind you, before we go too far, of the confidentiality agreement you signed before we started talking. Kyle and I have opened up quite a bit. The three of us in this room are the only ones who know about how far this goes."

"I remember, and I've always been a man of my word. Please don't question that again," Jack responded aggressively.

It had been a few months since they used the lab upstairs but it was still immaculate. The air filtration system Dr. Lewis had installed when he was first given the lab had been top of the line and it still worked flawlessly. Not a spec of dust rested on any surface and the air still smelled sterile as he walked into the lab and turned the lights on. Dr. Lewis was nervous, but was keeping himself busy enough to distract himself from the doubt that often entered his mind with new experiments. He had asked Kyle to help Jack get prepped for the treatment, which allowed Dr. Lewis the lion's share of the work. Dr. Lewis made two separate trips back to the second floor where their materials were stockpiled, grabbing an IV, bags, needles, and Dr. Stelious' scanning machine.

When Dr. Lewis returned from the second trip downstairs, Jack was already resting comfortably on the treatment table, his hands behind his head, and Kyle was starting up the electronics in the observation room.

"You seem relaxed," Dr. Lewis said smirking. He was taken back by the man's matter-of-fact attitude. Just thirty minutes earlier the man was ready to storm out because they had asked him a few very direct questions.

"Well if I'm being honest, I've secretly always wondered about that sensation. I'd love to see what the draw was."

"I doubt you'll get your answer tonight Jack," Kyle said entering the treatment room. "Mine didn't get answered until I went deep. This might give you a clue though. We're ready in here Doc," Kyle said gesturing toward the observation room.

"Thanks Kyle. Ok Jack here's the deal. We record everything, so if that's not ok, we can end this."

"Nope. Fire away."

Dr. Lewis nodded toward the observation room and Kyle walked back and started recording. He gave a thumbs-up through the window.

"This is Jack Reimers, volunteering for a baseline treatment for The Beyond Experience," Dr. Lewis said out loud for the recording. "Are you consenting to this treatment Mr. Reimers?"

"Yes."

"Ok. You'll feel a slight pinch, followed by a cold sensation as the cocktail enters your body."

"Fair enough. Thanks for the warning Doc but is all that necessary?"

"Old habits I guess," Dr. Lewis said with a shrug. He grabbed the needle and quickly found a vein on Jack's forearm. He plunged the needle through his hairy flesh and entered his vein on the first try. Dr. Lewis then attached the IV bag to the line and fed it through the pump. They knew the dosage based on Jack's height and weight, which they had gathered earlier.

"That is cold Doc," Jack said with a chuckle as his eyes slowly bounced open and shut as the drug took effect.

"How are we looking with everything Kyle?"

"Stellar. Input his parameters. Now we're waiting."

"What's the over under on Jack going deep?" Kyle asked after ten minutes.

"I'm not even gonna give odds."

"Oh come on Ethan!"

"It's not a fair bet."

"Why's that?"

"Did you see his eyes? The way he lit up when we said we could take him back? He's just like you. He's hiding something."

"You think he saw someone?"

"I think he knows who's calling him," Dr. Lewis said as he crossed his arms and stared at the monitors. Number 4 had turned on which indicated movement. Kyle saw it too, a simple twitch of the hand.

"That's nothing," Dr. Lewis said with a bit of frustration in his voice.

"To be fair, I came clean," Kyle said smiling.

"After the fact. Yes, you came clean."

"Well maybe he's waiting to see something."

"Let's hope it's nothing major."

Dr. Lewis was nervous. He still wasn't confident Kyle had told him the truth about Lily. Dr. Lewis refused to ask the lab assistant, refused to discuss the treatment with him at all. Inside he was afraid of the answer he may get, but terrified of its implications.

*Bing. Bing. Bing.* The alarms began to chime. "Ok Doc his BP hit the mark. Let's bring him back."

Dr. Lewis entered the room, stopped the cocktail, and injected the epinephrine.

Quickly, Jack's eyes sprung wide open and he stared directly at Dr. Lewis. "I cannot tell you how much that experience meant to me," he said as several tears rolled down his face.

"What do you mean?" Dr. Lewis asked as Jack reached out, grabbing Dr. Lewis' left hand, squeezing it firmly between his own.

"This just validated every emotion, the heightened experiences, and all the conversations I've had with non-believers of my story. It was almost exactly how I remembered it, but not all the sensory details were the same. The external stimulus were all different. The smells were now sweet, like apple pie and spring. What I saw was snow, deep and powdery, the kind a skier like myself would die for. It was warm though, I felt that same comforting warmth. All the internal feelings, the happiness, the confidence and strength was all there. And I felt the pulling. The guiding. I tried to follow but I barely got anywhere."

"Would you like to go?" Kyle asked from the doorway into the observation room. He didn't seem to care what Dr. Lewis would have thought of the answer. He was finally talking to someone who understood his desire to go deeper into the treatment.

"Hell yes. Can we do it now?" Jack asked looking back to Dr. Lewis, his eyes full of wonder, like a child waiting for Santa.

"Not today, but we can try next Friday. We need at least a week to ensure the drugs are out. The dosage is precise."

"How long will that treatment take? I'm guessing longer?"

Dr. Lewis looked over to Kyle, who returned the gaze. "It takes quite a bit longer. On the order of eight to twelve hours."

"Wow. That may be a bit of a problem. How do I explain that to my wife?" Jack's shoulder slouched forward, disappointed. He sat at the edge of the bed staring once again at the floor, but this time he traced the thin precise lines of grout that separated the white tiles.

"We'll tell her you have to do a sleep study. It'll give you the chance to stay overnight. It's the only time we could run the long test anyways. Secrecy is key. We three only know of this."

"Actually, it's a great idea. I've been nagged quite a bit about doing a sleep study. My wife says I don't sleep well at night. Nightmares."

"It's settled then. You have a sleep study next Friday. Have your wife drop you off at 6:00 p.m. She can pick you up at 10:00 a.m. Saturday morning."

## Thursday, December 14, 2006

It was Thursday night and Dr. Lewis was laying in bed. The week went by slowly and sleep came in short bouts, eating was forced, and he couldn't imagine what Jack would experience when Friday came. But beyond that, he worried for Jack's safety. They hadn't allowed individuals with heart conditions to be administered the cocktail and now they were going to take him to the edge of death once again.

The glow from the lamp on the end table was casting yellow light throughout the room, but it lit his book poorly. It was 2:00 a.m. and already he had been awakened three times without cause, greeted by the same anxiety-ridden questions. *What if his heart stopped like Kyle's had? Could we bring him back? Would he die like Lily?* There was no walking away from this one. The book of poetry by Jackie Ellis seemed to always do the trick, forcing him to focus on the words rather than his thoughts.

These tides show

no notion of relief

as urgent they flow
and ebb my exhaustion
I can barely hear
but for their roar
the spilling of waves
on to coveted shore
and I dare not dip
in these waters deep
for fear I submerge in a
swell of unspoken need
So I breathe back longing
and beg this release
to gift tired bones
a momentary peace.

Eventually he grew tired, shut his eyes, and went to sleep and began dreaming. In his dream, he was in the treatment room, but on the table. Jack was standing over him and was beginning to titrate the treatment. Suddenly, Dr. Lewis was surrounded by blue sky in all directions. He was floating through the air, tasting clouds, and feeling the warm sun on his face. He smiled and allowed himself to lower his guard and enjoy the experience of flying. He could hear the wind rushing by, the smell of rain and ozone, and felt a sense of exploration. He glanced downward and could see land through gaps in the puffy white clouds. There were islands far below.

He circled around and around as he descended closer to the land masses that dotted the deep blue ocean. Finally breaking through the clouds, he had an uninterrupted view of blue and green. He slowed himself down enough that he could barely hear the wind any longer. He panned from left to right in an arc across the horizon. Quickly, he realized it was French Polynesia. He looked toward the northwest and saw the islands spread out before him, as if it was a treasure map leading to Bora Bora. Ethan's heart began to race as he grew closer.

He felt drawn there, pulled there by something. With Lily it had been their dream location for a vacation, but since losing her he rarely thought of it. When he had, it brought up the scene from the lab at Harvard. Her beautiful eyes, which once reminded him of the cove surrounding Mount Otemanu had been haunting, almost pale green. But now, in this dream, he was happy.

He reached the island and flew several circles around the mountain, only feet above the surface of the cove. The water was unbelievable, the blue-green hues appeared manufactured, mesmerizing him. He could clearly see the sand far below the surface of the water, the stingrays spreading their wide bodies along the ocean floor, and the thousands of fish that swam within the coral. He then flew vertically to the top of Mount Otemanu and, for the first time in the dream, placed his feet on solid ground. No one had ever set foot where he stood admiring the beauty spread out before him. The several hundred feet to the summit was unscalable due to the crumbling rock.

He stayed there while the sun set behind him. His back was warm but in front of him the island became lost in the dark shadow of the mountain. It was incredible to watch the mountain cast a longer shadow as the sun sank deeper toward the horizon. The hues of orange, pink, and purple added a depth of color to the natural life below him. Ethan knew his dream would end soon and took in one last panoramic view. He then faced the low, red sun as it sat perched on the horizon. He looked down and saw nothing but a lush emerald and green landscape below. He closed his eyes and the warmth from the sun left him and darkness took him over.

When he opened his eyes he was in his bed. The happiness he felt a moment earlier was replaced with anxiety and fear. It reminded him of the times when his mother would bang through his bedroom door. He could smell whiskey in the air and the stale smell of a Camel cigarette. He looked to his bedroom door and it was dark, no light highlighting the doorframe that preceded the beatings as a child. He looked to his left and saw the blanket rising and falling rhythmically.

Ethan hesitated. The smell of whiskey had given way to flowers, and the cigarettes gave way to the smell of the sea. His heart leapt into his throat and he began to smile uncontrollably. He reached with a trembling hand toward the comforter. He could barely breathe and his heart was beating so strongly he heard the swirling of blood in his ears.

Ethan placed his hand down and the blanket failed to rise again. He squeezed and felt an arm. He slid his hand up toward the top of the blanket. Breathing heavily, he grasped at the top of the comforter and closed his eyes. Very slowly he began to slide it down a centimeter at a time. His right eye opened just enough to spot her dirty blonde hair and he gasped. He tried to scream but wasn't sure why. Part of him was happy whereas the other was petrified. He lay frozen staring at her hair not knowing what to do next. *What should I do? How did she get here? Is she alive? Did I do the right thing back then?* The questions began to melt together and he began to panic. He pulled his hand back and tried to turn from the person he knew was Lily in the bed next to him.

Ethan stared at the ceiling trying to work out every possible scenario when out of the corner of his eye he saw movement. It wasn't the rhythmic movement of breathing but a voluntary, muscular movement. He turned toward her and a hand grasped the top of the blanket and pulled it down, revealing her face and body. Her eyes were closed, and she looked peaceful, almost calming to him. Then she opened her eyes. The pale blue-green eyes with wide pupils that haunted him for many years now stared at his own. They weren't lifeless now, but full of apathy, disgust, and judgment. She threw the blanket off and sat up in bed rapidly, never averting her gaze. Ethan lay frozen in bed, his jaw slightly ajar and his entire body shaking involuntarily.

"Oh Ethan, did you think I'd let you dream about Bora Bora without me? Come on sweetie, that was our place right?" Lily said straddling Ethan's waist. "What's the matter, cat got your tongue?"

"I, I love you Lily. It was just a dream. Don't hold it against me," he responded not knowing what to say as he reached for her hand.

"Oh, I guess it's ok. Go ahead and be happy. You might want to keep Jack alive though. Can't just leave him in your lab. Might draw some suspicions."

Ethan sprung up from bed and panicked. He backed away from the bed and elbowed his lamp, sending it hard down to the floor. He ran to the wall and turned on the lights. It was bright, so much so that he needed to squint his eyes while he strained against it. After several moments he had scanned the room and realized that the whole encounter had been the latest episode of sleep paralysis.

The first occurrence had been when he was thirteen. His father came charging through the bedroom door screaming at him, which was normal. "You ate my leftovers!" he shouted and pounded him several times in the abdomen. "How they tastin' now!" he yelled as his silver chain dangled in open space, the cross twisting in air, glimmering as it caught the light from the hallway. Ethan remembered snapping up in bed and his father suddenly not being there. He cried for an hour at the horror, but, even moreso in relief. Ethan hated the cross.

Every episode he had was in some way related to his mother or father, until this morning with Lily. In fact, he realized this was the first one he had since meeting Lily. The first night he spent with her was hallmarked by a terrible episode where both his mother and father had entered his room and proceeded to beat him without mercy. He had woken Lily up during the encounter with the noises he made. She calmed him down, made him some tea, and that was the first time he had opened up about his parents. Ethan hadn't talked to his friends, his social workers, or the court appointed psychologist regarding the extent to which he was abused by his God-fearing parents.

Lily had read about a higher consciousness which is what led them to the lab. She had also been a Christian in her youth, guided by her parents, but she fell away from the church when college came along. Her parents blamed Ethan for that, too. The two grad students wished to find a way to achieve a thoughtless state of mind, which drove them to experiment with anesthetics, and ultimately, to the cocktail. Once Ethan tried it the first time he had been completely set free from the anxiety and depression he felt. Most of the anxiety came from his mother and father, but it hadn't mattered after the experience he found in the drug. It was why he wanted her to feel it too. It was one of the reasons he loved her so much. She knew everything about him, the only one who ever had, and she fixed him.

He walked to his side table and checked his phone, 3:45 a.m. He decided it was acceptable to wake up, plus, he wasn't going to be able to fall asleep anytime soon. Guilt had once again taken over and he resented waking up with sleep paralysis—not because it had returned, but because it was her and not his parents. He sat at his kitchen table, basked in the iridescent blue light from the coffee maker as it gurgled; his eyes focused on the table, his mind on Lily's soulless eyes.

## Friday, December 15, 2006

Kyle was excited. The week had finally passed by and Jack was scheduled for his trial in The Beyond Experience. His bedroom curtains were open and he was lying in the indigo light of an early morning when his alarm chimed softly, and began its crescendo. He reached over and stopped the noise, hopped out of bed, and grabbed his gym bag.

He got in the pool, swam his 80 laps, and toweled off after a shower all before 7:00 a.m. He got home and changed, grabbing a couple pieces of avocado toast, left the apartment and arrived at the clinic at 7:45 a.m.—the whole time with a smile on his face and a glimmer in his eyes.

"Hey everyone," he said stepping out of the elevator onto the second floor.

"What's this guy all smiles for?" Traci asked holding a clipboard with the pre-treatment questionnaire fixed to the top.

"I don't know," Veronica said nudging him in the side. "You all good?"

"Of course I'm good. What the heck's all this about?" Kyle said wrinkling his face, still smiling widely, like a kid who had a secret he was dying to tell.

"Ok kids we're all done with the jokes. We've got four people in the rooms. Let's get to work," Dr. Lewis said looking at the team with his hands on his hips over his long white coat.

"Ok, fair enough. But we're not done with you yet, Kyle," Traci said.

"Yeah, I think someone may have had fun last night. That's all I'm sayin'," Veronica said and looked to Adam, who smiled and kissed her.

The workday went by quickly for Dr. Lewis, but slowly for Kyle. It was 5:00 p.m. and the sun was already behind the large hospital building to the west. The sky was still blue, but they knew it would soon be changing to orange, pink, and purple. Christmas was right around the corner and the biggest gift to both of the researchers would be answered questions.

Dr. Lewis sat in his office with Kyle reviewing other applicants for The Beyond Experience. They had ordered pizza, eating it sparingly, as it was to be their meals for the next fifteen or so hours.

"So sweatpants, huh?" Kyle said as Dr. Lewis came out of the treatment room and toward the couch.

"You'll see."

"I'm not judging. I just wish I would have thought of it too."

"Next time maybe."

"Maybe?"

"Yeah, maybe. If this guy dies on our table, you'll likely be wearing prison orange for the rest of your life."

"That much confidence? I'm impressed."

"What time is it?"

"It's five," he said pausing to pull out his cellphone.

"Should be here soon," Dr. Lewis said as he sighed heavily. "I'm going to check our supplies in the lab. Make sure we've got six bags ready to go just in case."

A short while later, there was a knock at the steel office door.

"Who's there?" Kyle asking jokingly.

"It is I, Jack."

Several seconds passed and the door swung open. Jack squinted a little, despite the sun setting, the change in light was dramatic from the black box he'd been standing in.

"Doctor," Jack said extending his hand.

"How you feeling, Jack?"

"Excited to do this. Haven't slept much this week."

"Me neither," Dr. Lewis responded, faking a smile, his anxiety starting to get the best of him.

"Jack!" Kyle yelled from the other room quickly covering the ground to shake Jack's hand. "Excited?"

"Took the words out of my mouth."

"Don't mind him," Kyle said pointing a thumb back toward Dr. Lewis, "He's all business."

"I can see that." Jack and Kyle had a shared laugh while Dr. Lewis stood waiting for a moment to intercede.

"Let's get started then shall we? Jack why don't you take yourself into the treatment room and throw the gown on. We'll grab the necessities and meet you in there. No playing with the equipment though, ok?"

"I'll sit my butt right down on the table after I finish changing," he said playfully serious, then winking at Kyle. He walked directly to the treatment lab.

"Kyle please grab the IV bags, bring them into the treatment area.

I have a small refrigerator in there. Place five in the fridge, and hang one. Then get the AV equipment running."

"You got it Doc."

Dr. Lewis walked toward his office and grabbed the deep brain scanner. He then paused for a moment, thinking of an excuse to pull the plug on the whole experiment. Methodically he went through the list of things he needed to perform as he walked toward the treatment room. He felt the whole moment was surreal. After reviewing everything thoroughly multiple times in his head, he convinced himself they were ready to go.

He walked into the white treatment room and saw Kyle had hung one bag and was now talking with Jack. He paused for a moment listening to the two men. They were discussing their loved ones, the ones they missed. For Kyle, it was his father, who he was able to see again, but for Jack it was his grandparents. He missed Colorado, the smell of the wild and the excitement of the hunt. He wanted to go back to a place where technology didn't exist and one could lose a whole day watching the clouds climb over a mountain range. They began to talk about heaven, and how both believed it to be real.

"I think I met my dad in heaven, which was incredible. I even started going back to church," Kyle said to Jack who smacked Kyle on the shoulder.

"Good on you, boy. Good on you. That's what I was trying to get at the other night when we were all talking. My NDE made me feel like there was a God."

"Ok gentleman here we go," Dr. Lewis said breaking up the talk about religion. "Kyle put those bags in the fridge please. We need them cold. Fire up the computers."

"Ok Doc," Kyle said and moved to do his work, but not before shaking hands with Jack once more.

Dr. Lewis approached Jack slowly with a small but present smile on his face. "Jack, I want to make sure you're on board with this. I realize you and Kyle share something which I'm not a part of. Please don't let this clog your vision." The men stood and stared at each other for a brief moment.

"Doc, listen. I already cheated death once. Each day has been a blessing. But, I'm not afraid to die. If I do, I know where I'm going, and from what Kyle said, it sounds like I've already been there twice."

"Let's not get ahead of ourselves, I think you'll come out of this or I wouldn't be considering it. I just want to know you're on board, and it sounds like you are."

"I am."

"Good. Let me get you prepped."

Dr. Lewis placed the pulse ox on Jack's finger, the EEG with deep brain scanning on his head, and the blood pressure cuff on his arm. Lastly, he placed the IV in Jack's arm, hitting a vein on the second try. "Might bruise a little from that first miss Jack."

"I'm good with that Doc."

"Kyle are we ready in there?"

"Cameras just went live. We're good," he said giving the thumbs-up as he stood with one hand still on the desk supporting his weight.

"Jack Reimers, do you consent to this experimental treatment?"

"I do."

"You'll feel a chill when I administer the drug—"

"What is this guy, a robot?" Jack interrupted pointing to Dr. Lewis and laughing while looking toward Kyle. Even Dr. Lewis had a chuckle. It helped loosen them all up.

"Here we go Jack. See you when you wake up."

The pizza was long gone by the time Dr. Lewis and Kyle started watching reruns on television. They settled on *Requiem for a Dream* after a short discussion. Drug addiction seemed fitting for the researchers, but was almost too close to home for Dr. Lewis. His early addiction to the drug led him to show Lily what the treatment was all about. Both Kyle and Ethan sat in silence watching the start of the dramatic story unfold.

The credits rolled at the end of the fifth episode. Both men wiped their tired eyes. It was 3:00 a.m. and time to perform another check.

"BP is 65/42. Heart rate 37 beats per minute. Pulse ox is 98 percent and he's receiving 10 liters. Respiratory rate's eight. His brain waves are still showing all delta, two hertz, slightly lower than at 2:00 a.m.," Kyle said sighing heavily.

"He's gonna need a new IV bag. I'm going to take care of that now," Dr. Lewis said grunting as he stood from his chair and stretched. "I'm getting old Kyle. The knees get stiff sitting here so long."

"Take a walk old man."

Dr. Lewis did just that as he entered the treatment room and opened the small refrigerator grabbing the fourth bag of the treatment session.

"Haha." Dr. Lewis heard a laugh startling him from behind. He turned and sat on the floor.

"Haha." He heard it again, this time more loudly, and he located the source. Dr. Lewis closed the refrigerator and walked quickly to the IV pole, hanging the bag.

"Dr. Lewis!" Kyle said in a whispered scream from the doorway. He waved aggressively motioning the doctor to come.

"Did you hear the laugh, too?" Dr. Lewis asked as he got close.

"Yeah, and you really need to see this." The two researchers walked into the observation room and to the computers. "After I heard him laugh I checked the vitals. Check this out," Kyle said pointing to the screen. "His brain waves are gone."

"What the hell?" Dr. Lewis was confused. "I'd love to ask someone about how this is possible but who can we trust? His other vitals are ok?" he asked looking over the monitors, seeing everything was still stable.

"Grandpa," they heard followed by more laughter. Both men sat watching the monitors. Jack was smiling, moving his hands, and mumbling. He was also still showing a complete lack of brain activity; no delta waves whatsoever. His vitals were still in the designated safe zone as defined by Dr. Lewis: BP was above 40/25, heart rate was still above 30, pulse ox was over 85.

"This is incredible," Kyle said watching Jack who was essentially dead from the neck up.

"I agree."

"Dr. Lewis, what do you think this is?"

"I've got no idea. None."

"I have a clue. It's something I've been looking into for a few weeks now."

"What?" Dr. Lewis looked at Kyle, confused.

"Since I saw my dad, I went back to the church. First time back into church the sermon was on a vision of heaven. It was Revelations—"

I'm stopping you there," Dr. Lewis said frustrated.

"What'd I say?"

"Religion? This is a religious experience?"

"Yes. Maybe. What if we found a way to tap into something spiritual; a back door to heaven?"

"You can't be serious."

"Well I'd love a better explanation," Kyle said, crossing his arms as he sat back in his chair.

"I don't have one Kyle. That's why it's called research. We don't get the cop out answer of religion."

"Hear me out."

"Fine, I think we've got some time. Humor me."

"I'm not a biblical scholar, but I do know there are places in the Bible that discuss visions of heaven. One of those was in Revelations, Chapter Four I'm pretty sure. Goes into a detailed description. Frankly, though, I've had a hard time finding more. Isaiah mentions it, Ezekiel does too but both are very brief."

"Ok, so far you aren't exactly wooing me."

"You're coming at me pretty harshly Ethan. I had no idea you were such a staunch atheist."

"I, I wouldn't necessarily say that. Just have a hard time believing some religious ideas."

"Why's that?"

Dr. Lewis paused, taking the time to allow a well thought out answer. He reflected on his parents and their abuse having been backed up by their "biblical" rationale, and the cross they both wore around their necks. He remembered Lily's parents, their judgment and criticism, a total lack of love for him, and their refusal to talk to him, except to say he couldn't attend Lily's funeral, and that was in a notarized letter from an attorney.

"Let's just say my past hasn't allowed me to warm up to the idea of a god."

"Fair enough. A lot of people start like that."

"Anything else you want to add?"

"Just to say that these visions biblical men had. We're obviously wired to receive them. What if we've unlocked the door, allowing us to see things we otherwise wouldn't be able to see? Like this, a computer program, or game simulator, which we hacked into. We're in the program, but without the game coding, allowing us to have our own unguided experiences."

"I'd say I'm glad we're not letting you back in."

*Bing. Bing. Bing.* The monitor chimed. "That's it Kyle we're done," Dr. Lewis said as he ran into the treatment room and administered the epinephrine and stopped the drip. Slowly, Jack came back, opening his eyes and turning his head left to right.

"His stats are good and stable. Back to 90 percent of his pre-treatment numbers," Kyle shouted from the observation room. Dr. Lewis gave Kyle a thumbs-up and went back to watching Jack's recovery.

It took several minutes, but Jack was sitting up straight and smiling. The events of the experience still crystal clear in his mind. He sipped on water, his mouth and throat were dry from the high levels of O2 that were being pumped into his airways. He was far from dehydrated, however, due to the large volume of IV fluids that had been pumped into him over the last ten hours.

"So how was your grandpa?" Kyle asked entering the treatment room and walking to Jack's bedside.

"How'd you know?"

Kyle brought out a tablet. He had spent the last fifteen minutes cutting and splicing videos from when Jack was active, the highlight was when he had said "grandpa" and laughed.

"Well that's just weird," Jack said watching the video.

"Can you remember a moment when that happened in your experience?" Dr. Lewis asked.

"I can actually. It was when I saw him for the first time in 25 years. I could hear him for a while, talking to me like he did when I was young, whispers, but I could hear the words plain as day."

"What were they?"

"Stay downwind."

"Why?"

"I was hunting big game, a moose. We never downed a moose but it was always something we planned on doing together. I had a recurve and it was strung with 80-pound draw. That's the hardest pull I've ever used. I have a 60 now. Anyways, I heard him keep telling me to stay downwind. I was tracking this huge bull through the trees. Heard him snortin' and callin' to a female. Then I'd hear my grandpa again, 'stay downwind.' I did it all right. I stayed downwind then all of a sudden, a clearing in the evergreens. He was a big bull and he stood out like a sore thumb. Unlucky for him."

"How'd he stand out?"

"Strangest thing I'd ever seen. He was albino, almost translucent.

I could see his red heart beating through his skin. The green trees, the grass and stone, even the rolling peaks behind him couldn't mask any part of his form. It was incredible his size too. Massive creature. The moose paused and called again. Made my hair stand up on edge," he said holding his arm up and pointing. "See, it's doing it again," Jack said as his own hair stood on end. "That big bull looked right at me and I knew he saw me. It was like he was telling me it was ok to take the shot. So I did. Hit him right in the heart. He walked for several yards and I tracked him. Wasn't tough."

"That's incredible." Kyle said with a look of longing in his eyes.

"No. It wasn't," Jack said smiling widely.

"Why's that?" Dr. Lewis inquired, waiting for the punchline.

"Seeing my grandpa standing there with the moose's rack in his hands was. When I tracked the moose behind a row of trees my grandpa was there. I forgot all about the moose and we talked for what seemed like hours." Jack took a moment and reflected on the conversation.

"Everything was good huh Jack?" Kyle asked softly, placing a hand on his shoulder.

"Perfect," Jack responded, staring at the sheets that still covered his lap.

"Hungry?" Kyle said breaking the short silence.

"Starved."

The three men sat in front of the TV, drinking coffee and eating ramen. The sun had already come up bathing the top floor in a dense orange glow and the conversation was relaxed. They mostly talked about sports, but only Kyle really understood what they were talking about.

*Buzzzz. Buzzzzz. Buzzzzz.* Dr. Lewis' phone rang on his desk. He meandered over, assuming it was an accidental dial. He knew of nobody that would be calling him at 9:00 a.m. on a Saturday. *Dr. Stelious?* he thought as he saw the man's chubby face on the screen.

"Hello?" he answered.

"Is everything ok at your lab Dr. Lewis?" the doctor asked getting straight to the point.

"Yes, we are all good. Why do you ask?"

"Oh, well maybe I have a glitch. Did you use the deep scanner all through the night last night?"

Dr. Lewis froze. He knew he forgot something and now he realized what it was. All the results from the deep scanner were going immediately to Dr. Stelious. It was the agreement they made in order to secure the machines for their shared research interests. His knees weakened and he grasped for his chair, finding it just before he fell to the ground.

"Are you there, Dr. Lewis?" Stelious said in a high voice.

"Yes I'm here. Can you give me a moment to call you back? I'll look into it."

"Of course Dr. Lewis. If you say things are good, I believe you. I just want accuracy in my study. I'm counting on these results to make my conclusions for the paper."

"I realize that Marcus. I will call you back as soon as I can."

He hung the phone up and looked up at the exposed beams in the ceiling above. They were ugly and bare, like dirty secrets being brought into the light. Nothing could show flaws like the sun, and at this time of morning, it was coming straight through the east windows. The spray insulation was bubbled, uneven and ugly, and dust had collected in the crevices. Long strands of filth even hung down like small articles of clothing being hung to dry. Just below the metal beams, thousands of dust particles sat suspended in air, glowing in the orange light like small planets floating around in their own universe, their backsides darkened.

"Kyle, come here for a second," Dr. Lewis insisted as he rubbed both hands through his hair.

"What's going on Ethan," he said walking up with a smile, his eyes burning bright green against the orange glow.

"That was Dr. Stelious."

"Ok, what'd he want?"

"Wanted to know if we were using the deep scanner last night. He saw some weird activity."

Dr. Lewis watched as Kyle's expression changed from happiness to concern. The same thoughts and questions that were running through his own brain, were now swimming through Kyle's. "What'd you say?"

"The only choice I had. I told him I'd call him back later after I looked into it."

"Good idea."

"Yeah, maybe for a few hours. Then what?"

"Can we just lie to him? Tell him we accidentally turned it on at the end of the day?"

"Sure that'd be great, but we were getting delta waves for hours before it shut down. How do we explain that?"

"Good point." Kyle said. "Why don't we just tell him we had an experiment run long?"

"What about the lack of all brain activity for those hours?"

"We just tell him. I think the best solution is to tell him. He won't know why we did it for that long."

"Ok, but he will publish a paper, and it will include this outlier in the discussion. It will stick out like a sore thumb for sure," Dr. Lewis said sighing heavily, realizing for the first time this would likely have much further implications.

"We just can't use the deep scanner again for these."

"No. We will be using it. It tells us precisely when someone goes into their Beyond Experience. His talking started the moment brain activity ceased. We need it. I'll make the call. Tell him what we did. Let him decide what he wants to do," Dr. Lewis said.

Dr. Lewis and Kyle walked back to the office after breakfast. The air was crisp and the wind played music with the remaining leaves in the trees. The clouds hung low in the sky, giving the illusion one could reach up and grasp them; their shadows were long and dark, but not as dark as the thoughts looming in the men's minds.

The two had discussed many options. The first plan was to lie and say that one of their lab assistants was caught after hours playing with the device. The idea sounded great, initially, until they had to find a way to account for the actual readings overnight. Explaining that began to grow exceedingly complicated. The last idea wasn't an idea at all, but rather the truth. They decided to tell Dr. Stelious the truth, that they were conducting a new experiment and hadn't accounted for the change in data.

Dr. Lewis sat at his desk in the office, Kyle standing next to him. He keyed the numbers for Dr. Stelious, and turned on the speakerphone.

"Dr. Lewis, it's been some time. I hope you have an idea of what happened," Dr. Stelious said with a wide inflection in his voice.

"I do Marcus. I know what happened."

"Well let me hear it Ethan," he said excitedly.

Dr. Lewis looked to Kyle who returned the gaze with a reassuring nod. "First allow me to ask you a question."

"Sure."

"Are you still planning on coming down at the end of the month with the scanners?"

"As long as this explanation is adequate."

"We're partners in this Marcus. I don't understand why you're being so condescending," Dr. Lewis shot back, frustrated with the tone in the doctor's voice.

A pause, then Dr. Stelious cleared his voice and offered his best apology. "I'm sorry Ethan. I just hate not being in control of my own statistics. That's all there is to it."

"Thank you Marcus. I was only asking because I would rather show you than tell you. We were performing an experiment with our treatment cocktail, and the results were extraordinary. We are going to look for a second subject, and will wait till your arrival to show you what we are doing. I would exclude the results from last evening. It wasn't a controlled trial."

"Well, I must say Dr. Lewis you have piqued my interest. I'll have the deep scanners ready in three weeks. We'll see you in Saint Louis. I can't wait to see what you're doing out there."

"It's worth the wait doctor," Kyle said trying to add to the moment.

"Who was that?" Dr. Stelious asked suspiciously.

"I'm Kyle, Dr. Lewis' lead assistant. Nice to meet you."

"You as well. Talk to you gentlemen soon."

# | FIFTEEN |

## Early 2007

Adam stood in his apartment bathroom staring at the mirror. He had just finished shaving, and was inspecting his smooth face from every angle, his wet skin shimmering as he turned left to right, tilting his chin up and down. He rubbed his cheeks and chin with both hands ensuring not a single piece of stubble was felt. He then lazily tossed his new, shorter hair with his hands, trying to get an idea how he should wear it that evening.

He walked into his bedroom to throw on his clothes, which were already laid on his bed: a white t-shirt, navy pants, a white button down shirt with a dark blue knitted silk tie. He grabbed his phone and turned on some music, a soothing blend of old classic crooners to set the mood, and relax his mind. Adam strutted as he put his clothes on, jumping back and forth from the bathroom to the bedroom, inspecting himself after each article of clothing was added. Each time he saw himself, he appeared better looking, but it could have just been the fog from the mirror gradually lifting. He enjoyed getting dressed up. The lab work and college classrooms weren't conducive to his taste in high-end clothing.

He finished the knot on his tie and pulled it snug to his neck. His clothes looked almost tailored as he stood smirking in the mirror. He danced to the closet and grabbed his hair pomade, dabbing his finger inside and quickly spreading it around his dark hair, enjoying the rough and messy look it left behind. *Screw it*, he thought as he pointed at himself in the mirror. He began to hum *Come Fly with Me* by Frank Sinatra as he sprayed two squirts of John Varvatos Artisan Blu on the front of his shirt.

Adam grabbed a three-quarter length black coat from his closet and looked at his phone. He turned off his music and texted Veronica, "I'm leaving now. Can't wait to see you." He walked out the door and toward the VW in the outdoor parking lot. He continued to hum to the music in his head as he placed his coat in the back, closed the hatch, and jumped into the front seat. He turned the music back on in his car as he drove toward Veronica's place on Pershing Avenue, near the park.

Adam was nervous. He tried to listen to the music in the car, but he couldn't stop thinking about her. He played with the stations, dug his nails into the stitching on his steering wheel and, in between shifts, bit his nails and bounced his clutch foot onto the floor mat. He stopped himself at least a half dozen times before he got to her place, which was only fifteen minutes away. He parked in front of her condo and waited for her to come out.

Veronica bounced around her apartment frantically trying to decide what to wear. Adam was taking her to Kemoll's, an Italian restaurant that resided on top of the Met, allowing expansive views of the city and the Arch. She finally settled on a dress and threw her hair up haphazardly, having run out of time to do anything else with it. After throwing on her black heels, she turned and ran, hands swinging out wildly for balance, back into the bathroom to turn off the hair straightener she hadn't even used. Her first glance in the mirror forced a twisted expression. She opened the drawer and made quick work of applying a light foundation, penciled her eyelid, and placed a slight hint of rose on her cheek. She finished the look with a shade of lipstick that matched the dress.

Three songs played in the time Adam sat in the u-shaped concrete drive in front of the building but he hadn't heard a single one. Finally, she exited the glass doors. She was head to toe gorgeous, wearing a tight, red dress with black heels. Her hair was half up and curly, like he always told her he liked. She wore a long black coat, but hadn't bothered to button it. He got out of the car, walked around, and opened her door.

"Oh, that's sweet, honey," she said smiling and kissing him gently, trying not to remove any of the red lipstick. "I'm not leaning over to unlock your door. I've seen *A Bronx Tale* too, don't try to test me," she said playfully.

"Well, I have no idea what you're referring to. But if you say it's a good movie, we can watch it sometime," he said carefully closing the door behind her. Adam entered the car and sat in the driver's seat staring at her for a moment.

"What?" she said softly, her eyes turned upward in a loving arc.

"You're just so beautiful. I hope you know that." It took all the strength he had not to tell her he loved her right in that moment. He planned this evening in order to say the three words he never told anyone. It was bubbling up inside him, trying to fly out from his mouth and into her ears.

Adam finally found the strength to turn away and put the car in gear. He knew he could make it through to dinner, he just couldn't look into her eyes. *That's all,* he willed himself.

Adam pulled the car up right in front of the venue. The valet held Veronica's hand gently as she stood and exited the car. Adam smiled at her as she waited, both hands clutching her handbag as she tried her best to look relaxed. As the VW pulled away, they walked into the restaurant with linked arms and Adam placed the valet ticket deep into his pocket.

"Good evening," the man behind the small desk said as they entered the venue.

"Hello, we have a reservation," Adam said softly as his eyes darted around the room involuntarily.

"The name?"

"Adam Nicholson."

"Adam . . . Nicholson," the man said softly to himself as he scanned the computer.

"For what time sir?"

"Seven."

"I'm sorry sir. Could you have put it under a different name?"

"No, that's not possible. I called a few weeks ago. Is there a way to try and figure this out? I know I called."

"Sure, give me one moment. I'll look you up by name, see if somehow the reservation was cancelled. Spell your last name for me."

"N-I-C-H-O-L-S-O-N."

"Ok, I had the spelling correct."

Adam began looking around the waiting area, a short but impatient line was forming behind him; all seemingly fixated on his conversation with the host.

"Oh, here it is Mr. Nicholson," he said with a smile and a glance through the top of his eyes. "You're here on the wrong Friday. It's next Friday."

Veronica erupted with laughter and pointed it right at Adam who quickly smiled himself. Veronica couldn't control herself and continued to laugh so hard she had to place her hand on his shoulder to stop herself from doubling over. A landslide of giggling spread out over the waiting area, all at Adam's expense.

"Fair enough I guess," Adam said now chuckling himself. "See you next week then."

"Yes, sir, Mr. Nicholson, 7:00 p.m., next Friday."

Adam and Veronica walked back to the street and he handed the valet his ticket.

"Done already sir?" the valet asked him sarcastically.

"Yeah, afraid so. We'll be back next week."

"Ok, sir. We'll get the car. No charge."

"I really appreciate that."

The car came around and stopped right in front of them. Adam once again opened the door for Veronica. He then handed the valet a ten.

"So, I'm sorry," Adam said to the steering wheel, flushed with embarrassment.

"Oh don't be sweetie. It was worth the laugh."

"Maybe we can salvage the night."

"We can. Take me to get some ice cream."

"Dressed like this?"

"Yes. It'll be fun. Then surprise me. Take me somewhere."

Adam and Veronica drove out of town. He knew where to take her, and she knew she didn't have to specify. It was a place he took her on multiple occasions, as they had both fallen in love with it when they moved to the city. Ted Drewes was an icon in the Saint Louis area and Adam had heard Veronica talking about it one afternoon in the lab. It was the custard that led to their first conversation outside of work.

Adam turned into Ted Drewes and had his choice of spots. The lull in the business was a welcome sight for the two overdressed custard lovers.

"Vanilla?" he asked confidently.

"Let's get nuts, chocolate, and vanilla."

"Oh, two scoops, didn't see that coming," he said rolling his eyes playfully.

"You should come in with me. Let everyone see how beautiful you are."

"I love you," she slipped and quickly covered her mouth with wide eyes.

"What!" he responded smiling ear to ear, his face once again flushed.

"I'm so sorry," she giggled and said through her hands.

"Why are you sorry?" he reached to bring down her hands. The laughter stopped and the moment became intense. Her hands slid down guided by his. He touched her face gently, stroking her soft skin with the back of his fingers. She looked into his eyes as he traced her details with his fingertip. Adam gently grabbed a strand of curl that rested just in front of her ear and placed it behind with the rest. "I love you, too. I've honestly never said that to anyone before."

"I have, but—"

"I don't care. Don't even finish that sentence. I want to focus on you now. Not who you were before, or who you've been with before. I want now and forever with you. Only you."

"I want now and forever with you too. But I'm nervous."

"I'm ok with that. It'll go away. The nervousness won't last forever. I am so confident in us Veronica."

She leaned toward him and Adam watched her lips. Her eyes closed as her lips gently caressed his, not caring if lipstick was left behind. A simple outward mark for the monumental place she held within him. He pulled back after a moment. "So, two scoops huh?"

She gently shoved him back into his bucket seat, "Yeah two scoops, and I'm keeping my pretty self right here in the seat so leave the keys."

They sat in the car for hours, their eyes never tiring of looking at one another, both excited to be in the moment. The sweet treats had been expertly scraped from plastic cups long ago, and the couple secretly clung to questions they desperately wanted answers to, but were too nervous to ask.

"How many kids do you want?" Veronica asked, her feet on the seat as she sat sideways in the car, staring into Adam's eyes. Her heart was pounding, nervous that she allowed the question to slip.

"Three."

"Oh, that's a good number, I was thinking four."

"Four! That's a lot. I picked three 'cause I figured you'd pick it. Four seems like a lot."

"I was one of six honey. Four isn't bad."

"Four it is then, as long as you're confident you can handle it."

"I've got names picked too."

"Let's hear it."

"No," she said sitting up.

"Why?"

"Don't you know it's bad luck to discuss baby names before your baby's born?"

"Not true. So tell me."

Reluctantly, she began to recall the names. "If it's a girl, Valarie, McKenzie, Savannah, and Rosa."

"All girls?"

"For the boys," she said as if she didn't hear the question. "Mario, Theodore, Anselm, and Adam Jr."

"Anselm?"

"My grandfather is from Spain. It's his name."

"Ok, well we've got our names, now let's get to making these babies." Adam crawled over the stick and onto Veronica's chair.

"Um, this is not going to happen here like this," she said uncomfortably.

"You're right, let's get you home. I love you, you know that?"

"I love you too you big nerd," she said wrinkling her nose and grabbing both sides of his face. She playfully kissed him two more times in quick succession and he fumbled at moving himself back into the driver's seat.

The sun began to rise behind them as they drove, willing them to stay awake a little longer. They walked into her apartment, closed the shades, and fell asleep in each others arms, still wearing their clothes; secretly thinking if they changed their clothes, the night would end.

Kyle woke Sunday morning with the sun shining in his face. He buried himself in the blankets as he checked his phone, 7:40 a.m. His decision was quick, no swimming this morning. If he did, he wouldn't make the church service. His nose was cold and moist, like a dog, and no matter how deep he buried himself in the blankets there was no changing that. Quickly, he shot out of bed, ran to the windows, and closed them. He loved the fresh air, but clearly it was a terrible idea in January.

He ran to the bathroom and willed the shower to warm before jumping in. Finally, he entered with a shiver, feeling the chill give way to steamy warmth as the water ran down his body. He made quick work of readying for church, and left the house with time to spare.

The drive west out of the city was empty, the highway seemingly his own. The radio was off and he was reflecting on his conversations with Dr. Lewis. He knew the man well, or so he thought, but after their last conversation in the treatment room he realized Ethan had been very superficial with him for years. Kyle didn't know where Ethan was from, if he had both parents, if he had he ever dated anyone. Surely in the last seven years he would have heard of a woman, or even met one or two; but nothing.

*Let's just say the past hasn't allowed me to warm up to the idea of a god.* The phrase was powerful, revealing a vulnerability that Kyle hadn't seen before. Both men were affected by the comment in the lab, feeling on edge in a typically comfortable arena. They had spoken very little to each other during the last three weeks, and Kyle wondered what he should do. *Do I ask about his past? Do I act like I don't care? He helped me with my dad, how can I not ask him? Will he be angry with me? Will he fire me?*

He pulled into the church parking lot and all thoughts quickly melted away, a sense of peace overwhelmed him. Exiting the car, he waved to a young couple he saw regularly, but hadn't talked to. He hadn't talked to many people at church, only the ones who said hello to him, and those conversations had been fairly superficial. He still felt distant, out of place, an outsider who had snuck in and was waiting to get caught; *just keep your head down.*

The music began and he was filled with confidence. Kyle felt alone, in a way that allowed him to feel completely unjudged. He focused on the music while the band played and all those around him sang along, but he remained silent. Things were becoming more clear with the music. Questions were being answered by the same solution: *talk to someone who knows better than you.* Kyle knew in that moment that he had to talk to the pastor. He needed to know what to say to Dr. Lewis next time the topic of The Beyond Experience was discussed. Kyle knew, just as Jack, the experience was revealing of something more than just synaptic events deep within the brain. It was real, felt with all the senses the world around him allowed, but at an even deeper more fulfilling level.

He continued to think while the pastor delivered his sermon and by the time the benediction came, he had only one goal in mind. As the music played he walked toward the front of the church, fighting upstream against the current of people leaving as he approached the pastor. The man was short, with a white goatee, neat hair, and brown eyes. He was pleasant, shaking hands with dozens of people and chuckling with a few who were conversing as only close friends could. After several minutes, the crowd around him dispersed and left Kyle right in the sightline of the pastor.

Kyle nodded to him with a slight smile, "Morning sir," he said finally taking the three steps forward to shake his hand.

"Morning," he responded with a firm grasp and flick of the wrist.

"I'm Kyle. Wondering if I could ask you a couple of questions."

"Sure Kyle, let's start with the first," he said winking.

"You got me there. I was wondering if you thought we could all see what the prophets see?"

"I'm not following, Kyle."

"I'm sorry," he said a bit embarrassed. "What I mean is, do you think we all are capable of seeing what the prophets saw from biblical stories."

"Of course I do. Anything is possible with God. I'm sure you must mean something different."

"I'm a researcher, been performing studies on a new treatment. Unfortunately, I can't get into the details, but it's gotten me back into the church. With a lot of questions."

"As far as I'm concerned, that's a good thing."

"I know, I'd have to agree at this point," he said chuckling. He felt he was getting nowhere, the pastor giving the ninety-nine cent answer he'd been given dozens of times on YouTube, and searching the internet for sermons. "What I want to know, is how do I tell someone the afterlife is real? How do I convince them God is real and there is a higher place for us where all our experiences are magnified to unimaginable heights?"

The pastor froze, his smile no less bright. He crossed his arms and glanced down at the ground in front of Kyle's feet for several seconds. "You've got the million-dollar question right there, son," he said looking back at Kyle and pointing to his chest.

Kyle was frustrated. Clearly the pause was for dramatic effect. "Thanks," he said extending his hand.

"You seem frustrated, Kyle."

"To be honest, I am."

"What can I do son?"

"You can stop giving me the party line. I really need to get some answers here."

"Can you give me a more specific question?"

"Sure, do you think that someone can experience heaven without actually going there?" The question came out clear and without premeditation. Kyle had never even thought to ask it in that way, but it was the heart of the matter. Almost 90 percent of those finishing a treatment session described their experience as "heavenly" or that they had "gone to heaven."

"What kind of research are you doing again?" the pastor joked, but noticed Kyle's frustration being undaunted by the attempt. "If you are referring to near death experiences, I would have to think those are not biblically founded. In my opinion, someone may be having a synaptic event in their head."

"Ok, well, what about the accounts in the Bible where there are visions of heaven?"

"Like Revelations? You were listening several weeks ago I see. Well, yes. Those were visions of heaven, not an actual physical visitation. At least that's my interpretation, which is in line with a large majority of evangelical pastors."

"Well, going back to my original question, do you think we are all capable of this vision? Like, could we all be wired to experience this from a physiological perspective?"

"I certainly don't see why not."

"Well that's that then, sir," Kyle said extending his hand and smiling widely.

"Glad I could help. I've got to say I'm very intrigued by your research now. Do me a favor, if and when you can divulge, please let me know?"

"I will. It should be relatively soon, but who knows. It's medicine."

Kyle sat in his apartment in silent thought. Heaven was on his mind, but so was its antithesis, hell. In every single experiment the description was that of a heavenly place. *Statistically,* he thought, *if we're dealing with a glimpse of the afterlife, someone would have to experience hell as well.* He desperately wanted to answer that question.

He went online into the forums for a solution. He read post after post about individuals who were shown a glimpse of the terrors awaiting them in the presumed afterlife. However, every one of them had turned back to the church following the incident so they would be worthless as a test subject. Kyle tried not to be frustrated. People were coming back to the church after all, which, in his current mind, was more important.

The weight of the question was slowly consuming him. The sun had set hours earlier and he hadn't left the computer for any reason. His eyes were starting to burn and the only light in the room was radiating from the screen he stared into, continuing to read account after account of near death experiences. He had several web pages open in different tabs, referencing a half dozen sites and even did a search on Amazon for books related to the topic.

The stories of hell were, for the most part, similar and terrifying. It wasn't the gnashing of teeth, the screaming, the ripping of flesh from bone, or the darkness that scared him. He actually found that to be quite annoying and almost hokey. What he did find horrifying were the stories of solitude and the feeling of complete nothingness that seemed to last forever. It gave him a nauseous feeling with a hint of panic.

Finally, after hours of reading, he saw a post. It was aggressively written. The woman clearly believed it to be an artifact her brain created and not a religious experience whatsoever. In fact, she went on to say that "anyone who believes in a higher power is clearly a weak willed and flawed human, who shouldn't be allowed to perpetuate the false ideology to a new generation, and therefore, should all be castrated."

Kyle smiled. He had his subject, but looking at the date of the submission, it had been close to five years. He sent a direct message to the woman, hoping that she hadn't unsubscribed from notifications. She had several dozen responses, all attempting to bring her to the church or condemn her for her thoughts. It was rather rough criticisms, he had to admit. It was this sort of judgmental tendencies he heard lots of people his age complain about. He wrote a short note, and crossed his fingers.

# | SIXTEEN |

Dr. Lewis sat in an SUV with Kyle waiting for the flight to arrive. Dr. Stelious was sitting in a plane ten-thousand feet above them, circling the airport. The weather had been poor the entire morning and bled into the afternoon. Every flight entering and departing Lambert was delayed due to heavy cross winds and ice.

Kyle hadn't heard back from the woman on the forums, which was no surprise, but Dr. Lewis had found another subject to use for that night's demonstrations, if they ever got back to Washington University. It was 2:30 p.m. and Dr. Lewis finally received a text from Stelious: "On the ground. Coming out soon."

Twenty minutes later the short doctor exploded out of the airport, feet moving quickly as he barreled forward, head down into the wind and sleet, wrangling his large wheeled bag into the back of the vehicle.

"I don't need your help young man but thank you," he said to Kyle as he saw the strong assistant run to the back of the car.

"No problem Doctor. Just thought I'd offer. I'm—"

"Kyle, I'm sure. But let's leave the introductions for a less wet environment," Stelious said interrupting.

"Makes sense," Kyle smirked. Dr. Lewis had warned him about Dr. Marcus Stelious and his lack of people skills. *All business.*

"Dr. Lewis," Stelious said entering the shotgun position forcing Kyle to the back. Kyle smiled broadly and shook his head. He caught a glance from Dr. Lewis in the rearview mirror and watched his eyes squint slightly, indicating a smile from the doctor.

"Thanks for coming Marcus," he said extending his hand. "I think it's better you see rather than having to explain it to you."

"I must say the month has been torturous. I'm very excited to see your work Ethan, but, more importantly, how this anomaly could be removed from my study."

"One bit of nasty business I'm afraid Marcus." Dr. Lewis reached back toward Kyle who had the papers already in hand. "I'm going to need you to sign this. It's a non-disclosure agreement."

"I already know what's going on, and we've both signed these already."

"No, this is not the same. It is a special project. You'll be the fifth person to know about it."

"Well I'm out here, I'm not going back without knowing." Dr. Stelious didn't even read the paperwork. Curiosity had led him to Saint Louis, not jealousy. He had no intention of working on duplicating the new study, only to learn.

"This is your research building?" Dr. Stelious commented as they arrived at The Shack. "Small and quite old, but if it gets the job done I suppose it'll work," he said smiling. The moisture had darkened the brickwork and the windows were veiled in a watery textured surface hiding the fresh interior. They entered, and Stelious nodded his head in approval. The three entered the elevator and a quick guided tour was given to the visiting Stelious, who was still white-knuckled as he wheeled the suitcase.

"Well Marcus what do you think?" Dr. Lewis asked as their visitor looked everything over.

"I think it is all very pretty." The three men laughed.

"Ok well we're going up one more floor. It's our office, and our original treatment suite. Nobody can enter except myself and Kyle. Even our assistants don't know it exists."

"Let's get on with it then," Stelious said motioning toward the elevator, finally taking his hand off the suitcase.

"You can leave those here Marcus. They are safe," Dr. Lewis said smiling and pointing to the deep brain scanners that resided in the luggage.

"You will be needing one I presume."

"Dr. Stelious, we plan ahead. We're ready upstairs and our subject will be arriving in," he paused to look at his phone, "thirty minutes. Let's go upstairs until then."

"This is intimidating," Stelious said as the doors opened to the third floor.

"It's the look we were going for," Kyle said and opened the door, allowing the light to flood into the black box. The clouds still dominated the sky but were allowing a few streaks of brilliant light to slice through.

"Great office Dr. Lewis," Stelious said extending his arms wide as if trying to reach both ends of the clinic with his hands. "Harvard couldn't have offered this."

"Yes it's nice. This was all we had until the funding came through."

"So it was just the one treatment room?"

"Yeah, just this top floor. We built out the rest several months ago before we started the study."

"Wonderful," Stelious said in awe. He wasn't jealous, but certainly craved the success of Dr. Lewis. Not because he wanted fame and money, but because it meant he was had discovered a solution to a problem worth solving.

*Knock, knock, knock.* All three men turned silently toward the door. "Hello!" a muffled female voice yelled sweetly through the door.

Kyle quickly reacted and jogged across the wood floor. "Hi Janice," he said to the woman smiling at him.

She entered and greeted Kyle and Dr. Lewis with a hug. She paused at Dr. Stelious. "You must be the visiting doctor," she smiled at him.

"I am. Is that ok?"

"What do I care. I'll be sleeping," she joked and shrugged her tiny shoulders. "When do we get going here Doc?"

"Well Janice, right now I guess. You're a little early, but we're all here. Kyle, take her into the treatment room. Show her the gown and once she's done, get the electronics running. Dr. Stelious, come with me please."

"So Marcus, this is our cocktail," Dr. Lewis said as he grabbed the IV bags from the refrigerator. "It's what makes it all work."

"What's in it?"

"Proprietary blend, it's going to be in the research paper. We can go through the details while she's under. Trust me, we'll have time."

"Don't see why I would stop trusting now."

The doctors walked into the room where Janice lay on the treatment table in her gown, her large white teeth drawing the attention of the men.

"I see you're ready," Dr. Lewis chuckled and hung the IV bag.

"Darn right I am," she said and cackled. The years of smoking had damaged her stage voice years ago, but she still knew how to project.

"Dr. Stelious, would you do the honors?" Dr. Lewis asked handing him the deep brain scanner.

"Absolutely," he responded and made quick work of the placement, aggressively setting the device down hard on top her head. She grimaced, but only for a moment. "I'm sorry. I'm used to placing these on persons who aren't able to give me feedback."

"That was subtle," Kyle said laughing in the observation room. A quick look from Dr. Lewis and the laughter ceased.

"Ok Janice, are you ready?"

"Ready."

"Kyle start the recording."

"Done."

"Ok Janice, let me just make sure . . . you've got . . . everything hooked up . . . ok, we got the pulse ox, the O2 coming into the mask, the BP cuff, heart monitor, EEG and deep scanner," he slowly listed the items out loud, double checking himself. "Well Janice. You consent to this treatment?"

"Yes I do Dr. Lewis," she said formally, without any showmanship.

"You'll feel a chill when the treatment is administered."

"I do remember the chill. Won't last any longer this time right?"

"No, no. Same as the time before."

"Ok doctor, I mean, doctors," she emphasized and winked to Dr. Stelious who stood back watching intently.

"Count down from 100 please," Dr. Lewis said as he pressed a few buttons on the IV pump.

"99, 98, 97, 9—."

"Ok Marcus, that's it. Hope you brought some reading material."

The hours went by quickly for the three men in the now small observation room. It had been designed to fit two men relatively comfortably, for a few hours at most. Not three men for an entire night. The office behind them had been dark for quite a while which made the observation room seem even more enclosed.

Dr. Stelious was peppering the researchers with question after question. Dr. Lewis had showed him Jack's videos, the EEG, the deep brain scan which was time stamped exactly matching the physical movements and talking seen on the videos. Dr. Lewis also showed him the post treatment video from Jack, the handwritten notes of the account, and, as if there was any doubt, Kyle was there to back up the evidence with his own experiences.

Dr. Lewis and Kyle also broke down their standard research, the parameters they follow, how they wake an individual, the cumulative results of thousands before the funding, and the hundreds since. It was important Dr. Stelious understand the previous parameters, in order to comprehend The Beyond Experience's parameters.

The third of six IV bags was hung about an hour earlier, and still no stirring from Janice. Her vitals were solid and Kyle continued to monitor the live videos for movement, as best he could. His wiped his eyes, hoping the daggers would go away. His body repeatedly made loud hollow noises emanating from deep within, angry with him for not fueling his body. His working out had driven his metabolism through the roof, and with them neglecting to account for an additional man, they were rationing food for the night. They were lucky it wasn't a survival scenario because the three researchers gave into their hunger and boredom over two hours prior.

Kyle adjusted his Cardinals hat and sighed heavily trying to drive the thoughts of food and sleep from his mind. When his eyes finally settled on the screens he noticed that camera four had switched on. It was focused on her left hand.

"Dr. Lewis, we've got some activity," Kyle said not taking his eyes away. Dr. Stelious burst up from his chair and strained his neck in order to get a close look at the large monitor.

"It's happening then, yes?" he asked rapidly, the smell of dry mouth and adrenaline quickly entering the air.

"It appears that way," Dr. Lewis said calmly while looking at Janice's vitals. "See there Marcus?" he said pointing to the EEG and the deep brain scanner.

"Oh my God. Nothing. Nothing at all? How is she moving her hand? How is she even breathing? She had a heart rate? What is going on Ethan?"

Suddenly they heard a muffled, but distinctly gravelly laugh. It was brief, so much so that the three of them each looked to one another for reassurance it had occurred. A second time, much louder and longer startled Dr. Stelious, and made him shiver.

"Dr. Lewis we need to know what is happening here. Can you imagine the ramifications? Without brain activity we are talking about systems that are intrinsic to the organs controlling themselves. This is undocumented, unresearched. Frankly, it's science fiction!"

"Marcus please, calm yourself. You see why I couldn't just tell you over the phone?"

"I do, indeed I do. Now. What do we do with this information?"

"Nothing, yet. I don't know how to. You'll see when she wakes. The experience is powerful, likely addictive, and let's face it," he said pointing to the monitors, "dangerous."

"I realize all of this Dr. Lewis but you have stumbled upon something quite unimaginable here. Remember, my research is focusing on whether people are capable of coming back from certain depths of brain inactivity. One must appreciate where I am coming from. This changes everything."

Dr. Lewis had heard enough. "You signed a non-disclosure agreement didn't you? I will decide what is important and what isn't. You're more than welcome to stay for this treatment, and many more if you'd like, but for now the decision has been made. The results stay in this room."

"You're right. I will stay true to my promise. But please, consider the possibilities."

"I already have."

Two more hours passed and the men were silent. Dr. Stelious was still trying to wrap his head around the idea of possible control centers throughout the body that had been unaccounted for in medicine, and, how that alone, could be a Nobel Prize.

Dr. Lewis sat considering Dr. Stelious' suggestions. He was focused on the experience however, not the ramifications. He knew the only person he would see in his session, should he ever go under again, was Lily. He had nobody else. He wasn't sure his father or mother were still alive, and they were the reason he suffered from anxiety and depression. At least that was before Lily treated him, so they wouldn't be there. Ethan even tried to predict what she would be wearing—a navy blue dress with white flowers. He always asked her to wear it. Her body wasn't curvy, in fact, it was rather like a rod, but in that blue dress she had noticeable hips. She would likely wear flats, being that heels always drove her crazy. She never enjoyed them, saying several times that she'd "rather be splashing around tidal pools in knee high boots looking for algae than walking downtown in heels."

Kyle was reflecting on the moments he was allowed to see his father, their conversations, the urge to see him again. Most days he fought off the jealousy for those being tested—especially Jack and Janice. It was difficult for Kyle to believe it wasn't happening for him again, that his father was just a treatment away. It seemed so close. He felt as though his father was waiting for him to come back. But, the thoughts that kept circling back were about the man sitting behind him, Ethan Lewis.

Kyle wanted to know the doctor's past. He wanted to talk to Dr. Lewis about the theory he had, that everyone was able to see the way prophets had seen. However, what ate at him was the last thing his father said in The Beyond Experience. "Lily still loves him." The look on Dr. Lewis' face was terror when he asked about Lily; and Kyle saying it was his own dead dog was the quickest lie he'd ever told.

# | SEVENTEEN |

Kyle sat on his couch watching television with his phone in hand. He continuously refreshed the page, willing an email from the anonymous woman on the forums. He had been refreshing his email every chance he had for the last two weeks since Dr. Stelious had visited and witnessed The Beyond Experience. Stelious was very concerned about the data, about proof of the theory, whether in support of a deep neural pathway, or a higher power.

"Imagine us who were created, finding a back door to experience the glories of the afterlife," he said smiling and patting Kyle on the shoulder. "Or maybe we just don't know what we're looking for yet Kyle. The proof will come. It has to."

Kyle was left anxious, distracted, thinking myopically about what he felt was the one way to turn Dr. Lewis and convince him of the theory. It had become a challenge, his calling. Kyle hadn't been swimming as much, spending most of his time sulking and praying for a response from the woman. It left him feeling frustrated. Most nights he would go to sleep telling himself *things will change tomorrow, you'll go back to the pool and refocus. If she writes, she writes.* But each morning came and went, finding himself staring at a spam filled Google mail account and barely catching any of the news.

Kyle was antsy, angry with himself and decided to stop sitting on the couch waiting and be proactive. He walked to the kitchen counter and stood there opening his laptop and opened the forum. He began reading post after post. It was all more of the same: individuals seeing heaven and a light, hell and darkness mixed with pain and suffering, all the stories ending in people going back to the church. He was bored, frustrated, and thinking only about that one woman's story. Over the next half hour, he had a hard time focusing on what he was reading, and only thought about her story. It was leaching into all the other stories, finding himself having read several paragraphs at a time, without retaining any of the information.

Finally, he decided to read her story once more. He read it methodically, feeling for her emotions, as if by some unseen force he would be reaching out to her. Kyle saw, once again, the anger in her writing. But, unlike the first time, he could see a soft spot in her. She seemed alone, unhappy, unloved, like she was left to just exist. The more he read, the more it sounded like she was angry that she survived. He began to wonder if this woman had tried to take her own life. He read the post again, from the beginning, realizing that after reading it twice, he hadn't seen a mechanism for her experience.

Every single post he read except for hers began with a backstory of how they ended up in their near death experience. Most often it was an accident: a car crash, electrocution, an illness, but in a few posts, it was self-inflicted. This woman, however, had no lead in. It was essentially a long angry post about how God didn't exist, and even though her experience was completely horrifying, she felt it was an experience generated by her brain. He decided to write her one more time.

Dear Anonymous,

I'm truly sorry for what you've been through. If I may be rude and ask the nature of how your specific near death experience began, I would love to know. To me, it appears as though you are angry that you survived and joined us back amongst the living. If that's the case, I'm sorry, and wish you felt happier here. I have written before, several weeks ago now, and this will be my last attempt. I am a researcher who studies a treatment for anxiety and depression, but we have also been working on these NDEs. Please feel free to respond, and understand I am not assuming you have been diagnosed with these diseases, nor am I saying you need treatment. I'm just being as transparent as I can be.

Sincerely,
Kyle

Kyle felt closure. He hadn't ever heard back from the anonymous woman but maybe this had been enough, for now. It was only 8:00 a.m., and he decided he would go to the later service at church. He strode into his room, grabbed his swim bag, a change of clothes, and a Clif Bar. He walked out into the crisp February air, taking a deep breath before heading to the pool. His phone vibrated in his pocket— an email.

Quickly he tapped the notifications and swiped in his security code. It was a response from the forums. It was hard to read with shaking hands and blurred eyes. He wiped his nervous tears away and tried to take deep calming breaths.

Kyle,

I appreciate you reaching out. I have been battling depression for as long as I can remember. I don't enjoy talking about my history, but you seem kind, so I guess I can share it. I did try to kill myself, and I was very angry I didn't succeed. I'm heavily medicated now, but on disability. I'm not sure what else I can tell you, or what I can do to help you, but I'm not really sure I want to either.

Annie

He stood frozen for a while. It seemed as though he was to be a sundial, his shadow moving around him as he stood rooted to the spot. Several people walked around him, preferring to take their chance on the wet grass rather than interrupt his deep thoughts as he stared into nothingness. His mind wasn't rushing, it was clear. He was simply shocked to have heard from her. Kyle walked to his car, threw the bag in, and headed to the pool. It was probably better he waited a few hours to respond, otherwise it may be too emotionally driven.

# | EIGHTEEN |

Twelve weeks had gone by and Kyle had spoken with Annie several times over email and messenger. He had even convinced her to enter the study. She was interviewed by Dr. Lewis, who passed her and allowed her to continue into the study. Kyle instructed her to lie about the history of suicide. Annie had grown very unpredictable while weaning off her meds for the last six weeks.

"Annie please, I promise it'll be ok."

"I'm just not sure I can do this. I doubt it's even going to work."

"Trust me just a little bit longer," Kyle said, his head in hand while leaning heavily onto the counter with his elbow.

"You don't know what this is like Kyle," she spat his name out. "I was fairly well controlled on the meds. Now that I'm off of them, who knows what I'll do right?"

"Ok Annie, please. We care. It's why we do this study. It has amazing results, you'll see."

"Speaking from experience? Yeah, I'm aware, you've told me several times now. Give up the party line and spare me. It's transparent. You're looking to make millions."

"Annie, I promise, nobody is making millions. We are researching and it's going very well, the results I mean."

"Do you think I'm an idiot?"

"Of course not," he sighed heavily.

"Oh that sounds convincing."

"Please just come, your appointment is at 10:00 a.m."

"Well if it doesn't work for me I'm telling Dr. Lewis everything. That you found me on a forum, that you convinced me to do the study, that you told me to lie about my overdose."

"If it doesn't work I'll tell him myself."

"No you won't either. Don't take that from me. I want to watch you squirm when he's ripping you a new one in front of all your friends."

She hung up and Kyle continued to hold his head in his hand. He wasn't going swimming.

As Kyle walked to his car he was distracted. The air from his lungs threw turbulent wind into open space, only noticeable on mornings like this. The heavy snow that dropped over the weekend was now piled high at the edge of the parking lots, creating a vastly different landscape as he walked to The Shack. He was forced to detour into the street for a block, traffic was typically minimal so he felt safe. He looked high into the grey skies that hinted at dropping another three inches. He blew a long, continuous breath outward toward the grey ceiling. He watched as fast air flew from his lungs straight toward the clouds above. Some of the molecules decelerated faster than others, and tumbled down the outside of the warm column of air creating rolling, twisting tails that only lived a moment. They disappeared into the overwhelming cold, waiting to be inhaled once more.

"You got frozen hair today?" Traci joked as she saw Kyle exit the elevator on the main treatment floor. He was always the last one to get to work but nobody cared.

"No swimming today. Slept in," he lied.

"Getting soft are we?" she snapped at him.

"Soft this," he said taking off his coat.

"All right kids let's get ready. First patients are coming in 20," Dr. Lewis said focusing the group.

Kyle was wrapping up with his first patient. It was 9:30 and he knew Annie would have to be there soon, if she was coming at all. He was also nervous about her response to the treatment. If it was negative, then he would have some serious explaining to do but, if it were positive, he wondered how would she react.

"How would you describe your experience?" he asked his patient, happy it was being recorded. He was taking poor notes, and barely listening to the response.

"Ok, how would you rate your level of happiness?" Kyle asked, once again not listening to the response.

"Well that does it for me, please take the written tests before you leave," he said forcing a smile, guiding her out of the room quickly, despite her trying to give him a hug.

Kyle sat in the observation room waiting for the 10:00 a.m. appointments to be called up to the second floor. His leg had a mind of its own, bouncing up and down as his eyes darted from the clock on the computer screen, to the clock on the wall, then toward Treatment Room One where Dr. Lewis would likely be seeing Annie. He began to feel warm, but all he had on was a polo shirt so there was nothing he could take off. He shifted in his chair as his abdomen began to cramp with anxiety.

*Bing.* The elevator chimed and in walked four people, three patients and Veronica. Kyle's heart sunk and his head fell down toward the desk. The months of reeling Annie in had failed. Heartbroken, he rose to his feet but then realized the only person he recognized was Veronica. Before him stood two women and one man he had never seen before.

"Wow big guy, never seen you excited about a no show before. You feeling aright?" Veronica asked Kyle who stood staring at the four of them.

"I'm just shocked is all." One of the women smiled.

She was cute, black hair, brown roots showing. She looked to be no more than 24, younger than her gravelly voice and her long history would suggest. Her posture was poor and her form was barely visible though her baggy clothes. Her eyes darted around the facility, searching, but seemingly looking for objects that couldn't look back at her in an attempt to avoid human contact.

"Hello Annie," Dr. Lewis said guiding his patient into Treatment Room One. "Thanks for coming in. That's Kyle over there, would you mind if he joined us? He looks a little bored and his patient has not shown up."

"Oh, the more the merrier," she said without affect, for the first time looking toward a person, and staring into Kyle's eyes with her own dark, lifeless orbs.

"Just like old times huh?" Kyle said to Dr. Lewis.

"Exactly what I was thinking," he said with his back toward Kyle, guiding Annie to Treatment Room One.

She stood for a moment, eyes locked onto Kyle. He felt as though she was willing the treatment to fail. It was almost as if she would prefer to live in misery so long as she had a companion, and right now, she wanted Kyle to keep her company.

"You coming Annie?" Dr. Lewis asked a moment later, now in the treatment room.

"Yes." She turned from Kyle and glided into the treatment room after Dr. Lewis.

"Kyle," Dr. Lewis yelled. "Can you get the electronics going? Old time's sake?"

Kyle nodded and headed into the observation room, and began entering Annie's information into the system, then readied the equipment. "Oh Lord please let this go well," he said aloud to himself as he watched Dr. Lewis begin his pre-treatment checks.

Kyle sat quietly in the observation room with Dr. Lewis. Kyle's eyes were glued to Annie's vitals, willing them to go down quickly but his prayers had no affect on her physiology. His own physiology, however, was a different story. His palms were clammy, his mouth dry, and his heart was racing. He felt his pulse in his fingers, neck, and foot, all seeming more intense with each passing moment. He thought about running away, hiding in the third floor office one last time before he was fired by Dr. Lewis for trying to influence the study.

Dr. Lewis was quiet as well, simply watching the monitors and waiting, Annie was just another patient to extract data from. Thirty minutes passed and finally Dr. Lewis saw something.

"Well there she goes," he said to Kyle, bumping him with a soft elbow to the arm. He pointed to camera four, "Her mouth is moving."

"Yup, good to know, I'll write it down in the log for you," Kyle said with a smile. It was forced, but Dr. Lewis hadn't looked over anyway.

"What?!" she exclaimed loudly from the treatment room. Both men shot up into their chairs and peered directly into the room through the glass.

"That was very loud," Dr. Lewis said not taking his eyes off of Annie.

"I've never heard anyone talk that loud in here," Kyle stated, focused only on her. His anxiety had left and curiosity had taken over.

"Me neither."

"What am I doing here?" she said even louder with a voice that was many times larger than her.

"This is strange, right?" Kyle said.

"It's fantastic."

"Oh how beautiful," she cooed, reaching upward with her hand, the movement noticed by all the researchers who now stood, at least for the moment, behind Dr. Lewis and Kyle.

"She's really feelin' it, isn't she?" Adam said smacking Kyle in the shoulder.

"Oh is she? I can probably get that loud," Veronica teased and pinched Adam's chest. He pulled away in pain and rubbed his chest furiously.

*Bing, bing, bing.* The machines chimed.

"Her BP hit the mark, time to bring her out. Everyone back to their rooms," Dr. Lewis said. He walked into the room and administered the epinephrine.

She awoke slowly, a smile emerging on her face.

"Annie, are you ok?" Dr. Lewis asked smiling.

"I'm incredible."

"How would you rate your happiness currently?"

"Ten."

"How would you describe your experience?"

Annie sat for a moment, reflecting on her experience. It had been years since she tried to take her own life. The clarity she had in this moment almost made her cry. She was angry with herself for considering her selfish act, forcing her parents to watch another child die. She looked toward the observation room where Kyle stood frozen in the doorway. Immediately she felt a connection with him which she hadn't felt in all their conversations.

A stirring in her stomach reminded her of a time in her childhood where she was standing at the top of a waterslide. She wanted to go down but in the moment she felt scared, excited. She felt that same way when she looked at Kyle.

"Like breaking out of hell and seeing there's a better life for me," she said continuing to look at Kyle, his blue eyes blazing in the light of the lab. She smiled and looked away.

"That's amazing, I've very happy for you. Anything else you'd like to say?"

"Thank you. I'm indebted to you. You have no idea."

"Thank you but that's not necessary. Please fill out the questionnaires before you leave, and make sure you set up your long-term follow-up." Dr. Lewis hadn't realized it but everything she said was directed at Kyle. She felt free of her burdens, her faults, her failures because of this treatment. She wanted to pay him back but didn't know how.

Annie began to change back into her clothes. She took her time and watched for Kyle to be behind the observation room window.

"Are the mics still on?" she said when she noticed it was just Kyle in the observation room.

"Yeah Annie, they are."

"Good," she said turning now fully dressed.

"Were you watching me get dressed you pervert?"

"Uh, no Annie, I wasn't, you know that. Please try and be professional. Others may walk in and hear this. Then we are screwed," he whispered from the doorway into the room. He quickly went back and turned off the AV equipment and slowly walked into the room with her.

"You're younger than I thought you were," he said crossing his arms.

"What does that change?"

"Nothing."

"Hmmm. Not sure I believe it."

"How incredible do you feel?"

"Beyond amazing. How long does this feeling last?"

"We're not really sure. Nobody's ever come back for a second treatment though. I can tell you that."

"Well ok. I'm done with meds?"

"Appears that way."

"I'm sorry I was so rude to you, you must hate me."

"Please don't apologize. Just come out to dinner with me."

She laughed and looked down at the ground. "Are you allowed to do that?"

"I don't care if I am or not. Hasn't been discussed. Plus, I can be a rule breaker once in a while right?"

"You have been known to do that. You have my number. Call me." She fought the urge to explode onto her tiptoes and kiss him on the cheek. He saw her hesitation and smiled.

Annie was feeling amazing. She had gone to a salon, had her hair dyed back to a medium brown, her natural color that hadn't been seen in years. She had a makeover and bought everything the women at Sephora threw at her, taking the freebies as well. She was amazed at how the world was treating her differently, or so it seemed. Maybe it had always been her outlook on life, or maybe she just focused on the negatives. Either way, she wanted to stay happy like she was now.

Kyle had called her two days earlier and made plans. He wanted to be outside of the city, away from prying eyes, and it made sense. The last thing she wanted was to screw up his career and the treatment made her feel so good again. Since she met him she fell hard for him. It wasn't the treatment, it was his physique, his smile, his honest eyes, and thick hair.

She wanted to be beautiful for him, which was foreign to her. She hadn't wanted to be beautiful for anyone, ever. She remembered having crushes, being made fun of, and sitting at home when prom came and went. Some girls had been nice to her in school, even more when in college, but she never allowed herself to be brought in. Her self doubt and shyness overwhelmed her every attempt. She hadn't gone to social events like football games and parties, too afraid of what others would think or say. But now, as she stood looking into the mirror at this stranger that stood before her, she felt energized and confident.

The sweater she chose to wear was form fitting, and her jeans were as well, but she still remained figureless, an effect of the limited body fat. The curves that presented themselves were an artifact of bony prominences more than anything else but she shrugged it off, a bit sorry for her old self. He'd be there in thirty minutes but she was all ready to go so she just sat and waited, watching out the window for a car she didn't recognize, keeping a man she wanted warm and safe.

The EdgeWild Restaurant was busy, even for a Saturday night. A live band, Restricted by Bluejeans, a local favorite, was playing. They played upbeat comical music for a middle-aged crowd. They played at the EdgeWild once a month and had developed quite the cult following.

"Reservation for two, Kyle," he said entering the restaurant.

"Ok Kyle, I've got you. Follow Cassie, she's going to take you to the firepit while you wait for your table. It'll be ready in about ten minutes."

"Thank you," Annie said beating him to the response. She grabbed him by the arm and pulled him along, following close behind Cassie.

"You seem so nervous Kyle. Don't be. It's gonna be so fun!"

"I'm not nervous," he lied. Seeing her tonight caught him off guard. She was beautiful, her hair wasn't dark and ignored, but lively, and it bounced when she walked. Her eyes sparkled since the treatment, beautiful instead of haunting, like a smoky quartz.

"Ok just wait here until your table is ready. The bar is over there and you can bring your drinks here. Just don't throw them on the fire."

"Seriously? You have to say that?" Annie asked with a laugh that she covered with her hand.

"Yeah, unfortunately some idiot did that last week. He got second degree burns too when the fire followed the alcohol back to the glass and caught his jacket on fire."

"What a jackass," Kyle said confused at humanity.

"Thanks Cassie, have a good night."

"Want a drink?" Annie asked before Kyle could.

"Uh, yeah, just a beer, whatever's on tap."

"Oh, classy guy," she joked and smiled, her teeth a bit pointy, but all in their places.

He smiled and watched her walk away.

"Oh God help me get through this night," he said quietly to himself. His nervousness was palpable, even to the strangers around him. Kyle was always a great friend to anyone, but he never was the dated guy; always handsome, but never in love, he wouldn't allow it. Not that he hadn't wanted to, but when it came down to a serious situation, he clammed up.

"Were you a dancer?" Kyle asked when Annie came back, two beers heavy.

"Yeah, how'd you know?" she said taking a sip, and making a face.

"I don't know actually. I was watching you walk. You're light on your feet."

"Well, you watched me walk away huh?" she winked and choked down another sip.

"What's wrong with you?" he asked holding back a laugh.

"How do people drink this crap!" She handed him the beer.

"What is it?"

"Beer stupid!" she said with wide eyes and a silly look.

"You've never had this kind before, or you've never had a beer?"

"I've lived a sheltered life."

"Wow woman. We're gonna break that shell of yours."

She slapped him on the arm and although he tried to absorb it, beer still vaulted out of the top of the stein and onto his sleeve. They both laughed and she leaned into him.

Dinner was great, the conversation was led by the music with lyrics that highlighted common misunderstandings between lovers and friends. Kyle ordered a few drinks, a margarita, a rum and coke, and a martini just to see if Annie liked any of them. She hadn't, but all the sipping gave her a buzz and so she was very giggly and touchy. She grabbed Kyle's hand several times across the table throughout dinner; each time a little more lasting and more comforting to both of them.

The ride home was fun, too. They sang loudly to songs that played years ago, taking each of them back to when they were innocent and naïve. For Kyle, it was days spent with his father and for Annie, it was days spent with her twin brother.

"Kyle," she said as the car came to a halt in front of her condo building.

"Uh oh, you aren't feeling sick are you?"

"No, well, a bit like everything is spinning."

"Do you want me to come up?"

"Not for sex if that's what you're getting at," she snapped.

"I wasn't thinking that. Honest. I'm a good boy," he smiled.

"Ok. Please come up. I don't want to be alone feeling like this."

Kyle drove around to the parking lot. He helped her to her feet and up the stairs to the fifth floor and into her two-bedroom apartment. It was expansive, he estimated it at 2,000 square feet, but sparsely decorated. A moderately sized LCD TV decorated one wall, a small entertainment stand beneath holding an Apple TV.

"Set me on the couch," she said pointing to the green furniture. There were two couches, the longer of the two was clearly worn and the other, barely touched. He walked her to the worn couch.

"I'll get you something to drink kid."

"Thanks," she said placing her forearm over her eyes, attempting to stop the spinning.

The kitchen had a sink full of dishes and an empty refrigerator. There was a box that used to have bottles of water, but they were all gone. Kyle began opening cabinets and found a glass. He had to remove several dishes just to get the glass under the faucet but finally he had something for her to drink.

"Here," he said handing it to her. She sat up slowly and took a few sips. "I'm going to do your dishes. Let me know if you need anything." She nodded and took another sip.

"I'm glad I sobered up a bit. The water helped," Annie said when Kyle came into the living room 20 minutes later.

"Good, glad to see you're feeling yourself."

"Not quite there yet, but yes, better."

"Good enough for a tour?"

"Sure why not. You've seen the living room and kitchen—"

"How 'bout the bathroom," he said cutting her off and smiling.

"Down the hall, first door on the right."

Kyle washed his hands and got a good look at himself in the mirror before leaving the bathroom. Silently, he thanked his father for advising him to get out and date. On the way back toward the living room he saw the only picture in the house, an image of two young children. He paused, studying it for a moment. It was an undefined beach, but that was merely the backdrop for the children. It was a black and white, but he could tell from the young girl's eyes, it was Annie.

"That's me and my brother," she said walking up from behind him.

"It's a great picture."

"I'm tired now Kyle, I think I should sleep."

"Fair enough. I had a really great time. Been a while since I've been out with someone."

"I did too, we can do it again. If you want."

"I'm in," he said getting close enough to feel her breath on him.

"Goodnight Kyle." She walked him to the door and locked it behind him. She felt sad. She thought about her brother and walked back into the hallway to see him. It was likely the last picture ever taken of Jeremy. Annie reflected on that moment. She closed her eyes and went back to that summer when she was eight and they were at their family vacation home in Michigan. It had been a long day of building castles, riding jet skis, and eating watermelon. She and Jeremy had run races on the beach, flown kites, and took a nap in the shade of an umbrella. The two had been inseparable that day more than any other. Or at least that's how she remembered it.

He woke her up early the next morning, whispering about going to the water while it was calm. She remembered grumbling at him in a sleepy haze, then closing her eyes to dream once more. A few hours later she was awoken again by screams from her mother who had found Jeremy's lifeless body on the beach. Initially her mom had blamed Annie for not coming to her about Jeremy's plan, but she ultimately apologized after realizing it wasn't her fault at all. Her mom continued to apologize for the next year as they all dealt with depression. Annie just hadn't gotten over it.

She tried to refocus on the day she had with Kyle. It was the first time she enjoyed someone else's company since her brother died. She thought about his smile as she brushed her teeth, changed her clothes, and allowed the spinning of the room to rock her to sleep.

# | NINETEEN |

The weeks had marched slowly, each day longer in the cold, dead air. The days were even longer when there was little to do. Dr. Brian Lacey sat behind his wide cherrywood desk. He wasn't a man of elegant taste. It was simply that the less expensive desks were too small for his frame. He was holding office hours but students rarely came. They all seemed to ask questions via email, having limited interpersonal skills in the digital era. Even licensed practitioners had computers with them everywhere they went leaving them with their faces glued to the glowing screen rather than their patients.

Dr. Lacey had spent the afternoon reading research articles, catching up on the latest findings in the world of neurologic research. He came across very little fresh material, more or less different versions of the same things, neural pathways being mapped through the brain, spinal cord neural regeneration or mechanisms to go around injured tissue. One article piqued his interest. It focused on a device worn on the head that picked up the neural signals from the brain that signaled movement. It then sent the signal to a device placed on the arm that sent electric stimulation to the corresponding muscles for the movement. Persons who had been unable to use their hands were then able to perform gross and fine motor tasks.

Reading the articles was only frustrating him more. He had recently been notified he wouldn't receive funding for his research. It was the second year in a row the disappointing news had been given to him, and seeing others with funding that were simply replicating others work was driving him to a deeper level of anxiety and jealousy. To add fuel to the fire, Dr. Lacey had also just received his invitation to attend this year's research conference, but not to speak. He did, however, remember one individual who was supposed to talk: Dr. Ethan Lewis.

The thought of Dr. Lewis' work was inconceivable to Dr. Lacey. He wasn't sure if it was boredom or anger that drove him to read Dr. Lewis' research article once again. Lacey was combing through the article, looking for any small argument to be made.

"Ketamine, propofol, etomidate, thiopental, methohexital, and *Convallaria majalis.*"

"Where did you pull this formula from?" he grumbled aloud as he read the ingredients in the treatment cocktail. "*Convallaria majalis?* Why that particular plant?"

He Googled it, Lily of the Valley. Then it hit him hard as a linebacker on the blind side of a quarterback. Lily.

Dr. Lacey then searched for any more information on the flower, where it's grown, the effects of the drug on the human system, where to buy it, if at all. He looked at pictures, read a few blogs, and even saw a couple sites highlighting how to produce a deadly poison from the extract. *Poison,* he thought and paused from reading. *Hallucinogenic?* His mind went back to the previous year's talk where Dr. Lewis showed a female on a table experiencing a vivid world she considered heaven.

Lacey began to laugh as a case began to build against his former classmate. It could be relatively easy to sway people who were so moved by Dr. Lewis' presentation. It was a distinct possibility the researcher had simply gotten people high while they were under, effectively being a very well funded drug dealer.

"Biomedical research greenhouses," Dr. Lacey searched, trying to determine who may be supplying Dr. Lewis.

His first hit was a press release from a company called Whitestone. It detailed how they stepped into the realm of research. The release was only a couple months old. It made Lacey smile and rest back into his large brown leather chair. He swiveled around and faced the small shelves that lined the back of his office and thought. His hands were folded, elbows on armrests and his index fingers supporting his smooth chin. As he sat, he gently rocked back and forth putting together a timeline of events. The longer he thought the more he was convinced it was Whitestone that was growing the plants for Dr. Lewis and his research.

It wasn't hard to find information on Whitestone. There were dozens of sites that popped up when he searched the company. He made quick work of navigating their official website and found the name Elias Grant, the CEO. He saw a general phone number and decided to call.

"Hello, thank you for calling Whitestone, this is Mariah, how can I assist you?" a buttery voice greeted him.

"My name is Dr. Brian Lacey. I am a researcher at Madison and I stumbled upon your company's release regarding biomedical research. I am looking for assistance as well. Who may I talk to regarding this?"

"I will put you through to Seth. He's Elias Grant's assistant."

"Thank you very much," he said through the receiver. She could tell by his voice he was smiling. It was the first time he smiled in months. He had written and rewritten submission after submission to get funding for his research. They had all come back "no." They even called him after his last submission to ask him to discontinue submitting without new findings.

"This is Seth. How may I help you Dr. Lacey?" a man's voice said.

"Hi Seth. My name is Brian Lacey and I've recently come across your press release regarding biomedical research assistance," he said as an idea emerged. "I'm looking to grow a specific plant."

"Well Dr. Lacey, I believe Mr. Grant may be willing to discuss this. Can I have you hold for a moment?"

"Sure," Dr. Lacey said in a drawn out way only a southerner could have.

"This is Elias Grant. Great to hear from you Dr. Lacey. I must say, we haven't worked with biomedical till very recently and I'm excited you're calling."

"I am too," Dr. Lacey said, veiling the truth. "I'm wondering if you could help me."

"What is it you need?"

"A plant to be grown, in a relatively large quantity. Does that sound like a possibility?"

A pause, brief, but noticeable. "We can help you out there I believe. You just need to give me a little more info."

"It's called *Convallaria majalis*."

"I know the name, Lily of the Valley. Somebody put you up to this?"

"I don't follow."

"Did someone ask you to approach me about this?"

"No sir, just doing some research with the plant, but now you've got me curious."

"Don't be. No need." Elias dismissed it quickly, trying to find his rhythm again.

"I think I know why you asked," Dr. Lacey said not giving up. He could tell Elias was rattled, and not at all excited about it, but he also knew he was close. "You may know a paranoid colleague of mine, Dr. Ethan Lewis."

"I do."

"I'm also assuming you have a non-disclosure with him." A telling silence ensued. "Clear your throat if I'm on to something."

"Ehhem," Elias said and chuckled.

"Let's just say he wouldn't mind me expanding the growth so to speak."

"Well, I have to admit our last two quarters have done much better since we began the biomedical work. We'll talk more soon I think Dr. Lacey."

# | TWENTY |

## Chicago | Winter 2007

It was a beautiful night. Veronica huddled into Adam tightly for warmth, her medium length dress was lacking in that department. He enjoyed feeling her leaning into him as he wrapped his arm tightly around her. They made quick work of the walk into the John Hancock Building from their taxi.

Their reservation at the Signature Room was 6:00 p.m., a relatively early dinner but it was the easiest way to ensure a window seat overlooking Michigan Avenue. From ninety-five floors above the busy streets below he knew she would lose herself.

"I still don't understand where we're going," Veronica said as they entered the elevator that would shuttle them up to the restaurant without any stops.

"Just wait," he said, making sure she was always on his left side. In his right suitcoat pocket hid a special gift for her—a ring his mother, Julie, had given him when they arrived earlier that morning. It had been his grandmother's, whom he'd never met, and she had gotten it from her mother.

"I love you," she said reaching over to kiss his cheek, her tall heels helped her almost look straight into his eyes.

"Glad to hear you say that," he smiled.

The thousand-foot ascent was quick, highlighted by everyone yawning, trying to acclimate their ears to the pressure changes. The doors opened to reveal a panoramic view of the city at night. Far toward the east they saw darkest hues of purple and blue as the sun just set moments earlier. But, as beautiful as that palette was, it was a distant second to the scene Veronica was trying to take in: dozens of full tables, couples enjoying a romantic evening, waiters hustling elegantly, crisscrossing the dining area with precision. The windows stretched high all around, allowing limitless views of amber lights and small streaks slowly tracing their way down dark channels toward unknown destinations. Standing in the restaurant Adam felt apart from the city below, but craved its beauty and admired its precision.

"Mr. Nicholson," a man in a bowtie asked, his arm covered with a folded white towel.

"Yes," he responded with a smile, and felt Veronica squeeze his arm with hers.

"Right this way sir," he said gesturing him to follow. "I think you will be happy with your seating," he said looking back over his shoulder and smiling. "Here we are."

"It's incredible, honey!" Veronica said without taking her eyes off the city lights.

"That's Michigan Avenue," Adam said pointing down toward the bustling street below. "Thank you," Adam said turning to address the waiter, shaking his hand and placing a small cloth sack into his hand. He squeezed the waiters hand firmly, both men locking eyes, making sure they understood one another.

Veronica was transfixed by the lights, the structures, the lines. Adam had glanced out the window several times, but only because she was pointing things out to him. He found his happiness in hers, glad that he made this night possible, but was anxious knowing it wasn't quite over.

"Here is your dessert wine," the waiter said leaving two small glasses of white on the table.

"Thank you," Adam said nodding subtly at the waiter who winked at him from behind Veronica.

"Dessert wine?" she asked breaking her stare and looking at the table.

"Yeah. Nice place like this, figured we'd go for it you know?"

"I'm stuffed honey. I just don't want to leave this view."

"Well, sip the wine. We can milk it a while I'm sure. What are they gonna do, kick us out?"

She glanced back out the window and blindly grasped for the wine. Adam watched her bring it gently to her lips and take a tiny sip. The ring inside tilted and fell, clanking itself against the side of the glass. Veronica hadn't heard or seen. Adam smiled and watched. A second sip, another clink gone unnoticed. A third, fourth, and fifth, all unnoticed. Adam fought the urge to laugh, knowing that the romance would fizzle if he had to explain why he was laughing at her.

Finally, on the sixth repetition, she tilted the glass back far enough to feel the ring slide up the side of the glass and rest against her upper lip. Quickly, she brought the glass down thinking something was wrong. She glanced inside and saw something shimmering in the bottom. She snapped her head up and looked at Adam who was getting up from his chair. She looked down again and the image at the bottom of the glass had become clear. She quickly tipped the glass out saw the golden ring contrast dramatically against her plate covered in chocolate sauce.

"Veronica Martinez. The moment I first saw you I never even thought I had a chance. Your beautiful hair, your loving eyes, the way you make me feel is incredible. I can't go a day without a touch from you, and I love you. Just seeing you makes me feel weak and strong all at once." He reached onto her plate and grabbed the ring. Giggling, Veronica watched as he wiped the chocolate off of his great grandmother's ring.

"This ring made its way all the way here from England, worn by my grandmother I never met, given to her by her mother. When I told my mom I wanted to do this she insisted you have it." Adam paused, thinking of his mother for a moment and how she begged to come with tonight but he said no over and over again. "Will you marry me?"

Veronica was crying and smiling. It was difficult, but she could see him just over the top of the wall of tears that rested on her eyelid. She couldn't speak, but she could move. Her head was bobbing up and down as she opened her arms wide for him to come and grab her. He did, and lifted her gently off the ground, turning her slowly in a circle as the amber light silhouetted them against the window. A small avalanche of applause cascaded through the restaurant and the waiter brought out champagne for them.

"Can we stay here a while? Maybe just go up to the lounge?"

"Whatever you want, fiancé," Adam joked. Typically, that would have gotten him an eye-roll but tonight, it got him a kiss.

## Saint Louis | Winter 2007

Annie sat in her apartment, happy with her latest changes. Kyle had helped her paint nearly every wall in the house and it really changed the way it felt. It was now a home. She also covered the walls with a few bargain pieces of art from Hobby Lobby, as well as several pictures.

The wall in the living room now displayed a dozen pictures of Kyle, both with and without Annie. One picture had Kyle's face covered in food, another was the two of them kissing gently in a bar. Annie had taken the picture herself so the image wasn't great but captured a moment in time she loved. Another was from the zoo on a snow filled day. Kyle hadn't been impressed with the experience but she loved every minute because it was with him. Her favorite picture was from their first double date at Anthonino's Taverna. They were sitting, leaning in toward one another for a group shot. Kyle was nervous to do the double date, but she convinced him it would be ok. As soon as Veronica and Adam showed up Kyle was relaxed, the anxiety was gone, and they had a great night. In fact, it had been the night Adam told her and Kyle he was going to propose. Veronica had stepped away to go to the bathroom which gave him the chance. Annie loved that moment. It wasn't because it was a dream she had for herself, it was the fact that she was trusted to hear such an intimate detail of someone's life. It was the acceptance she had never felt before.

*Knock, knock, knock.* Someone was at her door. She checked through the peephole and saw Kyle. Her heart quickened and she let him in. She couldn't help feeling excited, despite her nervousness.

"Hey baby," he said kissing her on the cheek and showing her a bottle of red wine. He looked into the living room and spotted a glass already half empty on the new end table. The bottle rested next to it, a cork gently placed back inside. "Started without me I see," he said smiling.

"Um, yeah." She smiled playfully.

She had buried her pain for long enough and tonight was the night, she promised herself, for the third time in a row.

"Everything ok?"

"You're here. Everything is amazing," she said wiggling her tiny body in next to his, squeezing him hard around the waist, but leaving Kyle feeling little pressure.

"What d'ya wanna do?"

"Movie?"

"Fine with me. I'll grab a glass and meet you on the couch."

The movie wasn't memorable. Annie spent the entire time thinking of how to tell the story of her brother's death while Kyle's head bobbed in pitiful attempts to stay awake. He had been working long hours trying to gather the research data and begin sorting through it for statistical analysis. He was also swimming regularly again, which meant getting up earlier than he'd like because he prioritized his evenings with Annie.

The movie finally ended, but not before the two bottles of wine. Annie was laying on Kyle's chest as it rhythmically lifted and dropped her shoulders. He was asleep but she was finally ready to talk. She had gotten used to the room spinning, having felt it now on several occasions, but her concern at the moment was how to wake him without feeling bad.

"Ahem," she cleared her throat. "Ahem!" Again a bit louder, but still nothing. She attempted to squirm, and he stirred and settled. She sat up and watched him, fighting the urge to push him hard. It was mesmerizing for her to watch him sleep, the steady flow of air in and out, the gentle rising of his powerful chest, trained for efficiency in breathing by years of work in the pool. She could hear the sound of turbulent air moving through the airways, the pause of gas exchange, and the slight change in pitch as the air rushed out of him.

She touched his arm gently, her nails finally long enough to gently scratch, almost tickle his skin the way he liked. She had always bitten her nails down but since the treatment she had progressively broken the habit.

She traced his veins, the ones raised from his skin like small blue hoses lying across a barren landscape. She imagined herself as a small being, flowing through his venous network, completely free of choices and following a current that ultimately lead to his heart—a heart that she desperately wanted to have all to herself. For the first time in her life she was in love; vulnerable. Loss wasn't something she'd handled well.

"Hey, I'm sorry I fell asleep. I think the wine got me. These hours have been killin' me," he said as he woke, gently kissing her hair.

"It's ok, I didn't mind."

"Well, both bottles are already gone. Sure you're ok?" he asked smiling.

She paused, holding her breath before she spoke, willing herself to say what she wanted with the very breath she held. "No," she said opening the gates to the conversation she had replayed in her head for weeks. Her heart was pounding and she wished she had the two-letter word back.

"What's wrong, sweetie?" he said softly, empathy spilling over into words.

"I need to tell you something about my brother," she said softly, not looking him in the eyes.

"You can tell me. Please tell me."

"That picture. The one you always stare at. It's the last picture he ever took. The next morning, he went out to swim in the lake by himself and drowned. My mom found him on the beach, dead."

"I don't know what to say." Kyle shifted in his seat, hoping the movement would cause her to sit up, and it did. He hugged her tightly, allowing her to cry into his shirt.

"It's all my fault Kyle," she said sobbing.

"What?"

"It is. It really is. He came to me in the morning and asked me to come with—"

"Then you'd both be dead," Kyle said interrupting, "and I wouldn't have met you."

"I should have stopped him, told my parents, anything other than fall back asleep!"

"You should have stopped blaming yourself a long time ago. How old were you, seven? Maybe eight?"

"Eight."

"So do you think it's fair an eight year-old goes their whole life feeling responsible for their sibling's death? It's not your fault sweetheart," he said calmly, holding her face in his hands and trying to grab a look into her dark eyes. Finally, she did, and his heart melted. He was drawn back into his own memory of guilt with his dying father. For a long time he felt he could have done more, maybe should have reached out to more doctors. But, since seeing his father in The Beyond Experience his guilt had evaporated. He was guilt free knowing his father was happy, safe, and where he belonged. Annie's red eyes were a reminder of how terrible grief was in people's lives, and was a window into her own personal torment.

"It's why I don't believe in God," she said sniffling, the last of the tears had fallen and she was recovering, the anger at a God allowing him to die helped drive the sorrow away.

"Why?"

"Because I asked him to save my brother. I asked hundreds of times while my father did CPR, while the paramedics came and used the defibrillator," she paused and her eyes welled up once again, "I asked him to let me die when I took those pills."

"What about the treatment? You saw amazing things right?"

"I'm not convinced I believe it's heaven, or that one exists at all."

"I won't force your hand," he said holding back his biggest secret. In Kyle's mind, he wanted Annie to go back in, to go into The Beyond Experience, but he needed to talk to Dr. Lewis first.

# | TWENTY-ONE |

## Summer 2008

Dr. Lewis was burning out. The long workdays were compounded by night after night of limited sleep. He was no longer distracted by the idea to test the limits of their treatment. Three different people had all enlightened him to the experience. A new need in him grew stronger by the day. It was one thing to witness and hear about the incredible sensory experience and the unimaginable excitement of seeing a lost loved one, but to experience it would be incredible. He sat reflecting on Lily as an old buried story from their past came to him.

They had been young, 24, and only knew each other for a few months but he was willing to go with her to New York to see her "stomping grounds." Lily had promised multiple times leading up to the trip that Ethan wouldn't have to meet her family; the staunch Christians who had no reservations about laying on the judgment. Lily knew his history. She was the first and only person who knew about his past. She had a way of making it easy for him to talk to her. Maybe it was her eyes, how they stared into his, so confident and focused he had no choice but to believe she was truly listening. Her empathy seemed to know no boundaries as she cried for him on many occasions. She would always hug him tightly after he stopped talking, which made him feel relieved, accepted, loved.

The two of them were staying at her friend Tiffany's house. Lily said her parents didn't really know Tiffany so there was little chance of word getting back to them that she was in town. The three of them went out to a bar that Friday night. It was their first, and ultimately their only night in the big city.

The bar was full, but comfortably so. Everyone who wanted a table had one and the music was upbeat, with a few throwbacks here and there to appeal to the young business men and women who frequented the establishment. The three of them were several drinks into the evening when Lily and Tiffany started to dance with each other. It was more playful than sensual, but sometimes that didn't matter. Ethan saw him. A lonely man at the end of the bar in a flannel shirt and jeans, a bottle was constantly at his lips which made it hard to see his face, but Ethan saw his eyes. This man's eyes never left the two women Ethan was with.

He watched the mysterious man while the girls went laughing on to the dance floor. Ethan saw the man turn his back to the bar top and continue tracking the women with his menacing eyes. It didn't take long for the stranger to stand and walk toward Lily and Tiffany on the dance floor. The two of them accounted for 40 percent of the dancers so it wasn't hard for the man to get close to them. Ethan saw his face now. It appeared he hadn't shaven in a week, nor made any attempts to calm his wild hair. He also had a tongue ring, which he wasted no time showing Lily and Tiffany. He was taller than Ethan, and broad, just like his father had been; or so he remembered; he had grown quite a bit since emancipating himself.

Ethan watched as the man made several attempts to dance with them, but they found ways to squeeze him out and move to another spot on the small dance floor. Ethan laughed with them as they maneuvered and dodged the man several times but the joke was getting old, especially for the stranger. He grabbed Tiffany by the arm forcefully. She pulled away and looked toward Ethan who was getting up from the stool. Then the man grabbed Lily by the arm and slapped her in the face.

Ethan felt an unfamiliar flame inside of him ignite. His breathing quickened and his heart was pounding. He was deaf to the world around him, his senses focusing only on what he was seeing. He wasn't a child any more but he remembered the sting of flesh on flesh, his mother had conditioned him to that. He grabbed the larger man from behind. With his right hand he swung him around and landed his left fist straight into the stranger's cheekbone. Ethan felt nothing in his hand, but knew all too well the feeling of knuckles to cheek. That he had learned from his father. The flannel-shirted man still stood, wobbling on his feet, he opened one eye, finding Ethan ready as landed another strong left into the man's face. By now, the stranger was bleeding over his right eye; a collapsed orbit deformed his face. A third time he struck the man in the face, this time drawing blood from his knuckles as he broke several of the man's teeth.

One of the bartenders came running over to the dance floor.

"I saw the whole thing. You guys just get the hell outta' here," he said quickly as he pressed into Ethan's shoulders, looking him in the eyes trying to gain his focus and trust. "I would have done the same thing, man. Get the ladies home. I'll handle the cops when they come. I have to call them."

"Thank you," Lily said to the bartender as she held her own face. The sting from the stranger still throbbing.

"Get her some ice, then we'll leave," Ethan said, still clenching his fists together. Ethan glanced down at the floor where the man lay, staining the floor with sticky, viscous blood.

The cab home was silent except for the driver, who insisted on telling jokes for the entire ten-minute drive back to Tiffany's. Ethan went up to her place, grabbed his things, and left, driving back toward Harvard.

Ethan hadn't calmed down. He was terrified at his response to the situation. He thought he might be turning into his father and knew one of two things would have to happen: he would leave Lily in order to protect her, or she would see his true self and leave him. Either way, he saw himself losing her and he began to panic. The road at night was dark, and a thick fog had rolled that further limited his vision. More than once he was surprised by curve to the right or left, leaving him panicked trying to stay on the road.

Finally, he was defeated and pulled into a rest stop. As he sat there alone, he thought through the evening's events. The excitement of the city, the way Lily interacted with Tiffany, and how comfortable she was to be back home. He felt foreign, both in geography and emotion, feeling accepted by more than just Lily and it made him feel exposed. He wanted to make sure everything went well. He had read Tiffany's look correctly, she wanted him to come and take care of the situation but when he saw Lily hurt he snapped.

Ethan realized in that moment that he wasn't his father. He wasn't a drunk, a manipulator, a deadbeat. He was motivated, intelligent, empathetic. His rage came from a need to help someone, not abuse. It was simply a manifestation of his need to protect and watch over another person. He had never experienced these primal emotions and reactions before. Lily was his only person, and he knew now what he was feeling: love.

He started the car and raced back toward the city. His clarity of mind seemed to lift the still present fog as he screamed down the highway without a glance down to the speedometer. He got to Tiffany's apartment and knocked on the door continuously until someone answered it.

"Ethan?" Tiffany groaned as she opened the door and saw it was Ethan. She was clearly half asleep and vaguely waved him past her.

He walked into the guest room and saw Lily lying on her side, eyes closed, her pillow moist from tears. He sat next to her for a moment taking in her silent beauty, feeling hollow for leaving. Ethan bent down to kiss her cheek and she awoke, just like in the fairy tales he never got to experience as a child.

"Ethan you came back," she said in a gravelly voice and stretched and rolled onto her back to look at him.

He stared at her for a moment, a building fire within him was being stoked by her eyes. Even in the moonlight he could see the beautiful blue-green wonder that kept him entranced. He would never understand why she fell for him, and they never talked about it.

"I love you," he said as a whisper, half doubting himself, not sure if she would return the sentiment.

She sat up in bed and smiled broadly, unable to squelch her childlike giddiness. She thought Ethan was gone for good, that he might escape back into himself and she'd never get him back.

"I love you too," she said and held him tight, relieved that he loved her too.

Now Dr. Ethan Lewis sat in his office, knowing he craved seeing her, and it would likely lead to an addiction. He needed a distraction, and it came in the form of a letter.

Dear Dr. Ethan Lewis,

Harvard would be honored to have you present at their Annual Research Report this year. We understand your withdrawal last year, wanting to focus on the research, but we heard back from dozens of guests in 2007 who were disappointed you couldn't attend. Please consider sending a brief outline of your talking points as well as your research paper within the next ninety days so that we may review it. We will be reserving a spot for you until then.

Sincerely,
Dr. Robert Kincade

The lab was quiet on Monday morning. Everyone was focused on their specific tasks: Veronica and Traci were taking their data and comparing it with known mappings of the brain through the Human Connectome Project, Dr. Lewis and Kyle were gathering the data from the objective tests, as well as the data points for heart rate, blood pressure, O2 levels, and so on. Kyle was even putting together a video where persons who were undergoing treatment were shown to have relatively low brain activity but still moving, talking, laughing.

"Listen up everyone," Dr. Lewis said walking into the lab. "I just got this little letter yesterday."

"What's that?" Traci asked.

"It's a letter from my alma mater. They remembered my impromptu presentation and they want me to come and give a talk. We have 90 days to submit our article and a brief outline for talking points. I think that's more than enough time right?"

"I think so. We could crunch the numbers and have a very good idea on the brain mapping by the end of the month, and the article could be finished two weeks later if we push it," Adam said confidently.

"I'd agree with that," Veronica said. "We're not seeing any correlations to established upper motor neuron pathways in the brain anyway. Our research might blow this brain mapping thing wide open."

"Yeah I agree too," Kyle said. "I've got the video almost wrapped up, and you would know better than I, but those numbers should be easy to crank through and work statistics."

"I love the enthusiasm!" Dr. Lewis said. For the first time in a while he was wearing a wide smile.

"Are you done with your announcements?" Adam said trying to hide a smile, his eyes giving the happy secret away.

"Yes I am, you have the floor," he said nodding and gesturing toward his assistant.

Adam grasped Veronica's hand and helped her stand. "Veronica and I are engaged!" Everyone cheered obnoxiously loud for the couple.

"I have a question," Kyle said while pretending to look over some papers.

"What's that?" Veronica asked sharply.

"Can I have a plus one?" he smirked and looked up from the papers with his eyes.

"Well lookie here Doc," Traci said slamming her hand on the table. "Looks like we got ourselves a sneaky one. Dr. Lewis, did you know he was dating? Come on buddy what's your secret? Where do you find the time Mr. All-American swimmer?"

Everyone had a good chuckle at the lighthearted banter. It had been a tough few weeks and the humor was certainly doing the trick to lighten everyone's spirits.

"Well we knew. Actually went on a double date a few weeks back. I guess she passed the test huh?" Adam asked and winked at Kyle.

"Yeah. She gets the job done I guess."

"All right let's finish the day. Plan is to have the data done by end of the month. That gives us three weeks. Get working."

The third floor office in The Shack was perfect for compiling data. Kyle used the entertainment area as a large place to stack his collections of paper. Thousands of tests had been taken since their new treatment center opened and he was still getting things organized. He needed the difference between the patients' scores from their initial test, the pre-treatment test, post-treatment test, and three-month follow-up. They would still have a lot of the long-term follow-ups for several weeks, but those could just be plugged in. Theoretically, they would still make the Harvard deadline.

Kyle was distracted. He was thinking about Annie's brother. On top of that, he lied to Dr. Lewis about Annie. Kyle was sitting on two lies that loomed over him: one was that Annie was someone who hadn't experienced death, and the second, he knew of Lily from his father.

"So Kyle. Who's the lucky lady?" Dr. Lewis asked breaking the cycle of thoughts the ran through Kyle's head.

"Her name's Annie."

"Lucky girl," he said pausing. "I'm proud of you."

It was crushing, compounding the lies with pride. "Dr. Lewis I need to tell you something."

"Ok?" he said smirking, confused at Kyle's seriousness.

"I lied to you."

"About?"

"Well, she lied to you. Annie."

"Your Annie?"

"Yeah."

"Enlighten me." Dr. Lewis swiveled around in his chair to face Kyle who was sitting 30 feet from him on the floor, the stacks of papers around him like a tiny wall.

"I told her—"

"I've met her?" Dr. Lewis said loudly, interrupting his lab assistant who was now standing up and walking toward him.

"She was in the study. I met her in a forum. I have to admit to you I had an agenda. I wanted her to react to the study differently than anyone else. She had a very traumatic NDE and she had tried to kill herself."

"What were you thinking?" Dr. Lewis said through his teeth. He was reacting more aggressively than Kyle had thought.

"I wasn't. She said she saw hell. We haven't had anyone who's had an experience like that." He looked down at his hands, and rubbed them together nervously. The sound of dry skin reminded him of the effects of swimming in the chlorine day after day. "I . . . I just wanted to find a way to prove God's existence to you. I wanted her to go into The Beyond Experience too."

"Well that's not happening. And we're taking her out of the study. No matter what her test results say I'm not hearing it. She wasn't qualified based on our inclusion criterion. She's out."

"Ethan please listen to me."

"I think I've listened enough. You're lucky I don't throw you out of this right now. Jesus, Kyle what am I supposed to believe? First you lie to me about what was going on during your initial deep experiences, now this thing with Annie, who's your girlfriend. How many other things have you lied about over the years?"

"Nothing I swear." Another lie.

"I'm not sure I can believe that."

"Ethan please. Let me finish because to be honest, I'm confident at this point you can't get any more upset with me."

"I'm waiting," he sighed heavily and wiped his eyes with his fingers.

"Her depression started when her twin brother died. Do you think we can allow her to go into The Beyond Experience and give her a chance to unburden herself?"

Kyle watched for any signs of weakening of Dr. Ethan Lewis. After working with him for the past several years he had picked up on a few tells; none of which were showing.

"Kyle, the answer now and forever will be no. The lies were enough, but we can't have this becoming commonplace where we perform deep treatments on everyone we know just because they lost someone. It could get wildly out of hand. Plus, who knows the long-term effects of exposing someone to that? Is it addictive Kyle? My argument would be yes," he said deflecting; thinking about his own previous issues.

"She's not just anyone. I'm really falling for this woman. I hope that someday soon you come to realize this is a life changer. Maybe you should go in yourself to see what I'm talking about. Anyone you want to see again? Talk to?" Kyle paused, staring at his mentor. "Come on Ethan there's got to be someone," Kyle asked raising his arms out to the side. He was frustrated and angry about the way Dr. Lewis so quickly and condescendingly told him no.

"You have no idea what you're talking about Kyle. I think you should leave. Take the rest of the week off and come back with a clear head."

"I think that's a great plan." Kyle said grabbing his coat and slamming the door shut behind him.

# | TWENTY-TWO |

## Boston, Massachusetts | October 4, 2008

The results were in and the numbers were incredible: a 100 percent success rate in over five-thousand tests. The experiences people were describing left anyone who read them mesmerized and wanting to enter the experience without asking questions. The deep brain activity during the treatments were consistent with comatose patients, except during the test, they required little more than oxygen.

It was a cloudy Thursday afternoon in Saint Louis, but in Boston, it was a sunny 65. Dr. Lewis and Kyle were flying first class from Saint Louis to Boston. As a group, the research team decided it would be too expensive to take everyone, plus Adam and Veronica wanted to take advantage of the free time and plan their wedding.

Dr. Lewis stared out the oval window. He was spending a considerable amount of time trying to eliminate the thoughts of Kyle, Jack, and Janice, fearing that in the heat of the moment he may divulge too much information.

Kyle was watching a movie on his DVD player and using his headphones. He loved comedies, but Dr. Lewis found them to be less comedic and more raunchy Since discussing Annie, the two men had focused on their work and avoided talking about personal issues. It was difficult for them both; Kyle thought of Ethan like a father, and Dr. Lewis saw Kyle as someone he could help. But now neither man knew where they stood.

"What you gonna watch next?" Dr. Lewis asked as he saw Kyle end his movie and open his case to select another.

"I don't know. Thinking about *Apollo 13*."

"Who's in that?"

"Tom Hanks."

"What's it about?"

"Astronauts go to the moon, but everything falls apart."

"Sounds interesting. Better than that crap you usually watch," Dr. Lewis said jokingly.

"You really haven't heard of *Apollo 13?*" Kyle asked, handing him an earpiece.

"Nope."

"You gotta get out more."

The remainder of the flight went by quickly, both men locked intently onto the plot of the movie. In fact, the movie hadn't finished on the plane, so they watched the rest in the cab on the way to the hotel. Dr. Lewis insisted on separate rooms when they got there. He required his privacy, especially in a town that held so much history for him. He had his appointment scheduled with Jimmy the next morning at 10:00 a.m. but he told Kyle it was a meeting with old, boring friends, and advised him to take a tour of the campus instead. Kyle was happy with the suggestion.

The conference was to officially begin on Saturday, but the speakers were invited to a dinner the evening before. Dr. Lewis lay in his bed, arms crossed behind his head, and thought only of the awkwardness he would surely endure as he talked to other researchers less than 24 hours later. He knew a large contingency from two years ago would likely be at the dinner and would try to talk to him concerning his latest findings. In an email from Dr. Robert Kincade just two weeks before, he stated, "Several people have inquired about your involvement at this year's Research Report, and my response has been to confirm your lecture will be given. Just wanted to pass along the buzz. Seems to me people are very excited about what you have to say."

It made him nervous, being the center of attention. He had spent so much of his life trying to be ignored, to be unseen, and unheard.

Ethan still felt guilty about Lily as well, and being back at Harvard he always felt eyes on him. It wasn't appropriate but he thought somehow being in the light would reveal his involvement in Lily's death, despite it being over fifteen years earlier.

He finally drifted into restless sleep once his thoughts focused on Lily. His dreams were punctuated with visions of her smile, her eyes, and her touch.

Jimmy stood under an awning smoking a cigarette on the soggy Friday morning. He saw Ethan coming from a long way off, his long frame silhouetted against a torrent of heavy rain. Ethan's shoulders were shrugged, head down plowing through the rain with long steps. He wasn't rushing, just intent on his commitment.

"Ethan," Jimmy said with a cigarette pinched gently between his lips, stuck in place by the moisture on his lips.

"How are ya Jimmy? Thanks for meeting with me."

"You say that every year like you're putting me out Doc. You have the only love story I actually believe in. Jesus you're soaked. Let me grab you a shirt and shorts. I'll throw that stuff in our dryer."

"I appreciate it."

"Here ya go Doc," Jimmy said handing him a shop t-shirt and shorts. "You can keep 'em too."

"I'm gonna be a walking billboard Jimmy. Thanks."

"I'm not asking you to do that!" he said with a joking tone. "But I'm not gonna stop you either."

Ethan and Jimmy talked for two hours, mostly about Lily, but when Ethan got emotional they talked about his lecture. Jimmy never pressed, just let the man vent. He knew Ethan had no one else to talk to and coming back to Harvard always brought the wounds back as fresh as the white ink being placed into his skin.

"You should come," Ethan said to Jimmy as he put on his dried clothes.

"Come where?"

"To my presentation."

"I don't know man. You think they'll let me in?" Jimmy had lifted his arms out to the side, rotating them back and forth and raising his head to display for Ethan the large amount of ink that covered his body.

"I know they will if I put you on the list. Come early though. Apparently they're 'excited' about what I have to say."

"Ok Doc, when is it?"

"Tomorrow afternoon at 4:00 p.m. Last slot of the day just in case there's a lot of discussion."

"Ok Doc I'll make it happen."

Kyle and Dr. Lewis arrived 20 minutes late, purposefully. They both felt it was the best idea because neither one of them liked social situations, especially if they felt as though they would be peppered all night with small talk and research driven questions trying to poke holes in their study.

The dinner was packed. Dozens of men and women filled the private room meant for 150 people. The venue had several tall tables with stools, four long wooden tables covered with a variety of seafood, chicken, and steak. In addition to the meat was every variation of cooked and raw vegetable, potatoes in various forms, and a fifth table all to itself to hold an assortment of sweet treats. It was ironic how in a room full of researchers who are trying to improve the health of humanity, the dessert table goods were depleted the quickest.

Kyle was younger than everyone in the room, and very handsome, especially with his lean, muscular frame filling out his navy suit. Several heads turned and looked him over wondering who he was associated with. Dr. Lewis on the other hand, hadn't shaved for several days, his stubble was long and lacking the fullness for a handsome appearance. His black suit and tie left something to be desired. He ignored Kyle's advice to have it tailored, leaving his thin frame buried in the lines of the suit.

"You said open bar right?" Kyle said through the side of his mouth not taking his eyes off the room.

"Yup."

"Problem is I don't see a karaoke machine."

"Me neither, but I think we can manage."

The conversations went without effort or confrontation, even moreso as they continued to consume whiskey. Slowly the two men were approaching other groups, engaging in meaningless interactions and laughing about it to themselves. Often times, they would wager with one another how long another researcher would talk about themselves, keeping a close eye on the ornate clock positioned on the wall directly opposite the door to the room. Both men had to watch the clock because their vision was becoming blurry and their focus was less than optimal.

By the end of their night they had talked to nearly everyone in the room, remembering little of the evening except that they felt like a team again. It had been several weeks since they talked about anything other than the research reports, and even longer since they had a good time. When they got to their hotel, Kyle pulled out his phone and played *Total Eclipse of the Heart*, while in the lobby. It was 1:00 a.m. and the desk employees gave them a look of grave concern when they began to sing it out loud. The look was stern enough causing the two adult researchers to quiet down and go to bed.

As Dr. Lewis lay his spinning head down on his pillow he began to think of Lily. He sobered up quickly; the guilt acting as adrenaline cleaning his system of the poison he continuously swallowed throughout the evening. He went to the bathroom to shower and, being unable to fall asleep, set his clothes out for the morning. The last thing he remembered before his eyes finally shut was the clock that said 3:34 a.m.

*Ring, ring, ring, ring.* "Hello," Dr. Lewis said with a raspy voice.

"Good morning, sir. This is your wake up call. It's 6:30 a.m."

"Thank you," he said in a muffled voice through his pillow, his eyes remaining closed. It was only then that he heard his cellphone beeping from the alarm he set for 6:15.

The morning had come quickly and he wondered how long he would have actually slept had he not received the call. For the first time in several months he had slept soundly for almost three straight hours. For a brief moment he thought alcohol might be the answer to his sleep, but then he remembered his father and quickly dismissed the thought. He dialed Kyle's room to make sure he was awake.

"Hello," a displaced voice said.

"Kyle, we gotta get moving."

"Roger. Meet you in the lobby at seven."

"Sounds good."

Dr. Lewis had been telling Kyle about the fresh coffee he enjoyed on his last trip and wanted to share the experience. Unfortunately, it required them getting up early, and after the poor choices last night, it made for a difficult morning.

Finally, they reached the coffee shop and sat outside in the fog, watching the cloud drift past them. It was mysterious watching trees reappear from behind the dense fog, only to disappear a moment later behind another cloud.

"This is great coffee Doc. Gotta admit it."

"See what I mean?"

"I had a really good time last night. Been a while since I could say that with you," Kyle said too afraid to look up from his coffee.

"I agree. And I'm sorry for that. There's been a lot of stress on me and I was unfair. You're under the same stress as I am. The research is just as much yours as mine."

"Thanks Ethan. It really means a lot but I was stupid. Everything with Annie was stupid."

"Ok enough about it. We're good now. So true confession time Kyle," Dr. Lewis said leaning onto the small table.

"Uh oh."

"I never really go to these things. I mean, I come here, I just don't go to all of the talks. I feel like I have to this year though since I'm a speaker. People will notice."

"Ok. Makes sense."

"That means we need to go. It's already 8:15, starts at 9. You know when Stelious talks?"

"Yep. 9:00 a.m."

"Exactly. We shouldn't be late for him."

The conference room was unchanged from two years before, and neither was Dr. Kincade. He still bounced around the room and shook hands with everyone he saw. Dr. Lewis and Kyle decided to sit about half way down toward the front, along the left side of the room.

Dr. Lewis quickly spotted Dr. Stelious and waved. He returned the favor with little more than a forced, polite smile. He was prepping his talk, taking out the deep brain scanner, and setting up his presentation on the large screen behind him. Dr. Stelious hadn't told Dr. Lewis a thing regarding his research study, his finding, or what he planned on talking about, so both Kyle and Dr. Lewis were eagerly awaiting his results.

"Good morning everyone!" Dr. Kincade said to the packed room. Dr. Lewis scanned the room again and he noticed it was standing room only. He also noticed Dr. Lacey, the large broad man sitting in the same place he had two years before, two rows from the front directly in front of the podium. He appeared even larger, more looming and intimidating than ever, the memory of the confrontation two years ago still burning inside of Dr. Lewis. Seeing him brought back the rage. He had been distracted by his research but at that moment, being there in that room, on that campus, the emotions returned.

"Our first presenter today is Dr. Stelious. He will be discussing his deep brain scanner, as well as its accuracy in determining neural pathways in the brain."

"Well there we go," Kyle whispered, leaning in toward Dr. Lewis.

"Wish Veronica and Traci were here for this." They both smiled and watched as the short, stocky man walked to the microphone.

"Thank you all for coming today. I will get right to it. My deep brain scanner has been proven to detect neural pathways with a 95 percent accuracy. I received most of my data from an associate," the conference room chuckled at the comment remembering the deal struck between Dr. Stelious and Dr. Lewis. Stelious paused in front of the room, waiting for the chuckle to die down before continuing.

"I used the reference data from the Human Connectome Project, who represents the gold standard for neural mapping in the brain. The majority of this data was taken through MRI imaging, which as we know, is a frozen moment in time. My device will hopefully become the new gold standard. It allows us to monitor the events in the brain in real time, and plots them on an image of the patient's brain we have for a reference."

The room erupted in applause and Dr. Lewis couldn't help the goosebumps that raised the hair on his arms. The significance of this research was relevant in a wide range of medical fields from seizures, to stroke, to multiple sclerosis, traumatic brain injuries, psychological disorders, movement disorders, and the list would go on and on. But, what was most interesting to Dr. Lewis, was mapping his own patient's brain activities, and determining how they could be experiencing these vivid things without complex communicative pathways.

"My goal for future research is to increase the accuracy of the study by gathering a three-dimensional image of each individual brain tested, and map the pathways we see. I hypothesize we will increase the accuracy close to 100 percent. The pathways, at times, are very small and close to others within the same structures, so it's necessary to make the studies more individualized. I also would like to gather a more complex patient mix to see if my device can also monitor gross motor, fine motor, and sensory pathways. Thank you."

After several more lectures they broke for lunch. Dr. Lewis tracked down Dr. Stelious and the three of them went to out together.

"Very great study Marcus," Dr. Lewis said as they sat to eat.

"Thank you for the help Ethan. I will continue to use your data, if that's ok, but as you heard, I am looking to take on a broader scope of neural signals."

"I think it's fantastic. I have no doubts you will be up for a Nobel Prize soon enough. The idea of seeing neural pathways in real time is borderline science fiction."

"I appreciate your excitement but I am far from that honor."

"Marcus, I'm wondering if you could use some of my assistants. You met them, Veronica and Traci. I think they would love to hear about your research and even help you. What I'd like to propose is a long-term partnership."

Dr. Stelious sat for a few minutes digesting the information. He was a man who was quite driven in his desire for knowledge and not by self-indulgent ambitions. Dr. Lewis knew the key to getting Marcus on board was to convince him it would be beneficial for the research.

"Marcus."

"I'm considering your proposition Ethan. It may take some time you know."

"Of course. I wouldn't expect a response from you quickly and without thought. Spontaneity is not in your nature. My lecture is at 4:00 p.m. I hope you will be in attendance. After I reveal my research I am confident I will receive a large grant, and more likely than not, FDA approval for treatment. If that happens, I will start my own company. My contract with Washington University is almost up. My contract also dictates that any medical developments are mine. It was one of the reasons I decided to take my research there."

"I will be in attendance. You opened my eyes with that woman. Her experience was truly remarkable."

The men wrapped up their lunch, trying as best they could to engage Dr. Stelious with small talk, but had little success. The bearded researcher was perfectly content left to think quietly. It was almost 1:00 when they stood and shook hands, going their separate ways for the remaining break period before ending up back in the lecture hall.

It was quickly 4:00 p.m. and Dr. Lewis took his place at the front of the hall. The room seemed smaller than last time as Dr. Lewis stood in front, placing the mic on his collar. It was an illusion, brought on by the sheer number of people standing in the aisles on either side of the room, and across the back. As Kyle set the presentation up on the screen, Dr. Lewis scanned the room. He saw Dr. Stelious planted in the front row, nodding at him as they made eye contact. He saw Lacey, whose eyes like daggers buried themselves in Ethan. It gave him a chill and distracted him momentarily. Finally, he saw his old friend Jimmy, wearing a long sleeve blue button up, his neck tattoos still visible but only slightly. Jimmy waved politely and gave him a thumbs-up, Dr. Lewis smiled nervously back.

"Ok everyone here we go!" Dr. Kincade said smiling into the microphone. "I can see word has spread. This is fantastic!" again he exclaimed into the mic and clapped his hands one time. "So without much of an introduction required, Dr. Ethan Lewis. A transplanted Harvard man now doing his research at Washington University in Saint Louis. Back by popular demand!" Dr. Kincade clapped loudly and quickly into the air, his mic picking up the first several hand claps before they were able to shut it off. The aggressiveness of his clapping was piercing, but contagious as the room erupted.

"Good afternoon. I can't believe how many of us are in the room. Thank you, but I think the fire marshal would shut this thing down. Not sure he'd appreciate the fire hazard so we should probably have some of you go." He paused pretending to scan the room with his finger. "Ah, Dr. Lacey, let's start with you shall we?" he said joking, the entire room erupted with laughter. Even Dr. Lacey smirked at the first strike.

"Ok, it seems as though a lot of you have heard about what I revealed two years ago. I know a lot of you have been waiting to see a video. Kyle, please play the video."

Ten minutes isn't a long time, but for a room full of excited researchers to stay silent was a big ask. The video was well done, just as it had been before when Kyle showed Linda's video two years before. This time, they had Dr. Stelious' deep scanning device to assist with the visuals. The screen was split between the patient on the left side of the screen, the vitals on the upper right, and the generic brain model in the lower right with activity highlighted with a blue light marking the pathway and location. Even Dr. Stelious' mouth was slightly ajar as he watched the short video, a splicing of several dozen patients whose physical manifestations couldn't be explained through the deep brain scanner. According to what everyone in the room knew, the brain was required to be active during moments of speech, of movement, but there wasn't a blip to speak of, just a small blue glow in the brainstem and a reading of two to four hertz for brain activity.

The video ended and the room was silent for a moment. If thoughts were lightbulbs the room would have looked like Las Vegas with each researcher, tech, professor, or doctor reaching deep into their own brains to try and explain what was being seen.

Dr. Lewis took his place behind the podium. "Actually having my research this year, I'll show you the number," he pulled up the slide showing the results. "As you can see, we took four subjective tests. A test at our initial interview, one immediately prior to the procedure, then immediately following, and lastly a long-term test at three months. The data shows that with over five-thousand subjects now, we have a 100 percent success rate with a significant p-value at .0002. This result is the same for both tests immediately following the treatment, as well as at three months."

The room was audibly excited with the results, with loud applause. Dr. Lewis even heard a few whistles. Everyone in the room was excited except for Lacey, who sat with his arms crossed. Dr. Lewis had a difficult time avoiding eye contact with the large man. He was intimidating, angry, and continuously staring at him. His stares were not the kind that was associated with engaged listening, but rather malice and resentment.

## Poughkeepsie, New York   |   October 15, 2016

Lily's parents sat opposite Ethan and Annie on a small couch, holding hands and listening to Ethan talk continuously for hours as the sun slowly sank down toward the horizon.

"Excuse me Captain and Mrs. Fisch. I'm very exhausted," Dr. Lewis said, his voice straining from hours of non-stop storytelling.

"Ethan, you've talked for quite a while and I'm not sure we've gotten anywhere," Pat said sadly.

"I'm not exactly sure what your intent is," Ed said in agreement with his wife. "You said she saved you. In fact, you said twice she saved you but you haven't gotten to it."

"I realize that and I appreciate your patience with me. You have to trust me. The backstory is important. My resistance to Kyle's ideologies is important. The Beyond Experience is important. You really must know that."

"What we know is that our daughter is dead. We've spent over 20 years getting to know that. It still hurts, but the pain has become less frequent with time," Ed said squeezing his wife and kissing her gently on the head.

"The first time she saved me was with the treatment," Ethan said softly, his nervousness getting the best of him. His eyes began to well up and he felt a strong urge to run.

"She gave you the treatment?" Pat asked shocked.

"She invented the cocktail. She did it for me. We experimented a lot. When I say we, I mean she concocted the drug mix, creating all the drugs from scratch, and she gave them to me."

"So why was she the one that died?" Pat said sharply, a tear slowly rolling down her face, having overcome her strong will not to cry.

"I can only assume she wanted to see what I experienced," he said lying. He had wanted to take a break from the storyline. He needed a break. What came next was something he tried to bury in his own mind before it happened. After he and Kyle showed their results he was verbally attacked by Lacey, accused of being part of Lily's death, and then, in a drunken state, he told Jimmy and Kyle everything. He wasn't about to tell the Fisch family those details.

"Can we continue tomorrow? Please, I need to rest my voice. You need me to finish this story," he said picking up the black volcanic rock from the table and placing it in his pocket.

Ed and Pat sat looking at one another, conversing in silence as only two people could after fifty years of marriage. "I'll tell you what, Ethan. If you don't mind us calling Joey and inviting him over. We can have lunch and you can tell the three of us the ending of this."

"I'd love that," he said nervously. The last time he saw Joey was at the funeral, and he had showed him his sidearm.

Dr. Lewis lay in his hotel room reflecting on the story he hadn't finished. He allowed himself to relive those days in Boston, trying to grasp the moments he tried to bury deep inside, using it as a moment to process his past. Since his own time in The Beyond Experience he had decided to try and deal with his traumatic past, eliminating his anxiety one memory at a time.

He closed his eyes and he was back in the conference room on October 4, 2008.

"Dr. Lewis," a booming voice interrupted the applause as he stared at the speaker. It was Dr. Lacey, smirking.

"Yes, Dr. Lacey," he responded, his heart now pounding, feeling anxious instead of the excitement he had been experiencing.

"What's your secret?"

"I'm not sure what you mean."

"I think you do. But I'll elaborate for the sake of the room."

"Please do." Dr. Lewis crossed his arms and glanced down at the podium, trying to refocus himself before the attack.

"The ingredients you use."

"It's proprietary, but it includes ketamine, propofol, etomidate, thiopental, methohexital, and *Convallaria majalis*."

"That's quite a list doctor."

"Yes it is."

"What is *Convallaria majalis?*"

"A flower commonly known as Lily of the Valley."

"Poisonous if I remember from my botany so long ago. Correct?"

"Yes, in large doses."

"So have you measured the amount that enters the system? How did you study the safe levels? Have you ever had a poor outcome?"

Dr. Lewis began to sweat. He thought of Lily but tried not to show it. "You see the results behind me doctor. We haven't had a negative effect."

"Hmm. Nothing at all. That's impressive. Do you know Elias Grant?"

"Yes I do. CEO of Whitestone, why do you ask?" Dr. Lewis was furious. He knew right then and there Elias had violated his non-disclosure agreement.

"How did you convince a businessman to purchase a multimillion dollar greenhouse to grow you this plant?"

"I'm not discussing my arrangements with you here, or anywhere," Dr. Lewis' voice began to shake as his knuckles turned white, his hands grasping the podium firmly. "This isn't the time or place for something like this Dr. Lacey," he spat the doctor's name out through his teeth.

"Dr. Lewis, it's just a simple question," he said shrugging his large shoulders.

"But it's not," Dr. Lewis said walking out from behind the podium as he began to raise his voice. Pointing at Dr. Lacey, he said, "You've got something against me and I think everyone in this room feels the tension. I'm not sure what it is, but try and respect everyone in this room by keeping your issues to yourself."

"Sure, I'm ok with that," he said crossing his heavy arms and nodding his head up and down, his bottom lip protruding slightly. "Just one thought. I don't know, maybe not a big deal, but how do you explain a certain botany graduate student dying in a lab right on this campus, with ketamine, propofol, etomidate, thiopental, methohexital, and your ingredient *Convallaria majalis* in her system?"

The room began to spin for Dr. Lewis. His heart was pounding but it felt as though his blood wasn't moving. He was short of breath and his feet were numb. He flashed back to an interrogation room at the Cambridge police station. They had kept him in the room for hours, lighting him up with question after question, fatiguing him to the point of exhaustion, but he hadn't budged. He admitted to knowing she was using a few recreational drugs, which was a lie, and he admitted to knowing she often talked about manufacturing drugs in the lab for fun. Ethan never saw the police reports, never heard what they had found. There was no reason for him to. *How did Lacey know?*

Time seemed to move slowly, his mouth went dry and he thought he'd been standing for several minutes in silence. He willed himself to talk but nothing came out. He cleared his throat to reassure himself he was able to make a noise. He looked to Kyle, who sat stunned. He looked out to Jimmy who sat with both hands on the top of his head and Ethan imagined he was holding his breath, willing him to say something.

"I have no idea how to respond to that accusation," he finally said, his words reverberating through the room. "This is so out of bounds . . . she was my fiancé. She was taken from me by an accidental overdose I had nothing to do with. I have nothing more to say."

Dr. Lewis took off the mic. The noise from his hand and the feedback squeal caused several to place their hands over their ears. Kyle fumbled with the equipment in a hurry to follow Dr. Lewis out. The majority of the room sat motionless, silent, with empathy and confusion for the doctor who won the heart of the room only moments before. The same man now walked hunched forward, trying to hide within himself in an attempt to disappear in a room full of focused eyes.

He walked toward Jimmy who stood with his hands in his pockets, crying for the man he felt so much admiration toward. He knew more than anyone the pain Ethan was in. Jimmy held the door as Ethan walked out, and kept it open for Kyle who quickly snuck through as well. Jimmy paused looking into the room but decided not to open his mouth. The things he had to say weren't meant for a place like this.

The police called Dr. Lewis that evening and asked him to come to the station. Kyle had gone with him but the two sat in silence in the taxi. The officers were cordial, respectful, but confessed that someone had tipped them off to the incident at the Harvard Research Report. Ethan told the young officers everything he had said from the past. They probed more, and rightfully so, because the drug cocktail found in her system was exactly what he'd been giving patients now for over a decade. The shock and stress of the day had brought his armor fully down and he told another white lie, one that allowed him to save face, but destroy her even more.

"She had been taking the cocktail for a few months in an attempt to treat her anxiety," Ethan told them. "We researched the benefits of the hypnotic state, and how she was trying to get herself to a deeper level. I told her to stop, and she swore she had, so I didn't go to anyone to tell them."

"Why didn't you tell us this fifteen years ago Doctor?"

"Her family. They hated me already, I didn't want them to hate her too. They were very religious and for her to be depressed, let alone self-medicating for it, would have crushed them even more. I felt it was enough."

"All right Dr. Lewis I think that's fair. You have no priors, nor do you have any motives, but full disclosure, we will be reopening the investigation."

"I have nothing to hide guys. If you find anything else, let me know."

"One more question Doc, for me really. Off the record."

"Ok?"

"Why did you study the drug? I mean if you knew it might have killed her."

"Because she was the smartest person I know. If she believed in it, then so do I. So you see where it got me?"

"Thank you Doctor. We'll be in touch."

After exiting the interview Dr. Lewis checked his phone. He had a text from Jimmy.

"Sorry to see what happened to you up there. It wasn't right. Let me know if you need anything."

He responded, "Thank you, I'll be ok."

As he walked out of the building he saw Kyle leaning against the wall, playing on his phone.

"How'd it go in there?"

"Fine. They'll be in touch. Reopening the investigation."

"Wow, Doc I had no idea."

"You shouldn't. That wasn't anyone's business."

"We need to talk about this Ethan."

"We really don't," he said, sighing heavily looking into the night sky.

Kyle stared at him with his eyes hinting at a secret hiding just under the surface.

"You knew didn't you?" Dr. Lewis asked reading the expression.

Kyle shook his head no. "Another lie?"

"A lie about what? That I knew?"

"I'm not gonna play games Kyle, and I'm sick of this burden."

"I don't understand."

"You will. We're going somewhere. Grab a taxi. I gotta call someone." Dr. Lewis took out his phone and called Jimmy.

"Hey Doc how's it going?"

"I think you can imagine. You busy?"

"Nope, just put the kids down. The wife knows I'm on call tonight for you. If you need me, I'm here."

"Meet me at the shop? Bring some whiskey."

The street was dark and the stars were visible when Kyle and Ethan arrived at the shop. Jimmy was standing outside looking upward when they arrived.

"You see this Doc?" he said still looking upward admiring the stars he had forgotten existed.

"Yeah, Jimmy, I do."

"Had no idea how dark it got down here this time of night."

"Jimmy let's go inside."

"Who's your friend?"

"Jimmy, Kyle. Kyle, Jimmy."

"Nice to meet ya Kyle."

"Likewise," Kyle said and they shook hands.

"Ah, you've got some ink, Kyle. My kind of guy."

The three went inside not knowing what to expect. "I'm gonna need to drink," Dr. Lewis said to Jimmy who was already on his way to the back for some glasses. "Kyle, we're not going to the lectures tomorrow."

"Fair enough."

"I'm gonna tie one on hard. I've got something to tell you two."

Two hours passed and the men were at the bottom of the bottle. Jimmy had grabbed his tattoo gun and Kyle was looking through a book of examples. The two had hit it off and Ethan enjoyed watching them. It took the pressure off and allowed him to relax, the alcohol helped it happen more quickly.

*Bzzzzz.* The tattoo gun started and Kyle sat backward in the chair, his bare back presenting itself as a canvas for Jimmy. He had decided on a fallen angel, black and white, kneeling on one knee, his head buried in his hands. Wrapping around the angel's lean, muscular frame, were powerful wings as if to shield him from the surroundings.

Ethan felt like that angel, kneeling in remorse, his own thoughts and doubts overwhelming him. His wings were his walls for solidarity, not allowing others in, but the weight of it all had brought him to his knees. He needed an out, a friend, or in this case two, who could listen to his story, his painful past, and allow him a moment to stand back-up.

"You guys want to hear a story?" Ethan said plopping down in a chair next to the two men.

"That's what we're here for right?" Jimmy said pausing the gun and wiping the excess ink off of Kyle's back revealing which lines still needed work.

"Lily. I loved her. You know why?"

"Nope," Kyle said quickly, trying to press the story onward.

"Because she saved me."

"How's that?" Kyle said almost annoyed. Jimmy nudged Kyle forcefully into the chair.

"Can you let me speak?" Ethan said loudly in a slurred manner, throwing his arm awkwardly in the air toward the two men. Jimmy stopped the gun and laughed at the doctor.

"I emancipated myself from my parents as a teenager. Abusive people, I had nightmares, scars, and no childhood. They abused me almost daily. I had nothing and nobody until I met her. My life was motivated by anxiety and I was depressed. Until I met her. She cured me."

"How's that? She touch you in your special place?" Jimmy said laughing, the alcohol shut down his filter.

"No. She cured me," he said smirking at the stupid remark from Jimmy. Dr. Lewis bent down and got close to Kyle's face. "Kyle. I've been in the treatment."

"You have?" he said loudly jumping up to sitting. Jimmy reacted quickly despite the whiskey and avoided ruining the tattoo.

"Yes. More than you. A lot more than you. Lily and I experimented for an entire semester, manufacturing the drugs from scratch. She did it all. She was a genius. Linda was the first person to replicate the experience I had with Lily. That's when I knew we really had it." Ethan paused and reflected on the moment in the lab when Linda told him she experienced heaven.

"I killed her."

"What?" Kyle said. "Jimmy stop for a minute." Kyle sat up and looked at Ethan. Jimmy wasn't shocked. It hadn't been the first time someone confessed to murder in his shop.

"Kyle don't interrupt me again," Ethan said as he began retelling the events of that fateful day.

The research lab had been organized and quiet. Beakers, flasks, and test tubes sat in rows on shelves halfway up to the ceiling atop greenstone epoxy resin tabletops. The tabletops were black in color, but seemed almost translucent and deep, sometimes making it difficult to sense where the surface actually began. On more than one occasion, a student had slammed glassware hard down onto the surface shattering it, spilling its chemical contents onto the resistant surface. Against the far wall was a long wooden table with hundreds of potted plants sprouting upward toward a dozen full spectrum growth lights. Their growth was staggered, with the plants on the left being the tallest, while on the right the seedlings barely unfolding themselves upward toward the heavens, their branches still white.

Ethan sat in the dimly lit botany lab. Sunlight streaked the room through blinds that covered windows on the wall behind him. It was spring break for the graduate school and he knew the entire building would be empty. He borrowed her keys to gain access to the lab, saying he had a surprise for her. He looked at the clock, 11:30, and knew he had to get to work quickly. For the last several days he and Lily worked hard to manufacture several drugs: ketamine, propofol, etomidate, thiopental, and methohexital. She was the genius, being able to use her incredible knowledge of chemistry to build the complex chemical structures she researched. She could determine which ingredients and how many steps it would take to create each specific drug. With a few of them, the "impurities" could be precipitated out, placed in a second solution, then used to manufacture one of the other drugs they were playing with. It was incredible to watch how efficient and ingenious she was. He was infatuated by how easy it came to her.

Ethan was onto the final step, extracting the principle ingredient in the cocktail from *Convallaria majalis,* the Lily of the Valley. Ethan had watched her prep the cocktail many times, and this was certainly the easiest part. It involved mashing the flowers and berries with a mortar and pestle, pouring ten milliliters of deionized water into the bowl, mixing it together, then extracting the liquid. He fired up a Bunsen burner, distributed the fifteen or so milliliters of the pink liquid into a small beaker, and placed it over the heat waiting for it to simmer, indicating that it had become sterile.

Lily had mixed and matched their manufactured drugs with a variety of plant extracts. Her favorite, *Convallaria majalis*, always hit the hardest. He would go to a different world for what seemed like hours, but in reality, Lily said it had only been thirty minutes. Ethan came out of the experience much more refreshed and at ease, all trace of anxiety had been removed, and he was focused. He wanted her to feel the place he had been, understand the increase in sensory stimulus. It was impossible to explain, almost impossible to believe, but he had been there.

He sat on a stool, heart pounding and tapping his fingers on the black counter waiting for her to arrive. Ethan still wore gloves, ensuring no fingerprints would be left behind. It was their agreed upon failsafe, if any of the drugs were stumbled upon, they would have deniability. He checked the clock, 4:02, again, 4:05, again, 4:10. They had planned on meeting around 4:00 p.m. She had a habit of running a little late, but she always looked beautiful so he never minded. He hadn't told her tonight was her turn to experience the feelings she had given him so many times. *Syringe, needle, drugs in the refrigerator, epinephrine just in case, water, blanket, pillow.* He reviewed the necessities over and over again.

*Tap, tap, tap.* A nearly silent knock came at the heavy oak lab door. He sprung up from the chair to greet her. He took a deep breath and opened the door. There she stood with brownies and two bottles of water. Her full lips parted and small, soft islands of pink emerged between her teeth as she pressed her tongue nervously against them.

"Brought you brownies," she sung and her eyes glistened like a sun-kissed lake.

"Today was for you, not me!" Ethan responded in playful frustration. "You never let me win."

"It's cause I love you," she said kissing him on the cheek. His eyes closed and he sighed deeply in response to his heart quickening. The words would never get old. He grabbed her and held her as close as he could with the small glass pan of brownies between them. She smelled like flowers and the sea.

"Love you too," he said softly.

She pulled away lovingly, "You're gonna smash the brownies," then peeked around Ethan and into the lab. "Oh, Ethan," she said dropping her voice an octave. "What do we have here sweetie?" she asked pointing to the blanket and pillow lying on the clean tile floor.

"Well, I told you I had a surprise for you."

"What is it?"

"Well, I've watched you prep the cocktail several times, so I did it today."

"Oh I guess I should be proud huh?" she joked with a smile. "Ok, I guess I'll do it for you since you clearly want it so bad."

"No, Lily," he said softly and took her hand. "I want you to experience it. To feel what I feel. I'm sick of trying to explain it to you. It's impossible."

"I don't know Ethan. Never really liked getting high on the other stuff. Getting knocked out doesn't do it for me. I just like mixing it up and giving it to you."

"You'll like this," he said and gestured toward the blanket and pillow, still wearing the blue gloves on his hands. They were sweaty, his fingers wrinkled but he insisted on following the rules. She put gloves on as well and laid down on the floor.

"I'm only doing this because I love you. I swear to God if those brownies are gone when I come out I'm gonna kill you," she said and meant it.

"I'll be too busy watching you sleep sweetheart," he leaned into her and kissed her smooth forehead. "You're gonna feel a little prick—"

"Oh really Mr. Med School," she said cutting him off and laughed, her breath highlighted with a touch of mint from her gum.

"Spit your gum out," he said holding out his hand. She spat into his palm while staring at his eyes from underneath her furrowed brow. He threw it in the trash and walked to the refrigerator.

Ethan took out the small glass vial that contained the mixture of drugs and plant extract. Returning to the bench, he carefully opened the bottom of the sterile needle packet, and screwed it onto the plastic syringe. He then inserted the needle into the vial and drew up approximately 20 milliliters of the solution. He bent down and ran a cold alcohol wipe up and down her left forearm cleaning the area. The wipe left her arm cold and goosebumps cascaded up the arm and across her body. She shivered involuntarily and they both laughed nervously.

"You ready?" Ethan asked forcing a smile as his clothes were soaking up his sweat, leaving evidence under his arms and across his back.

"I trust you," she said smiling again, her eyes narrow, full of love. "If I'm being honest, I'm a little excited to see what the fuss is about," she bit her lip as if she said something she shouldn't have. They both giggled, revealing what little tension they had in the moment.

"Three, two, one," Ethan and Lily said together. He gently punctured her skin, feeling the skin pop as he broke through. He backed the plunger just a hair, and after seeing a sliver of pink swirl into the solution, he knew he was in her vein.

"Are you sure?" he asked without a smile this time. She looked at him, reached toward his gloved hand with her own, and pressed down on the plunger sending the drugs into her system. Within moments, she was asleep.

Ethan watched her breathe gently in and out. He sat next to her on the floor stroking her blonde hair. His fingers combed through the soft waves as he watched the strands fall one by one back down onto her cheek. Over and over he did it, watching closely, determining whether each strand was darker or lighter, which made up her diverse hues of blonde and brown that he loved so much. Several minutes passed and he quit playing with her hair and began to imagine what she was hearing, seeing, and feeling. *Would they be the same as mine? Would they be more intense? Would nothing happen at all?*

As the last thought entered his mind he stopped feeling her chest move against his leg. He quickly got onto his knees and bent down placing his ear next to her mouth. He heard nothing for several seconds. He checked her pulse with his left hand and got a good reading. Suddenly a rush of air went through her mouth and into her lungs. He rocked back onto his heels and looked up toward the drop ceiling in the lab.

"Thank you," he mouthed but it felt awkward. He never believed in God or a higher being, but suddenly he was thanking something or someone. He quickly dismissed the thought as his anxiety reduced. Then Lily did it again. She gasped for a breath and went silent once more. This time her pulse was very faint and Ethan began to scramble around the area, looking for something that would help her. Again she sputtered for air more shallowly and he could see her skin was becoming pale. He ran around the lab trying to find something, a drug, a plant, smelling salts, and then he remembered the epinephrine. He ran to her and popped the lid off the syringe and plunged it into her arm pressing the plunger down with all his strength. He wanted every last bit flowing through her.

"Forgive me," she said quietly, in a whisper but it was plain to hear. "Please . . . forgive me," he heard her say a little more clearly. Her eyes never opened, her chest never rose again. Her heart had stopped and she lay lifeless on the blanket he brought from his apartment.

"Lily, please wake up," he begged her with his hands on her shoulders. "No, no, no, please, no," he pleaded. "Please wake up, you'll never have to try it again, please God wake her up. I'll do anything I just want her here. I don't care if I get in trouble for this, if I get kicked out of Harvard I just want her to be here with me please make it happen," he begged aloud as he now sat with her lifeless body resting against his chest, he worked hard to keep her lifted to his chest, her face next to his, her skin growing cold.

Several minutes passed as he rocked her back and forth, his face buried in her wonderful blonde hair. He had a handful of it in each fist as he squeezed her tight against him. Her hair was saturated in his tears as he quaked from the crying. Her smell was fleeting and he took deep searching breaths attempting to gather as much of her into his nose, bottling it up in an attempt to remember it forever. Surges of anxiety washed over him and panic began to set in but he didn't know if it was from the fact that he'd never speak to her again, or the trouble that may be upon him soon.

He quickly glanced around the room and saw no evidence against him. He had already cleaned all the equipment that was used, he had worn gloves the entire time since setting foot in the lab. The only problem was his blanket and pillow being on the scene, but he could easily explain that away. *She borrowed them from him a few weeks back.* It was his fiancé for goodness' sake, only she had refused to move in with him, citing her religious parents and upbringing.

He kissed her softly on the forehead, the cheek, and finally on her pale lips. He held her head in both hands and tried to look into her face but it was sickening, too intense and surreal. He laid her gently down onto his pillow and placed the syringe on the blanket, along with her bottles of water and brownies. He placed the lab keys inside her pants pocket and went through a mental checklist ensuring he was leaving without any trace of evidence. He wanted to die. He wanted to run and jump right through the lab windows and fall 30 feet to his death. Instead, he grabbed one of the bottles of water, making her appear alone in the lab, and walked out of the room; the door locking behind him as it closed.

Instead, he walked out of the room and shut the door, locking it behind him as it closed. He walked slowly down the stairs, and out the rear of the building onto a quiet street. There were no security cameras here, no people walking down the streets of the ghost campus. He crammed his hands deep into the pockets of his jeans, and balled his fists tightly together. The walk felt endless, crossing streets, walking past a few groups of students who stayed on campus for the break. He avoided eye contact, rarely looking up from his feet.

When he got back to his apartment he climbed onto his bed, took off his clothes, and rubbed his finger on the wooden bedframe looking for the comfort he had as a boy. It was the only thing he had left in his life.

"It was an accident, and I swear to God I've never talked about this before so if this gets out I'll come after you guys."

"Don't worry Doc, we got you," Jimmy said nodding his head.

"It was an accident. She was so beautiful," he said pulling out his phone and accessing his secret app with her pictures. He showed the two of them who both nodded in agreement. "I wanted her to know what I was experiencing. She never did drugs, refused to. But she couldn't say no when I had everything set up that day to surprise her. I gave her the drug and she went to sleep. Kyle, just like everyone we have ever treated, but after several minutes she stopped breathing."

The men sat in silence waiting for Ethan to speak. Ethan sat in silence reliving the moment he decided to clean up and set the scene, making it appear an overdose. He reached for the second bottle of whiskey and drank straight from it, ignoring the glass that sat just to his left.

"What's always driven me wild is what she said."

"What?" Kyle asked softly. "What did she say?"

"Forgive me."

"Why did she say that?" Jimmy asked.

"That's what I can't figure out."

"Was she talking to you?" Jimmy asked again.

"No," Kyle said answering for the doctor. "It's an effect that happens. Just like in the video. Sometimes you see someone you lost, like in my case, my dad. I got to talk to him."

Dr. Lewis watched as Kyle explained The Beyond Experience to Jimmy who sat stunned.

"So only you guys know about this?" Jimmy said after Kyle finished explaining.

"No, but now including you, only three outside this room."

"Ethan why don't you go into the experience, see her, talk to her?" Kyle said.

"I can't. I was addicted to the treatment before. I can't imagine what I will do if I see her there. I would do anything to stay inside. I can't. Plus, who knows if it'll be her I see?" Ethan wanted to believe his last statement but he knew it would be her. It was always her he thought about.

"I have a confession," Kyle said folding his hands.

"I can't take this anymore, Kyle," Ethan said.

"Sounds pissed at you Kyle," Jimmy said jokingly and buzzed his tattoo gun a few times keeping the ink moist.

"My dad told me about Lily. A small thing that I didn't understand until we were in the conference room and Dr. Lacey said what he said."

"So when you said Lily, you weren't talking about your dog?" Ethan asked having already known the answer long ago.

"Exactly."

"What did he tell you?"

"He told me to tell you she still loves you. She isn't mad."

Ethan looked down at the floor. He began to cry.

Jimmy and Kyle knew Ethan needed time to reflect on the news. Kyle sat forward into the chair, his face in the port, and Jimmy went back to work on the tattoo. It took several more hours, the *buzzing* from the tattoo gun marked the passing of time as their sobriety returned. As Jimmy finished, the sun began to shine outside of the shop, marking the sign of a new day. Ethan lay passed out the couch, his sleep regenerating his emotional armor.

# | TWENTY-THREE |

## Poughkeepsie, New York | October 16, 2016

Dr. Lewis stood at the Fisch home for the second day in a row, nervous to knock. Yesterday was the first time he'd ever gotten to talk with Pat and Ed, but now he also had to sit in front of Joey, the one person in the family he had talked to. After Lily died, Joey had called him, stating if he ever tried to contact the family again he would take care of Ethan himself. Ethan knocked and held his breath. It only took a moment, but the door opened and there stood the 6'4" Joey Fisch.

"Ethan," Joey said as he took a sip of his lemonade. It looked refreshing, the condensation running off the glass and landing on the dark stained wood.

"Joey," he responded nodding his head. "This is Annie, and that little one is Junior."

"Yours?" Joey said smiling with his eyes and gesturing with the glass.

"No. Annie's, but I help out when I can."

"He's great with him," Annie interjected, smiling.

"Wait!" they heard a voice project from somewhere inside the home. Footsteps quickly came toward them, and Pat stood next to her son. "Annie . . . Kyle's Annie?"

"Yes Ma'am," Annie said, sighing heavily fighting back the tears.

Pat stood staring at Annie, her eyes darting from Annie's left eye and back to her right, over and over again, trying to read the young lady.

"Can I hold him?" Pat asked and stretched out her arms.

"Sure," Annie said handing Junior to Pat and quickly wiping away the tears that escaped her.

"Hi again," Pat said sweetly, smiling at the boy who smiled widely back, his brilliant blue eyes reflecting the skies above.

"What happened to Kyle?" Pat said staring at Ethan, her eyes firm as she bounced the baby gently.

"You'll know everything by the end of the night. I'm not leaving until I finish," Ethan said. The strength of his voice had returned.

"Come on in then. I made lemonade. It's on the table in the sunroom. Ed's already in there waiting."

They all gathered in the sunroom and took their seats around a table, except Annie, who went to put Junior down for a nap.

"Ethan, is Kyle gone?"

"We had a falling out," he said staring at the floor, trying to control his emotions. He promised Annie he wouldn't tell the Fisch family the story without her being present. She wanted to be there for him; she knew the guilt he felt was immense.

"What does that mean?" Ed asked, tired of the secrets.

"I promise we'll get there, but without the rest of the story you won't understand."

"Let's get on with it then," Joey said forcing a smile and pouring himself another lemonade.

"Joey, I spoke for hours yesterday and I—"

"Stoppin' ya right there Doc. They filled me in. I get the big points."

Ethan looked down at his pad of paper and quickly saw where he left off.

## Saint Louis | January 5, 2009

Dr. Lewis sat in his office Monday morning reading through emails. The group was on a well deserved break as they waited word from the FDA regarding the approval for treatment. Prior to submitting the results, they had discussed their futures, and everyone except Malcolm agreed to stay on board with the company if it moved forward. He wanted more variety in his professional life, so he took a job in the ER at Rush Hospital in Chicago. Dr. Lewis had written him a wonderful letter which got Malcolm a foot in the door. For the last month, Dr. Lewis was working with Michelle Adams on finding a proper patent attorney for their proprietary cocktail.

He closed his email and went back to reviewing the patent. Michelle had given him a preliminary outline of what the patent should entail, so he was making it as polished as he could before Michelle's attorney friend called him.

Then it hit him. A small flame of anger rose from deep within, reigniting a flame that lay dormant for some time. Dr. Lewis had always felt cautionary when dealing with Elias Grant, and now his feelings had returned. In the lecture, Dr. Lacey had brought up Elias, but because of the stunning revelations regarding Lily, he had forgotten until now. He picked up the phone and called Michelle.

"Michelle," she said picking up her private cell.

"Hi Michelle, sorry to bother you."

"Not a problem. I talked to my friend Nicholas, the patent attorney. He'll be calling you soon. Be patient."

"It's not about that," he said, having forgotten about the patent in the moment.

"What is it then, Doc?" she asked. A fluttering in her stomach almost revealed her secret. *Please let today be the day,* she thought as she sat straight up in her chair.

"I had an incident regarding Elias Grant while at Harvard a few months back. I'd been so distracted with things until now so I had forgotten. He violated our confidentiality agreement. I'd like to really go after him."

Michelle slumped in her chair and closed her eyes. She was angry at herself for once again getting excited. She had fallen for Dr. Lewis and his focus over the last three months. On the infrequent occasions where they actually sat in the same room going over the patent materials, she stared at his wavy hair, wanting to grab it with both hands and force him to look at her with his emerald eyes. She too had green eyes, and with her caramel skin she was often asked if she wore contacts. She hated that question, but when Dr. Lewis asked her three weeks ago she melted. It meant he actually looked at her.

"Email me the details. I'll take it from there Doctor. I hope you're right."

"Why's that?"

"'Cause I'll get 30 percent of the take," she said gathering her broken heart once again.

"Fair enough."

"Goodbye Dr. Lewis," she said sweetly, like a sassy teenage daughter who was with her friends.

He sat for a while following the phone call. For the first time, he allowed himself to imagine the possibilities of having his own company. He knew that leaving the university would present its own challenges: having to lease a building, pay for employees, their benefits, marketing, lab equipment, all added up, but for some reason he felt at peace. It could be that he felt he would ultimately have a donor, whether Elias liked it or not, he may be paying for the first treatment and research facility.

# | TWENTY-FOUR |

## October 2009

October twelfth and the weather was perfect. The church had been beautifully decorated in a variety of flowers, including, the Lily of the Valley. Thousands of them had come as a gift, from Elias Grant, a sort of peace treaty following the lawsuit for breach of contract.

The settlement in the case was Elias and Whitestone paying the twenty million dollars for The Experience Center. The Center was a massive one-story structure built in Chesterfield, Missouri. Elias had agreed to fund the project, so long as the lawsuit never made it to the public eye. Of course the company spun the information in a positive light through another one of their quarterly statements, but behind closed doors at Whitestone, Elias Grant was enraged.

Chesterfield was a town that was large enough to have its own airport, mall, YMCA, and dozens of chain restaurants, but it was also situated far enough outside of Saint Louis to be considered somewhat rural, so the cost for the land wasn't a premium. The facility had 25 treatment beds and a full state-of-the-art lab for creating the cocktail. It also had an even larger research area, where Dr. Lewis and Dr. Stelious could continue to perform their experimentations for brain mapping and treatment for anxiety and depression. Dr. Stelious had given his resignation to Harvard in the week following Dr. Lewis' presentation, stating that "this idea of us working together could be mutually beneficial," and signed on as a full partner once Elias Grant decided to fund the building project.

But that was all business, and as they sat in the beauty that was the Cathedral Basilica of Saint Louis, they tried to focus on the ceremony.

The surroundings were distracting and mesmerizing, the cost to build such a beautiful church would be incalculable in this day and age. They sat within marble pillars, golden walls, and ornate frescos painted on the ceilings stretching several stories above.

Adam stood in the front of the church, hands folded in front of him wearing a perfectly tailored tan suit. His tie was navy, and his undershirt was cream. The brown leather shoes he wore were bought for that day, and would forever rest in his closet, likely next to her gown.

He was flanked by two men, one was Kyle, and his best man, a close cousin he grew up with. Across the aisle were Veronica's maids, having two maids of honor, both her sisters, and another two bridesmaids, friends from school.

The organ began and the guests stood turning to see the beautiful bride walking down the aisle. Her arm linked as a chain to her father, a weak representation of their bonded souls that would soon be broken; hers would be reforged to Adam with love, her father's chain left to rust.

Adam was smiling, eyes welled up with joy as Dr. Lewis watched him, rather than Veronica. For a moment Dr. Lewis was transformed, brought to a place where he was standing in front of hundreds of people, saying the words that mattered little to him, but for Lily the imagery and religious intent meant the world. Dr. Lewis looked down to his hand where he had been unconsciously rubbing the skin at the base of his ring finger. The imperceptible change in color allowed him some solace as he remembered the only man witness of their commitment to each other: Jimmy.

The verses were read, the vows were said, and the two lab assistants kissed for the first time as Mr. and Mrs. Nicholson. When everyone exited the church they were met with a storybook scene. The iridescent glow of reds, burning orange, and yellow shimmered in the trees with the breeze. The smell of burning leaves brought childhood memories of sweatshirts and football. A wisp of air brought leaves afloat and women closer to their men as shivers rolled up their sun-kissed arms. The beauty from magic hour began to concede its rule over the chilled darkness.

It was beautiful how the purity of white stood out in the autumn palette, its rarity in nature causing everyone to take notice. Veronica wore it well with her dark bronze skin, the sun had done great work in making it glow. Her smile in the acute sunlight was shimmering as she turned and waved to everyone before kissing Adam and entering the Rolls Royce.

As the crowd waved, Kyle and Annie kissed. The joy of the moment left everyone feeling romantic. Even Dr. Lewis wished he had someone to hold. For the briefest moment he felt eyes on him as the car pulled away. From across the lawn he saw Michelle Adams standing with her plus one. A tall, lean African-American man dressed sharply with gold rimmed aviators on to block the sunlight. He smiled at her and waved, the two of them returning the favor and smiling. Dr. Lewis would never know how much she wished it were him she was locking arms with.

# | TWENTY-FIVE |

## Poughkeepsie, New York | October 16, 2016

"The next few years went very well for us at The Experience Center. Our drug was approved for treatment around the world. The company had a board of directors, a research and development group, a treatment branch, and even a team to determine where future treatment centers would be all over the world. We all stayed at the headquarters in Chesterfield, and asked Michelle Adams to work for us full time as the head of our legal department," Ethan said and paused, finally giving in to his urge to drink the lemonade that sat a few feet in front of him.

"When are we going to find out about Lily?" Joey asked frustrated. He took advantage of Ethan's loss of focus.

"Soon, very soon," he said holding up a finger as he took a drink. The lemonade was wonderful, sour with a hint of sweet, and bitterly cold. He could only sip it, but that was enough to feel refreshed.

Ethan reached into his pocket and pulled out the rock, allowing it to tumble around in his hand as he thought.

"Those first couple years were incredible. I'd been nominated to receive a Nobel Prize for our treatment, and Dr. Stelious for his work on neural mapping. We were financially successful as well, but that goes without saying."

"Yes we've all seen the money you've made," Ed said annoyed.

"I promise you, sir. It has never been about the money."

"Can we get on with it?" Joey asked watching Ethan, reading his body language.

"Sure, I'll just pick up where things started going south for us," Ethan replied, trying not to seem nervous, but Joey intimidated him.

## Puerto Vallarta, Mexico | December 2012

It had been a great week in Puerto Vallarta. The Riu Palace was everything it had promised to be. The food was good and the service exceptional. They were in the Jacuzzi Suite at the top of the left tower, giving them a sweeping view of the bay; the mountains closing in on the water from both the north and south like a large funnel.

Kyle and Annie climbed the pale flowered stairs, ascending to the open aired Jacuzzi that gave the suite its name. She wore a red bikini trimmed in blue, her narrow hips swinging side to side as she walked to the edge of the balcony. The howling wind that drove the undulating surf nearly drowned out the sound of the crashing waves. The early evening was Kyle's second favorite time, with the sun setting harshly against the tropical foreground, seemingly giving into gravity as it quickened its descent toward the horizon. This is what Annie loved, the amber glow before the heralding call, the shades of darkness that proceeded the shimmered blanket across the sky.

If it was up to him, he would have asked her in the morning when the waves thundered hard onto the sand in a gradual crescendo as it traveled the beachfront front, south to north. The predictability in the rhythm was soothing to him and the power was incredible. He enjoyed watching the stingrays in the waves, black kites in a blue-green sky, chasing sustenance and enjoying the speed as their world raced downward plunging to the hard sand below. It made him think of all the millions of imperceptible things that had to go right in order to make the world work—the pull of the moon bringing in the tides, the wind that swept down the mountains and across the water as the temperature drove molecules to excitable states causing them to vibrate and travel at higher velocities.

But it wasn't up to him, because he knew what she'd prefer. He watched her at the balcony for several minutes as she watched the sun. Kyle knew the time was right, the week had gone well and he promised himself he was ready when he bought the ring three weeks ago. He reached into his pocket and pulled out the ring, a blue sapphire, six carats in size. The emerald cut was what she wanted and she made it very clear that diamonds weren't her thing. She liked blue, just like his eyes.

"Don't you love the sunset?" she asked without taking her eyes away from it.

"I do," he said with a small questioning in his voice. She heard the awkwardness, and the direction his voice came from made her spin around.

"Annie I love you. Since the moment I saw you in our treatment room I loved you. I love you for coming on this trip with me and getting past your fear of the beach. I love you for listening to me, even when I make no sense. I love you for trusting me and coming to church. Please, let me marry you?"

She stood frozen for a moment, stunned by the spontaneity, the beauty of the fading sun and the way the blue stone complimented the orange sky. She smiled and raised him from the ground with a loving tug. She kissed him on his lips.

"When?" she asked, still smiling.

"After we get home. I want to ask Ethan to come with us. To be our witness."

"You do listen don't you?" she joked.

"I don't want a big wedding either. I just want him there. He's been so much like a father to me."

"I know. He's been great to us both."

## Chesterfield, Missouri | February 1, 2013

Adam and Veronica sat in their large, five-bedroom home. They built it large with the intention to fill it with children. Now, they sat waiting at the kitchen table, staring at a cellphone that hadn't yet rang. Adam held her hands in his as he comforted his crying wife. The table was littered with Kleenex, a side effect of the fertility drugs from her most recent bout of *in vitro* fertilization. The bills had been coming in for two years, but that hadn't mattered. Their insurance was good, and they had more than enough money to afford it, but the failed attempts had been hard to bear. Three times now they had performed the stimulation process, the egg retrieval, and six times they implanted two embryos, but not once had they even heard a heartbeat. The doctor told them this would be that last time for the stimulation. The more she was stimulated, the more estrogen was placed into her system, and the more estrogen, the higher the likelihood of developing cancer.

They sat at the table waiting for the call to come. They had done a five-day embryo transfer two weeks ago, and just got back from having blood drawn for a pregnancy test. They had taken three home pregnancy tests that very morning, all of which were negative. Adam and Veronica had heard it all before, several times, not to take the pregnancy test as it could lead to false positives and negatives, but they really wanted to see.

Suddenly the phone rattled on the table. Veronica started to cry and Adam held her close as he stood up, bringing her head gently into his abdomen. After three rings he picked up the phone.

"This is Adam . . . mhm . . . wait, what? Are you sure?" He reached down and squeezed Veronica's hand.

"Tell me," she whispered shaking his hand.

"Hang on, can you say it again? I'm gonna put you on speakerphone."

"Ok, can you hear me well?" the nurse said through the phone.

"Yes," Veronica said loudly toward the table where the phone rested.

"You're pregnant, and although we can't be sure, the level of hCG at this stage is very high, which could mean twins."

"Oh my God really!" Veronica exclaimed covering her mouth with both hands. She sprung up from the table and squeezed her husband as hard as she could. She was crying again, but this time it was the release of three-years worth of anxiety that she was shedding. Life felt easier to bear, the world outside seemed sunny and warm despite the winter storm watch.

"Ok you two, congrats. It's still a possibility that this may not go full term, but once we make it to twelve weeks we're at a greater than 90 percent chance."

"Thank you thank you thank you!" Veronica said again giggling and hopping in the kitchen, her feet slapping down against the tiled floor.

When Kyle walked into The Experience Center on Monday morning, he was met with jealous eyes. His bronze skin was in stark contrast to everyone. It was February and by now the entire midwest was angry with winter, its long cold nights, the ice and snow, and the misleading warm days.

He finally reached the white steel door at the far side of the treatment hallway and scanned his ID tag allowing him into the research area.

"Dr. Stelious," Kyle said nodding.

"Off wasting time again I see Kyle," he responded dryly.

"It was productive," Kyle said walking by and straight toward the far wall where Dr. Lewis' office was.

*Knock, knock, knock.* "Enter," Dr. Lewis said from behind the solid walnut door.

"Ethan," Kyle said as he entered the large office, quickly shutting the door behind him. The room was ornate, bright, not the style you would expect to see in the office of Dr. Ethan Lewis. It always threw Kyle off to see Ethan there.

"Kyle, trip went well I take it? Back ready to work?"

"It was great thanks. I actually do have some news if you have a minute?"

"Yes I do have a minute. Tell me the news," he said pushing away from his glass desk to give Kyle his full attention.

"I'm engaged," he said smiling widely, his face the color of the bright rug that rested on the black tiled floor.

"Haha!" Dr. Lewis exclaimed and hopped up from his chair to embrace his good friend.

"Why didn't you tell me you were going to propose?"

"I'm not really sure to be honest. I think I just didn't want the pressure of other people knowing. I had to do it when I wanted to do it."

"Amazing Kyle. Seriously happy for you." Dr. Lewis placed his hand on Kyle's shoulder. "You know your father is too."

"I do. But he's not here."

"I'm sorry Kyle this must be a bit bittersweet for you."

"I do wish he was here. I miss him with the big stuff," Kyle said looking at Ethan.

"We're all here for you, Kyle. I think I can speak for anyone."

"Thanks," Kyle said forcing a smile. He thought of Annie and the wedding and remembered why he came into the office. "Ethan, will you be our witness? We don't want anything big, just a small ceremony at the courthouse. I want you there."

"You have no idea how happy that makes me Kyle. I'm going to tell you a story. One that I've never told a soul, but it involves Jimmy."

"This's gotta be good then."

"Come on over and sit down." The two of them went to the far west side of the office, where he had large floor to ceiling windows and the same blue couch from their old treatment suite. He told the decorator that had to stay, no questions asked.

"When I was at Harvard and Lily and I were together we made a promise to one another. We said our own vows, never went to a courthouse but I did make her a promise to have a real wedding one day. We just had to wait until her parents didn't hate me. They were very religious, and, as you know from your constant attempts, I don't believe in church or God. Anyways, so we went to a tattoo shop, a young artist—"

"Jimmy," Kyle interrupted and Ethan nodded.

"He took us right away. We got these done," he said raising his left hand and pointing toward his ring finger."

"I really don't see anything."

"You see the slight discoloration of a band around my finger?"

"Wow, yeah I do now that you're pointing at it. You've had that since before we met? How have I been with you this long and haven't seen that?"

"Lily and I got matching white ring tattoos. Our secret pact with one another. Wanna know another secret?"

"Yup."

"I go back every year to get it redone. With the Harvard Research Report. That's the reason I go, and that's why I'm so close with Jimmy."

"Incredible."

"Yes it is. All of this is," Ethan said sulking low into the worn couch, the years had been hard on them both. He reflected on how far the treatment had come and the speed it went. He thought of Lily and her parents. He thought of The Beyond Experience and how that may affect them. It was an idea that for some reason he'd never had.

"Kyle," Dr. Lewis asked quietly. "Knowing what you know, would it be a good idea to let Lily's parents into the experience? To see her again?"

"I thought that treatment wasn't an option Dr. Lewis," he said coldly, remembering how both Dr. Lewis and Dr. Stelious confronted Kyle at their first partners meeting. The three of them held 75 percent of the company, the remaining parts were with Adam and Veronica. Traci had been bought out after the first year. The two doctors explained the negative ramifications of allowing The Beyond

Experience to become a regular occurrence. It was exceptional from a research standpoint; however, imagining a society that could be ushered into the presence of a loved one reeked of negative consequences. Kyle finally agreed, and the doctors asked Kyle to sign papers with Michelle.

"You're right Kyle, don't be upset. I just had the thought is all. I'm very grateful for you including me in your wedding."

"No, thank you. You've been like a father to me for a while now. The good and the bad that comes with it."

The men shared a warm embrace, both feeling their roles for one another.

Kyle left the room but Dr. Lewis stayed velcroed to the spot he sat. The thought of Lily's parents seeing her again was enticing. It was almost closure for him. *They may see the good in what we've done; they may believe I'm not a bad man.*

# | TWENTY-SIX |

Madison was cold, white, and quiet. The snow had accumulated several inches a day for the last week but the snow still filled the sky. Classes remained in session, government still went to work, and research continued to be conducted for Dr. Brian Lacey. After two years of begging, he had scraped up enough private funding to begin another trial on the effects of anesthetics, as well as the effects of Lily of the Valley on individuals who were treated with it. He had been poaching patients from Dr. Lewis' studies, trying to find a pattern of disease, and frankly, found very little.

It was frustrating him, the success of a former colleague, a former competitor. Lacey had seen Lily first at the Union one spring day. She was petite, blonde, bubbly in a cute way; his polar opposite. Lily was contagious and he grew obsessed. He talked to her a few times, even took her on a date once, but that all ended when she met Ethan, the quiet, first-year med school kid.

Dr. Lacey watched from a distance as she slowly fell for the skinny Ethan Lewis, the loser who hadn't talked in class and never socialized with anyone. Even with her he was awkward, his shoulder slouched forward and his hair fell into his eyes. What she saw in Ethan, he couldn't figure out, so he approached her one day but she refused to talk to him. Things became heated and he yelled at her. It was a story she never told Ethan, but she didn't have to. Her brother, Joey, had been visiting that weekend and she mentioned the altercation to him. After Joey Fisch talked to Lacey, he wasn't hovering around her anymore.

A sinister thought crept into Lacey's mind. One that would cost him his license and likely a prison sentence, but it was a revenge story.

He accessed the data from his most recent study on brain O2 levels in persons being treated with Lily of the Valley, both currently and previously. He played with parameters, exclusion criterion, inclusion criterion and selectively started to build his sample. He began to discard any subject that didn't skew itself toward his hypothesis. Eventually, he had over three-hundred data points that indicated, at a slight but present level, oxygen was negatively affected by immediate and ongoing treatment using Lily of the Valley. He did the same selective data point searching for several of the other anesthetics used by Dr. Lewis and found another drug, propofol, also decreased O2. Putting these two ingredients together made for a truly significant likelihood for decreased oxygen to the brain—at least in theory.

Lies, doctored data points, small probabilities, and the fact that the oxygen decrease during these short periods of treatment meant essentially nothing without follow-up studies to determine the long-term effects. Dr. Lacey knew it was a stretch, but, if it put a bump in the road for Dr. Lewis' global success, it was worth it.

He picked up his office phone and dialed. He had committed Elias Grant's private cell number to memory a few years back. Following the quiet court proceedings involving Dr. Lewis, the CEO of Whitestone reached out to Dr. Lacey. He offered to sell Lily of the Valley to him, if he was still requiring any, because they now had a greenhouse with no one to sell their goods to. Dr. Lacey initially passed, not having any research money, but two years prior his begging for money stopped when Elias stepped in and gave him a greenhouse, three million dollars, and any further assistance he could manage, just to take Dr. Lewis down.

"Dr. Brian Lacey," Elias said happily, his mouth biting the end of a half-smoked cigar. "Do you wish to tell me good news?"

"Elias, good afternoon. You seem happy."

"I am good Doctor. Playing golf in Naples as we speak. Every time I come down here I get a stronger urge to hang it all up and retire. We should get you down here Doc. I bet you can swing a club."

"I can, but don't get to much. Not a lot of time these days I'm afraid."

"Well, we gotta change that. What good is making money if you're not spending it?" he asked as he lined up his tee shot, earpiece snugly in place. He swung waiting for Dr. Lacey's response.

"Point taken."

"Ah!" Elias groaned into the earpiece. "You talked during my backswing doctor."

"Apologies."

"So what's on your mind. You need more money?"

"No, not yet. Just wanted to let you know I think I have a way to sting our friend. I'll be conducting additional trials, but it looks like I can put a few ripples in his pond."

"Excellent. Get on it. The sooner the better. I've been watching their little company, and it's not so little anymore. It appears that people will soon be able to pay out of pocket for the treatment without a doctor's referral. They're about to get a whole lot more business."

"Where'd you hear that?"

"I've got friends in high places son. You do your part, I'll do mine. Maybe your research will stall this proposal. Get it out there. The sooner the better."

Elias grant stood on the tee box at the number seven hole at Augusta. He turned toward the other men in the foursome, "I'm taking a mulligan. You fellas don't have a problem with that do you? After all, that was our boy Lacey who sent my ball into the hazard."

The three men smiled and waved him on. It was these men who had invited Elias out onto the golf course. His smooth talking had convinced several big pharmaceutical companies to allow him to head the attacks on Dr. Lewis' treatment. The drug companies stood to lose billions, so Elias gathered them together, convincing them to fund a research project that would create problems for the Nobel Prize winner, Dr. Lewis.

Now Elias got to reap the benefits of being pampered by billion dollar companies as his boy, a pitbull named Dr. Brain Lacey, went straight for the man who embarrassed him.

# | TWENTY-SEVEN |

## Saint Louis | June 20, 2013

Pi Pizzaria in downtown Saint Louis was relatively quiet. The weather was cold, and the city was dead after 5:00 p.m. this time of year when the Cardinals weren't in town. The décor was a pleasant change from the traditional pizza place, with tall, stainless steel chairs, a black bar, and slate floors. It also lacked the exuberant attempts at Italian flash, no grapes, no paintings of wine bottles or cityscapes. It had once been a tradition for the couples when they lived in apartments near the city, but since moving a year had gone by without a double date.

Veronica and Adam sat nervously waiting on the same side of the small metal table. Veronica had been waiting months to tell someone about their pregnancy, and since they hit the 20-week mark, they felt it was safe. She also had been starting to show so it was only a matter of time before the questions came.

After several minutes Annie and Kyle entered the restaurant and walked to the table where their friends sat waiting.

"I see you guys in the office all the time but I never got a chance to tell you how much I hate you two," Veronica joked as Kyle and Annie sat down.

"Oh come on now, is that any way to greet your only friends?" Kyle shot back lovingly, grabbing Annie and turning her as if they were leaving the restaurant.

"No, leave Annie here!" Veronica said reaching forward to grab her friend's arm. "You can go, Kyle. I already see you at work but I never get to see this beautiful lady!"

"Thanks Vero," Annie said walking around the table to hug her.

"No!" Annie exclaimed and placed her hand across her mouth. She began to tear up. "Why didn't you tell me? I pray for you every night!"

"What's going on?" Kyle said still locked hand in hand with Adam, the men frozen in a handshake.

"Look at her tummy!" Annie said twisting Veronica around and pointing at her belly.

"Adam didn't think you'd notice, but I wanted to wear a tight shirt just to test you. Told you honey," she said sticking out her tongue.

"Wow you guys. Congrats. How far along?" Kyle asked and sat down.

"They're 24 weeks now—"

"Twins!" Annie shouted and ran around the table again to hug her seated friend. The few people who were in the restaurant all turned to see who was yelling. "She's having twins, I'm excited," she said responding to their looks.

"A boy and a girl," Adam said smiling and holding Veronica's hand.

Kyle looked at Annie, who met his eyes. The two of them agreed on the way over that it was wrong of them not to invite Adam and Veronica to their ceremony. Over the last five years they had grown close to the couple, spending the middle three years together almost every weekend.

Annie reached into her clutch and slid the ring onto her finger under the table. She turned back to Kyle and nervously bit her lip and nodded.

"We've got some news too," Kyle said smiling.

"You're pregnant?" Veronica joked placing both hands flat on the table. She knew the couple had decided to wait until marriage.

"Dear sweet baby Jesus," Adam joked along.

"Close," Annie said raising her hand from under the table and showing the blue sapphire.

"I want your job," Adam said to Kyle admiring the ring. Annie took it off and placed it into Veronica's hand. She tried it on, only getting it over her first knuckle on her wedding finger.

"Are your hands that small or am I just that pregnant?" she joked showing the ring.

"So when is it?" Adam asked.

"Hope you don't have plans tomorrow afternoon," Kyle said with an uneasy smile.

Adam and Veronica were happy the next morning. The couple had discussed how they knew it was a last minute realization on the part of Kyle and Annie to invite them, but were honored to go nonetheless. They cancelled their birthing class and were getting ready to go to the courthouse early Saturday afternoon.

The courthouse was bland, with light linoleum tiles throughout with dark oak woodwork accenting the walls, desks, and lobby. One of the clerks at the main desk told them the ceremony would take place in a small room down the hall.

As they entered the room they saw Kyle and Annie facing one another, Annie's hands inside Kyle's. The two standard windows that were allowing sunlight in seemed to focus the rays on the loving couple. Seeing the two of them, Veronica leaned into Adam, like a puppy trying to cuddle. Adam jumped on the opportunity to reach around with his right hand and squeeze her close; he swore felt his son and daughter reach toward him too.

Annie turned to see Adam and Veronica walk through the doorway. "Hey guys! So glad you made it." Annie trotted the few steps toward the door and hugged them both. Kyle was shortly behind him and shook Adam's hand.

"I got the car running out back. Still got a chance," Adam joked, as some friend always does at a wedding.

"I think I'm good."

"You'd better be," Annie said slapping him playfully.

"Ethan!" Kyle said yelling past Adam.

"Hi Kyle," the doctor said reaching around Adam who bent out of the way to allow the men to shake hands.

"I've got my car running out back. Last chance," Dr. Lewis joked.

"Adam beat you to it, but like I told him, I'm good."

The ceremony was short and they exchanged rings. Adam and Dr. Lewis signed the marriage certificate as witnesses. The only negativity in the room was between Dr. Lewis' ears. Ethan had spent his whole life hiding his emotions deep within. So strong the memories of imagined events had been, that they were etched into his mind, as vivid as any moments he had with her. The wedding should have made him happy, watching Kyle, the closest thing he had to a son, getting married. Dr. Lewis was also distracted—and upset—about an email he read from Michelle Adams earlier that morning. A recent research article was being cited as a reason to shut down his work, every center, worldwide. The author was Dr. Brian Lacey.

# | TWENTY-EIGHT |

## Spring

Michelle Adams walked the streets of Madison looking for an address. She had used the research article to hunt down the lab assistants who were working with Dr. Lacey when he gathered his results that demonstrated negative findings related to drugs incorporated in Dr. Lewis' study. Michelle thought the study was too neat and tidy. She read it as soon as she heard about it and nothing felt right. She had taken it upon herself to investigate the research, which led her to Madison, and at the door to an apartment building where Karen Osborne lived.

Karen was an undergrad student who helped Dr. Lacey during the study. She was one of three assistants listed on the research paper, and the only one still attending UW–Madison. Michelle quickly reviewed her own questions regarding the study before knocking on the apartment door.

*Knock, knock, knock.* She struck the door with her knuckles taking a deep breath. It had been some time since she interviewed someone. Lately she had been exclusively defending patents and overseeing overseas contracts for the company.

"Who is it?" Michelle heard from the inside of the apartment. She could hear music getting softer and then footsteps getting louder.

"My name is Michelle Adams. I read a research article you were a part of recently. I'd love to come in and chat about it if that's ok."

"Hi," Karen said opening the door and continuing to dry her wet hair. "I just got out of the shower. Sorry," she said extending her small hand.

"Not a problem. So, do you remember the study?"

"Of course I do," she said rolling her eyes.

"Not much fun huh?"

"Um. No. You ever work research?"

"Yeah, did a few years back," Michelle winked at her. "Being in your forties has its advantages too. I don't remember the bad stuff as much now. Can I come in?"

The young research assistant paused and contemplated the request.

"I've got to be somewhere in 20 minutes. Wanna walk with me?" Karen asked with veiled discomfort.

"Sure I get it. I won't bite, and I won't be pushy. I'll be right outside. If you want to avoid me and sneak out the back I understand. I just wanted to ask a couple questions is all. I'll wait out there for 30 minutes. If you don't show, I won't be upset. Talk soon," Michelle smiled as she walked away, waving her painted pink nails at Karen while she turned away.

Ten minutes passed and Michelle waited outside enjoying the sunny spring afternoon.

"You've heard of Dr. Lacey?" Karen said as she walked outside, her backpack resting on her shoulders.

"Only from the article," Michelle said smiling and walking alongside Karen. "Thanks for letting me walk you."

"He's a huge man, but a bigger jerk. He never even paid me my stipend," Karen said dismissing Michelle's politeness.

"How much were you supposed to get?"

"Tweny-five-hundred dollars! I worked the whole fall semester in that stupid lab writing down answers to stupid questions."

"So you're clearly not happy. What a dick!" Michelle said, being as empathetic as possible.

"I know!"

"Ever ask him for it?"

"I wrote him at least five emails. Haven't heard back once. I gave up. I didn't even realize he published it."

"Yep. Brought you a copy."

"Thank you!" Karen said as she grabbed the paper. She quickly scanned over the work, a puzzled look started to develop on her face.

"What is it?" Michelle asked.

"These numbers seem small," Karen said furrowing her brow.

"Why's that?" Michelle asked as Karen was leading her right to an answer.

"The sample. I swear we saw more than that many people."

"Let me see again. Do you mind?" Michelle asked reaching out for the paper.

Michelle pretended to go through the paper again, but already knew what to ask.

"How many people did you see a day?"

"I didn't see them. I just plugged numbers in."

"How long did you spend working on these every day?"

"At least two hours."

"How many people would that mean per day?"

"Around 20, 25."

"Wow that's quite a few. You did this the whole semester? Five days a week?"

"Yes."

"That's literally thousands of people!" Michelle said genuinely surprised. "The results section doesn't really speak about thousands of people being excluded from the study. If I have any more questions, could you be available?"

"Yeah. I can help out."

"Here's my card," Michelle said handing it to her.

"A lawyer? Am I in trouble?"

"Did you get any money sweetheart?"

"No!"

"You'll be fine. It's him I'm after."

Michelle put her sunglasses on as she walked down the street enjoying the sunlight on her face. She was smirking, excited about the conversation she just had with Karen. Clearly Dr. Lacey had tampered with the research. She took out her phone to call Dr. Lewis.

"Hey Doc!" she said happily as her heels clicked on the uneven pavement.

"Morning Michelle."

"You don't sound happy. Well here, let me brighten your day. You can thank me later," Michelle said her pace quickening to match her heart. She loved hearing his voice.

"What do ya have for me?"

"I have Dr. Lacey's lab assistant telling me that she was inputting hundreds more values into the study's data than he was claiming. He also didn't explain any persons being excluded from his findings in his results or discussion section."

Dr. Lewis sat for a moment, processing the information. "So he's a liar?" He felt the rage he experienced at the last Harvard conference return. "What's with this guy!" he said loudly into the phone.

"Calm down honey we got 'em."

"What's next? How do we handle it?"

"That's what you pay me for Doc. Speaking of, I think I deserve a raise."

"Are you serious?" he asked laughing.

"We may have to talk about a few percentage points of the company."

"I'll just hire someone else," he joked.

"Not a chance honey. Nobody can do what I do for you. I'll keep you posted," she said and hung up, but not before blowing a kiss into the phone.

*Why do I do that?* she thought as she hung up the phone, embarrassed that she made a kissing sound. She sighed, as she reached her car and drove away; her mind filled with thoughts of Ethan and how she could make him happy.

# | TWENTY-NINE |

## Chesterfield, Missouri | August 29, 2013

It was dark, 2:30 a.m. when Veronica woke up to a strong pulling in her abdomen. In her foggy state she had mistaken the contraction for an aggressive kick from Tyler and tried to fall back to sleep. They often blamed the kicking on the boy. Veronica and Adam imagined him a soccer player, and Elle, would follow in her brilliant mother's footsteps, running her own research lab one day; Tyler, after Veronica's dad, and Elle, just because they liked the name. They decided to forgo the superstitions practice of not revealing their unborn children's names, putting their names on the shower invitations. The haul was substantial, and several of the gifts had their individual names on them.

It was 3:45 a.m. when Veronica woke again, but this time, it was the feeling of a cold, wetness around her hips that brought her to a full alert. She reached over and turned the lamp on, lifting her blanket to reveal the source.

"What's going on?" Adam said confused and unable to open his eyes, the sudden brightness overwhelming his retina.

"No!" Veronica screamed, her echoes reverberating around the master bedroom.

"What, what, what!" Adam said sitting up in bed still fighting to maintain a grasp on what was real and what may have been a dream.

"Oh my God Adam it's only 34 weeks! Is this normal?" She said clawing at the wetness that was displayed on the dark sheets.

"Baby it's ok. Let's get to the hospital."

"Ow!" she bellowed, realizing that her pain from earlier may have been her first contraction.

"Let's go. Throw your sandals on I'm gonna grab the go bag and help you to the car."

As she swung her feet over the end of the bed she saw it. The liquid that had been slowly spreading across her bed wasn't, in fact, the calling sign of labor, but rather blood. It was bright red, masked by the similar color of their sheets and the shadows from the blanket had hidden variance in the tint well. Now, as her feet hit the white rug below, she witnessed the blood trails navigating from her womb to the floor.

"Adam!" she screamed and began sobbing and froze in her spot. "Adam!" she screamed a second time as he came out of the closet.

"Oh my God," he said. Adam tried to be calm for her but he was struggling. The words had come out before he filtered through the thoughts. "Veronica," he said getting down on his knees to look her in the eyes. "We need to go, now!"

The two of them raced toward the hospital, weaving through the minimal traffic that presented itself. Thoughts raced through Adam's mind. *What if they died, what if she died, what if they all died? The gifts at home, the blood everywhere, how can I come home to that? What do I do with it all if they die? Oh my God. Oh my God!*

Veronica lay as flat as she could in the front seat. She was lightheaded, cold, and curled her arms around her children. It was as if she was trying to hold them closer to her, keeping them as long as she could, squeezing every drop of life giving fluid to Tyler and Elle.

As they arrived at the ER, Adam parked in the drop off zone, ran around the car, grabbed Veronica, and ran her through the doors in his arms.

"We need someone now!" he hollered and his voice seemed to carry through the entire hospital. Several staff members ran to help them, placing Veronica into a wheelchair and immediately brought her back. A nurse came quickly and tested her vitals, which were low,

85/50, with a pulse rate of 135. A doctor rushed into the large room, cramped full of people.

"What happened?" the doctor asked Adam without pleasantries.

"She woke up and we saw she was bleeding."

"How much?"

"A lot, I couldn't tell you an amount."

"How far along is she?"

"34 weeks."

"Ok, well we're gonna have to get these babies out," he said watching the nurse struggle to find a pulse through the abdominal ultrasound.

"Please doc, save them."

"Rachel, call the OR and someone call Dr. Hartford. We've got a c-section to do stat," the ER doctor barked. "Mr.–"

"Adam."

"Ok, Adam. We're going to have to do an emergency c-section on your wife and get these babies out right now. We haven't been able to get a heartbeat on them so this needs to happen now. Someone will talk to you about the complications while we prep for the surgery—"

"Please do what you have to do."

"We will."

It had taken an hour and a half before Dr. Hartford met with Adam. Veronica was stable and they had been able to get the babies out. Adam refused to see them until Veronica was awake and able. Adam sat frozen in a chair, staring at the ground for two more hours after that.

Thousands of thoughts flew through his mind about Tyler and Elle. *What would their nicknames have been? Would they have had the same friends? Would they have had a secret language only twins could share? Would they be strong willed or pushovers like me?* The list went on and on. He thought about Veronica too, how she would react when she heard the news, and how much he wished it were better.

"It was an unexpected complication that can come late in the pregnancy," Dr. Hartford said. "When your son began to have complications, it set off a cascade of events that ultimately affected your daughter as well. I'm truly sorry for your losses."

Adam sat in a chair holding Veronica's hand as she began to stir. He collected himself, dried his eyes, and stood to watch for her eyes to open.

"How are my babies? Can we see them?" she asked with a weak voice. Grimacing, she vaguely reached for her abdomen.

"Oh Vero," he said, struggling to get the words out. "Sweetheart . . . I don't. . . ." Adam lost control. Tears began to roll down his face. A sudden avalanche of reality hit him at once. The stress had allowed him to block his emotions, his thoughts of what might have been distracted him from what had actually occurred.

"Adam?"

"They're gone sweetheart. The doctors said it wasn't our fault."

They cried together for what seemed like the whole afternoon. Adam even crawled into bed with his wife and they consoled one another. They were silent, except for the sniffling and sobbing, both processing in their own way but being in the terrible moment together.

"How?" Veronica finally asked.

"They said Tyler had the cord around his neck and it got tighter. Once his body went into panic, it sent Elle's there too. They think you bled because they pulled the placenta from your uterine wall. It was a terrible surgery too. They said we may never be able to conceive again, but that's something to discuss months down the line. I almost lost you too. You lost a lot of blood."

"Have you seen them?"

"Not without you, sweetie. I couldn't do it."

The couple spent an hour holding their lifeless children in silence. For them, time had stopped its race allowing them a brief intermission to soothe their grief. They had been guaranteed nobody from the hospital would enter the room until they were finished visiting with their babies. Veronica stroked Elle's dark hair gently, committing each stroke to memory, while Adam rubbed Tyler's tiny feet, the ones that were supposed to strike the ball.

"Adam," Veronica said softly. "Do you think it's strange to take a picture?" she continued with tears rolling down her face. The etiquette for such a situation isn't defined. It was awkward to think of.

Adam didn't respond verbally, but pulled out his phone. He handed Veronica both children, then sat on the bed next to her. She brought Elle and Tyler up into view of the phone and the couple did their best to put a smile on. It would be the only photo of the family.

"I'll send it to you," Adam said briefly looking at the image, then instinct quickly advised him to turn the image away. He couldn't process the moment they were frozen in, let alone the moment their breathless children would be taken, and even worse, knowing the image would be the only visual reminder of this tragic time. *How quickly would their tiny faces fade from memory?*

"Adam, I want their footprints."

"Me too."

They stayed huddled on the bed, the family of four, slowly feeling time start to march on once more. Heaviness in their eyes, physiology reminding them both they couldn't avoid sleep forever. They tried as long as they could, but ultimately they fell asleep, dreaming of a better day.

# | THIRTY |

Monday was quiet. Everyone in the Chesterfield research office had heard about the loss of the twins. The whole company had been following Adam and Veronica's story. In fact, Adam and Veronica had started a blog about their pregnancy and fertility issues to try to spread awareness. It was as if work was a grief center as they formed small groups throughout the office talking about the couple, commiserating in their own way. Everyone was trying to find a way to donate their own time or money, to send a card, flowers, or even just figure out if any of that was right. Everyone at the office, as well as tens of thousands of other strangers, had followed along thanks to social media.

Dr. Lewis sat in his office, behind his desk staring blankly at the screen at an email from Michelle Adams, stating the investigation had been completed on Dr. Lacey. He was found guilty of scientific misconduct, fired from the University of Wisconsin–Madison, and lost his ability to apply for federal research finding for five years. The news barely registered for Dr. Lewis. He was focused only on Veronica and Adam, their babies, and what to do next.

He had already considered calling Kyle. The thought of taking Adam and Veronica into The Beyond Experience was unshakable, however, he knew bringing it up to Kyle would be Pandora's box. He had already turned Kyle down multiple times when he asked to allow Annie inside to talk to her brother.

"Dr. Lewis," Kyle said walking into his office, arms folded and staring at the floor.

Dr. Lewis looked toward his door, a small wave of anxiety crept over him, his thoughts now seemingly becoming actions.

"Hi Kyle."

"Adam and Veronica are home now. They've decided to cremate the babies and bring them home. No funeral."

"I think that's a good idea."

"Me too. Not sure what else you would do to be honest."

"Yeah me neither. I talked to him today. Told them not to bother coming in till they feel like it. Can't imagine they'll ever be the same."

"I agree. I think Veronica is really messed up. The way Adam is describing her is crazy."

"I can't even comprehend it, thank God."

"Hmm. Funny to hear you say that."

"Say what, God?"

"Yeah. Huh."

"Get past it Kyle, it's a figure of speech."

"I know, just an observation. Ethan . . .," he paused.

"Kyle?"

"Do you think we should treat them?"

"I do. If they're up for it. Close the door would you Kyle? Come have a seat." Kyle followed the suggestion. "Between you and me, they may feel too guilty about wiping it away so quickly. I've chosen not to go back. I want to feel that guilt. It's what keeps me driving forward. Plus, I was addicted before. I can't get back to that."

"Don't you want to see Lily at all?"

"Of course I do. But I don't trust myself."

"Ok, but please, consider offering them the treatment?"

"I am Kyle, but they likely won't take it."

"I'll feel better if we try."

"So will I," said Dr. Lewis. "Go ahead and ask them. Let's see what they say. You guys are close friends right?"

"Yes."

"He's gonna be more likely to say hello to you. Time it out however you want. Tell them to call me if they want the treatment. I want you to stay clear of it. You'll likely lose objectivity treating them. To be honest, I may as well, but I trust myself."

"I get it. I'll let them know."

Shortly after Kyle left, Dr. Lewis carefully walked to Dr. Stelious' office, making sure nobody, especially Kyle, saw him enter.

"So sad," Dr. Stelious said shaking his head. "That shouldn't happen to anyone. I have no idea what to say Ethan."

"I think we're all struggling right now Marcus."

"What do you need?" he asked Dr. Lewis who had already closed the door behind him, sitting down in the green chair opposite the aluminum desk where Dr. Stelious sat.

"Discretion."

"Regarding?"

"Things to come. I will also need your help."

"What is happening Ethan? Should I be worried?"

"No, nothing concerning. Adam and Veronica may be calling me."

"Ok?"

"For treatment."

"I see nothing wrong with that. In fact, I would recommend it."

"I have, so has Kyle." Dr. Lewis froze, his mouth became dry as the ruse began to unfold. His heart quickened and he pleaded silently for Dr. Stelious to understand his true intentions.

"Ok Dr. Lewis. I think I am understanding."

"You always were a smart man Marcus."

"You are wanting to take them into The Beyond Experience? To see their babies?"

Dr. Lewis nodded, afraid that if he actually said the words out loud then Kyle would hear and come charging into the office.

"This is why you need my help?"

"Yes. I can't ask Kyle. We all agreed not to take people into the beyond, and it was largely due to Kyle and Annie. I didn't want that to become an uncontrolled, unregulated, and abused phenomenon."

"And I agreed. So why are we doing it then?"

Dr. Lewis really hadn't thought of a reason. He was more or less flying by the seat of his pants, falling victim to the pains of persons he knew well. He knew Annie too, but not like Adam and Veronica. Annie was still an outsider, a lie that Kyle had told. Dr. Lewis still felt bitter about the lies from Kyle, but at the end of the day, he understood. It was simply taking a while to warm up to Annie who was rarely around.

"I think it's only fair for them. Think of everything they've gone through just to have a child. If we surprise them with the experience, then explain to them everything we've known over the last few years, they may be ok with not going back. Plus, we haven't sent two people back at the same time. This could get interesting."

Dr. Stelious sat in thought, as he often did, a pursed lip and eyes that were open but not seeing the world around him. They were simply acting as a visual aid, telling all those around him that he was awake, but not necessarily present, focused solely on his thoughts.

"I will help you."

"Great, and we need—"

"I won't speak with anyone about it. I can hold a secret Dr. Lewis. Can you?"

Adam had taken all the gifts from the baby shower and shoved them into the far corner of the basement. After an argument regarding what to do with them, he spent forty-five minutes storming around the house and gathering them together. Veronica didn't have the strength to help, her body still feeling the aftershocks of a birth void of life.

She lay on the couch, silent, her hand covering her tired swollen eyes. The house was dark despite the midday sun. The silence made the home seem much too large now for the young couple. Adam sat 20 feet from his wife, arms extended in front of him endlessly staring at a slideshow of photos. The first, their two embryos, the second, the initial ultrasound, a third, their 3D image of Tyler and Elle, and the last was their only family photo. Adam recalled how eagerly he awaited the birth of the twins to see how close their 3D scan was to their actual faces. It was remarkable how accurate the ultrasound had been. In the moment at the hospital the thought hadn't crossed his mind but now, seeing the images flashing before him, he saw it.

He wanted to tell Veronica, but couldn't. She hadn't wanted to talk about the babies for three weeks. She hadn't wanted to talk to anyone in three weeks. The few words they spoke were when she needed help taking care of herself, which Adam didn't mind. He loved her and although he was hurting, he knew she was worse. The bond between a mother and her baby is unrivaled, her bond to them being more than emotional, having felt them moving, reaching, and as one ultrasound had proven, hugging each other. Adam fought the urge to tell her, to remind himself, that they had three more embryos frozen. Neither was ready for the discussion. Not for the immediate future.

Adam's slideshow was interrupted by a text notification at the top of the screen.

"I know it's rough and I've left you some voicemails the last week, but if you want to talk, let me know."

Kyle had left several messages for Adam. Each of them had been shorter than the last. The first was very informative, how the Chesterfield office was all behind them, supporting them with anything they need. Kyle had also told him Dr. Lewis wanted to talk to them about treatment. Adam thought it was a good idea, but Veronica, as predicted, felt guilty about wanting the emotional pain to go away.

Adam had allowed himself to be treated two weeks earlier. After Kyle reached out, he called Dr. Lewis, who scheduled a secret treatment session. Dr. Lewis told Adam to have Veronica's mother come down and stay with her for the night. He also advised Adam to tell Veronica he needed a night away to clear his head.

Adam paused after reading the text from Kyle. He ached inside being unable to talk to his friend; but Dr. Lewis made Adam promise not to tell Kyle about the treatment. "Kyle will be furious if he knew you were treated this way. All treatment for The Beyond Experience had been stopped, so we are doing this behind his back," Dr. Lewis had said. Adam was struggling with the secret, but had to keep it—at least until Veronica was treated.

"Thanks for reaching out Kyle. She's still not doing great. I'll try and call you later. No promises."

"Fair enough. Annie misses you guys. Just tell her you did the treatment."

"I don't know how," Adam responded, recalling the hours he sat in the house trying to find the right words to say to his struggling wife.

"You just have to get it out man. Tell her how it felt. Tell her you still think about the kids."

"Ok," Adam responded, and the texting ceased.

Adam sat for a few moments. The thought of the treatment was weighing heavily on him. His heart quickened as anxiety drove his body's response. He wiped his clammy hands on his pants and looked toward his sobbing wife, whose dry eyes robbed her of the emotional release. Adam stood and walked toward his wife. He wasn't able to stop one foot from following the other forward. He sat on the floor in front of her and began to stroke her thick, tangled hair. She turned to him, looking into his eyes but not seeing him. Adam's eyes became a wall of water as he looked back into her swollen eyes.

"Sweetheart," he said softly, continuing to stroke her hair.

"Adam," she said squinting hard, her burning eyes yearning for moisture. She began to sob.

"Sweetheart we need to do something. I'm not going to do it without you."

"I don't want to feel this way anymore, but I can't forget my babies," she said reaching up and squeezing the hand that was rubbing her head.

"We won't. You know we won't. You've seen people come in for treatment. You know their stories. I don't want this to ruin us. I still need you."

"I love you Adam. Thank you for everything you do to help me. I never say it."

"You don't have to sweetie. I know."

"Tell me what to do Adam."

"We call Dr. Lewis."

"Call him for us."

It had only taken 24 hours, but Dr. Lewis had the room prepped. Dr. Stelious was present as well, splitting the time performing the observations with him. The experimental wing was shut down for the afternoon in order to prevent those who typically worked late into the evening from seeing the young couple enter the back door and head into the treatment room.

The treatment rooms were almost identical to those in The Shack at Washington University. The walls were a variant of cream on drywall instead of the white tile, and the floors were large rectangular tiles versus the square ones at the old clinic. The smell of alcohol lingered, the echoing was minimal, but the familiarity was important to Dr. Lewis. Doctors Lewis and Stelious both sat silently in the observation room waiting for the moment the couple would arrive.

It was 5:00 p.m. when they saw the broken mother and supportive husband. She wore sweat pants and a shawl over a baggy hooded sweatshirt. Her hair was loosely fixed on top her head in a large, brown bun, and her eyes and cheeks conveyed the look of someone who spent too much time on a boat, the wind and sun having had its way.

"I'm glad you decided to come," Dr. Lewis said standing and walking toward her, posturing for a hug but not pressing the offer.

"I don't want to forget my babies," she said beginning to sob. It had been a consistent theme Adam had heard for the last 24 hours. Adam stroked her back gently while he looked to Dr. Lewis.

"Adam, I'll give you a minute," Dr. Lewis said and turned, walking back into the observation room. Adam nodded and sighed deeply. He heard his own heart racing, pulsing deep in his ear. His mouth was dry and he shuffled his feet in place.

"Adam?" Veronica asked, distracted by his apparent anxiety in the moment. He paused, his head raced with so many things to say to his wife. She didn't know he had been treated, she didn't know he was treated beyond what millions have experienced. She didn't know The Beyond Experience existed, nor did she know the most unbelievable thing had already occurred to him, and would soon happen to her.

"Veronica I already had the treatment. Two weeks ago when your mother came down."

She glared at him, her face turning a varied shade of red as her tears began to flow once more. "How stupid am I? Thinking we were in this together. How could you have done that and not told me!" she said through grinding teeth, her mouth quivering, attempting to be strong in her moment of solitude. "So what's this then? Everyone come to convince me this will work? Where's Kyle? Hiding in the back laughing?" The tears stopped flowing and her face was firm.

Adam reached down and grabbed his wife's hands. She tried to quickly pull them away but he held on strong. Adam stared into her eyes, not looking away, waiting for hers to meet his. "What is this Adam? Let go of me!" she hollered, squirming to loosen his grip.

"Sweetheart, no. I'm not letting go. Not of your arms, not of our marriage, not of Tyler and Elle. You need to listen to me," he said calmly, despite her thrashing.

"Don't say their names. You cannot say their names now," she spat.

Adam looked toward Dr. Lewis who nodded and gestured with his hands to calm down. "Kyle's not here, because he can't be," Dr. Lewis said.

"Why can't he be here? Too busy having fun somewhere with

Annie? Can't believe she's not here either trying to drag me onto that bed over there."

"He can't be here because he can't know what we're about to do," Dr. Lewis said walking toward her.

"What's that supposed to mean?" Veronica stopped thrashing and her face softened.

"He can't know we aren't doing the normal treatment."

"What are we doing? I don't want to forget my babies," she said sobbing, finally looking Adam in the eyes.

"Honey, you won't believe me now, but these men are going to let you see Tyler and Elle but you cannot, under any circumstances, ever tell Kyle. Understand?"

"What?" Her mouth stayed open just slightly.

"Please sweetheart. Just say you won't. You'll never forget your babies. I promise."

"Ok. Dr. Lewis, please let me see my babies. I won't tell anyone. You can do that?"

Dr. Lewis nodded and walked into the treatment room. "Ok Veronica let's explain some things. Adam, you listen too. Kyle was the first to experience this, we did experimentation on it a while ago, before you two were brought on. Anyway, it changed his life for the better. He saw his father, three times in fact, and then I felt like he was becoming addicted to the treatment so we discontinued it. If he knew we were doing it for you two he would likely get upset. Do you both understand not to talk about this with Kyle, or anyone else for that matter?"

Adam and Veronica nodded.

"Good. Ok Veronica. Please go into the bathroom and change into that gown on the bed. Adam, you're more than welcome to stay and watch. It's actually quite incredible, but long."

Like thousands of times before, Dr. Lewis looked down at a patient on his table, and like thousands of times before, the patient looked up at him longing for a solution to a sorrowful problem. Dr. Lewis' problem had been his parents, the abuse, the drunkenness, the absence of a role model, and the necklaces they wore around their necks reminding him that if there was a God, Ethan Lewis wasn't on His radar. That ideology had been driven deeper into his mind by the loss of his only love, and the rejection of those who shared her life: the Christians from New York who looked down their noses at Ethan, the atheist who killed their Lily. Dr. Lewis always allowed those thoughts into his mind before administering the drug—a constant reminder of its origins in his own treatment, and the subsequent search for why she said "forgive me."

"You're going to feel a chill when the drug enters the arm," Dr. Lewis said after Dr. Stelious and Adam placed all the necessary items needed for recording her vitals.

"This is one elaborate trick Dr. Lewis," she said forcing a smile.

"Oh Veronica. You'll see. This is no trick," he said starting the drip and watching her fade into the experience.

Adam sat in the observation room with Dr. Lewis. Stelious had stepped out for the next few hours to sleep, his shift wouldn't start till 1:00 a.m. Adam had watched his wife breathe slowly in and out for over an hour. He remembered countless times lying next to her in their bed, watching her sleep. This was the first time since the twins had been born she was sleeping soundly. He looked around the room. Her vitals on the wall monitors were frighteningly low but the numbers that were looming large and red above them were even more terrifying: heart rate 15, BP 35/18, O2 80.

"Dr. Lewis are those her cut off numbers?"

"Yes. We've experimented before. We know those are the numbers based on her baseline. However, Dr. Stelious' device will trigger our alarm too. It'll sense the moment we need to bring her out."

Adam sat quietly as if asking more questions would lead to further anxiety. He'd rather take his chances watching.

Veronica felt it immediately. Her senses were heightened, she heard the sound of wind through leaves was surrounding her. She perceived the variations of their different sizes, the smaller leaves vibrating at higher frequencies, the large ones sounding like a standing bass being massaged with a bow. A colossal waterfall rumbled far off in the distance, quaking the soft dirt she stood on. She felt drawn to it, the churning water vaporizing into a heavy mist filling the area around the deep pool below. A small stream of water began to flow right in front of her feet, washing away the soft earth. The trench deepened as more water flowed quickly over the ground turning erratically following the path of least resistance as it continued further away from Veronica. She took a step back as the earth began to tumble down into the stream that continued to widen in front of her.

As she stared down into the clear smooth water she saw herself. She was beautiful again, a smiling flawless face, thick long hair and a body that remained void of the signs of a failed birth. She knelt, leaning over the widening stream for a closer look. She gently stroked her cheeks and her hair. She reached down into the fast flowing water and grabbed a scoop of the clear water, sipping the cool refreshment. She felt it run through her, recharging her, and allowing her to feel happiness once more. She took another drink and a second wave of the sensation flowed through her. The stream continued to widen, to deepen, to accelerate as the water that cascaded down from the large waterfall flowed downstream past Veronica.

Veronica closed her eyes and listened to the trees once more. She raised her head toward the sky, a yellow glow caressing her skin as it broke through the tree canopies high above. She took a cleansing breath and turned her gaze back toward the water, opening her eyes. Ten feet below the ever-changing water lay a rich golden shimmer. At first, Veronica thought it was a beautiful glow from the sun above reflecting off the water but when her eyes adjusted, she saw the source was from deep below.

Veronica held her breath, her hands stretched up above her head as she dove down into the water. The symphony of wind and leaves was replaced by the sound of water rushing and the muffled sound of bubbles and turbulence as she took long pulls through the water and reached the bottom. The golden glow from the riverbed was rich and substantial. She reached through the dark earth below and pulled out three golden balls. She then swam to the surface and exited the water, holding the three golden balls close to her. They felt warm to the touch and she felt a strong affinity to them.

Veronica suddenly felt drawn to the waterfall. She followed the river upstream climbing over fallen trees and rocks as she moved closer toward the waterfall. The water became louder, overpowering the noise of wind through the trees, as it crashed over the rocks. White foam highlighted the water revealing where it flowed against the current, forming eddies.

As she continued further upstream the noise of the rapids calmed as the water became deep and fast. The trees also became less dense and the canopy began to open. The waterfall dominated the horizon, a thick wall of royal blue, behind a misty veil. She focused on the falling water as she hiked on, attempting to trace the water from its initial fall, through its accelerating descent into the large, dark lake below.

Finally, she reached the lake. There were no trees, no brush surrounding the water. She had an uninterrupted view of the waterfall, which seemed to fall from the sky. It stretched for a thousand yards across the horizon, but to the immediate north and south, there was nothing—not a solid structure to hold the massive flowing body of water that was crashing down to the earth. She felt a strong pull from within her to continue toward the falls. The golden balls she held began to grow warmer as if responding to her thoughts.

She began to jog, slowly. The earth beneath her feet growing more firm with each heel strike. Veronica began to feel the golden balls quaking within her hands. It was exciting, the feeling of them moving.

She hugged them close to her abdomen and they felt as though they were rolling over, twisting, grasping at her, but when she looked, there was no movement. She felt a kick in her abdomen and her heart skipped with it. Her breath was stolen from her as the memory of Tyler's kicks entered her mind. She ran harder, sensing her son and now, her daughter Elle, calling her silently onward. The golden balls began to shrink allowing her to grasp them all in one closed hand, their heat growing even warmer. She saw a narrow path of river rock that lead her to the falls. On each side was deep lake water. She began to run down the path toward the falls.

Veronica didn't know how long it had taken but she was finally at the base of the waterfall. Hundreds of feet above her was the mouth, a spewing cascade of smooth flowing water tumbling down to the ground below. She stood at a point where the falls took a ninety-degree turn. She looked east, and water was falling for as far as she could see. To the north, falling water for what seemed like eternity as well. Her hand began to burn. The balls inside became incredibly hot and she opened her hand revealing her palm and the three hot, glowing balls.

The balls leapt out of her hands into the falls, quenching themselves as they entered. She reached forward into the smooth water to catch them but was unsuccessful. The water stopped falling. It froze in mid air and the flow of the lake and the river slowed to a stop. There wasn't a sound to be heard and she stood there staring into the mirror of water that was draped in front of her.

She saw something in the mirror moving behind her: a boy with light hair jumping and kicking river rocks, a small girl chasing the boy with bouncing dark curls and a red dress. Veronica watched the image of the children coming closer, too afraid to turn around and see for herself what was so hard to believe.

"Slow down Ty!" she heard a tiny voice yell, the sound carrying over the motionless water. Veronica turned without thinking. She saw the two children and knew. She began to run to them, her heart beating faster than her feet could go. She felt limitless. Suddenly the waterfall behind her began to flow upward toward the sky, the lake began to dry up, and the river flowed backward.

"Tyler! Elle!" she called to the children as she ran to them.

"Mommy!" they both yelled and ran to her. The sound of the water was deafening but none of the three paid it any attention.

"I love you so much!" she said as she knelt down and hugged them both tightly. "Oh thank God," she whispered with her eyes closed, wishing the moment would last forever.

"Mommy don't cry," Tyler said with his chin bouncing off her shoulder.

"I'm not sweetie," she said sniffling.

"Yes you are Mommy," Elle said squeezing Veronica tightly and shrugging her little shoulder high into the air.

"I miss you guys."

"We're happy Mommy, don't worry about us," Tyler said and stepped back to look at her in the eyes. Elle followed her brother's lead.

"You are so handsome Tyler, just like your daddy. And you Elle, such beautiful hair just like your mommy!"

"I knew you'd like it," Elle said smiling wide, her tiny teeth spread out straight across her mouth. "I tried to make it look curly for you," she said playfully lifting it in the air as if it were a pile of Slinkys.

"It looks wonderful sweetheart," Veronica said touching Elle's hair gently, the silky texture caused her heart to race.

"Mommy you're going to go back soon. Please take care of daddy. And please keep trying to give us a brother—"

"Or a sister!" Elle said, interrupting her brother.

The water had all gone back upward into the sky and suddenly the three small golden balls were flying around their heads.

"No more tears Mommy. We miss you too, but someday we will be back together. We're safe," Tyler said hugging her one last time.

"Yeah Mommy, please be happy," Elle said reaching up for Veronica who lifted them both up and squeezed them tightly.

"I love you guys," Veronica said as she opened her eyes in the treatment room.

"Love you too," Dr. Stelious said as he began to remove the devices from her body.

"Where's Adam," she asked with a dry mouth.

"I'm here sweetheart," he said smiling. "So?"

"They're so beautiful. We can't go back?"

"No," Adam said gently.

"Never?"

"Never," Dr. Lewis said entering the room. It was 5:00 a.m. and he had just been woken up by the alarms. "Remember what we talked about before you went in. We cannot allow you to become addicted to the experience. You're aware that they're safe and happy. Please let's leave it at that."

"Thank you Dr. Lewis." Veronica said extending her hands toward him.

"Don't thank me Veronica. It's the least I could do. Please remember our agreement. That's how you can say thank you."

"Why is it so important for Kyle not to know?"

"Because the three of us agreed it would no longer be performed," Dr. Stelious said. "Myself, Dr. Lewis, and Kyle."

"Why?" she asked softly.

"The physical danger, the addictive nature of the treatment. Plus, what would happen if the world knew about it? Some things are better left alone."

The room was quiet. Dr. Stelious had hit on something that Dr. Lewis, Kyle, and everyone else who knew of The Beyond Experience hadn't thought of before. People would be hysterical, some would try to profit from replicating the research and some would likely die. As Dr. Stelious said, maybe some things are better left alone.

# | THIRTY-ONE |

## Saint Louis | October 5, 2013

The entrance to the Saint Louis Zoo was incredible. A massive rusty structure arched skyward over the entryway, displaying dozens of animals from all over the world. The weather was a crisp 65 degrees, and a slight breeze cut the bright sunlight's warmth allowing everyone to enjoy the afternoon. Annie thought it would be fun for the foursome to get outside and walk around. The men had split off from the ladies about an hour earlier, electing to grab an early lunch while the ladies went to see the big cats.

Veronica walked slowly, watching the families just as much as the animals. Since her treatment, the young couple decided they would try another *in vitro* fertilization with one of the three frozen embryos. Her body wasn't ready yet, but her mind was absolute. She loved the excitement in the children as they ran toward a peacock displaying his feathers for all the world to see. She remembered her own children, how they ran to her, the feel of their skin on hers as they embraced her with strong healthy arms. *What would their favorite animal be?* She thought as she watched.

"Veronica I'm glad we have time to ourselves," Annie said linking her arm onto Veronica's.

"Me too. I'm sorry I ignored you for so long," Veronica said forcing a frown as she looked at her close friend.

"Don't apologize. I'm just glad we're together again. Trust me, I've been where you're at."

"I almost forgot!" Veronica said suddenly remembering the first time she saw Annie; the scared, solitary girl who stood drowning in her clothes. "You've come so far since then."

"And found myself a hunk," she joked and nudged Veronica with her elbow as she leaned in toward her. "I never told you the truth did I?"

"About what?"

"How we met."

"At the clinic?" Veronica asked as she stopped walking to focus on her friend.

"Um, no," Annie said smiling widely.

"Oh my God, Annie! How?" Veronica said playfully pulling her arm away. "Tell me now!"

"Ok, ok. He was on the forums, looking for people who had a near death experience. He found me and reached out." Annie paused for a brief moment, Veronica sensed her hesitation.

"Anyways, I didn't want to respond at first. My experience was rather bad. I tried to kill myself. While I was unconscious, I experienced terrible things. Darkness, completely alone, lacking all sense of a connection with anything. It was terrible. Kyle wanted to know about me. Offered to help me if I came to him."

"Why was he on the forums?"

"He never said."

"Ever ask?"

"No," Annie said smirking and looking away. "Maybe I should, huh?"

Veronica smiled to hide her inner thoughts. She knew what Kyle was looking for, experimenting on Annie. She wondered if Annie had ever gone into The Beyond Experience.

"Annie, when you were treated, how long did the treatment last?"

"Thirty or 40 minutes. Why?"

"Were you treated more than once?"

"No. Why?"

"Just asking."

"There has to be a reason. Do you guys normally do more than one treatment?"

"No, well, now we do, but only if people want the experience. It's become kind of thing to do for some. Like going to a show or an amusement park. I don't like it, but people will pay cash for it."

"But why did you ask about me? Is there something I should know?" Annie asked, nervously.

"No Annie. It's all ok. I think you may want to ask your 'hunk' about why he wanted to treat you if you want to know. I genuinely have nothing more to say. Except the treatment really does work doesn't it?" Veronica asked smiling wide as she genuinely felt happy and hadn't forgotten about her children.

"Yes. It does. I was depressed for a very long time Veronica," Annie said walking toward a bench and sitting down, Veronica sitting next to her.

"What happened Annie?"

"I was young, eight, and we were on a family trip. My brother came and woke me one morning. He wanted to go out to the lake and see the waves. I was tired and told him to go away. I woke up for a second time to the screams of my mother who found him on the beach, dead."

Veronica sat with her hand over her mouth, tears rolling down her soft cheeks. She placed her arm around her friend and gently stroked her back. "I'm so sorry Annie."

"I still miss him Vero."

"I'm sorry sweetie. I'll forever miss my babies too," she said gratefully. "I think it's good to miss him. It keeps him alive in a way."

"I get it. I do get sad still thinking about him. I just hope he's not mad at me."

Veronica felt a twinge of guilt rip through her. She knew Annie hadn't done The Beyond Experience based on that last statement. She fought hard not to let the secret come out. The closure Veronica was able to feel was immeasurable and here was her best friend sitting in the zoo on a beautiful afternoon, recalling the darkest day in her life, hoping her brother didn't hate her.

Annie cried for several minutes while sitting there in the shade, the gentle breeze giving Annie a chill as it blew on her moistened cheeks. Veronica continued to rub her back while she watched families walking by, some slow and methodical while the more entertaining groups ran from enclosure to enclosure jockeying for the best view, trying to awe one another by describing what they were finding.

"Let's go find our boys. What do ya think?" Veronica asked looking down toward Annie's face.

"I think it's a good plan," Annie said chuckling at herself and throwing her hands in the air. "At least now you know my story Vero."

"That's true."

The two friends walked back toward the food where Adam and Kyle still sat wearing sunglasses and drinking their soft drinks from lunch. Adam saw the girls first, and waved wildly overhead, calling them over. Kyle saw them after the gesture, and immediately read the distress in Annie's eyes. He got up from his chair and hugged her as they came close, the tight embrace always made Annie feel calm and safe.

"What's wrong," Kyle said softly into her hair as he kissed her head.

"We were just talking."

"About what?" Kyle looked down toward her and she looked up, telling him with her eyes what he already suspected. "How'd that come up?"

"We were talking about the treatment. Kyle, why were you on the forums? Why did you look for people like me?"

"I don't know," he said smiling through the lies.

"And why was I only treated once?"

"That's all we ever did," his smile was fading fast, but his thoughts, his anger, exponentially increasing. He knew Adam and Veronica had been treated, but now he was starting to question everything. *Why wasn't I allowed to be there? Why was the clinic shut down? Was Dr. Stelious there too? Did they go into The Beyond Experience? What did Veronica tell her?*

"Where are all these questions coming from?"

"Like I said sweetie. We were just talking."

"Hey Veronica. Come over here a minute, would ya?" Kyle said gesturing with his hand and grinning.

"What did you guys talk about?"

"Her brother, how you guys met, the treatment—"

"How was your treatment? Good?" he asked cutting her off.

"Kyle!" Annie said shocked at the manner in which the question was asked.

Adam heard the exchange and got up from his chair and walked toward the small group. "What's the issue Kyle?" he asked, guarded.

"Just wanted to know how it was. I could ask you too. We never really talked about it."

"What do you want to know?" Adam said sternly, trying to appear frustrated rather than scared.

"Who was assisting Ethan?"

"Stelious," Adam snapped.

"Huh," Kyle replied with a chuckle.

"What's so funny?"

"You ever had Stelious assist you Veronica? How about you Adam, ever had him assist you?"

"No," Veronica said and Adam shook his head, indicating the same answer.

"Well I have. I can tell you two right now what happened and I'm not happy at all."

Kyle was furious. His hands were shaking and his eyes were

welling up with tears. Annie squeezed his hands but it was as if he didn't feel her silent pleas for an explanation.

"Kyle let's get out of here. We don't need to make a scene," Adam pleaded with his friend.

"I'm done Adam. I'm not mad at you or Veronica. I'm pissed off for me and Annie."

"What's going on Kyle?" Annie said, worried, confused at why her husband was so angry with her friends and Dr. Lewis. "They're better now right?"

"Oh tons better. Tell her Veronica. Tell her why you're so much better."

"Kyle—"

"Don't Kyle me. You owe Annie this. She was worried about you every minute of every day since you lost the twins! Now you know her story too. Do you think it's fair?" Kyle said pointing at Veronica.

"No," Veronica said softly. "I've thought about it nonstop."

"Well that makes two of us. For almost five years now I've dealt with not being able to show her what I know, to bring her to that conclusion we've all gotten to have," Kyle said, a tear rolling down his face. Annie had never seen him cry before and it was overwhelming her.

"Someone tell me what's going on, please!" Annie said as she herself began to cry, reaching up to wipe Kyle's eyes.

"Do it Veronica or I will," Kyle spat.

Veronica looked to her husband who stood stunned. The courtyard around them was relatively empty, nobody was listening to the four of them argue.

"I met my babies Annie. I met them in the treatment. It was incredible, an experience I couldn't even describe. I'm sorry I couldn't tell you. Dr. Lewis made me swear not to tell Kyle—"

"Why?" Annie asked cutting her off.

"Because I asked if I could let you see your brother right after you told me about the drowning. I wanted you to see him, to talk to him, to see that he wasn't mad at you."

"How?"

"The Beyond Experience. That's what Dr. Lewis called it," Adam said quietly, still scanning the area for eavesdroppers.

"I named it that," Kyle said frustrated about the entire situation. "I'm leaving. Annie please, come with me," he said reaching out his hand for her to grasp.

"I'll text you later Vero," Annie said looking back as she was whisked away by Kyle.

Kyle slammed the door of his M4 and sped away as Annie struggled to get her seatbelt on. The turbos began to whistle as he aggressively accelerated onto the highway.

"Kyle you're scaring me," Annie said as her body pressed hard against the leather seats.

Kyle remained silent, checking his side mirrors for a hole in the traffic. Once he was on I64/40, he began weaving between cars; the German precision that was perfected on the racetrack was finally unleashed.

The traffic was thick but his aggressive style was allowing him to drive west at a quick pace. The setting sun rested at the peak of several hills, limiting the vision of the hundreds of drivers and this made Annie feel more anxious. She had one hand firmly pressed against the ceiling of the car while both feet were off of the floor in anticipation of a crash. She rarely opened her eyes and when she did, she held her breath watching the car weave through the lanes until she couldn't manage the sight any longer.

"Kyle talk to me," she said between squeals.

"Ok. Well, Adam and Veronica got to see their kids."

"What?"

"Yeah. Well, I know it's hard to believe but it's true," he said flooring the gas pedal and hit the paddle shifter placing it into third gear at 90 miles per hour, continuing to accelerate as traffic finally opened up.

"Slow down!" she screeched, as did the tires when he quickly hit fourth gear, the dual clutch was faster than the trees going past the window.

"The faster we get there the sooner we'll get answers."

"You're scaring me Kyle!"

"Nothing to be scared of," he said finally allowing the car to coast, the triple digit speeds seemed a bit aggressive for the moment. "They saw their babies, I saw my dad, other people saw their loved ones," Kyle said calmly.

"I'm so confused Kyle. What are you—"

"Several years back, when it was just me and Ethan, he asked me if I would have a problem taking the experiment further, just to see where it went."

"Ok?"

"I went so deep into the treatment that I saw my father. It changed my life. I went back to church, I found you."

"So why did you search for people like me on the forums?"

"To find someone who's had a negative near death experience. To see if what they were witnessing was hell. Everyone describes heaven, but nobody experienced hell."

"Why'd you need that?"

Kyle paused, reflecting on the times he spent with Dr. Lewis while they were vulnerable, emotional, awkwardly connecting with each other. They had a unique but working bond, as close as a father and son.

"I wanted to show him that heaven was real, that the experience was something more than a deep-seated manifestation in the brain. I wanted you to go deep into the experience and have those same things happen."

"Well that's great," she said hurt by the thought of feeling the solitude, the darkness.

"That was before we connected."

"Mhm."

"It is!" he said frustrated, squeezing the steering wheel and accelerating once more.

"Kyle stop it!" she said, this time with anger and force.

"We're going to the office. Time to have a conversation."

The Chesterfield office was relatively barren at 5:30 p.m. A few employees still remained but Kyle knew his two partners would still be in their offices. He walked in front of Annie, dragging her more than walking with her as they stormed through the treatment area, through the large, white double doors that required his access key, and into the research facility. He walked straight to Dr. Stelious' office.

*Knock, knock, knock!* He pounded on the door.

"Come in," Stelious said from behind his computer. He had been putting together some of the research findings on brain pathways from the last quarter.

"Marcus," Kyle said as he and Annie walked into his office.

"Hello Kyle, Annie," the small doctor nodded politely in her direction, a forced smile on his face. Stelious hated interruptions as they often cost him precious time.

"We're going to have a meeting. Now." Kyle said, a fire burning in his eyes as he tried to steady the quaking in his voice. He hadn't been angry in years, and certainly never to this level. It was the first time he shook with anger, the first time he felt like crying out of frustration, the first time he truly felt betrayed. He wanted to talk to his father and ask for advice, but that thought only caused a higher tide of anger to roll through him.

"What is it Kyle?"

"In Ethan's office," Kyle said as he left the room with Annie.

The three of them took the short trip to the office of Dr. Lewis. As they approached, they noticed the door was already opened. Kyle didn't hesitate to enter. After all, they had shared an office suite for years, this wasn't abnormal.

"Kyle," Dr. Lewis said as he saw him enter. "Annie, how are you my lovely lady," he said and stood with a large smile on his face. Then he saw Dr. Stelious and knew. "Close the door Kyle."

"Why?" Kyle said throwing his hands in the air. "Don't want anyone out there knowing what's been going on?"

The two techs in the lab stood in silence, giving each other an uncomfortable glance.

"Please," Dr. Lewis said gesturing toward the door.

"Ah, please. Did you hear that honey? He said please. I should close the door then, right?"

"Kyle please just close the door," she said looking at her husband; confused at his demeanor.

"Ok." He slammed the door.

"What's wrong Kyle?" Dr. Lewis asked as he sat back in his chair. He knew the answer but was forcing Kyle to say it and hoping he was wrong.

"Why was Dr. Stelious present for Veronica's treatment?"

"I wanted an assistant."

"Since when does Marcus help? He's got his own research doesn't he?"

"It was to keep others away. You have to understand that right?" Dr. Lewis said frustrated, trying to put on a good show.

"Yeah, I'd buy that if I didn't already know what I know."

"And what's that?"

"I know you could do at least two treatments by yourself with your eyes closed. I also know the only times Dr. Stelious has helped is when you took people into The Beyond Experience."

"Kyle—"

"I know what you did Ethan," he said cutting him off. "And we're going to let Annie see her brother. Tonight. Right there in that treatment room on the other side of this lab. You and I, just like old times. What'd ya say?" Kyle said dropping down into a chair right in front of Dr. Lewis.

The two men stared at each other for a long moment. A defiant son and a stubborn father, both silently making a statement, both silently heartbroken. Ethan was crushed seeing Kyle so angry with him. He knew he could rectify the situation by giving in, but what would he be asked next? *Would they both want to continue going back to see her brother or his father? How many times would be enough? Where do you draw the line?*

"No."

"It's happening Ethan, with or without you." Ethan knew from his own experience the treatment could be addictive, and Kyle's aggressiveness solidified it.

"Kyle, I don't want it. I don't understand it," Annie said, her eyes wet with tears.

"You want it Annie, I promise you want it. You've asked for it so many times. You've wanted closure for so long. Wouldn't it be nice to talk to your brother? To see if he actually blames you for what happened?"

"Yes," she conceded. The thought of that possibility was life changing. She couldn't recall a day in which she hadn't felt some guilt. The treatment had worked for her the first time, but now, to have the hypothetical so achievable was intoxicating.

"I've said no at least a half dozen times now Kyle and I won't say it again."

"It's my company too!" Kyle spat.

"I agree with Dr. Lewis, Kyle. We make the 60 percent majority. We have decided it will not be happening. Where will we draw the line, Kyle?" Dr. Stelious said, breaking the silence with his cold affect.

Kyle sat stunned. The fight was gone from him. He was defeated and shocked at the coldness in Dr. Stelious' tone. The doctor had always been by the book, never wavering, always thinking analytically at every situation. He was unbiased, unemotional, and supportive of Kyle in the past. Now, hearing him speak those words, he knew it was over.

"I'm done Dr. Lewis," Kyle said quietly.

"I'm glad Kyle. And Annie, it's nothing to do with you. We just have to define when to stop. If we allow you to go in, then maybe you will ask again, or, more likely than he'd care to admit, Kyle would want to go back and see his father too."

"I haven't forgotten your secret either Dr. Lewis," Kyle said breaking into the monologue.

Dr. Lewis sat silent, staring hard into Kyle's blue eyes. "Let's not make this personal, Kyle."

"It's been personal for a long time. But don't worry, Lily is safe. She's not mad, remember? Must be nice to have closure."

"You're right Kyle, you're done. I'm going to have Michelle draw up some papers. I'm buying you out of your part of the business."

"No you're not," Dr. Stelious said still standing near the door, arms crossed and resting on his abdomen. "You can't afford it. I'm going to buy his part as well. We will split it."

"You can't be serious?" Kyle asked as his eyes filled with tears. Memories overwhelmed him as he recalled the earliest days in The Shack. He remembered meeting Dr. Lewis for the first time, the skinny, quiet doctor who barely shook his hand. He remembered the man who sang karaoke while getting drunk with him after proving the experience worked, and the long nights they spent crunching through data. He thought of the Ethan at the tattoo shop in Cambridge, opening his heart and remembered why he was there. Kyle thought of all the times he wanted to know Ethan even more, wishing the doctor had shared those distant memories that seemed to keep him so far from God, so closed off to the world.

"We are," Dr. Lewis said. "Like you and I both said, you're done here. Michelle is a fair woman. You'll get a great price."

"This is just as much my research as it is yours. I'm the one we tested on," Kyle paused, reflecting on the moments from years ago where the two men worked long hours alone, finally achieving the success they wanted, and the closure Kyle received with his father. "I'm sorry—"

"Don't be. I just don't think you can work here anymore without conflict. This will forever be a wedge between us and I'm truly sorry for that. I just can't risk you coming in after hours and doing something stupid either."

Lily's face as she lay on Ethan's lap in the botany lab quickly flashed into his mind. "I'm hoping to still talk to you from time to time. You're genuinely my only friend," Dr. Lewis paused fighting back emotions that were confusing him. He reached out his hand.

"I'll do what I can. I can't promise anything," Kyle said wiping his eyes with his free hand.

"I understand."

Kyle placed his keys on Dr. Lewis' desk and walked out with Annie.

The two lab techs stood frozen in the same spot they'd been for thirty minutes as the discussion inside Dr. Lewis' office boiled over. They watched as Kyle and Annie walked out of the lab, taking in the research facility. Kyle took a deep breath of rubbing alcohol and solvents, smelling them for the last time. He was set to clear nearly fifty million dollars for the buyout and never needed to work again. In some ways it was satisfying, but in truth, he was still very raw. The decision was shocking to him, to throw away their long friendship over one treatment session for his wife. The couple walked through the double doors, never to set foot in the facility again.

# | THIRTY-TWO |

It took a couple of weeks to make it official but Michelle was able to get a team of corporate attorneys together to decide the value in the company. Based on their expansion, the number of treatments being performed that year versus the previous, they estimated global growth of 20 percent annually for the next five years, despite the bad press from Lacey's study. Dr. Lewis told Michelle to be generous with Kyle, by determining the company's projected worth over the next five years and find a number based on that. The number was seventy-five million dollars. Both Dr. Lewis and Dr. Stelious had to take out a loan to cover the large sum of money, but placing their investment in the company up as collateral made it easy.

Michelle sat in her spacious office surrounded by bright colors. A blue desk, a red couch, and multicolored abstract works of art covered the walls. She usually listened to music, cheesy pop songs that were often overplayed, but today she sat in silence. She was holding the paperwork for Kyle to sign, reading it over for the third time, making sure she did exactly what Dr. Lewis had asked. But she also wanted to ensure the financial safety of Ethan.

She looked up at the glass coffee table in front of her red couch. Resting in the center of the table was a vase full of plastic flowers, a variety of lilies making a brilliant array of colors. It was something she habitually stared at when feeling stressed, the colors relaxed her, helped her feel bright and cheery like they were, but in the moment she was struggling. She had known both Kyle and Ethan for years, and witnessed their symbiotic relationship flourish. Dr. Lewis filled Kyle's need for a father, Kyle forcing Ethan not to be alone. The doctor was an easy read, a loner, a person who refused to allow others in, but somehow Kyle had made it. She was heartbroken to see the turn. Michelle had held onto the idea that Dr. Lewis's armor had a weak spot, and Kyle had represented that. Now, she sat wondering if she would ever be with Ethan.

Michelle's phone chimed a cute noise that sounded like a kid's toy rather than a lawyer's phone. Looking at the notification, she saw Kyle's name.

"I'm in the parking lot, white M4. Not coming in."

Michelle took a deep breath, a wall of tears formed in her light green eyes, a delicate representation of her unspoken resistance to the buyout. She knew there was nothing for her to say, nor was it her place to fight on either behalf, but she now knew it was truly happening. She gently slid the file off the desk, placed it into her bag, and walked out of her office.

She spotted the white BMW at the far end of the parking lot. As she walked, the strong wind that raced across the open field adjacent to the facility swept her long coat up. Kyle saw her coming and got out of the car, but didn't walk toward her. Instead, he leaned against the car and waited.

"I'm sorry Michelle," Kyle said as he gave her a heartfelt embrace.

"It's ok. I needed a little walk," she said winking.

"I just can't go in there," he said sighing.

"Let's not talk about that. Let's talk about . . . this," she said pausing briefly to take out the papers.

"That's it huh," he said grabbing the small stack of papers with several pink sticky notes marking locations to sign.

"Yep. Pretty easy job right?" she said smiling as she folded her arms.

"You're ridiculous, you know that?" he asked, unable to stop himself from chuckling. "Wow!" he exclaimed as he saw the final total.

"Dr. Lewis asked me to determine the company's wealth. Then he asked me to chart its predicted growth over the next five years. He told me to pay you that amount based on your 30 percent."

"Seriously?"

"Seriously," she said softly, reading the emotion in Kyle's posturing.

"Well I guess that's what guilt does," he said trying to anger himself.

"Kyle, I don't know what happened, but it's genuinely breaking my heart. I couldn't hold it in anymore. I'm sorry for saying it." Michelle stung from the insult toward Ethan. She hated herself for feeling emotions.

"It's ok Michelle. You didn't do anything wrong. We had a difference of opinion. It's just not going to work anymore."

Kyle took a moment and reviewed the paperwork one last time. "You got a pen?"

She handed him one from her bag. He made quick work of signing over all the pages and handed it back to Michelle.

"Thanks big guy," she said grabbing the paperwork.

"Watch out for him would you?" he said, his eyes fighting back emotion.

"You're not gonna stay in touch?" she said fighting back the urge to squeeze Kyle, to scream for joy at the thought of taking care of Ethan.

"Probably for the best."

"I'm going to tell you something Kyle. I don't care how bad you think things are between you and Ethan. I've watched you two for a long time and if you ever need anything, I know he'll be there for you. Without a doubt."

"I appreciate you reminding me." They hugged, Michelle stood on her toes despite the heels she already wore just to grab around his neck. Kyle turned to open his car door. "By the way," he said pausing. "You should just talk to him."

"What?"

"I know you love him. I see it in your eyes when you're around him."

"Kyle don't say another word," Michelle said nervously smiling.

"Seventy-five million," he said as he took a deep breath and winked at her.

"I need a raise," she said, smiling widely as he closed the door and drove away.

Michelle walked back into the treatment center and sat at her desk for several minutes, allowing her emotions to calm down before calling Dr. Lewis. He asked her to call when Kyle arrived, but she made the decision not to involve the doctor when Kyle elected not to come into the facility.

She picked up the phone and called Dr. Lewis.

"Hi Michelle, should I come by now?" he asked, the excitement in his voice was unmistakable. He hadn't heard from Kyle since the day in his office despite his multiple attempts.

"I'm not sure how to tell you this, but he's gone."

"Gone?"

"He wouldn't come in the building so I met him outside. He signed the papers. He's gone already." She paused, allowing the doctor to reflect. "I'm sorry."

"It's ok Michelle. Thanks for letting me know . . . I'll, ah. We'll talk later. Thanks."

"I can come by and we can talk if you'd like?" she asked, her heart thumping through her chest while she held her breath, her eyes squeezed shut, shocked that she even asked. *I hate you Kyle!* she thought.

"That's all right Michelle. Thanks for the offer. Maybe another time."

Michelle had enough. It wasn't even lunch but the emotional toll the day already had on her was too great. She left the office and drove home back to the central west end, walked into her kitchen, and grabbed her favorite red wine. She sat at the kitchen table, silenced her phone, and thought. It hadn't taken long, but she finished the bottle and sat staring at the smooth steel refrigerator until she fell asleep on the table.

# | THIRTY-THREE |

## Chesterfield, Missouri | Spring 2014

Kyle sat in his home, bored, reading online about the growth of his former company. The money was nice but the work had been more rewarding. Six months dragged by since the money was wired to the couple and Kyle hadn't spoken a word to anyone from the company. He was depressed. Annie saw it too. Kyle wasn't working out, he wasn't being fun, he just spent money and sat. It was difficult for Annie to watch. She had always loved how excited Kyle got over little things, a package coming in the mail, a new clinic site opening, a good dinner.

Dr. Lewis had reached out to Annie a few times, but Kyle saw the messages once and was so angry that he left the house for the night, electing to stay in a hotel rather than be with someone who, "schemed with the enemy."

Kyle walked outside. The setting sun was brilliant as its hues highlighted the various stages of brown, orange, and red of the fall palette. Behind his home was a rich landscape of rolling hills, trees of various species, wild prairie flowers, and grass that grew hip high. There was wildlife too, and this time of the day the birds began to give way to coyotes and deer, often seen as close as ten yards from his back patio. He sat in his deck chair and began to feel a vibration in his pocket. He ignored the ringing, assuming it was someone he'd rather not talk to, which for him, was a safe assumption. The only person he didn't mind talking to was Annie, and she was just inside the kitchen getting dinner ready. His phone beeped so he decided to take his eyes away from the wilderness to look at the phone. A voicemail lay in wait.

"Hi Kyle, my name is Aaron. I've heard you recently had a falling out at the company. I've been watching from afar, and I know you may have had a disagreement with your colleague. If you're interested in hearing what I have to say, please give me a call back. Any hour of the day. I'm willing to allow you to lead a research team performing whatever you'd like, so long as its related to the experience. Talk soon."

Kyle placed the phone screen down on the arm of his chair and continued to watch the light change the colors in the field. The sun had dipped below the horizon, the colors fading into limited hues of purple, brown, and green. His mind was dominated by the thought of allowing Annie to see her brother, him to see his father, and to show others the miracle that was The Beyond Experience. His decision was made but he had no idea how to tell Annie. He concluded that patience was his best option. He was going to wait until Annie was gone the next afternoon. She had plans with Veronica, and he would call Aaron back, and hear what he had to say. *It can't hurt to have a conversation*, he convinced himself.

Kyle slipped into the house and walked to Annie, hugging her from behind, the smell of sweet flowers filling his nose. He closed his eyes and kissed her hair.

"Well, what happened out there?" she said smiling and holding his arms that were crossed over her abdomen.

"Just a great sunset."

"Well then. If it was that good I'll join you next time," she said turning around and grasping him around the neck.

He leaned in and kissed her once again, this time on her lips.

"Wow a kiss too?" she said giggling at him.

"Oh come on," he said gently pushing back but allowing her to hold him tight.

"I'm so happy to see you happy, Kyle."

"Well I'm happy to know that," he responded looking down his nose at her, his eyes narrowing in the comfort of her love.

He wanted to tell her. He felt the urge to just explain the voicemail and the possibilities. He fought it off, wanting to stay in the moment, not spoiling her thoughts of his possible turning point outside. She had desperately wanted him to get past the experience, and, possibly even respond to Dr. Lewis' multiple attempts at communications. He could never get over the experience or the idea that the treatment could allow Annie to have closure. But for now, he would live in the happiness they shared in this moment, standing next to a hot stove with his beautiful wife.

The last night had been wonderful, and the morning had been the sequel. Annie and Kyle had spent the majority of the last several hours lovingly entwined, but the morning sun reminded them the world still turned. Kyle got out of bed and made breakfast. The coffee was strong, but was required following the night they had shared.

Annie sat opposite Kyle at their barnwood kitchen table. She sat cross-legged in his shirt, sipping the coffee, and glancing up at her shirtless husband. She was excited. Kyle finally seemed to be coming back to her, but she was also reserved. She knew it might ebb and flow for a while, and for now she was holding her breath.

"So what're you and Veronica doing today?" Kyle asked between bites.

"I don't know. Lunch and some shopping probably." She paused and glanced at the table, a smirk emerged.

"What?" Kyle asked.

"Nothing," she said still staring at the plate and smiling, using her fork to play with her eggs.

"Don't you make me come over there, woman," Kyle said jokingly, pointing his fork toward her.

"Do you notice anything different about me?"

"No?"

"Hmm. You don't know me well at all do you?" she asked playfully standing up and spinning in his large t-shirt.

"No," he said; not because he was agreeing, but because he had picked up on her hints.

"Yup!" she said excitedly, placing her hands over her mouth.

"When!" he said standing and coming around the table, lifting her high into the air and spinning her.

"Don't make me sick, I'm eating for two."

"How far are you?"

"Eight weeks."

"Eight weeks!" he said, excited, but disappointed he hadn't known before then.

"I don't know exactly, but I've been late for at least six."

"So what are you guys shopping for?"

"We're not," she said softly, avoiding his eyes.

"What's wrong Annie?" he asked gently lowering her back to the ground.

"We're going to an OB," she said. "Going to make sure the pregnancy is real."

"Why didn't you tell me?" he asked, hurt.

"You've been so absent, stressed about everything. I didn't want to tell you something unless I knew for sure."

"Annie, you could have told me."

"I just did," she said cheerfully hopping onto her toes and kissing his cheek, a tear sliding down her face.

"I can come with?"

"Please," she said smiling.

"Is Veronica gonna be mad?"

"I don't care."

"I'll tell her to meet us there, then she and I can still go to lunch and you can go home. Fair enough?" Annie asked.

"Yup," he said kissing her quickly on the lips.

The examination room had pastel green walls, a linoleum counter with a steel sink. The walls were covered with images and models of pregnant woman and developing babies. Luckily, the room had several chairs, including the stool for the doctor.

Kyle and Veronica were both sitting in the room when the obstetrician entered.

"Hello," the doctor said. "Oh, is this a surrogacy?" She asked noting Veronica and Kyle in the chairs while Annie sat on the bed swinging her feet.

"No doctor, that's my husband and my best friend," Annie said smiling.

"Well, I had to ask you know," the doctor said smiling. "I'm Dr. Humboldt," she said reaching her hand out to Annie, Kyle, and finally Veronica. "So you're several weeks late?" she asked Annie reviewing the iPad she held.

"Yes, and I took three pregnancy tests this week, all positive," she said smiling at Kyle and biting her lip.

"Well that's news to me," he said playing along.

"Ok," Dr. Humboldt said. "Let's see if we can hear a heartbeat shall we?"

Annie lay on her back, staring at the drop ceiling. The gel was warm when the doctor began the ultrasound. Seconds turned to minutes while the blonde doctor continued to search. Annie soon became anxious and she reached her hand toward Kyle who quickly stood to be with her staring at the screen. Veronica stood also, catching a quick glance from Annie and winked, reassuring her it was normal to take a few minutes to find the heartbeat.

"There it is," Dr. Humboldt said breaking the silence. She turned the volume up. "Looks like 127 heart rate, perfect. That's your healthy baby," she said smiling at Annie who sat up on her elbows as tears of joy filled her eyes.

"Time to start thinking of names honey," she said looking at Kyle who still stood holding her hand. He was lost in the moment, his mind was struggling with the idea of a small life being formed inside his beautiful wife; half of her and half him.

After the appointment Kyle sat alone in his car. He pulled out his phone and reviewed Aaron's number. He dialed the man who left such an enticing voicemail. The ringing in his car was encompassing, as if he were inside the phone. It was awkward, so he turned his Bluetooth off and raised the phone to his ear.

"Hello," a deep voice said.

"Hi, this is Kyle returning your call."

"I recognized the number. I have to admit, I'm a bit surprised you called."

"Me too. Now if you wouldn't mind telling me exactly what it is I'm being offered, I'd appreciate it," Kyle said in his best attempt to sound disinterested.

"You haven't even asked me how I knew you had a falling out," Aaron said, a hint of disappointment in his voice.

"I guess I'm full of surprises."

"I would hope so. It's why I called. I feel as though there's more to the treatments than the public knows."

"I'm not sure I follow," Kyle said anxiously.

"Let's say I know a person who told me there were a few strange nights several weeks ago. Night closures, people being dismissed early, and then, you leaving the company."

"How do you know all that?" Kyle asked, curiosity getting the better of him.

"Finally, a question I was waiting for. I'm excited to say, I've had someone who works in the research lab at the Chesterfield office, who works for me. I mean, I pay them for information."

"You sound like the kind of guy I'd hate working for. Deception, lies, illegal activities."

"Nothing I've done is illegal."

"You called about the experience program, our treatments, you want me to replicate them for what? That sounds illegal to me."

"I'm not asking you to do what you did before. I'm asking you to take it further." Aaron paused, waiting, making sure Kyle was anxiously listening to what he was about to propose. He had rehearsed this part of the speech multiple times.

"Still not following," Kyle lied. He could barely hear Aaron's rumbling voice through the phone over his own heartbeat.

"Let's be honest with each other. I know you've experimented with the treatment. I know you've tested what it can do. All I'm asking is for you to bring that experimentation to me. I'll give you my lab, get you test subjects, and anything else you need. I just want that information."

Kyle was struggling to process the offer. He wanted to lead a team, conduct the research, perfect The Beyond Experience. He wanted to let Annie go in but now she was pregnant. There was no chance of her being put under any time soon, but he knew it would be safer with more research. Slowly he began to allow himself to consider taking the job. By they time their child was born, he could safely treat Annie. After her closure, he could walk away, or, maybe they could both come and go into The Beyond Experience as they wished. It would be his lab, his decisions, no oversight from Dr. Lewis. No more hearing about what was best for him from Dr. Lewis.

"Where do I go?" Kyle asked after a long silence.

"Come to Chicago. We'll get started right away."

"I'll consider it. Give me a week."

"That's all I want is for you to consider it. Talk next week."

It was early evening when Annie finally came home, struggling with several shopping bags as the door closed behind her.

"Hi Daddy," she said smiling and dropped the bags in the mudroom and ran on her bare toes toward Kyle. She jumped into his arms and knocked him back slightly, kissing him repeatedly on the mouth.

"Hey Momma," he said chuckling through the kisses.

"I'm so glad you're happy," she said squeezing him tightly around the neck.

"You're killin' me," he said in a gravelly voice. She loosened her grip. "I don't want you to be worried, but we have to talk about something."

Annie unwrapped her legs from around Kyle and her feet slapped the hardwood as she landed. The smile on her face was replaced by concern.

"I was offered a job."

"For what? We have money?"

Kyle looked at her, trying to say with his eyes what he was thinking. She was ignoring his eyes, making him say the words.

"For us. I'll be in charge of the research. I'll get to say what happens." He paused and gently grabbed both of her shoulders stroking them gently with his thumbs. "I want you to see your brother again Annie. I can make it happen now."

"I'm not doing that. I'm pregnant," she said annoyed. "Are you planning on leaving?"

"Yes," he held his breath.

"Great. I thought you'd be a present father."

"I will be."

"Please don't go," she said softly.

"It's my chance to change things. Trust me. It'll be for the good."

"Kyle I've always trusted you."

He rounded his shoulders and slumped down in an attempt to meet her gaze. Finally, their eyes hooked. He could see immediately the redness in her eyes, the moisture that was slowly building at her bottom eyelids.

"If you don't want me to go, I won't go," he said hoping she would tell him to go.

"I don't know Kyle. I don't want you to miss something. I don't want any regrets for either of us."

"I'll come home every weekend. I'd regret not doing this for you."

"Promise me you'll come home. No excuses."

"None. But you can't tell anyone either. Not even Veronica. Tell them I'm working on my own, a new idea to clear my head from all this business. Tell her, if she asks, I needed to do it before the baby came so I would be ready to be a father."

"Sounds stupid," she laughed, and he did too. "But I guess it will give me a lot of free time to paint."

"Good. Paint a whole bunch. Let's fill a studio full of your work before the baby comes. Just promise me you won't tell anyone?"

"I promise. Now take me upstairs."

# | THIRTY-FOUR |

## Chicago, Illinois | Fall 2014

The weeks went by and, as promised, Kyle came home every weekend. Their twelve-week appointment was incredible, allowing them to see their baby for the first time. The technician made an unofficial sighting, stating the baby was likely a boy, but it would be more certain at 20 weeks. Between weeks 12 and 20, Kyle became less consistent, having skipped coming home each weekend, citing that week 16 and 18 were "trial weekends" and would prove crucial to making certain the treatment would be safe for her. At week 20 Kyle made it home where they once again saw the baby. This appointment verified the baby was a boy.

Kyle sat in the basement of the warehouse just south of the city. He hadn't slept for two days and his eyes burned from staring at the computer screens. The engineering was incredible, but the programming was even more unbelievable. He had found a way to bring himself out of The Beyond Experience without someone being present. He hadn't, however, told Aaron.

"Did you ever go home?" Aaron asked from the doorway, his deep, booming voice filling the concrete room.

"Is it morning already?" Kyle said rubbing his eyes. He'd been sitting in the same place for the last eight hours.

"That's what my watch says," he said bringing his slender wrist up and pointing at the watch he wore. "Got any news for me?"

"No, unfortunately not yet." Kyle lied, wanting to keep his latest breakthrough a secret. He hadn't felt comfortable with Aaron like he had with Ethan. Aaron's motivations had been unclear for some time. When he revealed The Beyond Experience to Aaron, it was met with a sort of psychopathic giddiness you would see in a film. Aaron had giggled and stomped his feet quickly on the ground, then grabbed Kyle's face and kissed it. "We're gonna change the world with this, Kyle!" he exclaimed.

"Well keep me posted," Aaron said biting his tongue. He knew Kyle was lying, but it was only a matter of time before he pulled the plug on Kyle.

Aaron left the concrete treatment room in the basement of the abandoned warehouse and went outside. He got into his car and began to drive away from the facility and toward the gym. It was more than just fitness he required, but a complete change in appearance. He knew Kyle would likely recognize him from the lecture at Harvard, since he did make a large scene. He'd also tried to sabotage the experience treatment and lost his license because of it. He was now 80 pounds lighter, a vegan, and unrecognizable even for the few people who knew him. Pressing the Bluetooth button, he called Elias Grant.

"Dr. Lacey, or should I say Aaron? How're things going in the dungeon?" Elias said as he sat at his desk in his office, eating a plate of fruit.

"Very well," Lacey replied as he ignored the playful sarcasm. "Kyle's been working long hours and I've seen most of the data coming in. Seems he's made a real breakthrough."

"Excellent. So when do we get to crucify Dr. Lewis?"

"Looks like probably before the end of the year."

"You're such a good man, Dr. Lacey."

"When should I get paid my last installment?"

"The minute you capture that data from Kyle. Then we can have a few more doctors, licensed ones, no offense, look through it and replicate the findings."

"I'll try and grab it soon. Take care."

Dr. Lacey had no intention of getting the data from Kyle and giving it to Elias Grant. His life had been ruined by Elias when he convinced him it was in his best interest to make a study to prove Dr. Lewis was potentially harming patients. He played on Lacey's weaknesses, his own studies that showed the potential negative effects of anesthetics on brain O2. Lacey was angry at himself, but his true motivation was rooted in finding out if Dr. Ethan Lewis was involved in Lily's death. Kyle had shown Lacey he could talk to her again, now he was waiting for the proof.

For the next several weeks Annie's belly began to grow, as did the number of weeks Kyle stayed in Chicago. He still hadn't told her where he was, but the Facetime conversations allowed Annie to see that the weather was beginning to turn cold. She saw trees without leaves, wool coats, and Kyle's breath as he often talked to her while walking down the street. When Kyle initially went away they conversed multiple times a day, flirting, talking about the baby, discussing his name, but now conversations had become less frequent, spanning several days.

Kyle sat in his car with bloodshot eyes trying to see the small screen on his iPhone. He had just woken up from being under treatment for several days and his body was fairly weak.

"Kyle please come home," Annie said via Facetime as he struggled to focus on the screen, his eyes straining to relearn how to focus.

"I'm so close to having it ready sweetheart. I'll be coming home soon."

"You keep saying that but I don't believe you anymore," she said standing up. She wore a tight white shirt so he could see how large her abdomen was getting. She hoped he'd eventually realize the importance of coming home. For weeks he avoided the discussion of coming home.

"Oh wow, you're so big now," he said with a soft voice, feeling guilty.

"I'm aware!" she said playfully. "I need you to come home and rub my back," she said pouting and plopping back down on the bed.

"Are you at Vero's house?" Kyle asked after watching her sit on the bed.

"I've been here for weeks Kyle," she said disappointed. "I've been here for months and now you finally see."

"Why?"

"I'm lonely, Kyle. I can only paint by myself for so long. I need someone to help me with things. I get tired so fast. I was over here all the time, so they asked me to stay."

"I get it," he said. He felt anger, but wasn't sure why.

"Please come home Kyle."

"I've got one more trial to do sweetheart then I've got it," he said begging for her to understand. He wanted to hold her, to feel the baby move more than anything, except Annie's closure. He knew she battled it all the time, and wanted to finally bring her to a place where she didn't have the guilt.

"I'm 34 weeks now Kyle. I need you here."

"I'll be there, soon."

"Do not make me take Veronica with me to Dr. Humboldt."

"I won't. I love you, baby, and the baby."

"That reminds me. We still need a name. I need you here for that."

"I'll be there no matter how many tests I need to do. After this one I'm comin' home."

# | THIRTY-FIVE |

## Chesterfield, Missouri | December 11, 2014

Two dozen researchers sat at the long wooden table in the conference room. The Chesterfield office was quiet, all researchers staring at the screen at the far side of the room. Dr. Stelious was presenting his latest discoveries in mapping the brain, practicing his speech for an upcoming event hosted by the Human Connectome Project. Dr. Lewis had helped quite a bit, performing the tests on hundreds of patients in order to help his partner develop stronger statistics. It seemed selfless, but in reality, helping Marcus allowed him to distract himself from thoughts of Kyle.

Ethan was heartbroken. His closest friend wouldn't return his calls, his texts, or his emails. He had even asked Annie to talk to Kyle on his behalf several times but it only drove a wedge into their marriage, so Annie asked him not to request that of her anymore. Ethan was out of options. He had thought about going to church, where he knew Kyle would still be every Sunday morning, but he had decided against a confrontation at a place Kyle felt so happy.

"Good afternoon," Dr. Stelious said at the front of the room. "We're excited to reveal our latest breakthroughs in brain mapping. Dr. Lewis and I, as well as many of our assistants, have tested thousands of individuals as they experienced tactile stimulus in designated places throughout the body. We have determined a subtle, but present difference between these various sensory stimuli in terms of how they travel up through the brainstem and into the large gyrus we know as the somatosensory cortex—"

"Dr. Lewis," a page came through the loudspeaker on the table.

"I'm sorry Marcus," he said holding up his hand. "Yes Donna, what is it?"

"Can you please come to your office. It's important. Someone is here to see you."

His heart leapt. *Kyle!* he thought. "Marcus, do you mind?" Dr. Lewis asked as he outwardly showed disgust.

"Not at all Ethan. I will fill you in later."

"Thank you. Ok Donna, I'll be there shortly."

Dr. Lewis walked briskly down the hall, fighting the urge to jog. It had been years since he ran, the thought of him not remembering how to do the functional task briefly crossed his mind. His black, plain-toed shoes made muffled clicks across the tiles as he walked through the lab.

Finally, he saw his office, the door open fully and two men in suits were standing inside. His heart sank, and his cadence slowed. He wished he would have dismissed Donna and stayed in for the lecture. At least he could have given his colleague feedback making the afternoon productive.

"Dr. Lewis?" the tall man asked reaching out his hand. "I'm Mike Sims and this is Agent Giles. We're with the FBI. Can we have a moment?"

"Uh. Well yeah." Ethan said as he showed the men to the seats in front of his desk. He closed the door and walked to his desk chair sitting down. "I have to say I'm at a loss here guys. What can I help you with?"

"To be clear, you're not in trouble in any way. We are here simply to ask for your cooperation," Mike said with a raspy voice.

"Anything."

"Your research involves individuals being placed under anesthesia, correct?"

"Yes."

"Ok. You have hundreds of clinics worldwide at this point, correct?"

"Yes. Four-hundred twenty-seven."

"Do you have records for all these places?"

"Yes. Our digital system allows us to access the global database. Helps us continue to gather research about hundreds of thousands of treatments. It's quite remarkable."

"I'm gonna cut to the chase here in a minute Doctor, just trying to establish a few things."

"I'm in no hurry gentlemen," he said forcing a smile.

"You had a girlfriend, a woman named Lily Fisch."

"Yes," Dr. Lewis began to feel himself sweat. His palms became clammy and his mouth dried up. He swallowed hard, but was convinced Mike Sims hadn't caught the sympathetic response.

"How'd she die?"

"She overdosed on drugs in the lab. I've told the story before to Saint Louis PD."

"I understand that Doctor. I'm getting there," he said with a subtle smile. "Remember, I'm not after you. Not at this point."

"Ok."

"So, was the drug the same as you're currently giving patients?"

"Yes, but I didn't give Lily the drug. She did it to herself."

"I know. I've read the report Doctor."

"Why are you asking me then?"

"Twenty-seven reasons why Doctor, not including Lily."

"I don't follow," he responded.

"Come on Doctor you're a smart man. Twenty-seven lives are missing after being treated."

"That's simply not accurate," Dr. Lewis said, anger raising up within him.

"No?" Mike said throwing a file onto Dr. Lewis' desk. "Those are the individuals who stated they were receiving treatment and then went missing. Twenty-five are from our country, two were visitors from outside the US."

"It's coincidental," Dr. Lewis said, reeling to find an explanation.

"How can you prove they weren't being treated Doctor?"

"I can have these individuals looked up in our system. Can I get back to you gentlemen?" he asked flipping through the file.

"Absolutely."

"Thank you, Mike."

"I still have a few questions. If that's all right."

"Yes, sir."

"Made any enemies lately? Had any falling outs?"

"No," Dr. Lewis replied, thinking of Kyle.

"What I'm looking for are enemies. Someone as successful as you, gotta have some enemies. Jealous ones?"

"There was one guy a while back but he's been taken care of."

"Define 'taken care of' for me Doctor," he said with a chuckle. "Say that phrase in the wrong circles and we get broadly different answers."

"He was convicted of falsifying research studies. He can't receive federal funding for quite a while, lost his license, his job."

"You don't think he's a threat?"

"I can't imagine him killing people if that's what you're asking."

"Well that just about does it Dr. Lewis. Thank you for your time," he said standing, Agent Giles standing along with him. "Here's my number. Anything you think of, call me directly."

"Will do Mike. I'll get on these 27 names today."

"I appreciate your help. I know it's not easy to swallow these things."

"I'm not happy with the idea of people going missing."

"Neither are we Doc."

The agents left and Dr. Lewis sat at his desk. He began to page through the names and information. They truly were from all over the country. "Donna," he said into the speakerphone.

"Yes, Dr. Lewis."

"Can you please have someone look up the treatment history of 27 possible patients in our database? I have the folder with me in here."

"Is everything ok?"

"Yeah. These people apparently said they had treatment with us and then went missing. I'm not sure any of them ever came to us but we'll see."

"I'll be right in Doctor."

"Ok Donna," Dr. Lewis said when his office manager stepped into the room. "Nobody knows about these names and why except for you and me."

"Why don't I just look it up?" she asked holding the folder under her arm.

"You're busy enough."

"I can handle it Ethan. It's not that hard."

"If you insist."

"I do, since you insist on secrecy."

"It's the upmost importance."

"I'll get this to you by the end of day tomorrow."

"Thanks Donna."

Dr. Lewis arrived the next morning at 8:00 a.m., and sitting on his desk were 27 individual files, one for each of the persons the FBI had listed. He paged through each one, carefully noting when each individual had been treated. All 27 had been treated over two years earlier, and all had very strong outward manifestations during treatment. Ethan's hair began to rise on his arms as a chill quaked his body. Someone was clearly replicating his research and hand selecting persons with strong outward experiences. *How would they know? Who could get them the information? How were these people being contacted?*

Ethan quickly picked up his phone and dialed Mike Sims.

"Sims," a gruff voice sharply answered on the other end.

"This is Dr. Ethan Lewis. I have information regarding those names. Do you have time to stop by?"

"I can swing by within the hour. See you soon Doctor."

The hour passed quickly while Ethan worked on scenarios. He narrowed it down to a few possibilities. Someone had hacked into their results and began reaching out to persons who had these outward manifestations and convinced them to come for another treatment; someone was fishing through the internet for people who had been treated; or someone from inside a treatment center was feeding the copycat information about the patients. What he absolutely refused to believe was that Kyle had anything to do with it.

Kyle couldn't hack the system, he couldn't have stolen information, nor did Kyle ever talk to anyone at the Chesterfield office except for Adam and Veronica, and they certainly wouldn't have been leaking patient information to him.

"Dr. Lewis, Mike Sims is here for you," Donna said through the phone.

"Send him in please."

"Mike thanks for coming in. Figured it be easier in person," Ethan said standing and shaking Mike's large calloused hand as he sat. "No suit today?"

"Nope. It's my day off."

"Sorry to drag you here then."

"No biggie. What you got for me there, Doc?" Mike said pointing to the stack of files on the desk.

"Twenty-seven prior patients. They were all seen over two years ago. I have a couple theories—"

"Not your job Doc, that's mine," Mike said cutting him off. "No offense."

"None taken," Ethan said biting his tongue. He grabbed the stack of files and handed them to Mike.

"Ok Doc you got me," Mike said. "I'm curious. What are your thoughts?"

"Someone got my research. I don't know how they got it, but every one of those 27 individuals had very intense outward manifestations during treatment."

"Translate that for me Doc."

"They talked or moved a lot while under."

"Is that a big deal?"

"We didn't think so. There's a lot of variability in the outward manifestations. Most people have mild ones, some don't have any."

"Someone seems to think it's a big deal though, huh?"

"I'm guessing so, but I've been doing this quite a while now and I can't see what it is."

"Thanks for the info Doc. Let me know if anything else comes your way."

"Can you do the same? I'd love to know what the heck's going on here."

"Sure can Doc, as much as I can."

# | THIRTY-SIX |

Thirty-eight weeks into the pregnancy and Annie was in Dr. Humboldt's office with Veronica. Annie was trying hard not to get emotional, but the hormones and the fact that she hadn't heard from Kyle in two weeks was weighing on her. She wasn't sure if he was working hard, hurt, or dead, but the flood of thoughts overwhelmed her. Veronica had done a great job of trying to put her mind at ease, talking through scenarios with Annie, but it was hard. Annie had lied to her friend for months now, the only people who were there for her, and she was ready to snap.

"Ok sweetheart let's check on that baby," Dr. Humboldt said walking into the room with a smile. "Where's the hubby today?"

"Working," Annie said smiling. "Trying to get some things finished before the baby comes."

"Well all righty then. Let's measure you. That belly is getting pretty sizable." Dr. Humboldt took out her tape measure to assess the size of Annie's belly, measuring from sternum to pubic bone. "He's a big boy! Looks like he might be over eight pounds already." The doctor sat back in her chair and looked at Annie's chart. "We might need to set an induction date for you, missy."

"Why? Is everything ok?" Annie said, scared.

"He's just a big boy. We're not gonna let him go any later than 40 weeks. He's healthy, you're a small person. You won't stand a chance at a ten-pound baby."

"When?" Annie was grasping the treatment table firmly. She blinked hard and looked toward Veronica. Annie's eyes were empty.

"Annie?" Veronica asked standing up.

"Are you ok?" Dr. Humboldt asked seeing Annie's face becoming pale.

"Yeah, I just feel a little strange."

Dr. Humboldt quickly placed a blood pressure cuff on Annie. "Sweetie lay down," she said noting her high blood pressure, 185/150, and her heart rate was over 100. "I think you're just having some anxiety."

Annie lay down on the bed and slowly the room began to stop spinning. Her thoughts became clear and all she thought about was Kyle. She needed him there to help her, to be with her for the birth. The experiment meant nothing to her, it never really had, but he needed to know she would never forgive him for being absent at the birth. In a way, an induction was a blessing in disguise. Kyle would have a date he needed to be home. She just had to set it.

"Dr. Humboldt," Annie said while remaining on the bed.

"Are you ok, Annie?" she asked still seated on her stool, watching over her patient.

"What date can we schedule the induction for?"

"I'd like you to make it to 39 weeks. So . . . five days, January second."

"I'll let my husband know."

Annie texted Dr. Lewis from the examination room after Dr. Humboldt left.

"Dr. Lewis. I wouldn't ask, except it's a serious situation. I haven't heard from Kyle in several days, and I'll be induced on January second. Can you please try and contact him as well?"

Annie's phone vibrated shortly after she got in Veronica's car, on their way to her house.

"I will do my best but I haven't heard back from him since our last conversation in my office. Best of luck. Hope you are healthy. Thanks for reaching out."

# Chicago, Illinois | Late December 2014

Kyle woke up in a treatment bed. The room was dark and he felt a soreness in his nose. He reached up to feel a tube going into his left nostril. He pulled the tube, breathing out as he did it. Looking down toward his weak, stiff legs, he saw swollen feet that were wrapped in boots that massaged his calves, preventing blood clots. He pulled off the EKG leads, the EEG head wrap, the pulse ox, and blood pressure cuff.

He finally stood up and felt a rush of dizziness set in, which he had been prepared for. It was why he had a bar installed on the wall two feet to the left of the bed, just in front of the entrance to the observation room. However, nobody was observing the experiment. Kyle had been working on an automated treatment that maintained a steady state, allowing The Beyond Experience to last forever, in theory, so long as there were enough bags to hang and food to pump through a nasal tube.

Looking at the computer, he stopped the timer. It had been five days, fifteen hours, twelve-minutes since he went under. The system had worked, maintaining his safety levels until he was ran out of the cocktail. On several previous attempts, the titration hadn't stopped him from bottoming out his vitals, but the failsafe brought him out of the experience. The failsafe was a double shot of epinephrine which was automatically administered if his vitals went too low. The first three attempts at using the automated system, Aaron was present to ensure it happened as planned. The last three attempts, he'd been gone, performing other research.

Kyle felt his heart sink when he saw the date. He had missed his son's 38-week appointment. He scrambled to check his phone. After several moments he realized he wouldn't get a signal in the basement of the building. He left the musty treatment room and began walking down a long corridor lined with concrete bricks. The ceiling was low, and the walls narrow, but the single light bulbs placed every 20 feet still left the hallway dark.

There was a white metal door at the far end of the hall that was always locked shut. But this day was different. This time a bright light was shining through the doorway as it rested slightly ajar. Kyle felt a knot in his stomach as he approached. The whooshing sound of an IV pump was unmistakable to Kyle, having heard it thousands of times before. He could even tell the manufacturer based on the difference in noise. He pushed gently on the heavy door, opening it just enough to see what hid behind.

Inside the room were ten people being treated, each one of them with a nasogastric tube, a full array of hanging bags, and a clock above them marking time. The sound of oxygen flowing through facial masks reminded him of white noise on a television and the smell was rancid.

Kyle walked into the room and read the time over several of the treatment beds: Four beds had ten days; two were twelve days; another two, six days; and the last two beds had been under for eighteen days. He looked at the patients more closely, each of them had a colostomy bag and were catheterized. Blood was also present near the buttocks and feet of those who had been under the longest, a strong indication of bedsores. He touched their feet, which were ballooned masses of flesh that choked off tiny, nearly absent toes. Their hands were purple and cold to the touch.

A moan from across the room caused him to spin around quickly, making him almost fall. Kyle's legs were still weak and his vestibular system hadn't been challenged like that for days. He took a deep breath and walked toward the woman at the front left of the room. She was one who had been in for eighteen days. He grabbed the chart from a basket on the end of the bed next to her feet.

Sarah Williams: 46, mother of two. Requested time with her father and her grandmother.

Kyle felt sick as he placed her chart back into the rack and continued to scan the room. He walked toward the back of the room and grabbed another chart.

Chad Ford: 37, single. Requested to see his friend who died in a motorcycle accident.

Kyle slammed the chart back into bin. He began to breathe heavily as he stood in the center of the room. He clenched his hands and ground his teeth. Anger was an emotion he had become familiar with in recent years, but this was something different. He was angry at himself, feeling guilty about being taken advantage of. Dr. Lewis had been right to shut The Beyond Experience down. Kyle hadn't seen the negative ramifications until this moment, his mind had been myopic, focusing only on the good it could have done in ethical hands.

He felt a wave of anxiety overwhelm his as he realized he would be responsible for a future full of people living in their versions of heaven, choosing to be placed under anesthesia and live there, versus the real world in which they lived. It would be addictive. He felt jealous, inspired, shocked at Dr. Lewis' ability to stop himself from entering the experience. How easy it could have been to be with Lily or to make sure she wasn't mad at him. *I use the negative thoughts as motivation to do my work right* Ethan had said many times after he told Kyle the story.

Kyle looked toward the far side of the room and saw a large window. The glare from the bright lights in the treatment room didn't allow him to see into the dark world behind the glass. A dim desk light illuminated a tall figure. A moment later, a large man rose steadily from his chair and the silhouette moved toward the doorway. Aaron ducked down through the low doorway and stood in the expansive treatment room.

"Kyle," the booming voice said from across the room. "You've seen it now. No turning back. Can you imagine what you've helped me create? How many people will love you for it? How many people we'll help?"

"This is insane!" Kyle shouted at the man.

"Why?" he asked, his face morphing into a look of disgust.

"Look at what you're doing to these people," he said pointing into the room. "I'm ending this now."

Aaron chuckled. "You're not in charge. Now that I know everything, I have no need for you anymore. I was kind of hoping you wouldn't wake up," Aaron said walking toward Kyle. "I turned off the epinephrine, but I guess this time your little experiment worked. A shame really, because now I'll have to kill you myself."

Kyle didn't hesitate. Life sprung into his dead legs as he raced up the stairs and out of the basement of the abandoned warehouse. He reached his M4, grabbed the keys out of his wheel well, and hopped in the car. He hammered the gas and left a trail of rubber on the concrete floor of the warehouse as his car screamed out of the building, sending echoes throughout the facility. He was scared, hungry, and shaking. His breathing was rapid and deep and he couldn't stop looking into the rear view mirror. The thoughts of the large treatment room were categorically crossing his mind, reviewing everything he had seen. He had made this possible, he had to end it. *Annie,* he thought and quickly called his wife.

"Kyle!" Annie said through the speakers, her beautiful voice coming in clear and surrounding him, bringing his anxiety level down for the moment. "Are you ok? Where have you been? I need you here—" she continued to ask questions without waiting for an answer.

"Annie I'm so sorry I wasn't there. I'm coming home right now. I'll be there tomorrow. I'm never leaving again," he said crying.

"Kyle is everything ok?" she asked hearing the emotion in his voice.

"I'll explain what I can to you when I get there but right now I have to call Dr. Lewis."

"Why?"

"He's the only one that can help me right now."

"Kyle talk to me, you're scaring me."

"Baby, there's nothing to be scared of. I'm driving right now. I'm heading to the apartment first to grab a few things but I'll be coming straight down after that."

"Ok. Please don't lie to me. I can't take that anymore," she said with her head in her hand.

"Sweetheart I'm not lying. Trust me. Please."

Annie sat in silence. The thought of her husband finally coming home was putting her at ease. Annie hadn't realized how on edge she was until she began to calm down. She began to sob.

"Annie?" Kyle asked hearing her sniffling.

"I'm ok Kyle, just happy you're finally coming home."

"Nothing is keeping me from coming home. I don't care about this experiment anymore. I'm coming home. You and Kyle, Jr. are the only things that matter to me," he said with clarity of mind as tears rolled down his face. He squeezed the steering wheel as he drove his car hard toward his apartment.

"I love you," she said kissed the phone.

"I love you too, so much sweetheart. See you two tomorrow."

Kyle hung up the phone and immediately called Dr. Lewis. The phone rang several times and his voicemail picked up.

"Ethan it's Kyle. I'm sorry but something has happened. I can't explain it all on the phone but I'm coming home tonight. I need to meet with you. It's bad."

Kyle parked the car at his high-rise apartment and ran inside. He skipped the elevator and ran up the stairwell. The adrenaline was beginning to wear off and his legs were heavy and nausea was settling in. He thought he just needed to eat something. As he got into his apartment he walked immediately into the kitchen and grabbed a protein bar. He took a large bite and walked into the bedroom turned on the light, and began to pack a bag: several pairs of underwear, two pairs of jeans, a handful of shirts and socks. He reached over his bed, unplugged his phone charger, and threw that into his bag as well. Throwing the large duffle bag over his shoulder, he took another large bite of the bar and left the room shutting the light off.

Snow had begun to fall heavily outside as he looked out his bedroom window. The room was dark except for the welcoming winter glow that was entering the far side of the room. He paused for a moment admiring the soft, slow falling of the first snowfall of the year. He took another bite of the bar as he walked across the room and peered outside. White had already covered everything in the five minutes he'd been in the building. It was humbling, the power of nature, its ability to change everything in sight within a moment.

Kyle sighed heavily, his shoulders rounded and he looked toward the carpeted floor. "Oh Lord please forgive me for what I've done. I have no idea the possibilities and allow me to right the wrongs I've committed."

"That's cute," a voice from behind Kyle said causing him to drop his bag and whip around looking for the voice.

"How'd you get in here?" Kyle asked staring at the small, chiseled man standing in the doorway.

"You didn't think it through young man. Brian had this plan in place."

"Oh yeah, you had no idea did you?" the man said smirking. "Aaron."

It only took a moment for Kyle to weave it all together. Aaron was Brian Lacey.

"What plan?" Kyle said hiding the anxiety he felt growing larger within.

"In case you made it out of the treatment."

"Don't do it. Please don't do it. My son's going to be born any day! I'll do anything—"

"Anything?" the man said taking out a 1911. He began screwing on a suppressor.

"Yes," Kyle said raising his hands in the air in front of him.

"Shut up," the man said as he raised the gun into the air. *Pop, Pop!*

Two shots fired into the quiet apartment. The murderer stood over Kyle right next to the apartment window that was now spattered with blood. The crimson red a stark contrast to the delicate beauty of the pure snow outside.

"We've got nothing to worry about," the man said into the phone as he looked out the window. He stayed for a moment sitting on Kyle's bed before gently rummaging through Kyle's apartment looking for any clues that may lead back to Brian Lacey. It had taken the better part of an hour, but he was satisfied nothing would come back to his employer. He locked the apartment door on the way out and took the stairs into the cold, white world.

# | THIRTY-SEVEN |

## Saint Louis | January 2, 2015

Annie was a mess. She had arrived at Barnes Jewish Hospital an hour earlier and was sitting in her room waiting for the pitocin to induce her labor. She was scared. Kyle hadn't come home, hadn't called, and his voicemail was full so she couldn't leave anymore messages. She wasn't alone however, Veronica was sitting next to her squeezing her hand, knowing that the moment was far from wonderful for either of them. The last time Veronica was in a room like this, she was delivering stillborn twins.

"Call Dr. Lewis again for me please Veronica," Annie asked as her mind continued on, unsettling thoughts dominating her mind.

"Ok Annie, but promise me after this you'll focus on the delivery. We can do this without them. I'm sure he's ok."

"Fine," Annie said as she let go of her friend's hand so she could go out to the lobby and call the doctor.

"Veronica," Dr. Lewis said as he answered the phone. "How's she doing?"

"Terrible Ethan. She's scared for Kyle, and frankly, so am I."

"Me too. I haven't heard from him. I was disturbed by his message. He sounded scared Veronica. He wasn't ever scared. Don't repeat any of this to Annie. She doesn't need that right now."

"You think I need you to tell me that?"

"Sorry," he said, realizing, as best he could, Veronica's position. "How're you handling it Vero?"

"I'm ok," she said, sighing and reflecting on the family picture she had taken with her two babies before having them taken away.

"I can't imagine what you're going through."

"It's ok Ethan, really. I want to be here for Annie."

"Do you need me to come down?"

"No. Do you think we should call the police?"

"Who do we call? Nobody knows where he was," Ethan said frustrated. It hit him. *Mike Sims.* "Vero I've got an idea. I'll call you later."

"Mind sharing the idea?"

"It'll take too long. Trust me, I'll fill you in. We'll talk soon. Give Annie my best. Tell her I'm working on things and that it'll be all right."

Dr. Lewis sat at his desk and dialed Mike Sims.

"Sims," a response came after three rings.

"Agent Sims this is Dr. Lewis."

"Hi Doc, been meaning to call you. So far no real hits on these files you gave us but we're still working on it."

"Not why I called. I've got something new for you."

"Ok," Mike said then waited in silence. It took a moment for Dr. Lewis to realize Mike wanted him to speak.

"I received a call from my former assistant. He said he had some bad news for me that he couldn't tell me on the phone. He said he was coming home that night from God knows where, but we haven't heard from him since."

"You think something happened to him?"

"Yes. His son is being born today and we haven't heard a thing. He told his wife he was coming home too, promised her work wasn't important to him anymore and all that was important was them."

"What was his work?"

"Nobody knows."

"Where?"

"Nobody knows."

"Well Doc I can't help much without more info."

"His name is Kyle Braun."

"OK Doc. I'll look for him and have someone try and hunt him down."

"Thanks Mike. Call me as soon as you hear anything please."

"Of course Doc. You do the same."


"One, two, three, push!" the doctor directed Annie as she stood between her legs. "One, two, three, four, five, six, seven, and breathe," she said allowing her to rest for the moment.

"Come on Annie you can do it girl," Veronica said holding onto Annie's left leg; Annie's epidural had made it impossible for her to control her own legs.

"Ok Annie get ready to push again," Dr. Humboldt said. "Push! One, two, three."

Annie wasn't focusing on the baby, or the contractions. She wasn't focusing on Dr. Humboldt or her friend speaking sweet encouraging words into her ear. It would have all been so wonderful had Kyle not been absent once again. She silently worried for her husband and what she thought was his addiction to the treatment experience. He hadn't told her, but she knew it was likely the cause of his absence. Dr. Lewis had made his concerns clear that day in his office, and now she laid in bed understanding the truth to his words.

"Three, two, one, push!" Dr. Humboldt yelled once again as Annie made a weak effort to play along.

Annie thought of Kyle's smile, the crooked one that hinted at an uncomfortable shyness when she gave him a compliment. She thought of his hands, the soft firmness in them as he rubbed them against her skin and the strength his arms possessed when he held her close. She craved his warmth despite her currently sweaty state. As she thought of him being close, she caught a faint hint of his smell, causing her to feel butterflies in her stomach as she took a deep searching breath for more.

"Her stats are dropping," Dr. Humboldt said as she saw Annie close her eyes.

Veronica looked at the monitors and saw Annie's BP was 60/20 and her heart rate was 42.

Annie was in front of a white light, a silhouette of a man stood in front of it walking toward her. She knew it was Kyle, the way he walked was unmistakable as he waddled subtly from side to side. He walked right up to her so she could see his face and feel his warmth, smell his scent, and grasp his hands.

"Where are you, sweetie?" she asked him, smiling largely.

"I'm right here, he said smiling back."

"I've missed you so much. You missed everything," she said squeezing him tightly.

"Annie push. You need to push," Kyle said grabbing her face with both hands and staring into her eyes.

"I don't want to leave you," she said kissing him forcefully.

Suddenly she was back in the delivery room. "How are you feeling," Dr. Humboldt said looking into Annie's eyes with a penlight. "Had to give you two shots of epinephrine. You must have liked wherever we lost you to," Dr. Humboldt joked.

"I'm ok, I'm good," Annie said looking at Veronica who returned the gaze, asking with her eyes what her words couldn't.

"Glad to hear it sweetie. Now let's get this baby out. I'm gonna need you to push with everything you've got. He's crowning now."

"Gr-ah," Annie growled as she bore down forcefully and listened to her friend count the seconds.

"Ok, breathe, Mama. Great push let's do another one like that," Dr. Humboldt said giving Annie the thumbs-up.

"Gr-ah!" she growled again as she pushed hard, her face turning a deep shade of red.

"Heads out honey let's keep it rollin'. You good?" the doctor asked.

"I'm good," Annie said blowing a bead of sweat from her nose.

"Three, two, one," Dr. Humboldt shouted and so did Veronica as the three of them pushed together.

Out came Kyle, Jr., a crying eight-pound nine-ounce mess. Annie let the staff clean him up and cut his cord, something Kyle had always talked about, saying it would make him nervous. The room cleared except for Veronica. The two of them stared at Kyle, Jr. for a while in silence. Annie smelled his head over and over, his fine hair tickled her nose every time she did.

"You want to hold him?" Annie asked Veronica who couldn't stop crying happy tears for her friend. Veronica nodded and reached her hands out for the tiny boy. Veronica took a deep breath through her nose, smelling Kyle, Jr.'s head. She remembered how her twins smelled, how they felt, what they looked like. She thought of her experience with them during her treatment and felt a warm surge of happiness cascade though her entire body. She thought of Annie and her vitals.

"Annie," Veronica asked not looking up from the baby. "Where'd you go?"

"When?"

"During the delivery. Where'd you go?"

"I don't know."

"What did you see?"

"I saw Kyle," she said, her chin beginning to quiver and she looked away.

"What did he say?"

"He told me to push, so I did."

# | THIRTY-EIGHT |

Two days had passed before Mike Sims received a phone call saying they found where Kyle Braun was living. They traced his credit card to several locations throughout Chicago, which ultimately led them to checking recent checks from his bank account too. There had been several that were made out to a property management company. The FBI office in Chicago sent one of their local guys to the leasing office and reviewed recent rental agreements, finding Kyle's apartment.

Mike sat thinking, his cell phone still in hand as he stared at the oak veneered desk. He stroked the glass on his phone with his thumb, sliding the greasy smudge around on the screen. He pressed the on button several times, and each time he watched the screen until it timed out and turned black once again, indicating a minute had gone by. He knew what he had to do, and he knew it needed to happen soon, he just hated this part of the job. Finally, he unlocked his phone and called Dr. Lewis.

"Hello?" Ethan answered seeing "restricted" on the caller ID.

"Dr. Lewis. This is Agent Sims. Can you talk?"

"Yes sir. Did you find Kyle?" he asked, nervously.

Mike paused for a moment and rubbed both eyes with his right thumb and first finger. He ground his teeth and grimaced saying, "Unfortunately we have Dr. Lewis."

"Unfortunately?"

"Yes. We found him in his apartment," Mike said sighing.

"What was he doing?"

"He was lying on the floor Doc, dead."

For Ethan the room began to spin. It had been almost a year since seeing his friend. He hadn't even received a text from him. Then, out of the blue, Kyle needed his help. Ethan thought of Jimmy's tattoo shop the night he told Kyle and Jimmy what had happened to Lily. He thought about the night they succeeded with Linda, and how Kyle was so eager to help him push the research further. He remembered the Missouri tattoo on Kyle's arm and how for years it had brought such heartache but then, after seeing his father again, it became a steadfast reminder of his father's love and pride. Ethan felt guilt, anger over not answering the phone a week ago. He tasted bile when he thought of how easy this could have all been avoided had he just allowed Annie into The Beyond Experience.

"He was shot in the head twice. We currently have no clues as to why, but that's being looked into by the local authorities. Unless you can prove that it was connected to our investigation Doc."

*That's it,* he thought and realized he was still on the phone with Mike. "I've got to tell you something Mike, but not right now. I need to be with Annie and the baby right now. Please don't call her till I get there."

"I can't promise that Dr. Lewis. They're going to be notifying next of kin once they get the body examined."

"How long do I have?"

"I'd estimate about three hours from now. Tops."

"I'll call you soon, Mike. Please trust me."

Dr. Lewis drove to Veronica and Adam's house, arriving there with a little over two hours to spare, according to Mike's calculations. He walked through two tall pillars as he approached the front door of the large home and rang the doorbell. He felt bad, knowing the bell might wake everyone in the house, but this was no time for pleasantries.

"Dr. Lewis," Adam said quietly shaking the doctor's hand as he stood in the door.

"Hi Adam, can I come in?" he said smiling.

"Sure," he said stepping out of the way and noting Dr. Lewis' appearance. He looked worn, unhealthy. He had always been on the lean side but he appeared malnourished as he walked into their home. "Everything ok?"

"No, I need to talk with Annie."

"Is it about Kyle?" Adam asked holding his breath unknowingly.

Dr. Lewis simply looked at his colleague, which told the story.

"I'll uh, I'll get Veronica. Maybe she can take the baby so you guys can talk." Adam walked away quickly, which gave Dr. Lewis a moment to think.

Dr. Lewis wanted Annie to go into the experience and talk to Kyle. He was scared to do it himself now more than ever. He saw Kyle become addicted, just like he himself had been so long ago. He knew how much more powerful The Beyond Experience had been for all those who lived it. He couldn't imagine himself being able to control the situation if he was able to be with Lily.

He heard footsteps echoing throughout the main level as Adam walked back toward him across the natural stone floor.

"She's upstairs," Adam said gesturing with his head toward the wooden staircase he just descended.

Ethan walked up the stairs slowly, quietly, each step he took more stressful than the last. He wanted to run away, never show his face again, bury himself in guilt and sorrow far away from this place. He felt it was his fault and now he had to look Annie, the widow, the single mother in the face and tell her what happened to Kyle before the FBI called her and asked her questions. Ethan needed to ask her if she would go into the beyond to see Kyle, to see her brother, so he wouldn't have to.

*Knock, knock, knock.* Dr. Lewis tapped gently on the door and entered.

Annie sat rocking in a large, soft chair, Veronica standing beside her. Annie held Kyle, Jr. with her eyes closed as he whimpered. Fortunately for Annie, Adam and Veronica hadn't made any rash decisions after losing their twins, and the room meant for Tyler was still decorated for a little boy.

Annie opened her eyes and glared at Dr. Lewis. For the first time in the last two days her thoughts were clear and she felt alive, but full of anger.

"Why are you here?" Annie asked softly as Junior stirred.

"I've heard some news."

"Funny how news travels Dr. Lewis," she said huffing.

"What do you mean?"

"You're here to tell me Kyle's dead, that he was shot twice, right?"

"How'd you know?" he asked, shocked at her demeanor.

"I'm his wife Ethan, you don't think they'd call me?"

"I knew they'd call you. I just thought—"

"Thought what exactly? That you'd be the one to tell me? That you'd somehow make me feel better? Please Ethan tell me what the plan was?"

"I don't know Annie. I just wanted to be here."

"Tell me the real reason or please leave. I know it's more than you wanting to help, because I've been on my own for months now and you haven't once shown up. Why now?"

Ethan was reeling. He knew the answer would be no, but he couldn't help himself. He needed to do everything he could not to go into the experience himself. "I wanted to know if you wanted to see Kyle?"

Annie looked to Veronica and handed her the baby. She stood, slowly, pressing down into the arms of the chair to help herself. Ethan began to walk over to help her.

"No," she said defiantly, releasing one arm from the chair and held it in front of her. Finally, she was standing, her thin legs supporting her weakened body.

"You want me to go into the experience now? Why? Because you're guilty? Because it's your fault I'm a widow and a single mother?

Because you drove my husband, your only friend away to do some experimenting on a project you killed supposedly years ago?"

"I just wanted to know if you wanted to talk to him. You could help find his killer."

"No Ethan, you can help find his killer. It's your responsibility now. I'm not going to let the treatment run my life like it did my husband's. I have a baby, a responsibility, unlike you."

Ethan was hurt. Her words cut deep, but there was truth in them. It was even worse than she said. He had no responsibilities, but he also had no true friends. He was expendable, useless to those around him. If he died it would be talked about in the news for a few days, but after that, nobody would mourn for him, or visit his grave, or think about his life.

"You're right Annie. It's my responsibility. It's all my fault he's gone and there's only one thing I know I can do about it. I'll go in, I'll talk to Kyle, and I'll come back to you and tell you everything he says." Ethan began to cry. For the first time in a very long time he was unable to control his sorrow and the walls that surrounded his heart came crashing down. He whimpered, hugging himself in the little boy's room. He looked around, thinking about his own room when he was a child and began to feel the anxiety rush over him. He knelt to the ground as waves of terror slithered through him, just as he did on his old worn mattress just before he received his beatings. His eyes closed and he imagined the amber glow from below the door. He reached out in front of him, his motor memory acting on its own accord as he ran his finger in circles around an imaginary wooden bed post that remained unseen by Annie and Veronica.

The two women looked at each other in disbelief as the confident, secure man they once knew now knelt in front of them suffering from an anxiety attack. Annie approached the doctor from the side and cautiously placed her hands gently on his shoulders.

"It's ok Ethan. I'm sorry for the things I said. They were out of line. I know you loved Kyle and this must hurt you very much. I just can't be treated. Not now, not ever. I need to live here and be present for my son."

Dr. Lewis reached up and grabbed her left hand with his right. His shoulders still bounced up and down as the sobbing continued, but he nodded his head yes. He stood and hugged Annie tightly. Before he left, he came close to Veronica and Junior, looking closely at the baby's face.

"He looks like him doesn't he?" Ethan asked smiling.

"He's handsome," Annie said.

Dr. Lewis called Agent Sims from the car on his way to the office.

"Dr. Lewis," Mike said answering the phone. "That was faster than I thought."

"Me too. She already knew by the time I got there."

"I'm sorry Doc. Some things you can't predict I guess," Mike said in a somber tone.

"Can you meet me at my office? We need to talk in private."

"Now?"

"Now."

"I think I can manage that. Be there in an hour."

The early evening was dark and cold. The threat of a snow was moderate, but unlikely for that time of year. If anything, the precipitation would create a very slick roadway for the morning commute. However, if everything went as planned, none of them would have to worry about going anywhere in the morning.

Ethan sat at his desk reading through the email he had spent the last 20 minutes preparing. It was short, simple, but believable. He and Dr. Stelious had recently closed the research lab twice in the last year for "improvements," which he thought the staff hadn't really fallen for. This time, he was using the excuse of a deep cleaning, stating that an independent lab evaluation team had come in to test the facility and found that it was unsatisfactory. He sent the email anyway, giving the researchers a day off, and allowing Stelious to take him into The Beyond Experience.

It had taken exactly one hour for Agent Sims to arrive at the facility. In that time, Ethan had sent the email to the staff and convinced Dr. Stelious to come to work in order to treat him. The three men sat in Dr. Lewis' office around the coffee table.

"Mike this is Dr. Marcus Stelious," Ethan said introducing each to one another.

"Nice to meet you Doctor," Mike said, partially standing to shake his hand.

"Pleasure is mine, sir," Marcus responded with a practiced smile.

"Ok Dr. Lewis, you have the floor."

"I'm about to explain something to you that only a handful of people know about. I suspect it's what Kyle was working on when he was found dead."

"Why didn't you come to me with this before?"

"I had no idea it was a possibility Mike."

"Well let's get on with it," Mike said sitting back in the chair and crossing his arms, a puzzled look on his face.

"We stumbled onto something years ago, Kyle and I, that could change the world, but it sounds like science fiction."

"Come on Doc let's get a move on here. Patience isn't something I do well."

"I can talk to Kyle."

"Come again?" Agent Sims asked, not understanding.

"I can talk to Kyle. Marcus will help, but you have to stay and witness it."

"Yup, sounds like hocus pocus to me."

"It is not hocus pocus, sir. We have done it several times. I guarantee you will believe when you see," Dr. Stelious said with a straight face.

Agent Sims read people well, and as soon as he met Marcus

Stelious he had him pegged for an honest guy who worked hard, and never wasted time.

"I guess I don't have an option here guys. What next?"

"It takes several hours," Dr. Lewis said.

"Let's get started then," Mike said placing his hands on his knees and looking back and forth to each of the doctors.

The treatment room was cold with only a gown on. Ethan had never experienced the chill in the air when he was administering the drugs, but he would remember now. His clammy feet stuck to the cold floor with every step along the tile as he approached the bed, and the waiting Dr. Stelious. He was thinking only of Lily as he lay onto the bed. Dr. Stelious began placing the vital equipment on: the blood pressure cuff, the pulse ox, the deep brain scanner, and the oxygen mask.

"Do you want me to record it?" Dr. Stelious asked as he situated the wires coming off of Ethan and began to prep the drug cocktail.

"I think it's better that you do," Ethan said forcing a smile, but not looking at Marcus.

"You seem nervous," Dr. Stelious said as he rubbed the alcohol onto Ethan's left forearm.

"I am Marcus."

"Don't be. Tiny prick here, then the cold. You'll be in heaven soon right?" Dr. Stelious said as he looked down his nose through his bifocals and watched the tip of the needle enter Ethan's arm.

Ethan felt the chill go into his arm, up to his chest, and throughout the body. His mind slowed and he couldn't stop his eyelids from falling as he strained to focus on the LED lights that shone brightly downward in the treatment room. He was under.

Ethan felt the surge of stimulus, the heightened sense of being, the immeasurable space that surrounded him as he went deeper into the unconscious state. He began hearing the crashing of waves and the salty smell of the ocean before he saw anything. Then the visual stimulus came hard, the brilliance of the light around him was shocking, blanketing everything in a monochromatic haze as he looked around the vast plain where he stood. Slowly, the contrast began to increase as he was able to make out a lonely mountain far off in the distance. He looked around him and saw the tropical blue-green water in every direction he turned. He realized he was on an islet that surrounded the main island of Bora Bora. He knew the view, having dreamt of it many times, using the thousands of pictures he and Lily had looked at during their short time together.

Ethan felt the urge to move toward the mountain, but he refused to swim. He scanned the area and saw a solitary boat about a mile to his right, just up the coastline at a lonely dock. He began to walk toward it, slowly, watching the clouds tumble over the peak of Mount Otemanu as he closed in on the white and blue boat. He began to see fish through the clear water as he walked—an orange one and a group of four long thin fish with blue stripes down their bodies. He saw a stingray gracefully swimming side to side along the sandy bottom, which appeared to be deep below the water.

The wind swept across his face and although it felt thick and strong, he was able to walk through it as if it had no power over him as his clothes were popping in the wind. He took a deep cleansing breath and allowed himself to smile. He felt the stress, the anxiety, the sorrow, disappear. He remembered why the treatment was so effective and craved the freedom that came with happiness.

He arrived at the boat and quickly hopped inside. The urge to go full throttle across the expansive lagoon was unbearable. He sensed Lily was on the other side calling him to her. However, a hesitation deep inside told him to look back toward the beach. He paused for a moment staring at the tan leather steering wheel that felt so soft and smooth in his hands.

Turning around he saw Kyle standing on the beach. He was dressed in white from head to toe, the clothes gently blowing in the wind. He waved and gestured for Ethan to come to him on the sand. Ethan exited the boat and walked quickly to his friend and the two men embraced for the first time in a while.

"It's not your fault Ethan," Kyle said into his ear.

"What happened?"

"I got a phone call one day to run a research lab. To do what I wanted to do, no questions asked. The man knew it all. He knew we had a falling out and he knew we were doing some kind of experimentations. Someone inside your facility told him."

"The Chesterfield facility?"

"Yes."

"Who was it?"

"No clue. Never asked. I'm sorry Ethan," Kyle said smiling. "How's my son?"

"He looks like you," Ethan said as he smiled at his friend.

"You have to look after him Ethan. I mean that. You're the closest thing he's got to a father and a grandfather."

"I don't know about that Kyle," he stepped back uncomfortably.

"You are. You'll be a good influence on him. I wish I would have listened to you more. You were always right. If I listened to you all this wouldn't have happened."

"I can say the same thing Kyle. If I let Annie in then you wouldn't have left."

"Ethan. It was Brian Lacey. He's the man who called me. He hired someone to kill me. He tried to kill me while I was in The Beyond Experience but I developed a fail-safe program."

"Dr. Lacey did this?"

"Yes. I'm sorry Ethan but he's killing people. I saw it with my own eyes after I woke up."

"Where's the lab?"

"An abandoned warehouse, just south of Chicago. It's in the basement of the building. My car has it marked on the GPS. You've got to go downstairs. At the base of the stairs there's a white door, which was always locked, except for the last time. Behind that door there were ten people being treated, and at that time, some had been under for eighteen days already."

"Eighteen days!"

"Yes. It was gruesome. Tell the FBI you need to come with because you're the only one who knows how to safely pull those people out."

"Why tell them that?"

"Because I want you to get my research. Take it home, go through it, see what I created."

"Why?"

"So you can come back and see her," Kyle said pointing to the main island. "She wants to tell you something but there isn't enough time right now. You're going to be leaving soon so we've got to hurry."

"Leaving where?"

"The experience."

"How do you know?"

"I've done it quite a few times," Kyle said smiling. "So go with the FBI and once you're done helping people wake up, tell them you need a minute to breathe. Walk down the hallway until you're about halfway down. On your left will be another door. That's my treatment room where I conducted all my research. In the observation room is a metal desk. Beneath the desk is a hollowed out piece of flooring. Inside will be three one-terabyte hard drives. Take them. You've got all that?"

"I do Kyle." Ethan stood frozen on the soft white sand looking at his friend for the last time.

"Take care of my family Ethan," Kyle said reaching out his hand.

"I will," Ethan said shaking his hand.

"You know Ethan, it's all real right? Everything I've been trying to tell you."

"And I told you I'm not so sure I'm one of the chosen. My life is terrible. Not sure the big man wants me, even if he's out there."

"If you can't believe now, then you'll never believe my friend. I love you Ethan."

"Love you too Kyle. Only told one person that before. Sad thing is you're both dead."

"You can see us again someday you know. Just gotta believe and ask for forgiveness."

"Forgiveness!" Ethan exclaimed as he came out of the treatment.

"What was that Doc?" Agent Mike asked watching as Dr. Stelious began to remove the equipment.

"Nothing, just a manifestation is all," Dr. Stelious said without looking away from his work.

Ethan sat in the bed recalling what Lily had said almost 20 years ago in the botany lab as she lay dying in his arms. "Forgive me." Those words had eaten away at him for years and now he possibly had an answer. He needed to get to Kyle's research; he needed to get to Lily.

# | THIRTY-NINE |

The snow had been impressive, dumping twelve inches onto Chicago over the previous week. The small but constant snowfall became a burden as city trucks continually worked, removing the accumulation that was perpetually just enough to make the roads slick. Ethan and Mike had arrived in Chicago the night before and were already losing their edge. The sky was an unchanging gray from morning to night, and had convinced them to share in its boredom and misery.

The two men sat silently in a Ford Explorer just outside of a large, steel warehouse. There used to be long steel piles that traveled from the larger warehouse to a series of smaller, round buildings, but had since fallen to the ground; their remnants standing as a fractured memory.

The warehouse had hundreds of small, filthy panes of glass encircling it. Thankfully, there were a few broken windows that allowed a visual of the inside. Unfortunately, with the snow steadily falling, Mike couldn't risk leaving tracks.

Mike had called the Madison field office when they arrived in Madison the night before. He hadn't been confident with Ethan's experience, but knew if they found the warehouse, even by chance, it was worth having some extra guys on the ground. Mike had texted the local guys once they found the warehouse.

"You're sure about this?" Mike asked turning his stiff neck toward Ethan who sat facing forward in the passenger seat, his mind still replaying the conversation with Kyle.

"Yes, Mike. I'm positive. This is the place."

"I'm gonna look like a big idiot if you're wrong. You know that?"

"I'm not wrong."

Ten minutes later, two more black Ford Explorers arrived. As they pulled up next to Mike, they rolled down the windows.

"We ready?" the driver of one SUV said to Mike.

"Yup. Let's hit it," Mike said putting the car into drive.

The three SUVs began speeding toward the building throwing large rooster-tails of white snow behind them. Neither the parking lot, nor the field they were racing the trucks through had been touched in quite some time. The snow was deep, at least a foot, but in some places where the ground dipped low, it was as deep as three feet, challenging the four-wheel drive in the vehicles. It was fun, distracting, and painful at times for Ethan, his bony extremities bumping into the interior of the car, but at least he wasn't focused on what he may see.

"We've got a car," Mike said gesturing with his head as they pulled into the loading dock of the warehouse. He then slowed to a stop and the two other SUVs did as well. Everyone exited the car slowly, and congregated at the Mercedes.

"Run the plates," a nameless FBI agent said, while yet another started talking into his phone, giving whoever was on the other line the license plate number.

"Where now?" Mike asked Ethan who stood staring at the car, unable to think.

"Uh, we have to go down. As low as we can."

"There's stairs over there according to this sign," someone said.

Ethan followed the men down the dark stairs. The air became warmer as they descended the stairway. A ninety-degree turn to the right revealed a faint light at the bottom of the stairs, and, the white doorway on the left. Ethan saw it and he felt a chill, despite the warmth below. Kyle had told him what lay beyond the white door, but he was nervous. *What if they're dead? What if whoever is behind the door has a weapon? What if it's not actually there?*

Slowly, they went, careful not to make a sound as the water from the melting snow dripped its way down the stairs, causing the rubber on the soles of their shoes to squeak.

"There's the door," Ethan finally said to Mike as his foot hit the floor that lay directly in front of the dingy white door.

"This white one?" Mike said pointing to his left with his thumb, and glancing back up the stairs to Ethan. Ethan nodded and the agents all squared their bodies to face the door.

Mike placed one hand in the air and held up three fingers. He dropped one leaving two, dropped another leaving only one, then he grabbed the doorknob. Locked. He then backed up and kicked the door hard, near the handle, with his large powerful leg. The deep sound echoed down the hallway. Mike wound up again, *bang!* His foot struck the door again and it sprung open.

The smell of feces and sickness spewed out into the hallway and caused the men to stagger for a moment. Mike was the first to go inside and witness the horror. The timers still ran over all the beds, ten in all, just as Ethan said there would be. The rest of the agents followed Mike through the door and swept the room.

"Clear!" the men yelled as each had looked over an area of the large treatment room.

"Ethan get in here and help these people!" Mike yelled.

Ethan ran down the stairs and into the room. He froze as he entered. The scene was too much. Bags hanging from the beds, overflowing with disgust, nasogastric tubes rubbing the patient's noses raw. Three of the people had infections running up their arms, indicated by a red streak highlighting the vein and leading directly to the IV.

"What?" a patient yelled jokingly from behind Mike, causing him to draw his weapon and point it in the general direction.

"No!" Ethan yelled. "It's a physical manifestation of the treatment. It's normal," he said placing his hand on the agent's shoulder, reassuring him. Ethan looked around the room at the blood, the bedsores, the infections, and the clocks that continued to run over the ten patient's heads.

"We're gonna need ten ambulances before I even consider taking these people off."

"Call it in," Mike said to one of the men.

"You know who did this, don't you?" Mike asked looking at Ethan.

"Yes."

"Who?"

"I need a minute. This is too much Mike. I'm feeling pretty dizzy."

"Why don't you step out. You've got about a half hour before we scrounge out these ambulances."

"Thanks Mike, for listening," Ethan said and reached out his hand.

After the handshake, Ethan walked quickly down the hallway and found Kyle's lab. He entered and froze. A large man was throwing Kyle's research equipment all over the room. The treatment table was on its side, the operative light was askew, pointing toward the observation room causing a large glare across the glass. The man was in the office now, mumbling noisily, his deep voice rumbling as it bounced around on the concrete walls. Before Ethan's feet became unglued from the wet floor, the man looked up toward him. It was Dr. Brian Lacey, but he looked wildly different.

Lacey burst out of the office and ran toward Ethan. The strength hadn't left the man's legs since playing college football, but the arthritis in his knees limited his speed and mobility. Ethan's adrenaline, however, had allowed him to become unglued and ran down the hallway toward the main treatment room and the seven FBI agents inside. As Dr. Lacey entered the room he was struck in the face by Agent Sims.

"This is how it's gonna be," Agent Sims said standing over Dr. Lacey. "You're gonna cooperate and let us know everything, start to finish. No deals. No phone calls."

"It's all his fault," Lacey said pointing to Ethan.

"If he'd had just listened to me about researching this project. I told him it would hurt people," Lacey said pointing at Ethan while he sat up on the ground.

"Take 'em topside," Mike said to the other agents. He walked over to Ethan who was standing in the corner, arms folded staring at Dr. Lacey.

"You all right, Doc?" Mike asked Ethan.

"Yeah—I just—I—he was so against what I was doing. He tried to shut me down so many times. Why would he do this?"

"I'll tell you why I did it," Lacey said hearing Dr. Lewis struggling to find the words.

"Because you're useless. You weren't gonna do it, were you? You had this big idea, this ability to unlock a better world for everyone and you chose to keep it a secret. I always knew you were up to something, just didn't know what. I know you killed her Ethan. I've always known."

"You think these ten are my only ten? Think again. I've used it on hundreds of my own patients. Some loved me, others didn't but I can tell you something. So many people experienced it Ethan it's incredible. Most reflect on how vivid the experience was, how incredible it was to see a loved one, how they'd do anything to experience it again, even if just for a moment." Dr. Lacey spat, a thick red discharge from his bleeding mouth. "And you weren't going to tell anyone."

"All right that's enough outta you," Mike said as he picked Lacey up by grasping his wrists, which were now tied behind his back.

The agents had all gone out to wait for the ambulance while Ethan stayed behind to monitor the patients. After the men had been gone for five minutes, he quickly returned to the room down the hall, went under Kyle's desk, and lifted the floorboards. Within, he saw three hard drives. He placed them in the inner pocket of his coat and walked back into the larger room. Shortly after returning, ambulance crews entered the room, one at a time, and Ethan slowly brought each patient around, handing them off to the emergency management team. It was difficult managing their pain, but thankfully they woke up quickly and safely, because Ethan's mind was on other things: the hard drives.

# | FORTY |

## Chicago, Illinois | February 3, 2016

Before the trial had even begun, Dr. Lewis was concerned for his research and the treatment for physiological disorders. The prosecuting lawyer knew the defense attorney was going to call Brian Lacey to the stand. If that happened in an open court, with a variety of media and other observers, then the entire world would soon be aware of the possibilities the treatment had if the limits were pressed aggressively enough. The prosecutor motioned, several times, to have the entire court proceedings private, as well as insisted on requiring the jurors to sign non-disclosure agreements regarding the ideas discussed in the courtroom. The judge was reluctant at first, but when Michelle Adams spoke on behalf of the prosecuting team in a closed door meeting the judge got the point. There was a large amount of proprietary information being released with Dr. Lacey was on the stand, and even more when Dr. Lewis had to sit, under oath, telling the jury of his unreleased and secret research projects.

Dr. Lewis sat in a suite at the Hilton in Chicago with Michelle. The two of them had been working for days, practicing his responses to possible questions from the defense, as well as rehearsing which questions the prosecuting team would be asking.

"Thanks for doing this Michelle," Dr. Lewis said taking a sip of water.

"It's not a problem Dr. Lewis," she said smiling. "I want you to feel comfortable out there and I'm not too fond of our prosecution team either."

"Yeah, they just don't seem to care much. Might be because nearly 20 years of their lives don't hang in the balance."

"You don't worry. I've talked with them about what questions to expect from the defense, and I've also added a few of my own, just to make sure it's all covered. I know you better than most," she said blushing through her dark skin.

"You do, Michelle," he said smiling. "It's going to be hard not to say something to him."

"Lacey?"

"Yeah."

"You can't do that. Don't even think about it Dr. Lewis," she said, knowing how hard watching the trial had been for him. Dr. Lewis had sat in the courtroom listening while Lacey took the stand. He heard Lacey explain the reasons for his experimentation: "to replicate the research." Lacey also explained how he always had a fascination with physics, the inability to control limitations that we have as humans, and he thought the treatment could unlock human's true potential. Ethan wasn't sure if the defense attorney told Lacey to appear insane, but the former doctor sure seemed to be leaning in that direction.

"And Elias Grant? I can't believe he was funding Lacey's study."

"There's more to that story, Doctor," Michelle said angry with herself for letting it slip at a time like this.

"Michelle don't tell me," he said with his lips, but his eyes screamed curiosity.

"Elias was getting paid quite a bit of money from some pharmaceutical companies to find a way to shut you down. You realize you've decreased their bottom line literally billions with your treatment? Think about it. No more pills, means no more revenue."

"I know, but I don't care about the money. Nor theirs."

"They do. That's a different story though Dr. Lewis," she said gently lifting her hair from her face and placing it behind her ear, revealing a pair of small emerald earrings.

"Those can't be the earrings I got you the Christmas we had at The Experience Center," Dr. Lewis said seeing them shimmer in the light from the morning.

"Yeah, matter of fact they are," she said, faking surprise. She was shocked at the gift from Ethan, but even more surprised when he said he got them because they matched her wonderful eyes.

"Enough about us Doc," she said to slow her heart. The thought of them being more than just colleagues had entered her mind and she needed it to leave. "You ready?"

"No."

"Get there. You're on in an hour."

The courtroom made Ethan feel nauseous, like a wild animal taken into captivity, the secrets he kept for so long now being brought into the light because of one man, the same man who falsified research in order to shut him down. He was reliving the moment he had to testify against his own parents leaving him in foster care.

Michelle had done an excellent job prepping him, however, he had gotten quite long winded in a lot of the answers he gave to the prosecutors. Dr. Lewis told the jury everything he and Kyle had done with The Beyond Experience from Kyle's times with his father, the persons who had near death experiences, and how he and Dr. Stelious went behind Kyle's back to treat Adam and Veronica. But what hurt Ethan the most was explaining to the court why he felt Kyle had gone with Brian Lacey, which was in his opinion, a direct result of him not allowing Kyle to show Annie the experience. He told the jury he had gone into the experience and talked with Kyle, and that's how they found the secret testing labs in the bellows of the abandoned warehouse.

"Good afternoon, Dr. Lewis," the defense attorney said as he paced the stone floor of the courtroom. Immediately Dr. Lewis' anxiety shot up and he searched for Michelle, finally locking onto her eyes. She smiled subtly at him and his fears subsided as he remembered the hours they spent practicing answers.

"Good afternoon," he responded into the mic with a forced smile.

"You revealed a lot today, about your research. Tell me Doctor, was anyone in your lab ever in danger during this, Beyond Experience?"

"No," he responded. *Short and sweet,* he reminded himself.

"How about any other lab?"

"I couldn't say."

"And why is that Dr. Lewis?"

"Because I'm not sure who else is out there trying to replicate my research.

"Fair enough," the defense attorney said as he paused, a puzzled look on his face. He turned toward Dr. Lewis and smirked.

"Dr. Lewis, who was Lily Fisch?"

"Objection," the prosecution team said.

"Overruled," the judge immediately responded.

"Lily Fisch has already been discussed. Her death was ruled a suicide," the prosecutor spoke again.

"Your honor this has a point," the defense attorney said, annoyed.

"I recall the testimony from Brian Lacey as well as the Saint Louis Police Department," the judge said taking off her glasses. "This better get somewhere in the next two questions or believe me I won't be overruling another objection. Answer the question, please, Dr. Lewis."

He was frozen, angry. "She was my fiancé."

"And what happened to her?"

"She died."

"What drugs were found in her system?"

"My cocktail."

"Objection, all of this has already been determined—"

"Well what I'm trying to get at, is that this treatment is dangerous, and millions are undergoing it on all over the world," the defense lawyer said addressing the jury and cutting off the prosecutor.

"Sustained. Prove your point," the judge said pointing at the defense attorney.

"My point is that my client did the world a service. He was merely trying to replicate research already performed by Dr. Lewis, and, due to Dr. Lewis's selfishness, my client was unable to foresee the inherent dangers of aggressive treatment. All of the persons in my client's study were willing participants, having signed waivers and evidence was presented showing videos of informed verbal consent."

`"Yes. One," he said looking toward the doctor. "How do you sleep at night knowing your treatment led to the death of so many people?"

Ethan became molten hot. Rage engulfed his insides and he sat squeezing fists together and struggling to let the air out of his lungs. He was frozen in the chair staring at the defense attorney, then his eyes darted toward Lacey who sat smirking in court, his black suit and tie making him appear confident and untouchable. The accusation was incredible. For 20 years Dr. Lewis had played it safe, gradually playing with the cocktail not to overdo it, and, when The Beyond Experience came, he quickly dismantled it knowing the long-term ramifications before he actually saw them in Lacey's treatment room.

"I haven't slept for years, sir, but it's a separate issue," he said thinking about Lily and his nightmares; his guilt.

"You're dismissed Dr. Lewis," the judge said from above.

As he left the stand, he looked to Michelle who exhaled for him, smiling because she knew it took everything Dr. Lewis had not to explode on the stand. He was well prepared, and they both knew it. "Thank you," he mouthed to her and left the courtroom.

# Chesterfield, Missouri | March 11, 2016

Dr. Lewis sat in his office, eyes closed as he relaxed, his head leaning back against the top of the couch. For the first time in months he was alone, allowing his mind to think about what it wanted. Brian

Lacey had been convicted on fifteen counts of murder, ten counts of false imprisonment, and 27 counts of medical malpractice, despite not having a license. The civil lawsuits were starting to come in, but Dr. Lewis would have nothing to do with those; his part was finished. Even Elias Grant was having troubles, sentenced to five years in prison for his involvement; but what stung the businessman even more, were the thousands of people who pulled out of his company, forcing them to file bankruptcy.

Ethan hadn't forgotten his friend Kyle's request, to take care of Annie and Junior. Almost every night he had gone to Annie's home and helped out with the baby, brought groceries, watched Junior as she went out for appointments, or just got away to clear her head. Ethan loved seeing Junior, his mannerisms, the way he smiled, all reminded him of Kyle. He talked to Junior, told him stories about Kyle, talked about Ray, his grandfather, what little he knew from Kyle's stories. It was depressing and fulfilling at the same time.

But now, Ethan was finally allowing himself to think freely instead of about Lacey and the trial, about Annie and Junior, or about The Experience Center's reputation having been slightly smeared by the trial. His first thought was about Lily's eyes, their blue-green beauty that was only matched by the tropical water in the cove of Bora Bora. He thought of the pull he felt when he was in The Beyond Experience, how great he felt giving in to her pull. Ethan knew she wasn't mad at him. He knew she wanted to see him, to talk to him, and finally find out why she said, "Forgive me."

Suddenly, Dr. Lewis remembered something else Kyle said to him when in the experience. He quickly sat up in the darkness of his office and ran to the eastern wall of his room where he had a small safe. Because the only light source in the room was behind him, he could barely see the biometric lock sensor where he had to place his finger. Opening the safe, he saw the three hard drives he hid there when he got back home from the warehouse in Chicago. Ethan told himself he wouldn't look at the research before the trial was over. He thought it would keep himself safe, undistracted, and leave Kyle's research as pure as he possibly could. But now was the time.

He quickly sat down and plugged in the first of the three hard drives. He noticed immediately that the information was all test trials for the same person. Having placed Kyle under anesthesia dozens of times, he noticed right away that every test was Kyle. Dr. Lewis saw the progression with each trial, Kyle staying under longer and he noticed his vitals would stabilize right at the point where his brain activity became completely absent. Dr. Lewis knew this was the point where everyone entered The Beyond Experience, and Kyle had found a way to maximize the time in that zone.

The desk lamp became obsolete as the sun began to pour in from the windows behind Dr. Lewis. He hadn't noticed the morning when it began, and he hadn't heard the dozens of people come in to work as the research center buzzed to life. He was myopic, obsessed, feeling the adrenaline he hadn't felt for quite a while. His devil was back, talking to him, convincing him the answer was in the research and all he had to do was replicate it.

Kyle was a problem solver; Dr. Lewis knew it, his father Ray knew it too. Kyle knew how to write a great research paper and how to use his charm to convince others he was right. Kyle organized the data well, clearly explaining every step of the process down to the milliliter and the second. He also recorded all the physical manifestations, recorded them in a separate file indicating the times they occurred and which camera they occurred on in order to find it quickly. This meant he watched every second of all four cameras after every test. The last few tests he had spent days, not hours in the treatment so it was an immense number of hours he had committed to the project.

Dr. Lewis had been scribbling down notes as he digested terabytes of data. After nearly twelve straight hours his eyes became so blurry and dry he had to take a break. He walked to the couch and lay down to sleep. He remembered Kyle laying in that same couch, his head cocked into an extreme position while papers were spread out everywhere in front of him. It was the night the two of them had penned their original research paper. How different the moment was now for Dr. Lewis. Outside his window he saw anvil clouds and an eerie green glow in the late afternoon sky. The ironies Dr. Lewis was searching for stopped after that, because he was now alone instead of having Kyle right there to question his research, to challenge the writing, and to create a video.

After a quick nap, Dr. Lewis reviewed his notes on Kyle's research. It was remarkable, and he knew what he had to do next, however, flashes of Lacey's lab entered his mind: the people on the beds, the sickness on the floor, the smell of death and infection in that air. Like a heroin addict he craved his fix, but knew chasing the dragon might kill him. He then remembered the island, how real it was, her pulling him in. Ethan thought of Kyle, and how he talked about Lily being right on the main island, waiting for him. *Kyle made it ok*, he thought, convincing himself to go in despite the mountain of evidence against it.

Ethan decided a secret lab of his own was in order. He realized he didn't need anyone to help him anymore, Kyle had found a way for him to treat himself. Ethan loved the idea of being alone, of disconnecting from the world around him, of being that same man he was before Lily. Ironically, the solitude is what would allow him to see her once again. He was going in as soon as he built his lab in the basement of his house. He didn't care if he became addicted to the treatment, all he knew was that the pulling had become stronger, even though he wasn't in the experience. But Ethan didn't care, Lily had always guided the research, and the research had stimulated his need for knowledge. He decided to succumb to both of them; it was time to see her again.

# | FORTY-ONE |

## October 1, 2016

The next several months went by relatively slowly, however, Ethan's inability to sleep allowed him to be productive while still maintaining his regular work schedule. It wasn't nightmares or guilt that kept him up anymore, nor was it attending to Junior, which did take its toll. It was the excitement of seeing Lily again. He knew the quicker he was able to build his lab the sooner he would be able to experience what he hadn't allowed himself to do in two decades.

He would usually help Annie with Junior by coming over after work three days a week. Afterward, he would head home and work in his basement on the lab. The other four days a week, he found himself leaving an hour early, that grew to two hours early after a week. He had even worked through the night several times, bringing back memories of The Shack, which made him smile as he reflected on good times with Kyle.

Ethan had ordered a variety of lab equipment and had it shipped to his home: a treatment bed with an automated air mattress to prevent bedsores, calf compressors to prevent blood clots, a BP machine, pulse ox and heart rate monitor, IV infusion pump, and large tanks of oxygen. He used his own computer and Kyle's hard drives which had the program to read the data that was incoming from the vitals, and regulate necessary changes to the output of the drug cocktail. Kyle had also found a way to keep the drug cocktail even longer, by placing the bags on a large, overhead refrigerator. Kyle had used a kegerator he mounted to the ceiling in his lab, so Ethan thought he'd do the same. Within the mounted cooling unit were fifty IV bags, rigged in such a way that when one bag finished, the next one began. It was part of Kyle's ingenuity and computer programming. The sensors he used were developed by another individual in Brian Lacey's group, however, that kid had no idea what he had built it for.

Ethan set up the lab and ran two separate trial runs for the drug delivery system, each one week in duration. Every morning and evening he would check to determine how well the fluids titrated out of the bags, through the IV pump, and how well the cocktail stayed consistent during the seven days. On the first trial, a terrible thunderstorm ripped through the area and Ethan lost power for less than thirty minutes, but the trial was ruined. He decided to have a second breaker box installed for 100 amps, adjacent to his standard 200 box. He also had the electrician install a solar panel behind his house for charging batteries that could last for approximately five days. He also installed a backup generator, which could work self sufficiently on gasoline for up to twelve hours, if the solar batteries weren't fully charged. It was a lot of redundancies, said the electrician, which also meant a lot of money, but Ethan didn't care. Money was worthless to him.

After the installation of the redundant power supplies he performed the second trial, which was flawless. The drip continued to flow based on the computer's output, the cocktail stayed at the same potency, and, for a complete check, he shut his breaker boxes down and forced the system to run for the last three days with only the solar power and gas generator.

The basement was dark but warm, and the only light Ethan allowed was coming in obliquely through the large window in the east side of the basement. It was the week of the Harvard Research Report but he wasn't going this year. He had, however, called Jimmy and told him he wouldn't be making the appointment this year, but would come by within the next few weeks to explain.

Ethan sat on the noisy mattress of the hospital bed, the motors for air bladders constantly buzzing, attempting to accommodate his bony prominences as he fidgeted. He had to call Annie, he had to lie, and that made him nervous and guilty. Without Lily none of this would have been possible, and he had also fought the urge for long enough. He deserved to see her, he needed to see her.

Holding onto that confidence he called Annie.

"Hey Ethan," Annie said on the end of the phone,

"Hey Annie, just wanted to remind you I'm going to be in Cambridge this week. I've got the conference I'm attending. Wanted to make sure you had things covered with Junior."

"I do Ethan, have a good trip. I'll keep a good thought for you as you travel. He's gonna miss you," she said referring to Junior.

"I'm gonna miss him too. I'll see you guys soon."

Ethan hung up. His hands were shaking and so did his chest as he took a deep, cleansing breath. He walked behind the bed, climbed the step stool and inspected the bags of fluid inside the kegerator. Satisfied with the connections he saw, he moved onto testing the power back-ups, and the computers, making sure they were receiving information from the vitals machines. He was once again satisfied with what he saw. Last, and most important, he placed two doses of epinephrine into an IV port, which he then attached to a mechanical clamp that would be triggered by the computer if his vitals finally hit low enough, or after one week in the treatment; whichever came first.

Ethan placed the leads onto his body for the heart monitor, the sensor on his finger, the BP cuff on his arm. He almost placed the mask around his face, but remembered he needed a feeding tube so he went to retrieve it. He had premeasured the length he needed, and had a small amount of lubrication to help it slide in. As Ethan sipped water he pressed the nasogastric tube an inch or two further each swallow until he hit the mark he made with a small piece of tape being just outside his nostril. He then placed a large syringe and drew up, seeing a slightly green liquid, which let him know he was in his stomach, as he should be. He taped the NG tube in place. He then performed the most unpleasant bits, a catheter and bags for waste.

He returned to the bed and turned the oxygen on, lastly grabbing several alcohol packs from the table next to him wiping his left arm. He grabbed the IV and placed it into his forearm, hitting the vein on the first try. He knew it was a good vein, Lily had always used it. He taped it in place.

The laptop sat immediately to his right. He hit the "begin" button on the screen.

"You're gonna feel a chill," he told himself aloud as the drug ran into his body. He had just enough time to smile before he slipped into a world he had been avoiding for so long.

The pull was intense and immediate. He felt Lily drawing him in even more than last time, as if she was just as excited as he was. Ethan found himself rooted in the soft white sand as the water gently kissed his ankles making a subtle splashing sound as sporadic waves launched droplets of water onto his legs. He looked down the beachfront and saw an old Chris-Craft. It was a 1941, 19-footer, mahogany in color with a red stripe down the side and pigskin seats. James Bond had first introduced Ethan to the high gloss wood and smooth lines of the nimble water glider. The color of the boat was beautifully contrasted against the blue-green water and white sand.

He began to jog down the beach, his eyes looking back and forth from the boat to Mount Otemanu. His bare feet were sending sand arcing up behind him like rooster tails from a jet ski. He knew she was on the central island where the mountain stood casting a soothing shadow. He felt the entire world was almost leaning in her direction, the gravity from her pull becoming stronger by the moment. He was much calmer being in the experience than he thought he'd be, as if everything he'd gone through before was meaningless: the research, the schooling, the guilt, the abuse from his parents, had all been for this one moment: a perfectly orchestrated life that led to this climax.

He leapt from the pale wood dock and into the Chris-Craft. Immediately, he hammered the gas and refused to look back toward the beach. Several months ago looking back allowed him to see Kyle, but this time was all about Ethan and Lily; just as it had been for them 20 years earlier. The boat was smooth over the water. The feeling of a wooden boat was different from the aluminum boats Ethan had been on historically. It seemed to cut through the water with very little fight, and grabbed an edge when turning a bit better; but he wasn't doing any turning, heading straight for the mountain.

The sunlight was intense but comforting, which made him want to take off his shirt. He always had a shirt on in front of people no matter the situation. It had been that way since he was 10. That was the point in his life he became self-conscious. The burn scars from cigarettes and the stitches from getting hit by his parents weren't looked well upon. When Lily saw them for the first time she covered her mouth and cried as he stood there allowing her to look over his body. She walked to him and squeezed him tightly, her tears falling upon his bare chest. But now, in this boat, in this cove, on their island of Bora Bora, he was taking off his shirt.

As he continued across the water a tremendous symphony of noise melded together from the wind and the water slapping the sides of the boat as he cut through the waves. Every so often a mist of salty warm water would hit him in the face, leaving him wishing for it to happen again. He couldn't stop smiling as the sensory experience continued to become more intense. He heard fish jumping, birds high above, and the sound of dolphins as they swam all around his quick boat almost guiding him toward the island. They were sporty and great companions as they launched from under water and arced their way across his bow, then dove deep down into the clear water below.

Finally, he saw her standing at the dock. Ethan was several hundred yards out but he could see her dirty blonde hair being whipped up into the wind. He also saw her dress, navy blue with white flowers. He had always asked her to wear it but they never had the right occasion. The wind changed directions and he caught a slight scent of flowers mixed with salty air. He inhaled deeply and slowed the boat trying to stay in the breeze, to not lose that familiar smell; the smell of Lily. As he slowed the boat the dolphins left, but not without jumping one last time as if to say goodbye. He was trying to process the moment, grabbing the last 20 years of his life in an attempt to gauge how fast time had gone. It was incredible to him how standing in one moment and referencing a time in the past he could eliminate so much of the monotony and convince himself it hadn't really been that long. Then she waved and his heart melted. He began to sob tears of joy at the sight of her moving body. He remembered the last time he saw her, the brownies, the reluctance in her consent to the treatment, and how her eyes looked at the moment she lay breathless in his hands. But now she was waving!

The boat entered the harbor and she stood patiently at the end of the dock. Ethan took his time parking the beautiful boat, not wanting to ruin the wonderful piece of art. He climbed onto the dock.

Ethan looked down into her eyes and held her at arms' length while his hands rested on her hips. He wanted to experience her again, take her in fully, test his mental capacities to remember every inch of who she was on earth. Her skin was smooth, soft, and tanned. Her hair felt like silk and had the slightest of wave to it. But nothing could capture the beauty of her eyes as he stood in front of her looking into them—neither the water in the cove which they often joked about being similar in color, nor the pictures he still had stored on his phone and computer. They were wonderfully brilliant, smiling eyes with small specs of brown within the green.

"I'm not mad Ethan," she finally spoke, her full tonality and subtle raspiness falling on starved ears. He had craved her voice for such a long time it caused his knees to buckle and almost fall down on the dock.

"I'm sorry."

"Don't be. I've been well," she said wiping a tear from his face. "I asked everyone to tell you but I know they didn't."

"I wouldn't have listened anyway," he said, the smile quickly evaporating as the thought of her lying dead in his arms flashed before him. "Why did you say forgive me?" he asked before the words even registered in his head. "When you died, you said it." The question had been more significant to him than he realized.

Lily smiled and stroked his chest with her hand, feeling the scars he displayed for her and no one else. "I think you'll understand soon enough, Doctor," she said smiling. "I'm so proud of you Ethan."

"I'd be nothing without you."

"That's not true," she said walking down the dock, her hand gently grasping Ethan's.

Ethan squeezed her hand and turned her back around to face him. He pulled her in close and squeezed her, allowing himself to smell her hair once more; the sea and flowers. The flowers he smelled were roses, jasmine, and lilies, the intensity and depth caused his head to spin and he squeezed even tighter to steady himself.

"I've missed you so much Lily," he said breathing deeply, allowing himself to let go of the world he left behind, the clinics, the stress, the memories, and the people. He closed his eyes but still saw the world that surrounded him in the experience.

"I've gotta change clothes."

"For what?" Ethan asked giggling.

"The hike. We're taking the path less traveled honey."

"To where?"

"Up there," she said gesturing with her head. She saw him looking deep into her eyes and she came close. "You want to count the spots?" she asked, remembering how he loved to count the brown flecks in her eyes.

"You remember that?"

"Obviously," she said smiling.

"I don't need to count. I've done it thousands of times staring at your pictures."

"How many are there then?"

"Twelve on the left and sixteen on the right."

"My right or yours?"

"Everything's yours, Lily."

They smiled together and embraced again for a moment before she pushed lovingly away. "Let's go," she said and walked down the dock, Ethan close behind.

They walked for hours, days, the sun neither set nor rose, remaining a constant intense light that lit their way. Ethan followed Lily as she steadily climbed upward through the thick green forest.

"Have you been here this whole time?" he asked as she climbed over a boulder.

"I don't understand," she said looking back at him and smiling.

"Here, the island."

"No, I've been a few different places, but I've been eager to come here with you. It was our place Ethan." She paused, turning her back toward the summit of Mount Otemanu and looked at Ethan. The harsh light of the sky above made her hair glow like a thousand LED lights and stood in sharp contrast to the black volcanic summit that sharply speared through the green jungle surrounding it. "You know that top has never been reached right?" she asked pointing toward the peak looming above. "The rock is too loose, crumbles very easily."

"And we're gonna make it?"

"Do you trust me?" she asked smiling with her beautiful eyes.

Ethan felt warm inside. Trust was something he had when he was with Lily for those few quick years, then it all crashed back down again following the accident. Kyle had filled that void momentarily, but even Kyle spawned a history of lies.

"Only you," Ethan said smiling at her.

Higher they continued to climb and the cove began to take shape across the horizon. While standing on the beach, the cove's immense size was overwhelming, becoming indiscernible with the open ocean that flowed between the small perimeter land masses that defined the outer banks. From where Ethan and Lily stood, just above the tree line, they could see the varied depth of water by its hues, as well as the reef that encircled most of the island.

"Perspective right?" Lily said as she walked back toward Ethan who was taking in the view.

"You have no idea how many times I dreamt this. You and me up here and looking over the water."

"You're right. How's it look compared to your dreams?"

"Better. The details are incredible here. Feels like I'm actually on this mountain with you."

"Who says you're not?" Lily said and continued to charge up the mountain, the terrain becoming loose under foot.

Ethan followed but was questioning everything. He felt the ground beneath him, smelled the air, heard Lily's voice, but continued to struggle with it being real. He had, for years, told everyone they were experiencing an illusion created by the brain. The problem was, Dr. Stelious' deep brain scanner had yet to find the specific pathway causing the sensory experiences.

He began to try and quantify his feelings, how he could hear, feel, touch, and see everything around him at an increased sensitivity. He placed some vegetation in his mouth while Lily wasn't looking and even that tasted more incredible than anything he'd had in life.

He began to feel confused, a slight frustration was settling in as he fought the thought of the experience being a real place, but how could he be somewhere other than the treatment bed in his basement in Chesterfield?

"Are you ok?" Lily said stopping and looking down at Ethan who was now more than 20 yards behind her.

"I'm good Lily, I really am."

"Let's keep going," she said and began hiking. "We're running out of time."

"Time for what?" Ethan asked.

"What I need to show you, honey. I don't really think of time anymore, but now that you're here eternity seems so much longer. You're going to be waking up soon."

"How do you know?"

"I've watched you do it before. I've watched Kyle do it dozens of times. There's a feeling I get. I can't explain it to you. Not worth the time. Now climb!" she said playfully, her voice echoing around the tall wall of rock that stretched toward the bright white sky.

After hours more of climbing the crumbling cliff face they reached the summit and an incredible 360-degree view of the cove below and the open ocean beyond. In the distance, a variety of other islands dotted the horizon, some named, others not, but all part of French Polynesia. Ethan turned slowly, taking in the view as he had done in some of his dreams. The effect in the moment was beautiful, surreal, inspired.

"Lily, this is incredible," he said quietly looking down toward the cove below.

"It really is something," she said in response taking it all in for herself. She had seen many incredible things since she passed on. "Are you happy Ethan?" she said walking to him and grasping his hand.

"I've fought this moment for a long time. I never wanted to forget you. I didn't want to treat myself. I needed to feel the grief. It kept me going."

"Release it all honey. Remember what we used to do? Remember how we'd meditate and help you relax it all away? It was all for you Ethan, the whole experience. It was always meant for you. I love you Ethan," she said smiling, herself now forming tears.

Behind her, Ethan saw a large object slowly forming. It was

massive, covering the entire skyline from horizon to horizon. It was glowing, golden with an intense brightness, causing him to squint and almost look away. Slowly, intricate designs and patterns were presenting themselves as his eyes adjusted to the intensity of the glow. It was a wall of gold, each brick was the size of a car and stacked as high as a 20-story building. It began to slide westward across the sky, allowing rubies of red, green emeralds, and lapis lazuli to glisten and bathe in the white light that continuously shined from far above. It was as if the emeralds were the mortar that held the golden bricks in place. The ground beneath them shook causing volcanic rock to fall to the ground.

Suddenly, from the east, a large arched doorway began to come into view. It stretched from the base of the wall and arced upward high above the top. Images of angels flying, trees, and animals decorated the twin doors. The images were highlighted with a variety of precious metals and stones, which Ethan could not recognize. The hinges on the door were the size of buses standing straight into the sky and were made of solid gold that matched the doors, but the handle was iridescent, glowing bright white. The faintest sound of singing could be heard where Lily and Ethan stood.

"What's going on Lily?" Ethan asked as he stared at the massive structure before them hovering in the air, clouds draping themselves lovingly around the walls and gate.

"You wanted to know why I said forgive me?" she asked and held onto both of Ethan's hands. She hadn't turned to look at the wall or its gates, only focusing on him in this moment.

"You know I do."

"This is why. To go home, to be with my God. I needed forgiveness to gain access to eternity Ethan."

Ethan stood stunned. It was absolution she had asked for as she lay dying on the dirty lab floor in his arms. The arms of an atheist who killed his only friend, the only person he trusted, the one who shared a secret bond that he tattooed onto his finger every year since. He felt guilty for not marrying her in a church, he felt sorrow for her family who watched their daughter fall for a man who was drawing her out of her faith.

"I want to come with you. I want to go in there with you," he said frantically, beginning to feel the distance growing between them. The magnetism was growing faint and he knew he was going to wake up soon.

Lily's hands let loose of Ethan's and she began walking toward the gates. They opened and Ethan was forced down onto his knees by the intensity of the light that passed through the crack in the doors.

"Lily!" he yelled as loud as he could, a chorus of singing beginning to drown out all sound as it intensified. It was magical, encapsulating but he frantically wanted to hear her voice once more. He wanted her to reassure him he could come with her. Ethan didn't understand religion, he didn't know the rules. He was desperate for an answer from her before he woke. He knew once she entered the golden doors she wouldn't be able to come back and see him again, as if the entire time she'd been dead, she was waiting for this moment to explain it all.

Lily turned to face him, her once glowing hair and beautiful eyes were now a black silhouette against the pure light behind her. "Ethan, Kyle was right!" she yelled.

"About what?" he yelled back.

"About everything. Listen to what he said Ethan! He loved you too! Now jump!"

"What?"

"Jump into the water! Trust me Ethan. You can't come in here unless you have faith. Make the leap. Trust that you'll be ok! Give up control. I love you honey so much! Please let yourself be happy!" she said and waved high into the air. She turned and walked up several stairs as the white light enclosed her and the doors closed behind.

Ethan stood at the edge of the peak looking down. He hesitated for a moment and turned back around. He grabbed a volcanic rock and squeezed it tightly into his hand, then ran. As he approached the edge, his heart was racing but he had become more open to trust, to faith. The idea of believing in something despite not seeing, the fact that he witnessed an unshakeable truth that had been presented to him time and time again by Kyle, by Lily, and recently by Annie. The image of Lily walking through the gates held more proof to him than any research that may eventually come in through Dr. Stelious' neural mapping.

He jumped, spreading his arms out sideways as he flew through the open air. The wind began to sing loudly into his ears as he accelerated downward. His pants flapped in the wind and he leaned, allowing himself to float forward on the breeze. He was attempting to hit the water where it was the darkest blue.

He hit the water with a cracking sound that echoed against the mountain as he broke the surface of the cove spreading a wide ripple of water in all directions. As he plunged deep into the water below, his sorrow fell away, then his guilt, his emptiness and loneliness fell away too, allowing love in. Then his physical and emotional scars were washed away, his hatred toward his abusive parents bubbled up and left him like air from his lungs. He finally hit the ocean bed, the soft sand covering his toes. He stayed for a moment on the bottom in quiet reflection while laughing. He opened his hand and looked at the black rock from the top of Mount Otemanu. He closed his eyes as the darkness completely overtook him.

He awoke, groggy, trying to feel his numb body. He moved, slowly, and struggled to open his eyes. Even the faint sunlight entering the basement window was too great for his eyes that had been shut for a week. He heard something hit the ground as he struggled to remove his feeding tube.

"You dropped something," a woman's voice said.

"Lily?" Ethan responded, confusion in his voice as he struggled to locate the sound.

"No, it's Annie," she said walking toward the bed. "Did you really think I didn't know what you were doing?" she asked as she sat on the bed, Junior in her arms.

"I'm sorry Annie but I had to do it. I—"

"Tomorrow's Sunday," she said cutting him off. "The least you can do is take us to church. It's what Kyle would have done. You can make it up to me by doing that."

"I think that's fair," Ethan said still envisioning the moment on top of the mountain with Lily.

"Here," she placing a black rock into his hand. "You dropped this."

Ethan smiled and stared silently at the rock, spinning it in his hands and taking in its details.

# | FORTY-TWO |

## Poughkeepsie, New York | October 16, 2016

Ethan, Annie, and the Fisch family all sat stunned in the sunroom. The sun had gone down an hour ago, but they hadn't budged from their spots in several hours. Ethan was playing with the rock in his hands, just as he had every day since waking up from the treatment.

"I think I get it now," Pat Fisch finally spoke, breaking the silence.

"Get what honey?" Ed asked having forgotten why Ethan had come in the first place.

"How she saved him twice. She treated you before she died. Then she showed you in the experience? Right?"

Ethan shook his head yes. "And this is the rock." He held it in front of him, the porous stone wasn't beautiful in the traditional sense, but its significance made it irreplaceable. "I had it analyzed," he said referring to the stone, "and it's a match for the islands of French Polynesia."

"I'm stunned," Ed said as he sat back into the couch trying to find a way to react to the entire story.

"You said the agent was Mike Sims?" Joey asked, arms folded. He knew FBI agents in the midwest and wasn't going to allow Dr. Lewis to lie to his family again.

"Yes, from Saint Louis."

"Be right back," Joey said, leaving the sunroom and walking into the house.

Ethan reached into his pocket and pulled out a check, and placed it on the table, folded in half. He remembered what Michelle had told him when he wrote it. He also remembered the disappointment in her face when he told her he already asked Annie to come with him to Poughkeepsie to deliver it to Lily's parents.

"I'm going to leave these here for you, and I won't be taking it back," Ethan said placing the volcanic rock on top of the check that lay on the coffee table next to the empty pitcher of lemonade.

"What is it?" Ed asked as he reached toward the table.

"I'm aware Pat started a charity after Lily's death, and I wanted to make a contribution. I'm hoping it stays anonymous. Like I said before Captain Fisch, the money meant nothing to me."

Mr. Fisch grasped the rock, feeling its warmth from being in Ethan's hand. He lifted the folded paper and opened it revealing the sum.

"This is outrageous," Ed said and folded it back, placing it on the table. "You trying to buy us?"

"Ed—"

"Don't Ed me, Pat. That looks like guilt money," Ed said pointing at the check and looking at his wife. Ed felt awkward about getting help from anyone, and certainly not from someone who was considered a suspect in his daughter's death, no matter the story he just heard.

"It is and it isn't, sir. This was always Lily's creation and it doesn't feel right that I'm the one who gets the money. I want it to go to help people. It's what Lily would have done."

"Take the money, Ed," Pat said flipping her finger toward the check. Ed slowly reached for it and handed it to his wife, refusing to look at it again.

Pat opened the check and began to cry, "This is too much, Ethan. I don't even know what to do with this; fifty million dollars? Are you sure?"

"Your story checks out," Joey said bursting back into the room. "Called a few guys, got a hold of Mike Sims myself. Great work Dr.

Lewis," Joey said extending his hand to the doctor.

"I appreciate that very much from you," Ethan said standing to shake his hand. "I think we should be leaving now. Kept you guys from your lives long enough. I appreciate you giving me the chance to talk."

"Take care of that baby," Pat said as she hugged Annie goodbye.

"I will," Annie responded and looked toward Joey, smiling.

"Can't say I want to see you again," Ed said shaking Ethan's hand firmly. "But I'm glad to hear what you said. Those gates seem mighty inviting don't they?"

"They really did, sir."

The drive back to Chesterfield was uneventful. Ethan had volunteered to do all of the driving while Annie slept. The quiet darkness allowed him to think, uninterrupted. He reflected on the story, on Kyle, on Lacey, on Lily. He thought about Stelious, and how, without his deep scanner The Beyond Experience would never have been stable. It truly was incredible all the people who had come into his life, seemingly orchestrating him toward that pivotal moment where he witnessed his love walk through the gates of heaven.

He felt more relieved and relaxed than at any other point in his life. Even with Lily he had stress from school and from her parent's dislike for him. But now, he had nothing held over his head. Not Lily's death, not the clinics, not the research or money. He was truly free of burdens and it made him feel lighter, his mind was clear. His treatment had worked.

Ethan thought of Lily again, the fleeting moments before she went into heaven. *Please let yourself be happy,* she had said.

*Michelle,* he thought. Ethan was confused. He never thought of Michelle unless he needed legal advice but for some reason, her name popped into his head. He thought about her emerald eyes and smooth caramel skin. He smiled remembering she was wearing his earrings before the trial.

During the last twelve hours of the trip, he allowed himself to focus on his history with Michelle. He recalled many times where she flirted with him playfully, *call me anytime, sweetheart, honey,* the winks, and the smiling eyes. He also remembered some of the bad times she had been there for him. When Kyle left, when he was prepping for court, and he also thought of Veronica and Adam's wedding, where he locked eyes with Michelle. She seemed so sad with the man she was with as she looked toward Ethan. Looking back at their time together Ethan finally saw Michelle was there for him, hinting at him all along.

## Chesterfield, Missouri | October 18, 2016

Ethan dropped Annie and Junior off at their house early in the afternoon.

"I'm just gonna head out. Talk to you soon," Ethan said without walking into the house.

"That's fair, you've gotta be tired," Annie said wiping her own eyes as she lay Junior down in a portable crib.

"Actually," Ethan said smirking. He was excited to talk about Michelle rather than bury her in his mind as he did with so many things from his past. He had finally unloaded most of his skeletons and it felt good.

"What?" Annie said crossing her arms and raising an eyebrow.

"I'm calling Michelle."

"Are you serious?" she said, a smile spreading wide across her face.

"Yeah. I thought a lot on the way home. I've been so focused for so long. I finally feel free from everything since seeing Lily again."

"Well it's about time, Doc!" she said walking toward him and squeezing him tightly. "You know Kyle told me she liked you."

"I miss him, Annie."

"Me too. We'll be all right, Doc."

"Call me Ethan."

"Nah," she said smiling and pulling away. "Kyle would love to see you squirm with it." They both laughed and he waved goodbye.

Michelle sat on her couch curled up in a ball reading over patent proposals for Dr. Stelious. She had on black-rimmed glasses and was quietly listening to classical music. It forced her to focus more on what she was reading when there was at least some background noise. Her phone rang as she reached for her tea.

"Dr. Lewis," she said, her heart leaping in her chest as she sighed, trying to gain composure. The unexpected calls from him were the worst, often getting her excited and causing her to emotionally collapse when the conversation ended as professionally as it started.

"Hi Michelle," he said smiling through the phone and she heard it.

To my family and friends.
Thanks for listening to me drone on about the book,
and other ideas for that matter.

|

To my wife, thank you for brainstorming with me and
guiding me with every decision.
Without you I'm lost.

|

To Annmarie, you made the book read, and look
beautiful on the inside. To Heather, thanks again for
your wonderful recommendations which forced me
to dig deep and bring the details.
Without you two, I'm not an author.

|

To Mosbrook Design for taking on the task of
working with me; an emotional, impulsive, anxiety
driven monster. Thankfully we have friends in
common because this cover was masterful.

|

To Jackie Ellis, also known as a.poets.quill on
Instagram. Thank you for allowing me to use your
wonderful poem. It put Dr. Lewis at ease, which
says a lot. And thank you for reading The Beyond
Experience in its infancy, assisting in bringing a solid
foundation to the story.

|

Thank you John. Forever and ever. Without your
nudge I'd still be playing videogames.

|

To Mike Grunst, thank you for the logo artwork.

# | ABOUT THE AUTHOR |

Mike's wide knowledge base helps drive his eclectic writing. He received his undergraduate degree in biology, with minors in both psychology and chemistry. He went on to Washington University in Saint Louis where he received his doctorate in physical therapy. Prior to this he worked at Great Lakes Naval Base where he interacted with a wide range of military personal, both past and present.

Outside of writing novels, he blogs professionally for Veritas Health, in their Spine and Sports sections. He also spent time in religious studies and grew up in the Christian church, which helped his unique writing style, allowing him to work across genres.

His interests include writing, woodworking, and exercise, and has been known to work on cars and motorcycles.

# | OTHER WORKS |

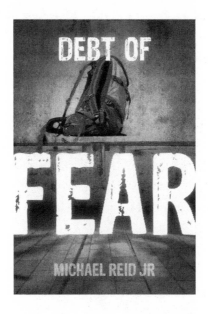

# | CONTACT |

Join Mike's email newsletter at his webiste for the latest information regarding new releases and upcoming work.

Web: **michaelreidjr.com**

Instagram: **authormichaelreidjr**

Facebook: **www.facebook.com/Authormichaelreidjr/**

# | COLOPHON |

This book was designed and laid out by kalzub design (Racine, WI), November 2016.

The cover and back covers were designed by Mosbrook Design.

Interior text is set in Frutiger LT Std family and Adobe Garamond family.

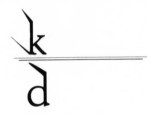

Made in the USA
San Bernardino, CA
02 May 2018